IN A LO

KARL EDWARD WAGNER was b
earned a history degree from Kenyon College in 1967 and obtained a ~~~~~
ical degree from the University of North Carolina–Chapel Hill, training to
be a psychiatrist before becoming disillusioned with the medical profession
and turning to writing full time. Wagner is best remembered today for his
series of fantasy novels featuring Kane, an immortal warrior-sorcerer, as
well as for his horror stories, several of which won or were finalists for the
British Fantasy Award and World Fantasy Award, and the best of which are
collected in *In a Lonely Place* (1983) and *Why Not You and I?* (1987). Wagner
was also a publisher and editor of horror fiction, republishing pulp horror
by writers such as Manly Wade Wellman and Hugh B. Cave under his own
Carcosa Press imprint and editing fifteen volumes in the long-running *The
Year's Best Horror Stories* series. He died in 1994 at age 48 as a result of long-
term alcoholism.

KARL EDWARD WAGNER

IN A LONELY PLACE

with a new introduction by
RAMSEY CAMPBELL

VALANCOURT BOOKS

In a Lonely Place by Karl Edward Wagner
First published as a paperback original by Warner Books in 1983
Expanded hardcover edition published by Scream/Press in 1984
First Valancourt Books edition 2023

Copyright © 1983 by Karl Edward Wagner
Introduction copyright © 2023 by Ramsey Campbell

All rights reserved. In accordance with the U.S. Copyright Act of 1976, the copying, scanning, uploading, and/or electronic sharing of any part of this book without the permission of the publisher constitutes unlawful piracy and theft of the author's intellectual property. If you would like to use material from the book (other than for review purposes), prior written permission must be obtained by contacting the publisher.

Published by Valancourt Books, Richmond, Virginia
http://www.valancourtbooks.com

ISBN 978-1-954321-78-6 (trade paperback)
ISBN 978-1-954321-79-3 (trade hardcover)
Also available as an electronic book and an audiobook

Cover art by Eli John, design by Vince Haig
Set in Dante MT

CONTENTS

INTRODUCTION

K arl Edward Wagner is among the most important and
accomplished writers of my era to have emerged from the
tradition of the horror story, and *In a Lonely Place* is one of the
most impressive horror collections of the 1980s (as indeed is the
companion volume, *Why Not You and I?*). Where many recent
horror writers appear to have learned too much of their craft
from their own generation, Wagner draws strength from his
considerable knowledge of the history of the field. Indeed, *In a
Lonely Place* demonstrates the development of the genre from the
landscapes of the Gothic novel through the ghost story and pulp
fiction to the modern self-consciously psychological horror story,
and does so with a good deal of individuality and unexpected-
ness.

Wagner isn't a writer who seeks to conceal his influences, as
the title of the book—with its clustering references to Bogart,
Nicholas Ray, Dorothy B. Hughes and Walter de la Mare—makes
clear. (The assumption that the reader will note the references
also implies that Wagner is a writer to be read attentively.) Thus
the earliest tale, "In the Pines," a ghost story which perhaps isn't
only that, acknowledges its echo of "The Beckoning Fair One,"
though the reader may be more struck by the ways in which it
prefigures *The Shining*, published three years later. "In the Pines"
is the first statement of one of Wagner's recurring themes, the
swallowing up of characters and their psychological conflicts by
a vividly imagined, almost hallucinatory landscape.

If "In the Pines" incorporates Wagner's tributes to several
aspects of British supernatural fiction, not least a piny whiff of
Algernon Blackwood, "The Fourth Seal" both reaches further
back, to Faust, and deserves to be hailed as a progenitor of the

modern tale of medical horror where the mad doctors are not so much visionaries, misguided or otherwise, as professionals who have sold their souls to the job. That the tale derives from Wagner's observations of medical school makes it even more dismaying. The reader may turn with some relief to "Sticks," one of the few original Lovecraftian stories of the seventies, a witty and touching tribute to *Weird Tales* and in particular to the artist Lee Brown Coye. With its enigmatic landscape strewn with lattices that seem on the point of turning into symbols, the story also reinvents the Gothic in terms of the psychedelic decade, and is often cited as a source for *The Blair Witch Project*—certainly a precursor.

".220 Swift" was written partly with a Lovecraftian anthology in mind, but found a home in an anthology of newer terrors. Karl used to describe himself as a very slow writer, a trait that ultimately saw his work fall sadly short of deadlines and advances, to be abandoned while he set about another abortive project to make ends meet. (I edited both anthologies, and so was ultimately happy to have lost the tale from one book only to accept it for its successor.) Though both Lovecraft and Machen loom in its shadows, it reaches back to an earlier myth, and its scenes of underground terror are all Wagner's own. "Where the Summer Ends" is the most sustained tale of terror in the book, but "The River of Night's Dreaming" may be the finest story; it is certainly the most variously disturbing, and a masterpiece. In this story Wagner uses Robert W. Chambers' mysterious symbol *The King in Yellow* for highly personal ends. "The River of Night's Dreaming" repays especially attentive reading, and offers Wagner's finest nightmare landscape to put the reader in the mood.

"Beyond Any Measure" is both an unusually powerful treatment of the confrontation with the Other and an enviably original variation on the theme of vampirism, firmly rooted in the conventions of such stories. With their erotic explicitness, these last two tales might have had difficulty being published much earlier, and the story that followed, "More Sinned Against," was rejected by a horror anthologist who lacked the courage of his genre on the grounds that the drugs used by the characters were insufficiently disapproved of, a doubly absurd objection to the story. "More Sinned Against" is the first example of a bleaker phase of Wagner's work, where the landscape is mostly psychological. Other examples may be found in *Why Not You and I?*, alongside such stories as "Sign of the Salamander" and its oblique sequel, "Blue Lady, Come Back," remarkable rediscoveries of the merits of pulp writing.

Some of Wagner's later fiction seemed limited by a bitterness akin to that apparent in Cronenberg's *The Brood* and Amis's *Stanley and the Women*. Karl explained to me that he was attempting to exorcise his inner demons. In retrospect it looks like an act of literary courage, and not to be dismissed. However dark his star burned, it illuminated areas of experience where few writers venture. The horror story would be much poorer without the full range of his intelligence and imagination and often audacious originality, all of which are exemplified in the present book. May its reappearance help to establish his reputation on the peak his fiction scaled.

RAMSEY CAMPBELL
Wallasey, Merseyside
January 21, 2022

RAMSEY CAMPBELL was born in Liverpool in 1946 and now lives in Wallasey. The *Oxford Companion to English Literature* describes him as "Britain's most respected living horror writer," and the *Washington Post* sums up his work as "one of the monumental accomplishments of modern popular fiction." He has received the Grand Master Award of the World Horror Convention, the Lifetime Achievement Award of the Horror Writers Association, the Living Legend Award of the International Horror Guild and the World Fantasy Lifetime Achievement Award. In 2015 he was made an Honorary Fellow of Liverpool John Moores University for outstanding services to literature. PS Publishing have brought out two volumes of *Phantasmagorical Stories*, a sixty-year retrospective of his short fiction, and a companion collection, *The Village Killings and Other Novellas*, while their Electric Dreamhouse imprint has his collected film reviews, *Ramsey's Rambles*. His latest novel is *Fellstones* from Flame Tree Press, who have also recently published his Brichester Mythos trilogy.

IN THE PINES

———

Prologue

There is an atmosphere of unutterable loneliness that haunts any ruin—a feeling particularly evident in those places once given over to the lighter emotions. Wander over the littered grounds of an abandoned amusement park and feel the overwhelming presence of desolation. Flimsy booths with awnings tattered in the wind, rotting heaps of sun-bleached *papier-mâché*. Crumbling timbers of a roller coaster thrust upward through the jungle of weeds and debris—like ribs of some titanic unburied skeleton. The wind blows colder there; the sun seems dimmer. Ghosts of laughter, lost strains of raucous music can almost be heard. Speak, and your voice sounds strangely loud—and yet curiously smothered.

Or tour a neglected formal garden, with its termite-riddled arbors and gazebo. The lily pond is drained, choked with weeds and refuse. Only a few flowers or shrubs poke miserably through the rank undergrowth. Dense clots of weeds and vines overrun the paths and statuary. Here and there a shrub or rambling rose has grown into a wild, misshapen tangle. The flowers offer anemic blooms, where no hand gathers, no eye admires. No birds sing in that uncanny hush.

Such places are lairs of inconsolable gloom. After the brighter spirits have departed, shadows of despair and oppression assume their place. The area has been drained of its ability to support any further light emotion, and now, like weeds on eroded soil, only the darker sentiments can take root and flourish. These places are best left to the loneliness of their grief. . . .

I

The road that climbed pine-hooded slopes was winding and narrow—treacherous with deep ruts and large stones. County work crews seldom came this far, and rains of many seasons had left the unpaved road with the contour of a dry stream bed.

In late afternoon sunlight the dusty Chevy bounced and rattled its cautious ascent of the pine-covered ridge. A rock outcropping struck its undercarriage and grated harshly. Janet caught her breath, but said nothing. Gerard Randall risked a quick glance from the wheel to note her tense fright. He scowled and concentrated on driving. Accustomed to wide, straight lanes of modern highway, Randall found this steep country road with its diabolical curves a nightmare. Rains had long since washed out whatever shoulder there was, and he watched in sick fascination as the road disappeared completely all too few inches from his jolting wheels.

"Can you see roads like this in Ohio?" he snorted, and wondered what would happen should two cars meet. With traffic almost nonexistent, that seemed unlikely. At any rate, he was barely crawling, as the light car wallowed over the rutted bed. Once again he felt a pang of regret for the Buick and its solid feel. But now life was strictly economy class.

The road made an impossible hairpin, so that Gerry had to stop the car to back and fill. He swore silently, keeping his anger to himself. What had this road been designed for, anyway—didn't these Tennessee hillbillies drive cars? The long drive from Columbus had been difficult. From wide interstate highway, the roads had steadily retrogressed down the evolutionary ladder—until now he followed a trail Davy Crockett would have scorned.

Their silence had been awkward, but conversation was a greater strain. Instead, he turned up the radio and pretended not to notice Janet's tight-faced nervousness. For miles now the radio had blared out twangy country music from the small-town stations along their route. When they left the paved road, it faded into static.

They were passing vacation cabins now, so he paid careful attention. "Help me find the place, Janet," he said levelly. "If we miss it, I'll never get turned around."

One of the last ones on the road, the agent in Maryville had told them when they stopped for the key. On the left, a good coat of green paint, with red fuel oil and water tanks in front. The sign over the door would read "The Crow's Nest" in red and white. Couldn't be missed.

"I hope it's . . . clean," Janet offered hesitantly. "Some of these look so run-down."

True enough, Gerry admitted. A few cabins were in good condition—fresh paint, aluminum screens, new car alongside. But most were half fallen apart—sagging wooden boxes perched on precarious stilts along the steep mountainside. A few had tumbled down the slope—pitiful heaps of crumpled and rotting timbers. Not encouraging. He voiced his annoyance: "So most of these places are fifty years old! What did you think seventy-five bucks a month would get you for a mountain cabin! In Gatlinburg we'd pay this much for a night!"

Her face drew tighter and her eyes looked damp. She was assuming her wounded-martyr expression. Gerry braced himself for the now familiar crisis. *Please God, not now, not here.*

"There it is!" He pointed suddenly. "Let's see if there's room to pull off the road." Cautiously, he edged the Chevy into a parking area beside the cabin.

Janet's face grew keen with interest. "It doesn't look too bad." she observed hopefully.

Gerry eyed the structure in quick appraisal. "No. No, it doesn't," he conceded. "At least, from the outside."

The Crow's Nest was a typical mountain cabin from the early twenties, days when this had been a major resort area. It clung to the steep slope with one end resting on the bank just below the road, while an arrangement of wooden posts supported the sections jutting out from the mountain. Its unlovely design was that of a stack of boxes anchored to the ridge. The top floor—on level with the road—was a large square; underneath was a rectangle about two-thirds the width of the first, and the bottom floor was an even narrower rectangle. Rusty screen enclosed porches running the length of each level on the side overlooking the valley.

"Well, we can't complain about the view," Gerry offered. "There's three porches to choose from. Hope it's not too drafty for you. Well, come on. You can explore while I unload stuff."

Getting out, he gratefully stretched his long body, then reached in. "Make it OK?" he inquired solicitously. She pulled herself erect unsteadily, tugging hard on his arm and gripping the door with the other hand. Gerry unloaded her walker, then went to unlock the cabin while Janet hobbled painfully across the pine-needle carpet to the door.

Inside she smiled. "Oh, Gerry! It looks so cozy! I know we'll be happy together here!"

"I hope so, darling!" He brightened.

The screen door slammed shut on squawling hinges.

Janet was exhausted and went to bed early. Gerry had not felt like sleep. The ordeal of driving had left his nerves on edge, and the strange surroundings made him restless. Instead he settled down in one of the huge rocking chairs, propped his feet on the edge of the porch screen and enjoyed the mountain night. Idly his fingers flicked the bottle caps nailed to the wide wooden arm-rests, while he thoughtfully nursed a Scotch and soda. He had brought several fifths down with him—the nearest liquor store would be Knoxville, and Tennessee liquor prices were terrible. He grimaced. Good Scotch was another luxury he could no longer afford.

The mountain breeze was cool and clean, and the night's silence astonished him. Dimly he could hear the whine, see the flicker of light as an occasional car passed along the highway in the valley far below. The house uttered soft groans and squeaks in the darkness, and the rocker answered with a rhythmic creak. From outside came the sounds of creatures of the forest night. Crickets, tree frogs, shrill insect calls. Mice, flying squirrels made soft rustlings in the quiet. An owl called from the distance, and a whippoorwill. Overlying all was the whisper of the pines. Gerry had often heard the expression, but until now he had never understood that pines actually do whisper. Soft, soothing whisper in the night. But a sound so cold, so lonely.

Even bad Scotch gets better with each drink. Maybe not Chivas Regal, but it does the job. Gerry rocked softly, sipped slowly, glass after glass. The night was soothing. Tension slipped from overstrung nerves.

Half in dream he brooded over the turn his life had taken. God, it had all seemed so secure, settled. His wife, their son. A rising position with the firm. Good car, good house, good neighborhood. Country club, the right friends. Bright young man already halfway up the ladder to the top.

Then a woman's inattention, a flaming crash. Only a split second to destroy everything. The funeral, weeks of visits to the hospital. The lawsuit and its cruel joke of an insurance executive whose own policy was inadequate.

All of it destroyed. A comfortable, well-ordered existence torn to twisted wreckage. He could never return to the old life. Despite the sincere best wishes of embarrassed friends, the concerned expressions of doctors who warned him about the emotional shock he had suffered.

Maybe it would have been best if he had been in the car, if he had died in the wreckage of his life.

No . . . that was a death wish. Part of the warnings of those concerned doctors after that scene in the hospital . . . Part of their reasons for urging this vacation upon him . . . "You both have scars that will have to heal . . ."

Gerry laughed softly at the memory of the psychiatrist's attempt to talk with him. In the stillness of the dark cabin his laughter was ghastly. He checked the bottle and noted it was almost empty. Drunk, by God. He supposed he should start bawling in his glass. Yes. Doctor, worry about me. Lose a little sleep in your $300,000 home. God knows how I've waited for the nights to end since then.

Time for bed. Try out that musty old mattress. He drew in a deep lungful of the mountain air. Curious fragrance he had not noticed before. Probably some mountain flower. Something that smelled like jasmine.

II

The cabin stairs were too treacherous for Janet, and so Gerry had to carry her—and then both nearly fell. But Janet insisted on exploring each drafty level of the old place as soon as the late breakfast was cleared. Hungover, Gerry reluctantly joined the game. Strange how frail she seemed in his arms—she had always been so solid. Maybe if she'd exercise her legs more, like the doctors had told her to do.

The cabin was in reasonable repair, but not much more. The floor sagged in places, and the roof showed signs of having leaked, but by and large everything seemed sound. Squirrels had slipped in and chewed up some of the furnishings. The furniture all was cheap, beat-up—caught in a limbo somewhere between antique and junk. None of it had captured the fancy of the countless prowlers who had broken in over the years. Disreputable iron-railed beds with collapsed springs and dirty mattresses, scarred tables and cheap dressers with many layers of paint, boxes and trunks of discarded items. A grimy bookshelf with several Edgar Wallace mysteries, a copy of Fox's *Trail of the Lonesome Pine*, a Bible, odd volumes of *Reader's Digest Condensed Books*, other nondescript items. Janet delightedly pawed through each new trove, and Gerry became interested despite himself. He joined her laughter when one drawer yielded a bedraggled two-piece man's swimming costume.

The first level included the kitchen with its ancient appliances, two bedrooms, a bathroom with an old chemical toilet, and a large open area for dining or sitting. Below were two more bedrooms and a narrower open space along the screened front. The lowermost level was a narrow porch with several army bunks and a room at one end that had once been a bar. The insubstantial posts that supported the cabin were a good twelve feet high at the far end, so that there was a large dry storage area underneath. This had been stuffed with boxes and piles of junk not worth the effort of hauling away.

Here Gerry returned after a light lunch; Janet was tired and wanted to lie down. The disorder was fantastic—a clutter of discarded trivia decades old. Gerry had an appreciation for the cash value of an antique, and with a treasure hunter's enthusiasm he rummaged through the tottering stacks of lost years.

More junk than any attic would attempt. Broken chairs, cracked dishes, boxes of Mason jars, heaps of newspapers, rusty tools, old tires, a wheel-less bicycle, fishing poles. Anything. Doggedly he worked his way from pile to pile, covered with a paste of sweat, red dust and spider web. Once he found a scorpion under a wooden box, and remembered that black widow spiders, too, liked these places. Maybe there were snakes. But he paid no more attention to such misgivings than to the dirt—although a year ago he would not have braved either just to rifle through old junk.

It had been profitable so far. He had pulled out a tool chest, in case he felt up to making repairs. There was a stack of crumbling pulp magazines—*Argosy, Black Mask, Doc Savage, Weird Tales,* and others—that would provide a few laughs. A crockery jug—just like the moonshine jugs in the cartoons—would make a nice lamp. An old copper lantern might be a nice antique, along with the cane-bottomed chair. Some of these picture frames might be valuable. . . .

He stopped. Against one post leaned a stack of old pictures— mostly mountain scenes and calendar cutouts behind glass opaque with dirt. But as he shuffled through them, one picture suddenly caught his eye.

It was an original oil painting, he saw on closer examination, and did not look quite finished. For a moment he remembered stories of undiscovered masterpieces, but laughed the thought aside. Carefully he blew away loose dust. Sandwiched between several larger frames, the canvas was undamaged. Critically he held it to the yellow sunlight.

The picture caught him—drew his attention in a manner he had never experienced. Inexplicable. Art had never meant anything to him, aside from a few tasteful reproductions dutifully purchased to fill wall space.

A woman's portrait, nothing more. Curiously blurred, as if the oils were somewhat translucent. Was it unfinished—or was it an attempt at impressionism? She wore a simple green frock—a light summer outfit stylish in the '20s. Her auburn hair was cut in the short bob popular then. Almost in keeping with the latest styles, but for an indefinable air that proclaimed an older period.

It was a lonely picture. She stood against a background of dark pines, cold and lonely about her. There was a delicacy about her and, illogically, an impression of strength. The face was difficult, its mood seeming altered at each glance. Indefinable. Sensuous mouth—did it smile, or was there sorrow? Perhaps half open in anticipation of a kiss—or a cry? The eyes—soft blue, or did they glow? Did they express longing, pain? Or were they hungry eyes, eyes alight with triumph? Lonely eyes. Lonely face. A lonely picture.

A song, long forgotten, came to his mind.

> In the pines, in the pines.
> Where the sun never shines,
> And I shiver when the wind blows cold . . .

He did shiver then. Sun falling, the mountain wind blew cold through the pines. How long had he been staring at the portrait?

Struck with a chill beyond that of the wind, Gerry cradled his find in cautious hands and started back up the dusty bank.

Janet was in a cheerful mood for a change. Not even a complaint about being ignored most of the afternoon. "Well, let's see what goodies you've brought up from the basement," she laughed, and glanced at the picture. "Oh, there's Twiggy! Gerry, how camp! Look—an original piece of nostalgia!"

He frowned, suddenly offended by her gaiety. In view of the profound impression the picture had made, laughter seemed irreverent. "I thought it was kind of nice myself. Thought I'd hang it up, maybe. Can't you just feel the loneliness of it?"

She gave him a hopeless look. "Oh, wow, you're serious. Hang that old thing up? Gerry, you're kidding. Look how silly she looks."

He glanced at her prefaded bell-bottoms and tank top. "Maybe that will look silly in a few years too."

"Hmmm? I thought you liked these?" She inspected herself in faint concern, wondering if she had gotten too thin. No, Gerry was just being pettish.

"Well, let me take a good look at your treasure." She studied the picture with a professional attitude. On Tuesday afternoons she had taken art lessons along with several of her friends. "The artist is really just too romantic. See—no expression, no depth to his subject. Pale girl against dark woods—it's corny. Too much background for a portrait, and that dress dates it too severely to be idealized—not even a good landscape. His greens are overused and too obvious. His light is all wrong, and there's certainly no imagination with all those dark colors. Is it supposed to be night or day?"

Gerry bit his lip in annoyance. Snotty little dilettante. He wished he knew enough about art to tear apart her prattling criticism.

"This is pretty typical of the sort of maudlin trash they turned out in the '20s. Probably some amateur on vacation here did it of his girlfriend, and she had enough taste to leave it behind. Let's see—it's signed here on the corner, E. Pittman ... 1951. 1951? That's funny ..." she finished awkwardly.

Gerry's mustache twitched sarcastically. "And when did they make you valedictorian of your art class? That gossip session where bored housewives can splash on gobs of paint and call it a subtle interplay of neo-garbage."

That stung. "Oh, stop sulking. So I insulted your male ego because I don't care for your little Twiggy-of-the-woods."

"Because you're too damned insensitive to get into the mood of this painting!" Why had she gotten him so riled over an old picture? "Because you don't feel the ..." *Damn!* How do art critics choose their phrases! "Because you're jealous over a portrait of a beautiful woman!" *What the hell sense did that make?*

"You're not hanging that piece of junk up here!" Now she was mad at him. Her lips made a white line across her blonde face.

"No! No, I'm not! Not where you can sneer at her! I'll hang her up downstairs!"

"Way downstairs, I hope!" she shouted after him, close to tears now. And things had been going so well ...

Dinner had been awkward. Both sheepish but sulking, apologies meant but left unspoken, quarrels ignored but not forgotten.

He left her fiddling with the portable TV afterward, making the excuse that he wanted to read without distraction.

Downstairs he had replenished the old bar. The portrait hung against the wall, watching him. In cleaning it, he had noticed the name "Renee" scrawled at the top. Maybe the artist's name—no, that was E. Pittman. Probably the title, then. Name suited her well. "Mind if I have a drink, Renee?" he murmured. "Wife says I have a few too many a bit too often. Cliché for the day: Bitter hero drowns his grief in booze." The eyes stared back at him. In pity? Loneliness? Hunger? How lost she looked!

Gerry flipped on a lopsided floor lamp and settled down to read some of the pulps he had resurrected. God, how ingenuous the stuff was! Were people ever so naive? He wondered how James Bond would appear to readers back then.

Bugs slipped through the rusty screen and swarmed to the light. Buzzed through his ears, plopped on the pages, fell in his drink. In vexation he finally clicked the lamp off.

His gaze was drawn back to the portrait, visible through the darkness by the glow of the bar light. He considered it with the careful patience four double shots of Scotch can bestow. Who was she, this Renee? She seemed too real to be only an artist's imagination, but it was curious that an artist of the '50s should paint a girl of the '20s. Had she once sat here on this porch and listened to this same wind? This cold, lonesome wind in the pines?

God. Getting sentimental from Scotch. Mellow over a painting that a few months back he'd have laughed at. He closed his eyes wearily and concentrated on the night, letting its ancient spell wash over him.

The cool, velvet-soft night. Pines whispering in the darkness. The sound of loneliness. And Gerry realized he had become a very lonely man. A lost soul—adrift in the darkness of the pines.

Again came the faint scent of jasmine, haunting perfume. Jasmine, antique like this cabin. Worn by enchantresses of another age. Fragrance lingering from dead years. Delicate floral scent worn when beauty was caressed by silken gowns, garlanded with pearls, glinted with lacquered nails. Gone now, vanquished by synthetics. Today a woman clothed, adorned, perfumed herself with coal tar and cellulose. No wonder femininity had declined.

He breathed the rare fragrance, the cool night, somewhere between waking and dreaming. Faintly he heard the rustle of silk behind him, a sound separate from the whisper of the pines. A cold breath on his neck, apart from the mountain breeze. Like the elusive scent of jasmine, sensations alien to the night, yet part of it. The wind brushed his dark hair, stroked his damp forehead, almost as if a cool, delicate hand soothed the lines of pain.

He sighed, almost a shudder. Tension softened, days of anguish lost their sting. A feeling of inexpressible contentment stole over him; anticipation of ecstasy came to him. He parted his lips in a smile of dreamy delight.

"Renee." The sigh escaped him unbidden. It seemed that another's lips hovered close to his own. Sleep came to him then.

III

The sign announced "Pennybacker's Grocery—Drink Coca-Cola." Maryville had modern supermarkets, and ordinarily Gerry would have driven the extra distance. But today the country grocery with its old-fashioned general store atmosphere appealed to him—and it *was* close-by.

The building was old. In front stood two battered gas pumps of some local brand. A long peaked roof overhung to form a sheltered enclosure between gas pumps and store front. Two wooden benches guarded the doorway. Their engraved invitation to "Drink Royal Crown Cola" was almost obliterated by countless carved initials and years of friction from overalls. The paint was starting to peel, and the windows were none too clean. Rusty advertising signs and a year's growth of posters made a faded patchwork of the exterior.

Inside was packed more merchandise than there seemed floorspace for. Strange brands abounded on the crowded shelves. Fresh produce from local farms stood in open baskets. Cuts of meat were displayed within a glass counter. Odd items of hardware, clothing, medicines, tackle augmented the fantastic clutter. Here was a true general store without the artificial quaintness of the counterfeit "country stores" of Gatlinburg's tourist traps.

Grocery buying was something of an adventure, and Gerry was glad Janet had not come along to quarrel over selections. A display of knives caught his eye as he waited for the proprietor to total his purchases on a clattering adding machine. Among the other pocket knives, he recognized the familiar shape of a Barlow knife.

"It that a real Barlow, or a Japanese copy?" he asked.

The storekeeper looked up sharply. "No, sir! Those knives are every one made in America. For your real quality knife you want your American one every time—though there's some likes the German. Take them Case knives there. Now you can't ask for a better knife. Lots of folks swear by a Case knife. Now that Barlow's a fine one too. It's a Camillus, and as fine a knife as any you could've bought fifty years ago. Cost you just four bucks. Want to see one?"

Gerry tossed the stubby knife in his palm and decided to buy it. He had never carried a penknife, and this one was too bulky for his pockets. Still, a good souvenir. The storekeeper was disposed to talk, and the knife led to a rambling conversation.

Lonzo Pennybacker had run this store since the Depression. His uncle had built the place about the time of the Great War, and the gas pumps were some of the first in the area. Lonzo was interested to learn that Gerry was from Columbus—two of his cousins had families up around there, although he supposed Gerry wouldn't know them. No, Gerry guessed he didn't.

Lonzo's expression was peculiar when Gerry mentioned he had rented The Crow's Nest. "So they've got somebody to stay in the old Reagan place again," he reflected.

"Oh?" Gerry's bushy eyebrows rose. "Why do you say that? Is the place haunted or something?"

Pennybacker scratched his pointed chin pensively. "Hants? No—don't think you can say that rightly. Far's I know, nobody's ever seen no hants around the old Reagan place. If it's hants now, you could've seen as many as you'd care in the old Griffin house. Everybody knew it was for sure hanted. Course it burned down in '61.

"No. Far's I know the Reagan place ain't hanted. It's just what they call unlucky."

"Unlucky? How do you mean that?" Gerry wondered if he should laugh.

Lonzo finished packing the groceries before answering. "Well sir, I was just through schoolin' back in '22 when David Reagan built The Crow's Nest. He was a mine owner out of Greenville and a wealthy man as we counted them in those days. Built the place as a honeymoon cabin for him and his wife. Fine handsome young lady, I can remember. She was maybe twenty years younger than David Reagan—he being in his forties and sort of stout. Renee, though, was a mighty prettysome girl."

"Renee?"

"Renee. That was her name. Quite a looker. Wore her hair bobbed and those short dresses and all. A real flapper. Women around here was scandalized with all her city ways and manners. Men though liked her well enough, I'll tell you. Red hair and the devil in her blue eyes. Used to draw a regular crowd down at the hotel swimming pool when she'd come down.

"Well, she liked it here in the mountains, so they spent the summers here. Back then this area was pretty lively. Tourists came from all over to spend their vacations here. Used to be some big fancy resort hotels and all the cottages, too. Yeah, this place was real busy back before they opened the park.

"Well, Renee was a little too much woman for David Reagan, they said. Anyway, summer of 1925 she took up with one of the tourists—good-looking fellow name of Sam Luttle, staying the summer at a resort hotel near here. Far as anyone can say, David Reagan must've found out about them—you know how gossip gets around. So one day Renee just plain vanished. And before anyone really noticed she was missing, David Reagan one night drove his Packard off the side of the mountain. Remember seeing that one. Threw him through the windshield, and his head was just about cut loose.

"When Renee didn't show up, they got to searching for her. But nothing ever did turn up of that girl. Disappeared without a trace. Since David Reagan was known to have a mean temper and a jealous streak besides, folks sort of figured he'd found out about his wife and Sam Luttle, and so he'd killed Renee and hid her body out somewhere in the mountains. All that pine forest—they never could find her.

"Some figured maybe she'd run off with Luttle, but he claimed he didn't know a thing. Anyway, he got chewed up by a bear out walking one night not long afterwards. So there wasn't nobody left who knew anything about the business. David Reagan had a brother who sold the cabin, and it's been passed around and rented ever since."

"And have there been stories since then of ghosts or something in connection with the place?" Somehow the idea did not seem as absurd as it should have.

"No, can't say there has," acknowledged Lonzo, his expression guarded. "Not much of anything unusual gone on at the Reagan place. Nobody's ever cared to keep the place for too long for one reason or another. Still, the only thing you might call mysterious was that artist fellow back in the early '50s."

"Artist? What about him?"

"Some New York fellow. Had some disease, I think. Kind of strange—crazy in the head, you could say, maybe. Anyway, he killed himself after living there a few weeks. Cut his throat with a razor, and didn't find him for a week. Had trouble renting the place for a while after that, you can guess. Fellow's name was—let's see. Enser Pittman."

IV

Janet seemed disgustingly solicitous during dinner, going out of her way to avoid mention of Gerry's long absence that afternoon. She had fixed Swiss steak—one of his favorites—and her eyes were reproachful when he gave curt, noncommittal answers to her attempts at conversation. If only she wouldn't be so overbearing in her attempts to please him, Gerry thought, then act like a whipped dog when he didn't respond effusively.

Dutifully he helped her clear away the dishes—even dried while she washed. Afterward she offered to play gin rummy, but he knew she really didn't like the game, and declined. Conversation grew more dismal, and when Janet seemed disposed to get romantic, he turned on the TV. Presently he lamely mentioned paperwork, and left Janet protesting her loneliness. He thought she was crying again, and the familiar flash of anger returned as he descended the precipitous stairs. Anyway, she'd perk up for the Doris Day flick.

Drink in hand, Gerry once again studied the strange painting which had captured his imagination. E. Pittman—1951. Enser Pittman who had once stayed here. And committed suicide. Artists were never stable types.

But why had he painted a woman dressed in the fashion of a quarter century previous? *Renee.* Gerry felt certain that this Renee was the unfortunate Renee Reagan who had probably been murdered by her jealous husband in this cabin years before.

Of course! Pittman had discovered an old photograph. Certainly he would have learned of the cabin's tragic past, and the photograph of the murdered woman would have appealed to his artistic imagination. A mind on the brink of suicide would have found sick gratification in the portrayal of a murdered temptress from a decadent period like the '20s.

She *was* a beautiful creature. It was easy to see how so much beauty could drive a man to adultery—or murder. Easy to understand why Pittman had been fascinated as an artist.

Moodily he stared at the painting. She was so vital. Pittman must have indeed been talented to incarnate such life within the oils. Strange how her eyes looked into your own. Her smile. If you looked long enough, you could imagine her lips moved, her eyes followed you. Amazing that he had painted it from only a photograph.

She would have been easy to love. Mysterious. Not a shallow housewife like Janet. Strange how things had changed. Once he had loved Janet because she was a perfect housewife and mother. A woman like Renee he would have considered dangerous, trivial—desirable, perhaps, like a film sex goddess, but not the type to love. So old values can change.

And Gerry realized he no longer loved his wife.

Bitterness flooded his mind. Guilt? Should he feel guilty for treating Janet so callously? Was it wrong to be unforgiving over an accident, a simple accident that . . .

"You killed my son!" he choked. Tears of rage, of pain, blinded his eyes. With a sob, Gerry whirled from the painting and flung his empty glass through the doorway of the bar.

He froze—never hearing his glass rip through the rusty veranda screen and shatter against a tree below.

Renee. She was standing in the doorway.

Only for a second did the image last. For an instant he clearly saw her standing before him, watching him from the darkness of the doorway. She was just like her picture: green summer frock, bobbed flame hair, eyes alight with longing, mouth half open in invitation.

Then as his heart stuttered at the vision, she vanished.

Gerry let out his breath with a long exclamation and sank onto a chair. Had he seen a ghost? Had they started bottling LSD with Scotch? He laughed shakily. An after-image, of course. He'd been staring at the painting for an hour. When he had abruptly looked away against the darkened doorway, the image of the painting had superimposed on his retina. Certainly! They'd done experiments like that in college science.

It *had* been unnerving for a second. So that was how haunted houses got their reputation. He glanced about him. The porch was deserted, of course. The wind still whispered its cold breath through the rhythmically swaying pines. Again came a faint scent of jasmine on the night wind. God! It was so peaceful here! So cold and lonely! He closed his eyes and shivered, unreasonably content for the moment. Like being alone with someone you love very much. Just the two of you and the night.

"Gerry! For God's sake, are you all right?"

He catapulted out of the rocker. "What! What? Of course I am! Damn it all, stop screaming! What's wrong with you?" Janet was at the top of the staircase. She called down half in relief, half in alarm. "Well, I heard a glass smash, and you didn't answer when I called you at first. I was afraid you'd fallen or something and were maybe hurt. I was about to start down these steps, if you hadn't answered."

Gerry groaned and said with ponderous patience, "Well, I'm

all right, thank you. Just dropped a glass. Turn down the television next time, and maybe I'll hear you."

"The TV's off." (So that was why she took time to think of him.) "It's started acting crazy again like last night. Can you take a look at it now? It always seems to work OK in the daytime."

She paused and sniffed loudly. "Gerry, do you smell something?"

"Just mountain flowers. Why?"

"No, I mean do you smell something rotten? Can't you smell it? I've noticed it several times at night. It smells like something dead is in the cabin."

V

Gerry had been trying to move an old trunk when he found the diary. The rusty footlocker had been shoved into one of the closets upstairs, and Janet insisted that he lug the battered eyesore downstairs. Gerry grumbled while dragging the heavy locker to the stairs, but its lock was rusted tight, and he was not able to remove the junk inside first. So it was with grim amusement that he watched the trunk slip from his grasp and career down the narrow stairs. At the bottom it burst open like a rotten melon and dumped its musty contents across the floor.

Clothes and books mostly. A squirrel had chewed entrance at one point and shredded most of it, while mildew had ruined the remainder. Gerry righted the broken trunk and carelessly tossed the scattered trash back inside. Let someone else decide what to do with it.

There was a leather-bound notebook. Its cover was thrown back, and he noted the title page: *Diary. Enser Pittman. June-December, 1951*. Gerry looked at the footlocker in alarm. Were these the possessions of that artist, left unclaimed after his suicide?

He set the diary aside until he had cleared away the rest of the debris. Then he succumbed to morbid curiosity and sat down to thumb through the artist's journal. Some of the pages had been chewed away, others were welded together with mould and crumbled as he tried to separate them. But he could read enough to fasten his attention to the tattered diary.

The first few entries were not especially interesting—mostly gloomy comments on the war in Korea and the witch hunts at home, the stupidity of his agent, and what a bitch Arlene was. On June 27, Pittman had arrived at The Crow's Nest for a rest and to try his hand at mountainscapes. From that point, certain passages of the diary assumed a chilling fascination for Gerry.

June 28. Went out for a stroll through the woods today, surprisingly without getting lost or eaten by bears. Splendid pine forest! After N.Y.'s hollow sterile canyons, this is fantastic! God! How strange to be alone! I walked for hours without seeing a soul—or a human. And the carpet of pine needles—so unlike that interminable asphalt-concrete desert! Pure desolation! I feel reborn! Extraordinary those pines. Can't recall any sound so lonely as the wind whispering through their branches. Weird! After N.Y.'s incessant mind-rotting clamor. If I can only express this solitude, this unearthly loneliness on canvas! Fahler is an odious cretin! Landscapes are not trite—rather, the expression has cloyed....

June 30. Haven't found those flowers yet. Guess the night breeze carries the scent a long way. Didn't know jasmine grew here. Weird. At nights it almost feels like a woman's perfume....

July 2. The horns are growing. Several times at night now I've definitely sensed a woman's presence in the darkness. Strange how my imagination can almost give substance to shadow. I can almost make myself visualize her just at the corner of my vision....

July 4. Wow! Too much wine of the gods, Enser! Last time I get patriotic! A little excess of Chianti to celebrate the glorious 4th, I drop off in my chair, and Jesus! Wake up to see a girl bending over me! Nice trick, too! Looked like something out of a Held illustration! Vanished about the time my eyes could focus. Wonder what Freud would say to that! ...

July 7. Either this place is haunted, or I'm going to have to go looking for that proverbial farmer's daughter. Last night I woke up with the distinct impression that there was a woman in bed beside me. Scared? Christ! Like a childhood nightmare! I was actually afraid to reach over—even turn my head to look—and find out if someone was really there. When I finally did check—nothing, of course—I almost imagined I could see a depression on the mattress. The old grey matter is starting to short out. . . .

(The next several pages were too mutilated to decipher, and Gerry pieced together the rest only with extreme difficulty.)

. . . seems to know the whole story, tho it's hard to say how much the good reverend doth impart. Banner's a real character—strickly old-time evangelist. Mostly the same story as Pennybacker's and the other loafers—except Rev. Banner seems to have known Luttle somewhat. Renee was a "woman of Satan," but to him doubtless any "fancy city woman" would reek of sin and godlessness. Anyway his version is that she married Reagan for the bread, but planned to keep her hand in all the same. She seduced Sam Luttle and drove him from the path of righteousness into the morass of sinfulness and adultery. In Banner's opinion Renee only got . . . (half a page missing) . . . no trace of Renee's body was ever discovered. Still it was assumed Reagan had murdered her, since she never turned up again in Greenville or anywhere else—and Reagan seemed definitely to have been on the run when he drove off the mountain. Here Banner gets a bit vague, and it's hard to tell if he's just getting theatrical. Still he insists that when they found Reagan with his throat guillotined by the windshield, there wasn't a tenth as much blood spilled about the body as would be expected. Same regarding Luttle's death. Superficial scratches except the torn throat, and only a small pool of blood. Banner doesn't believe the bear explanation, but I don't get what . . .

(pages missing)

. . . know whether my mind is going or whether this cabin is actually haunted.

July 15. I saw her again last night. This time she was standing at the edge of the pines beyond the front door—seemed to be looking at me. The image lasted maybe 15-20 seconds this time, long enough to get a good look. She's a perfect likeness of the description of Renee. This is really getting bizarre! I'm not quite sure whether I should be frightened or fascinated. I wonder why there haven't been any other reports of this place being haunted. . . .

July 16. I've started to paint her. Wonder what Fahler will say to a portrait of a ghost. It's getting easier now to see her, and she stays visible longer too—maybe she's getting accustomed to me. God—I keep thinking of that old ghost story. The Beckoning Fair One! Hope this won't. . . .

July 17. I find I can concentrate on Renee at nights now, and she appears more readily—more substantial. Painting is progressing well. She seems interested. Think I'll try to talk with her next. Still unsure whether this is psychic phenomenon or paranoid hallucination. We'll see—meanwhile damned if Enser will let anyone else in on this. Tho aren't artists supposed to be mad?

July 18. Decided to use the pines for background. Took a long walk this afternoon. Strange to think that Renee probably lies in an unmarked grave somewhere under this carpet of pine needles. Lonely grave—no wonder she doesn't rest. She smiles when she comes to me. My little spirit remained all of 5-6 minutes last night. Tonight . . .

(pages missing)

. . . to no one other than myself, and I think I understand. This goes back to something Bok once talked about. Spirits inhabit a plane other than our own—another dimension, say. Most spirits and most mortals are firmly anchored to their separate worlds. Exceptions exist. Certain spirits retain some ties with this world. Renee presumably because of her violent death, secret grave— who knows? The artist also is less firmly linked to this humdrum mortal plane—his creativity, his imagination transcends the normal world. Then I am more sensitive to manifestations of another plane than others; Renee is more readily perceived than other spirits. Result: Our favorite insane artist sees ghosts where countless dullards slept soundly. By this line of reasoning anyone can become a bona fide jr. ghostwatcher, if something occurs to make him more susceptible to their manifestations. Madmen, psychic adepts, the dying, those close to the deceased, those who have been torn loose from their normal life pattern . . .

. . . for maybe half the night. I think I'm falling in love with her. Talk about the ultimate in necrophilia!

July 26. The painting is almost complete. Last night she stayed with me almost until dawn. She seems far more substantial now—too substantial for a ghost. Wonder if I'm just getting more adept at perceiving her, or whether Renee is growing more substantial with my belief in her. . . .

July 27. She wanted me to follow her last night. I walked maybe a mile through the dark pines before my nerve failed. Maybe she was taking me to her grave. It's auditory now: Last night I heard her footsteps. I'll swear she leaves tracks in the dust, leaves an impression on the cushions when she sits. She watches me, listens—only no words yet. Maybe tonight she'll speak. She smiles when I tell her I love her.

July 28. I swear I heard her speak! Renee said she loved me! She wants me to return her love! Only a few words—just before she disappeared into the pines. And she seemed as substantial as any living girl! Either I'm hopelessly insane, or I'm on the verge of an unthinkable psychic discovery! Tonight I'm going to know for certain. Tonight I'm going to touch Renee. I'm going to hold her in my arms and not let her go until I know whether I'm mad, the victim of an incredible hoax, or a man in love with a ghost!

It was the last entry.

VI

Lonzo Pennybacker gave directions to the house of the elderly Baptist preacher. Eventually Gerry found the right dirt road and drove up to a well-kept house at the head of a mountain cove. Flowers bloomed in the yard, and dogs were having a melee with a pack of noisy children. The house presented a clean, honest front—a far cry from the squalor Gerry had expected in a mountain home.

Rev. Billy Banner sat in a porch rocker and rose to meet Gerry. He was an alert man in his seventies or better, lean and strong without a trace of weakness or senility. His eyes were clear, and his voice still carried the deep intonations that had rained hellfire and damnation on his congregation for decades.

After shaking hands, Banner motioned him to a chair, politely waited for his guest to come to business. This was difficult. Gerry was uncertain what questions to ask, what explanations to offer—or what he really wanted to find out. But Banner sensed his uneasiness and expertly drew from him the reason for his visit. Gerry explained he was staying at the old Reagan cabin, that he was interested in the artist Enser Pittman who had killed himself there.

"Enser Pittman?" The old man nodded. "Yes, I remember him well enough. He paid me a visit once, just like you today. Maybe for the same reason."

Plunging on, Gerry asked about the history of the cabin and was told little he had not already learned. Rev. Banner spoke with reluctance of the old tragedy, seemed to suspect more than he was willing to put into words.

"Do you have any idea what might have driven Pittman to suicide?" Gerry asked finally.

The preacher kept silent until Gerry wondered if he would ignore the question. "Suicide? That was the verdict, sure enough. They found him mother-naked in bed, his throat tore open and a razor beside him. Been dead a few days—likely it had been done the last of July. No sign of struggle, nothing gone, no enemies. Artists are kind of funny anyway. And some claimed he had cancer. So maybe it was suicide like the coroner said. Maybe not. Wasn't much blood on the sheets for a man to be cut like that, they tell me. All the same, I hope it was suicide, and not something worse."

"I thought suicide was the unforgivable sin."

"There's things worse." Banner looked at him shrewdly. "Maybe you know what I mean. The Bible talks about witches and ghosts and a lot of other things we think we're too wise to believe in today. That Renee Reagan was a daughter of Satan, sure as I'm sitting here remembering her. Well, I'm an old man. but no one's ever called me an old fool, so I'll just stop talking."

Feeling uncomfortable without knowing why, Gerry thanked the preacher and rose to go. Rev. Banner stood up to see him off, then laid a sinewy hand on his shoulder at the edge of the porch.

"I don't know just what sort of trouble you got that's bothering you, son," he began, fixing Gerry with his keen eyes. "But I do know there's something about the old Reagan place that gets to some kinds of people. If that's the way it is with you, then you better get back to where it is you come from. And if you do stay on here, then just remember that Evil can't harm a righteous man so long as he denies its power and holds to the way of Our Lord Jesus Christ and his Gospel. But once you accept Evil—once you let Evil into your life and permit its power to influence your soul—then it's got you body and soul, and you're only a plaything for all the devils of Hell!

"You've got that lost look about you, son. Maybe you can hear that Hell-bound train a-calling to you. But don't you listen to its call. Son, don't you climb on board!"

VII

With a strange mixture of dread and anticipation, Gerry broke away from Janet's mawkish attempts to make conversation and retired to the lower veranda for the evening. All afternoon he had thought about returning to Columbus, forgetting this mystery. Yet he knew he could not. For one thing, he had to stay until he could be certain of his own sanity. Barring madness, this entire uncanny business must be either hoax or genuine. If it were an elaborate hoax, Gerry wanted to know who, how and why. And if the cabin were haunted . . . He *had* to know.

But it was deeper than the simple desire to explore an occult phenomenon. Renee—whoever, whatever she might be—held a profound fascination for him. Her image obsessed him. He thought of this passionate, exotic woman of another era; then there was Janet. Bitterness returned, and again the memory of the son and the ordered world her moronic carelessness had torn from him. Right now she was sitting like a mushroom, spellbound by that boob-tube, never a concern for her husband's misery.

His thoughts were of Renee when sleep overcame him. In dream he saw her drift through the screen door and greet him with red-lipped smile. She was so vivacious, so desirable! Pittman's painting had held only the shadow of her feline beauty.

Gracefully she poured two fingers of Gerry's Scotch and tossed it down neat, eyes wide with devilish challenge. Bringing the bottle with her, she took the chair beside his own. Her long fingers cozily touched his arm. "Nice of you to offer a lady a drink," she grinned impishly. "Good Scotch is so hard to get now. Been saving this stuff in your cellar since before Volstead—or is this just off the boat?"

"Oh, the Prohibition's been repealed for years now," Gerry heard himself say dully, as in a dream. It was a dream. Renee cast no reflection in the barroom mirror.

"Sure honey." She laughed teasingly. "Say, lover—you look all down in the dumps tonight. Care to tell a girl all about it?"

And Gerry began to tell Renee the story of his life. As the night grew deeper, he told her of his struggle to become successful in his work, his efforts to build a position for himself in society, his marriage to a woman who couldn't understand him, his son for whom he had hoped everything, Janet's accident and the death of all his aspirations. Quietly she listened to him, eyes intent with sympathy. God! Why couldn't Janet ever show such feeling, such interest! Always too busy feeling sorry for herself!

When he finished, mechanical sobs shook his angular frame. Renee expressed a wordless cry of concern and laid a white arm around his shoulder. "Hey, c'mon now, Gerry! Get it all out of your system! You've really had a tough break or two, but we can work it out now, can't we? Here now—think about this instead!"

She slithered onto his lap and captured his lips in a long kiss.

Somewhere in the kiss Gerry opened his eyes. With a gasp he started from his chair. No one was there, of course.

God! What a dream! His lips felt bruised, unnaturally cold— even her kiss had felt real. Got to go easy on the bottle. Still if this was DTs, it was pleasant enough. God! Had he ever carried on! That psychiatrist would have had a picnic. He reached for the Scotch. Empty. Had he had that much to drink? No wonder the dream.

Was it a dream? Gerry looked about him suspiciously. The chair beside him seemed maybe closer, although he really hadn't noticed it earlier. An empty glass on the floor—but maybe he'd left it there before. That peculiar scent of jasmine again—wonder what perfume Renee had worn? Absurd—it was mountain flowers.

He touched his lips and there was blood on his fingers.

VIII

"I'm going out for a walk," he told Janet after breakfast.

"Can't you stay around here today for a change?" she asked wistfully. "Or let's go someplace together. You've been off so much lately, I hardly get to see you. And it's so lonely here without anyone around."

"Without a phone to gossip with all the bitches in your bridge club," he snapped. "Well, I'm not sitting on my ass all afternoon watching television. If you want company, then walk along with me!"

"Gerry," she began shakily. "You know I can't . . ."

"No, I don't know! The doctors say you can walk whenever you want to! You're just so content playing the invalid, you won't even try to walk again!"

Her eyes clouded. "Gerry! That was cruel!"

"The truth though, wasn't it!" he exploded. "Well, damn it, snap out of it! I'm getting disgusted with waiting on you hand and foot—tying myself down to someone who can't stop feeling sorry for herself long enough to . . ."

"Gerry!" Janet clenched her fists. "Stop it! What's happening to us! For the last several days you've been getting ever sharper with me! You shun me—avoid my company like you hated me! For God's sake, Gerry, what *is* the matter!"

He turned from her in wordless contempt and strode off into the pine forest. She called after him until he was beyond earshot.

The pines! How restful they were after her miserable whimpering! The dense shade, the deep carpet of fallen needles choked out undergrowth. The dark, straight trunks stabbed toward the sunlight above, leaving a rough shaft branchless for dozens of feet. It was so pleasant to walk among them. The needles were a resilient carpet that deadened all sound. The trunks were myriad pillars to support a vaulted ceiling of swaying green boughs.

It was eerie here in the pines. So unlike a hardwood forest, alive with crackling leaves and a wild variety of trees and underbrush. The pines were so awesome, so ancient, so desolate. The incredible loneliness of this twilight wilderness assailed Gerry—and strangely soothed the turmoil of his emotions.

The restless wind moved the branches above him in ceaseless song. Sighing, whispering pines. Here was the very sound of loneliness. Again Gerry recalled the old mountain folk tune:

> *The longest train I ever saw*
> *Was a hundred coaches long,*
> *And the only girl I ever loved*
> *Was on that train and gone.*
> *In the pines, in the pines,*
> *Where the sun never shines,*
> *And I shiver when the wind blows cold.*

What was happening to him? A year ago he would have laughed at the absurd idea of ghosts or haunted houses. Had he changed so much since then—since the accident?

No, this couldn't actually be happening to him. He must try to examine all the facts with the same clear, down-to-earth attitude he formerly would have taken. He had come here with his nerves in bad shape—on the verge of a breakdown, the doctors had implied. Then he'd found an unusual painting and read through the diary of a deranged artist. Nerves and too much Scotch had got the best of his disordered imagination, and he had assumed the same delusions as poor Pittman. Add to that the stories of the place he had gleaned from the locals, and his newborn romantic streak had run wild—to the point he was sharing Pittman's own mad hallucinations. Similarities were not surprising; the circumstances that induced the delusions were the same, and he had Pittman's notes to direct him.

Besides, if the Reagan place were haunted, why had no one else seen anything out of the ordinary? Pittman in his egotism had claimed his artistic soul made it possible for him to perceive what lesser minds had missed. But Gerry had no artistic pretensions or illusions of paranormal talents.

Pittman had suggested that someone might become susceptible to the spirit world, if he had somehow become alienated from his normal plane of existence. Gerry shrugged mentally. Perhaps then he had become receptive to the other world when the protection of his safe middle-class existence had collapsed about him. But now he was accepting the logic of a suicide.

He paused in bewilderment. The pine forest had suddenly assumed a sense of familiarity. Curiously Gerry studied his surroundings—then it occurred to him. Granted the passage of time, this section of the forest resembled the background in the painting of Renee. He had half assumed Pittman had done a stylized portrayal, rather than an actual landscape. How odd to happen upon the same grove of pines and then to recognize it from the painting.

Why had Pittman chosen this particular section of the pines? Probably he had simply wandered to this spot just as Gerry had done. Still, perhaps there was something that made this spot especially attractive to the artist.

Gerry stood in silence. Was it imagination again? Did the sun seem to shine less brightly here? Did the pines seem to loom darker, with a shadow of menace? Was the whisper of the pines louder here, and was there a note of depravity in the loneliness of the sound? Why were there no cries of birds, no sounds of life, other than the incessant murmur of the brooding pines? And why was there a bare circle of earth where not even the pines grew?

Gerry shivered. He hurried from the spot, no longer so certain of his logic.

IX

Janet was sulking when Gerry returned, and they studiously avoided each other for the remainder of the day. Monosyllables were exchanged when conversation was unavoidable, and whatever went through the mind of either was left to fester unexpressed. Mechanically Janet prepared dinner, although neither felt like eating.

"I can't take this!" Janet finally blurted. "I don't know what's happened to us since we got here, but we're tearing ourselves apart. This just hasn't worked for us, Gerry. Tomorrow I want to go home."

Gerry sighed ponderously. "Now look. We came here so you could rest. And now already you want to go back."

"Gerry, I can't stand it here! Every day I've felt you grow farther away from me! I don't know if it's just this place, or if it's us—but I do know we've got to leave!"

"We'll talk about it in the morning," he said wearily, and stood up.

Janet's lips were set. "Right! Now go on downstairs and drink yourself to sleep! That's the pattern, isn't it? You can't bear to be around me, so you get as far away as you can! And you stumble around all day either drunk or hungover! Always bleary-eyed, paunchy and surly! Gerry, I can't take this any longer!"

He retreated stolidly. "Go to bed, Janet. We'll talk this over in the morning."

"Damn it, Gerry! I've tried to be patient. The doctors warned me you'd made an unhealthy adjustment to the accident—just because you came out no worse than hungover! But if this doesn't stop, I'm going to ask for a separation!"

Gerry halted, angry retorts poised on his tongue. No, let her yell. Ignore her. "Good night, Janet," he grated and fled downstairs.

Angrily he gulped down half a glass of straight Scotch. God! This Scotch was the only thing that held their marriage together—made this situation tolerable. And, he noticed, his stock of Scotch was just about gone.

Divorce! Well, why not! Let the leech live off alimony for the rest of her years. It was almost worth paying to be rid of her! Let her divorce him then! She'd made a ruin of everything else in his life—might as well finish the job right!

Once again he thought of Renee. There was a woman to love, to desire—a woman who could stand on her own two feet, who could return his love with full passion of her own! She and Janet shared their sex with no more in common than a leopardess and a cow. No wonder Pittman had fallen in love with his phantasy of Renee!

Damn Janet! Damn the doctors! Bitching at him about his emotional stability. So he drank more than he used to! So he maybe threw a scene or two, maybe felt a little differently about things now! Well, it was a different world! A man was entitled to make adjustments. Maybe he needed a little more time. . . .

No! It wasn't *his* fault!

The glass slipped from his shaking fist, smashed on the floor. Gerry pawed at it clumsily, cursing the spilled liquor. He'd fix another and clear up tomorrow. Dully he noticed another broken glass. When had he . . . ?

It was late when Gerry finally drifted off to sleep, as had become his habit. Smiling, he welcomed Renee when she came to him. How strange to be dreaming, he mused, and yet know that it's a dream.

"Here again, darling?" There was secret humor in her grave smile. "And looking so sad again. What are we to do with you, Gerry? I so hate to see you all alone in a blue funk every night! The wife?"

"Janet. The bitch!" he mumbled thickly. "She wants me to leave you!"

Renee was dismayed. "Leave? When I'm just getting so fond of you? Hey, lover, that sounds pretty grim!"

Brokenly, Gerry blurted out his anger, his pain. Told her of the lies and insinuations. Told her how hard it was to get through each day, how only a stiff drink and the memory of her smile could calm his nerves each night.

Renee listened in silence, only nodding to show she understood, until he finished and sat quivering with anger. "It sounds to me like you've finally realized Janet has only been a nagging obstruction in your life," she observed. "Surely you've never loved her."

Gerry nodded vehemently. "I hate her!"

She smiled lazily and snuggled closer, her lips only inches from his own. "What about me, Gerry? Do you love your Renee?"

His Renee! "With all my soul!" he whispered huskily.

"Mmmmm. That's sweet." Renee held him with her glowing eyes. "So you love Renee more than Janet?"

"Yes! Of course I do!"

"And would you like to be rid of Janet so you could be with me?"

"God, how I wish that!"

Her smile burned more confident. "What if she died? Would you want Janet dead?"

Bitterness poisoned his spirit. "Janet dead? Yes! That would be perfect! I wish she were dead so we could be together!"

"Oh, sweetheart!" Renee squeezed him delightedly. "You really do love me, don't you! Let's kiss on our bargain!"

Somewhere in her kiss the dream dissolved to blackness.

From upstairs a shriek of black terror shattered the stillness of the night.

He started awake sometime later, groggily rubbed his head while trying to collect his thoughts. What had happened? The dream . . . He remembered. And suddenly he had the feeling that something was wrong, dreadfully *wrong*. Strangely frightened, he staggered up the stairs. "Janet?" he called, his voice unnatural.

Moonlight spilled through the rusty screen and highlighted the crumpled figure who lay in one corner of the room. A small patch of darkness glistened on the wood. Strange how small that pool of blood.

"Janet!" he groaned in disbelieving horror. "Oh, my God!"

Her eyes were wide and staring; her face set in a death grimace of utmost loathing, insane dread. Whatever had killed Janet had first driven her mad with terror.

It had not been an easy death. Her throat was a jagged gash— too ragged a tear for the knife that lay beside her. A Barlow knife. His.

"Janet!" he sobbed, grief slamming him like a sledge. "Who could have done this thing!"

"Don't you know, lover?"

Gerry whirled, cried out in fear. "Renee. You're alive!"

She laughed at him from the shadow, triumph alight in her eyes. She was just as he had seen her in the painting, in the dreams. Green silk frock, bobbed auburn hair, eyes that held dark secrets. Only now her lips were far more crimson, and scarlet trickled across her chin.

"Yes, Gerry. I'm alive and Janet is dead. Just the way you wished. Or have you forgotten?" Mockery was harsh in her voice.

"Impossible!" he moaned. "You've been dead for years! Ghosts can't exist! Not here! Not today!"

But Renee stepped forward, gripped his hand with fingers like frozen steel. Her nails stabbed his wrist. "You know better."

Gerry stared at her in revulsion. "I don't believe in you! You have no power over me!"

"But you *do* believe in me."

"God, help me! Help me!" he sobbed, mind reeling with nightmare.

Contempt lined her face. "Too late for that."

She pulled his arm, drew him to the door. "Come now, lover! We have a sealed bargain!"

He protested—willed himself not to follow. Struggled to awaken from the nightmare. In vain. Helplessly he followed the creature he himself had given substance.

Out into the pines Renee led him. The pines whose incessant whisper told of black knowledge and secret loneliness. Through the desolate pines they walked into the night. Past endless columns of dark sentinel trunks. Swaying, whispering an ancient rhythm with the night wind.

Until they came to a grove Gerard Randall now found familiar. Where the darkness was deeper. Where the whisper was louder and resonant with doom. Where the pines drew back about a circle of earth in which nothing grew.

Where tonight yawned a pit, and he knew where Renee's unhallowed grave lay hidden.

"Is this madness?" he asked with sudden hope.

"No. This is death."

And the illusion of beauty slipped from Renee, revealed the cavern-eyed lich in rotting silk, who pulled him down into the grave like a bride enticing a bashful groom. And in that final moment Gerard Randall understood the whispered litany of the merciless pines.

WHERE THE SUMMER ENDS

I

A long Grand Avenue they've torn the houses down, and left emptiness in their place. On one side a tangle of viaducts, railroad yards and expressways—a scar of concrete and cinder and iron that divides black slum from student ghetto in downtown Knoxville. On the other side, ascending the ridge, shabby relics of Victorian and Edwardian elegance, slowly decaying beneath too many layers of cheap paint and soot and squalor. Most were broken into tawdry apartments—housing for the students at the university that sprawled across the next ridge. Closer to the university, sections had been razed to make room for featureless emplacements of asphalt and imitation used-brick—apartments for the wealthier students. But along Grand Avenue they tore the houses down and left only vacant weed-lots in their place.

Shouldered by the encroaching kudzu, the sidewalks still ran along one side of Grand Avenue, passing beside the tracks and the decrepit shells of disused warehouses. Across the street, against the foot of the ridge, the long blocks of empty lots rotted beneath a jungle of rampant vine—the buried house sites marked by ragged stumps of blackened timbers and low depressions of tumbled-in cellars. Discarded refrigerators and gutted hulks of television sets rusted amidst the weeds and omnipresent litter of beer cans and broken bottles. A green pall over the dismal ruin, the relentless tide of kudzu claimed Grand Avenue.

Once it had been a "grand avenue," Mercer reflected, although those years had passed long before his time. He paused on the cracked pavement to consider the forlorn row of electroliers with their antique lozenge-paned lamps that still lined this block

42

of Grand Avenue. Only the sidewalk and the forgotten electroliers—curiously spared by vandals—remained as evidence that this kudzu-festooned wasteland had ever been an elegant downtown neighborhood.

Mercer wiped his perspiring face and shifted the half-gallon jug of cheap burgundy to his other hand. Cold beer would go better today, but Gradie liked wine. The late afternoon sun struck a shimmering haze from the expanses of black pavement and riotous weed-lots, reminding Mercer of the whorled distortions viewed through antique windowpanes. The air was heavy with the hot stench of asphalt and decaying refuse and Knoxville's greasy smog. Like the murmur of fretful surf, afternoon traffic grumbled along the nearby expressway.

As he trudged along the skewed paving, he could smell a breath of magnolia through the urban miasma. That would be the sickly tree in the vacant lot across from Gradie's—somehow overlooked when the house there had been pulled down and the shrubbery uprooted—now poisoned by smog and strangled beneath the consuming masses of kudzu. Increasing his pace as he neared Gradie's refuge, Mercer reminded himself that he had less than twenty bucks for the rest of this month, and that there was a matter of groceries.

Traffic on the Western Avenue Viaduct snarled overhead, as he passed in the gloom beneath—watchful for the winos who often huddled beneath the concrete arches. He kept his free hand stuffed in his jeans pockets over the double-barrelled .357 magnum derringer—carried habitually since a mugging a year ago. The area was deserted at this time of day and Mercer climbed unchallenged past the rail yards and along the unfrequented street to Gradie's house. Here, as well, the weeds buried abandoned lots, and the kudzu was denser than he remembered from his previous visit. Trailing vines and smothered trees arcaded the sidewalk, forcing him into the street. Mercer heard a sudden rustle deep beneath the verdant tangle as he crossed to Gradie's gate, and he thought unpleasantly of the gargantuan rats he had glimpsed lying dead in gutters near here.

Gradie's house was one of the last few dwellings left standing in this waste—certainly it was the only one to be regularly inhabited. The other sagging shells of gaping windows and rotting board were almost too dilapidated even to shelter the winos and vagrants who squatted hereabouts.

The gate resisted his hand for an instant—mired over with the fast-growing kudzu that had so overwhelmed the low fence, until Mercer had no impression whether it was of wire or pickets. Chickens flopped and scattered as he shoved past the gate. A brown-and-yellow dog, whose ancestry might once have contained a trace of German shepherd, growled from his post beneath the wooden porch steps. A cluster of silver maples threw a moth-eaten blanket of shade over the yard. Eyes still dazzled from the glare of the pavement, Mercer needed a moment to adjust his vision to the sooty gloom within. By then Gradie was leaning the shotgun back amidst the deeper shadows of the doorway, stepping onto the low porch to greet him.

"Goddamn winos," Gradie muttered, watching Mercer's eyes.

"Much trouble with stealing?" the younger man asked.

"Some," Gradie grunted. "And the goddamn kids. Hush up that growling, Sheriff!"

He glanced protectively across the enclosed yard and its ramshackle dwelling. Beneath the trees, in crates and barrels, crude stands and disordered heaps, lying against the flimsy walls of the house, stuffed into the outbuildings: the plunder of the junk piles of another era.

It was a private junk yard of the sort found throughout any urban slum, smaller than some, perhaps a fraction more tawdry. Certainly it was as out-of-the-way as any. Mercer, who lived in the nearby student quarter, had stumbled upon it quite by accident only a few months before—during an afternoon's hike along the railroad tracks. He had gleaned two rather nice blue-green insulators and a brown-glass coke bottle by the time he caught sight of Gradie's patch of stunted vegetables between the tracks and the house that Mercer had never noticed from the street. A closer look had disclosed the yard with its moraine of cast-off salvage, and a badly weathered sign that evidently had once read "Red's Second Hand" before a later hand had overpainted "Antiques."

A few purchases—very minor, but then Mercer had never seen another customer here—and several afternoons of digging through Gradie's trove, had spurred that sort of casual friendship that exists between collector and dealer. Mercer's interest in "collectibles" far outstripped his budget: Gradie seemed lonely, liked to talk, very much liked to drink wine. Mercer had hopes of talking the older man down to a reasonable figure on the mahogany mantel he coveted.

"I'll get some glasses," Gradie said, acknowledging the jug of burgundy. He disappeared into the cluttered interior. From the direction of the kitchen came a clatter and sputter of the tap.

Mercer was examining a stand of old bottles, arrayed on their warped and unpainted shelves like a row of targets balanced on a fence for execution by boys and a new .22. Gradie, two jelly glasses sloshing with burgundy, reappeared at the murkiness of the doorway, squinting blindly against the sun's glare. Mercer thought of a greying groundhog, or a narrow-eyed pack rat, crawling out of its burrow—an image tinted grey and green through the shimmering curvatures of the bottles, iridescently filmed with a patina of age and cinder.

He had the thin, worn features that would have been thin and watchful as a child, would only get thinner and more watchful with the years. The limp, sandy hair might have been red before the sun bleached it and the years leeched it to a yellow-grey. Gradie was tall, probably had been taller than Mercer before his stance froze into a slouch and then into a stoop, and had a dirty sparseness to his frame that called to mind the scarred mongrel dog that growled from beneath the steps. Mercer guessed he was probably no younger than fifty and probably not much older than eighty.

Reaching between two opalescent-sheened whiskey bottles, Mercer accepted a glass of wine. Distorted through the rows of bottles, Gradie's face was watchful. His bright slits of colorless eyes flicked to follow the other's every motion—this through force of habit: Gradie trusted the student well enough.

"Got some more of those over by the fence," Gradie pointed. "In that box there. Got some good ones. This old boy dug them, some place in Vestal, traded the whole lot to me for that R.C. Cola thermometer you was looking at once before." The last with a slight sly smile, flicked lizard-quick across his thin lips: Mercer had argued that the price on the thermometer was too high.

Mercer grunted noncommittally, dutifully followed Gradie's gesture. There might be something in the half-collapsed box. It was a mistake to show interest in any item you really wanted, he had learned—as he had learned that Gradie's eyes were quick to discern the faintest show of interest. The too-quick reach for a certain item, the wrong inflection in a casual "How much?" might make the difference between two bits and two bucks for a dusty book or a rusted skillet. The matter of the mahogany mantelpiece wanted careful handling.

Mercer squatted beside the carton, stirring the bottles gingerly. He was heavy-set, too young and too well-muscled to be called beefy. Sporadic employment on construction jobs and a more or less adhered-to program of workouts kept any beer gut from spilling over his wide belt, and his jeans and tank top fitted him as snugly as the older man's faded work clothes hung shapelessly. Mercer had a neatly trimmed beard and subtly receding hairline to his longish black hair that suggested an older grad student as he walked across campus, although he was still working for his bachelor's—in a major that had started out in psychology and eventually meandered into fine arts.

The bottles had been hastily washed. Crusts of cinder and dirt obscured the cracked and chipped exteriors, and within were mats of spider web and mouldy moss. A cobalt-blue bitters bottle might clean up nicely, catch the sun on the hallway window ledge, if Gradie would take less than a buck.

Mercer nudged a lavender-hued whiskey bottle. "How much for these?"

"I'll sell you those big ones for two, those little ones for one-fifty."

"I could dig them myself for free," Mercer scoffed. "These weed-lots along Grand are full of old junk heaps."

"Take anything in the box for a buck then," Gradie urged him. "Only don't go poking around those goddamn weed-lots. Under that kudzu. I wouldn't crawl into that goddamn vine for any money!"

"Snakes?" Mercer inquired politely.

Gradie shrugged, gulped the rest of his wine. "Snakes or worse. It was in the kudzu they found old Morny."

Mercer tilted his glass. In the afternoon sun the burgundy had a heady reek of hot alcohol, glinted like bright blood. "The cops ever find out who killed him?"

Gradie spat. "Who gives a damn what happens to old winos?"

"When they start slicing each other up like that, the cops had damn well better do something."

"Shit!" Gradie contemplated his empty glass, glanced toward the bottle on the porch. "What do they know about knives? You cut a man if you're just fighting; you stab him if you want him dead. You don't slice a man up so there's not a whole strip of skin left on him."

II

"But it had to have been a gang of winos," Linda decided. She selected another yellow flower from the dried bouquet, inserted it into the bitters bottle.

"I think that red one," Mercer suggested.

"Don't you remember that poor old man they found last spring? All beaten to death in an abandoned house. And they caught the creeps who did it to him—they were a couple of his old drinking buddies, and they never did find out why."

"That was over in Lonsdale," Mercer told her. "Around here the pigs decided it was the work of hippie-dope-fiends, hassled a few street people, forgot the whole deal."

Linda trimmed an inch from the dried stalk, jabbed the red strawflower into the narrow neck. Stretching from her bare toes, she lifted the bitters bottle to the window shelf. The morning sun, spilling into the foyer of the old house, pierced the cobalt-blue glass in an azure star.

"How much did you say it cost, Jon?" She had spent an hour scrubbing at the bottle with test tube brushes a former roommate had left behind.

"Fifty cents," Mercer lied. "I think what probably happened was that old Morny got mugged, and the rats got to him before they found his body."

"That's really nice," Linda judged. "I mean the bottle." Freckled arms akimbo, sleeves rolled up on old blue workshirt, faded blue jeans, morning sun a nimbus through her whiskey-colored close curls, eyes two shades darker than the azure star.

Mercer remembered the half-smoked joint on the hall balustrade, struck a match. "God knows there are rats big enough to do that to a body down under the kudzu. I'm sure it was rats that killed Midnight last spring."

"Poor old tomcat," Linda mourned. She had moved in with Mercer about a month before it happened, remembered his stony grief when their search had turned up the mutilated cat. "The city ought to clear off these weed-lots."

"All they ever do is knock down the houses," Mercer got out, between puffs. "Condemn them so you can't fix them up again. Tear them down so the winos can't crash inside."

"Wasn't that what Morny was doing? Tearing them down, I mean?"

"Sort of," Mercer coughed. "He and Gradie were partners. Gradie used to run a second-hand store back before the neighborhood had rotted much past the edges. He used to buy and sell salvage from the old houses when they started to go to seed. The last ten years or so, after the neighborhood had completely deteriorated, he started working the condemned houses. Once a house is condemned, you pretty well have to pull it down, and that costs a bundle—either to the owner, or, since usually it's abandoned property, to the city. Gradie would work a deal where they'd pay him something to pull a house down—not very much, but he could have whatever he could salvage.

"Gradie would go over the place with Morny, haul off anything Gradie figured was worth saving—and by the time he got the place, there usually wasn't much. Then Gradie would pay Morny maybe five or ten bucks a day to pull the place down—taking it out of whatever *he'd* been paid to do the job. Morny would make a show of it, spend a couple weeks tearing out scrap timber and the like. Then, when they figured they'd done enough, Morny would set fire to the shell. By the time the fire trucks got there, there'd just be a basement full of coals. Firemen would spray some water, blame it on the winos, forget about it. The house would be down, so Gradie was clear of the deal—and the kudzu would spread over the empty lot in another year."

Linda considered the roach, snuffed it out and swallowed it. Waste not, want not. "Lucky they never burned the whole neighborhood down. Is that how Gradie got that mantel you've been talking about?"

"Probably." Mercer followed her into the front parlor. The mantel had reminded Linda that she wanted to listen to a record.

The parlor—they used it as a living room—was heavy with stale smoke and flat beer and the pungent odor of Brother Jack's barbecue. Mercer scowled at the litter of empty Rolling Rock bottles, crumpled napkins and sauce-stained rinds of bread. He ought to clean up the house today, while Linda was in a domestic mood—but that meant they'd have to tackle the kitchen, and that was an all-day job—and he'd wanted to get her to pose while the sun was right in his upstairs studio.

Linda was having problems deciding on a record. It would be one of hers, Mercer knew, and hoped it wouldn't be Dylan again. She had called his own record library one of the wildest collections of curiosa ever put on vinyl. After half a year of living together, Linda still thought resurrected radio broadcasts of "The Shadow" were a camp joke; Mercer continued to argue that Dylan couldn't sing a note. Withal, she always paid her half of the rent on time. Mercer reflected that he got along with her better than with any previous roommate, and while the house was subdivided into a three-bedroom apartment, they never advertised for a third party.

The speakers, bunched on either side of the hearth, came to life with a scratchy Fleetwood Mac album. It drew Mercer's attention once more to the ravaged fireplace. Some Philistine landlord, in the process of remodelling the dilapidated Edwardian mansion into student apartments, had ripped out the mantel and boarded over the grate with a panel of cheap plywood. In defiance of landlord and fire laws, Mercer had torn away the panel and unblocked the chimney. The fireplace was small with a grate designed for coal fires, but Mercer found it pleasant on winter nights. The hearth was of chipped ceramic tiles of a blue-and-white pattern—someone had told him they were Dresden. Mercer had scraped away the grime from the tiles, found an ornate brass grille in a flea market near Seymour. It remained to replace the mantel. Behind the plywood panel, where the original mantel had stood, was an ugly smear of bare brick and lathing. And Gradie had such a mantel.

"We ought to straighten up in here," Linda told him. She was doing a sort of half-dance around the room, scooping up debris and singing a line to the record every now and then.

"I was wondering if I could get you to pose for me this morning?"

"Hell, it's too nice a day to stand around your messy old studio."

"Just for a while. While the sun's right. If I don't get my figure studies handed in by the end of the month. I'll lose my incomplete."

"Christ, you've only had all spring to finish them."

"We can run down to Gradie's afterward. You've been wanting to see the place."

"And the famous mantel."

"Perhaps if the two of us work on him?"

The studio—so Mercer dignified it—was an upstairs front room, thrust outward from the face of the house and onto the roof of the veranda, as a sort of cold weather porch. Three-quarter-length casement windows with diamond panes had at one time swung outward on three sides, giving access onto the tiled porch roof. An enterprising landlord had blocked over the windows on either side, converting it into a small bedroom. The front wall remained a latticed expanse through which the morning sun flooded the room. Mercer had adopted it for his studio, and now Linda's houseplants bunched through his litter of canvases and drawing tables.

"Jesus, it's a nice day!"

Mercer halted his charcoal, scowled at the sheet. "You moved your shoulder again," he accused her.

"Lord, can't you hurry it?"

"Genius can never be hurried."

"Genius my ass." Linda resumed her pose. She was lean, high-breasted and thin-hipped, with a suggestion of freckles under her light tan. A bit taller, and she would have had a career as a fashion model. She had taken enough dance to pose quite well—did accept an occasional modelling assignment at the art school when cash was short.

"Going to be a *good* summer." It was that sort of morning.

"Of course." Mercer studied his drawing. Not particularly inspired, but then he never did like to work in charcoal. The sun picked bronze highlights through her helmet of curls, the feathery patches of her mons and axillae. Mercer's charcoal poked dark blotches at his sketch's crotch and armpits. He resisted the impulse to crumple it and start over.

Part of the problem was that she persisted in twitching to the beat of the music that echoed lazily from downstairs. She was playing that Fleetwood Mac album to death—had left the changer arm askew so that the record would repeat until someone changed it. It didn't help him concentrate—although he'd memorized the record to the point he no longer needed listen to the words.

When he glanced at her again, something was wrong. Linda's pose was no longer relaxed. Her body was rigid, her expression tense.

"What is it?"

She twisted her face toward the windows, brought one arm across her breasts. "Someone's watching me."

With an angry grunt, Mercer tossed aside the charcoal, shouldered through the open casement to glare down at the street.

The sidewalks were deserted. Only the usual trickle of Saturday morning traffic drifted past. Mercer continued to scowl balefully as he studied the parked cars, the vacant weed-lot across the street, the tangle of kudzu in his front yard. Nothing.

"There's nothing out there."

Linda had shrugged into a paint-flecked fatigue jacket. Her eyes were worried as she joined him at the window.

"There's something. I felt all crawly all of a sudden."

The roof of the veranda cut off view of the windows from the near sidewalk, and from the far sidewalk it was impossible to see into the studio by day. Across the street, the houses directly opposite had been pulled down. The kudzu-covered lots pitched steeply across more kudzu-covered slope, to the roofs of warehouses along the rail yard a block below. If Linda were standing directly at the window, someone on the far sidewalk might look up to see her; otherwise there was no vantage from which a curious eye could peer into the room. It was one of the room's attractions as a studio.

"See. No one's out there."

Linda made a squirming motion with her shoulders. "They walked on, then," she insisted.

Mercer snorted, suspected an excuse to cut short the session. "They'd have had to run. Don't see anyone hiding out there in the weeds, do you?"

She stared out across the tangled heaps of kudzu, waving faintly in the last of the morning's breeze. "Well, there *might* be someone hiding under all that tangle." Mercer's levity annoyed her. "Why can't the city clear off those damn jungles!"

"When enough people raise a stink, they sometimes do—or make the owners clear away the weeds. The trouble is that you can't kill kudzu once the damn vines take over a lot. Gradie and Morny used to try. The stuff grows back as fast as you cut it— impossible to get all the roots and runners. Morny used to try to burn it out—crawl under and set fire to the dead vines and debris underneath the growing surface. But he could never keep a fire going under all that green stuff, and after a few spectacular failures using gasoline on the weed-lots, they made him stick to grubbing it out by hand."

"Awful stuff!" Linda grimaced. "Some of it's started growing up the back of the house."

"I'll have to get to it before it gets started. There's islands in the TVA lakes where nothing grows but kudzu. Stuff ran wild after the reservoir was filled, smothered out everything else."

"I'm surprised it hasn't covered the whole world."

"Dies down after the frost. Besides it's not a native vine. It's from Japan. Some genius came up with the idea of using it as an ornamental ground cover on highway cuts and such. You've seen old highway embankments where the stuff has taken over the woods behind. It's spread all over the Southeast."

"Hmm, yeah? So who's the genius who plants the crap all over the city then?"

"Get dressed, wise-ass."

III

The afternoon was hot and sodden. The sun made the air above the pavement scintillant with heat and the thick odor of tar. In the vacant lots, the kudzu leaves drooped like half-furled umbrellas. The vines stirred somnolently in the musky haze, although the air was stagnant.

Linda had changed into a halter top and a pair of patched cut-offs. "Bet I'll get some tan today."

"And maybe get soaked," Mercer remarked. "Air's got the feel of a thunderstorm."

"Where's the clouds?"

"Just feels heavy."

"That's just the goddamn pollution."

The kudzu vines had overrun the sidewalk, forcing them into the street. Tattered strands of vine crept across the gutter into the street, their tips crushed by the infrequent traffic. Vines along Gradie's fence completely obscured the yard beyond, waved curling tendrils aimlessly upward. In weather like this, Mercer reflected, you could just about see the stuff grow.

The gate hung again at first push. Mercer shoved harder, tore through the coils of vine that clung there.

"Who's that?" The tone was harsh as a saw blade hitting a nail.

"Jon Mercer, Mr. Gradie. I've brought a friend along."

He led the way into the yard. Linda, who had heard him talk about the place, followed with eyes bright for adventure. "This is Linda Wentworth, Mr. Gradie."

Mercer's voice trailed off as Gradie stumbled out onto the porch. He had the rolling slouch of a man who could carry a lot of liquor and was carrying more liquor than he could. His khakis were the same he'd had on when Mercer last saw him, and had the stains and wrinkles that clothes get when they're slept in by someone who hasn't slept well.

Red-rimmed eyes focused on the half-gallon of burgundy Mercer carried. "Guess I was taking a little nap." Gradie's tongue was muddy. "Come on up."

"Where's Sheriff?" Mercer asked. The dog usually warned his master of trespassers.

"Run off," Gradie told him gruffly. "Let me get you a glass." He lurched back into the darkness.

"Owow!" breathed Linda in one syllable. "He looked like something you see sitting hunched over on a bench talking to a bottle in a bag."

"Old Gradie has been hitting the sauce pretty hard last few times I've been by," Mercer allowed.

"I don't think I care for any wine just now," Linda decided, as Gradie reappeared, fingers speared into three damp glasses like a bunch of mismatched bananas. "Too hot."

"Had some beer in the frigidaire, but it's all gone."

"That's all right." She was still fascinated with the enclosed yard. "What a lovely garden!" Linda was into organic foods.

Gradie frowned at the patch of anemic vegetables, beleaguered by encroaching walls of kudzu. "It's not much, but I get a little from it. Damn kudzu is just about to take it all. It's took the whole damn neighborhood—everything but me. Guess they figure to starve me out once the vines crawl over my little garden patch."

"Can't you keep it hoed?"

"Hoe kudzu, miss? No damn way. The vines grow a foot between breakfast and dinner. Can't get to the roots, and it just keeps spreading till the frost; then come spring it starts all over again where the frost left it. I used to keep it back by spraying it regular with 2.4-D. But then the government took 2.4-D off the market, and I can't find nothing else to touch it."

"Herbicides kill other things than weeds," Linda told him righteously.

Gradie's laugh was bitter. "Well, you folks just look all around as you like."

"Do you have any old clothes?" Linda was fond of creating costumes.

"Got some inside there with the books." Gradie indicated a shed that shouldered against his house. "I'll unlock it."

Mercer raised a mental eyebrow as Gradie dragged open the door of the shed, then shuffled back onto the porch. The old man was more interested in punishing the half-gallon than in watching his customers. He left Linda to poke through the dusty jumble of warped books and faded clothes, stacked and shelved and hung and heaped within the tin-roofed musty darkness.

Instead, he made a desultory tour about the yard—pausing now and again to examine a heap of old hubcaps, a stack of salvaged window frames or a clutter of plumbing and porcelain fixtures. His deviousness seemed wasted on Gradie today. The old man remained slumped in a broken-down rocker on his porch, staring at nothing. It occurred to Mercer that the loss of Sheriff was bothering Gradie. The old yellow watchdog was about his only companion after Morny's death. Mercer reminded himself to look for the dog around campus.

He ambled back to the porch. A glance into the shed caught Linda trying on an oversized slouch hat. Mercer refilled his glass, noted that Gradie had gone through half the jug in his absence. "All right if I look at some of the stuff inside?"

Gradie nodded, rocked carefully to his feet, followed him in. The doorway opened into the living room of the small frame house. The living room had long since become a warehouse and museum for all of Gradie's choice items. There were a few chairs left to sit on, but the rest of the room had been totally taken over by the treasures of a lifetime of scavenging. Gradie himself had long ago been reduced to the kitchen and back bedroom for his own living quarters.

China closets crouched on lion paws against the wall, showing their treasures behind curved glass bellies. Paintings and prints in ornate frames crowded the spider webs for space along the walls. Mounted deer's heads and stuffed owls gazed fixedly from their moth-eaten poses. Threadbare oriental carpets lay in a great mound of bright-colored sausages. Mahogany dinner chairs were stacked atop oak and walnut tables. An extravagant brass bed reared from behind a gigantic Victorian buffet. A walnut bookcase displayed choice volumes and bric-a-brac beneath a signed Tiffany lamp. Another bedroom and the dining room were virtually impenetrable with similar storage.

Not everything was for sale. Mercer studied the magnificent walnut china cabinet that Gradie reserved as a showcase for his personal museum. Surrounded by the curving glass sides, the mementos of the junk dealer's lost years of glory reposed in dust-less grandeur. Faded photographs of men in uniforms, inscribed snapshots of girls with pompadours and padded-shoulder dresses. Odd items of military uniform, medals and insignia, a brittle silk square emblazoned with the Rising Sun. Gradie was proud of his wartime service in the Pacific.

There were several hara-kiri knives—so Gradie said they were—a Nambu automatic and holster, and a Samurai sword that Gradie swore was five hundred years old. Clippings and sou-venirs and odd bits of memorabilia of the Pacific theatre, most bearing yellowed labels with painstakingly typed legends. A fist-sized skull—obviously some species of monkey—bore the label: "Jap General's Skull."

"That general would have had a muzzle like a possum," Mercer laughed. "Did you find it in Japan?"

"Bought it during the Occupation," Gradie muttered. "From one little Nip, said it come from a mountain-devil."

Despite the heroic-sounding labels throughout the dis-play—"Flag Taken from Captured Jap Officer"—Mercer guessed that most of the mementos had indeed been purchased while Gradie was stationed in Japan during the Occupation.

Mercer sipped his wine and let his eyes drift about the room. Against one wall leaned the mahogany mantel, and he must have let his interest flicker in his eyes.

"I see you're still interested in the mantel," Gradie slurred, mercantile instincts rising through his alcoholic lethargy.

"Well, I see you haven't sold it yet."

Gradie wiped a trickle of wine from his stubbled chin. "I'll get me a hundred-fifty for that, or I'll keep it until I can get me more. Seen one like it, not half as nice, going for two hundred, place off Chapman Pike."

"They catch the tourists from Gatlinburg," Mercer sneered.

The mantel was of African mahogany, Mercer judged—darker than the reddish Philippine variety. For a miracle only a film of age-blackened lacquer obscured the natural grain—Mercer had spent untold hours stripping layers of cheap paint from the mahogany panel doors of his house.

It was solid mahogany, not a veneer. The broad panels that

framed the fireplace were matched from the same log so that their grains formed a mirror image. The mantelpiece itself was wide and sturdy, bordered by a tiny balustrade. Above that stretched a fine bevelled mirror, still perfectly silvered, flanked by lozenge-shaped mirrors on either side. Ornately carved mahogany candlesticks jutted from either side of the mantelpiece, so that a candle flame would reflect against the bevelled lozenges. More matched-grain panels continued ceilingward above the mirrors, framed by a second balustraded mantelshelf across the top. Mercer could just about touch it at fullest stretch.

Exquisite, and easily worth Gradie's price. Mercer might raise a hundred of it—if he gave up eating and quit paying rent for a month or three.

"Well, I won't argue it's a beauty," he said. "But a mantel isn't just something you can buy and take home under your arm, brush it off and stick it in your china closet—that's furniture. Thing like this mantel is only useful if you got a fireplace to match it with."

"You think so," Gradie scoffed. "Had a lady in here last spring, fine big house out in west Knoxville. Said she'd like to antique it with one of those paint kits, fasten it against a wall for a stand to display her plants. Wanted to talk me down to one-twenty-five, though, and I said 'no ma'am.'"

Linda's scream ripped like tearing glass.

Mercer spun, was out the door and off the porch before he quite knew he was moving. "Linda!"

She was scrambling backward from the shed, silent now, but her face ugly with panic. Stumbling, she tore a wrinkled flannel jacket from her shoulders, with revulsion threw it back into the shed.

"Rats!" she shuddered, wiping her hands on her shorts. "In there under the clothes! A great *big* one! Oh, Jesus!"

But Gradie had already burst out of his house, shoved past Mercer—who had pulled short to laugh. The shotgun was a rust-and-blue blur as he hinged past Linda. The shed door slammed to behind him.

"*Oh, Jesus!*"

The boom of each barrel, megaphoned by the confines of

the shed, and, in the finger-twitch between each blast, the shrill chitter of pain.

"*Jon!*"

Then the hysterical cursing from within, and a muffled stomping.

Linda, who had never gotten used to Mercer's guns, was clawing free of his reassuring arm. "Let's go! Let's go!" She was kicking at the gate, as Gradie slid back out of the shed, closing the door on his heel.

"Goddamn big rat, miss," he grinned crookedly. "But I sure done for him."

"Jon, I'm going!"

"Catch you later, Mr. Gradie," Mercer yelled, grimacing in embarrassment. "Linda's just a bit freaked."

If Gradie called after him, Mercer didn't hear. Linda was walking as fast as anyone could without breaking into a run, as close to panic as need be. He loped after her.

"Hey Linda! Everything's cool! Wait up!"

She didn't seem to hear. Mercer cut across the corner of a weed-lot to intercept her. "Hey! Wait!"

A vine tangled his feet. With a curse, he sprawled headlong. Flinching at the fear of broken glass, he dropped to his hands and knees in the tangle of kudzu. His flailing hands slid on something bulky and foul, and a great swarm of flies choked him.

"Jon!" At his yell, Linda turned about. As he dove into the knee-deep kudzu, she forgot her own near-panic and started toward him.

"I'm OK!" he shouted. "Just stay there. Wait for me."

Wiping his hands on the leaves, he heaved himself to his feet, hid the revulsion from his face. He swallowed the rush of bile and grinned.

Let her see Sheriff's flayed carcass just now, and she *would* flip out.

IV

Mercer had drawn the curtains across the casement windows, but Linda was still reluctant to pose for him. Mercer decided she had not quite recovered from her trip to Gradie's.

She sneered at the unshaded floor lamp. "You and your morning sunlight."

Mercer batted at a moth. "In the morning we'll be off for the mountains." This, the bribe for her posing. "I want to finish these damn figure studies while I'm in the mood."

She shivered, listened to the nocturnal insects beat against the curtained panes. Mercer thought it was stuffy, but enough of the evening breeze penetrated the cracked casements to draw her nipples taut. From the stairwell arose the scratchy echoes of the Fleetwood Mac album—Mercer wished Linda wouldn't play an album to death when she bought it.

"Why don't we move into the mountains?"

"Be nice." This sketch was worse than the one this morning.

"No." Her tone was sharp. "I'm serious."

The idea was too fanciful, and he was in no mood to argue over another of her whims tonight. "The bears would get us."

"We could fix up an old place, maybe. Or put up a log cabin."

"You've been reading *Foxfire Book* too much."

"No, I mean it! Let's get out of here!"

Mercer looked up. Yes, she did seem to mean it. "I'm up for it. But it would be a bit rough for getting to class. And I don't think they just let you homestead anymore."

"Screw classes!" she groaned. "Screw this grungy old dump! Screw this dirty goddamn city!"

"I've got plans to fix this place up into a damn nice townhouse," Mercer reminded her patiently. "Thought this summer I'd open up the side windows in here—tear out this lousy sheet-rock they nailed over the openings. Gradie's got his eye out for some casement windows to match the ones we've got left."

"Oh, Jesus! Why don't you just stay the hell away from Gradie's!"

"Oh, for Christ's sake!" Mercer groaned. "You freak out over a rat, and Gradie blows it away."

"It wasn't just a rat."

"It was the Easter bunny in drag."

"It had paws like a monkey."

Mercer laughed. "I told you this grass was well worth the forty bucks an ounce."

"It wasn't the grass we smoked before going over."

"Wish we didn't have to split the bag with Ron," he mused, wondering if there was any way they might raise the other twenty.

"Oh, screw you!"

Mercer adjusted a fresh sheet onto his easel, started again. This one would be *Pouting Model,* or maybe *Uneasy Girl.* He sketched in silence for a while. Silence, except for the patter of insects on the windows, and the tireless repetitions of the record downstairs.

"I just want to get away from here," Linda said at last.

In the darkness downstairs, the needle caught on the scratched grooves, and the stereo mindlessly repeated:

"So afraid . . . So afraid . . . So afraid . . . So afraid . . ."

By one a.m., the heat lightning was close enough to suggest a ghost of thunder, and the night breeze was gusting enough to billow the curtains. His sketches finished—at least, as far as he cared—Mercer rubbed his eyes and debated closing the windows before going to bed. If a storm came up, he'd have to get out of bed in a hurry. If he closed them and it didn't rain, it would be too muggy to sleep. Mechanically he reached for his coffee cup, frowned glumly at the drowned moth that floated there.

The phone was ringing.

Linda was in the shower. Mercer trudged downstairs and scooped up the receiver.

It was Gradie, and from his tone he hadn't been drinking milk.

"Jon, I'm sure as hell sorry about giving your little lady a fright this afternoon."

"No problem, Mr. Gradie. Linda was laughing about it by the time we got home."

"Well, that's good to hear, Jon. I'm sure glad to hear she wasn't scared bad."

"That's quite all right, Mr. Gradie."

"Just a goddamn old rat, wasn't it?"

"Just a rat, Mr. Gradie."

"Well, I'm sure glad to hear that."

"Right you are, Mr. Gradie." He started to hang up.

"Jon, what else I was wanting to talk to you about though, was to ask you if you really wanted that mantel we was talking about today."

"Well, Mr. Gradie, I'd sure as hell like to buy it, but it's a little too rich for my pocketbook."

"Jon, you're a good old boy. I'll sell it to you for a hundred even."

"Well now, sir—that's a fair enough price, but a hundred dollars is just too much money for a fellow who has maybe ten bucks a week left to buy groceries."

"If you really want that mantel—and I'd sure like for you to have it—I'd take seventy-five for it right now tonight."

"Seventy-five?"

"I got to have it right now tonight. Cash."

Mercer tried to think. He hadn't paid rent this month. "Mr. Gradie, it's one in the morning. I don't have seventy-five bucks in my pocket."

"How much can you raise, then?"

"I don't know. Maybe fifty."

"You bring me fifty dollars cash tonight, and take that mantel home."

"Tonight?"

"You bring it tonight. I got to have it right now."

"All right, Mr. Gradie. See you in an hour."

"You hurry now," Gradie advised him. There was a clattering fumble, and on the third try he managed to hang up.

"Who was that?'

Mercer was going through his billfold. "Gradie. Drunk as a skunk. He needs liquor money, I guess. Says he'll sell me the mantel for fifty bucks."

"Is that a bargain?" She towelled her hair petulantly.

"He's been asking one-fifty. I got to give him the money tonight. How much money do you have on you?"

"Jesus, you're not going down to that place tonight?"

"By morning he may have sobered up, forgotten the whole deal."

"Oh, Jesus. You're *not* going to go down there."

Mercer was digging through the litter of his dresser for loose change. "Thirty-eight is all I've got on me. Can you loan me twelve?"

"All I've got is a ten and some change."

"How much change? There's a bunch of bottles in the kitchen —I can return them for the deposit. Who's still open?"

"Hugh's is until two. Jon, we'll be broke for the weekend. How will we get to the mountains?"

"Ron owes us twenty for his half of the ounce. I'll get it from him when I borrow his truck to haul the mantel. Monday I'll dip into the rent money—we can stall."

"You can't get his truck until morning. Ron's working grave-yard tonight."

"He's off in six hours. I'll pay Gradie now and get a receipt. I'll pick up the mantel first thing."

Linda rummaged through her shoulder bag. "Just don't forget it's probably going to rain anyway."

V

The storm was holding off as Mercer loped toward Gradie's house, but heat lightning fretted behind reefs of cloud. It was a dark night between the filtered flares of lightning, and he was very conscious that this was a bad neighborhood to be out walk-ing in with fifty dollars in your pocket. He kept one hand shoved into his jeans pocket, closed over the double-barrelled derringer, and walked on the edge of the street, well away from the con-cealing mounds of kudzu. Once something scrambled noisily through the vines; startled, Mercer almost shot his foot off.

"Who's there!" The voice was cracked with drunken fear.

"Jon Mercer, Mr. Gradie! Jon Mercer!"

"Come on into the light. You bring the money?"

"Right here." Mercer dug a crumpled wad of bills and coins from his pocket. The derringer flashed in his fist.

"Two shots, huh?" Gradie observed. "Not enough to do you much good. There's too many of them."

"Just having it to show has pulled me out of a couple bad moments," Mercer explained. He dumped the money onto Gradie's shaky palm. "That's fifty. Better count it, and give me a receipt. I'll be back in the morning for the mantel."

"Take it now. I'll be gone in the morning."

Mercer glanced sharply at the other man. Gradie had never been known to leave his yard unattended for longer than a quick trip to the store. "I'll need a truck. I can't borrow the truck until in the morning."

Gradie carelessly shoved the money into a pocket, bent over a lamplit end table to scribble out a receipt. In the dusty glare, his face was haggard with shadowy lines. DT's, Mercer guessed: he needs money bad to buy more booze.

"This is travelling money—I'm leaving tonight." Gradie insisted. His breath was stale with wine. "Talked to an old boy who says he'll give me a good price for my stock. He's coming by in the morning. You're a good old boy, Jon—and I wanted you to have the mantel if you wanted it."

"It's two a.m.," Mercer suggested carefully. "I can be here just after seven."

"I'm leaving tonight."

Mercer swore under his breath. There was no arguing with Gradie in his present state, and by morning the old man might have forgotten the entire transaction. Selling out and leaving? Impossible. This yard was Gradie's world, his life. Once he crawled up out of this binge, he'd get over the willies and not remember a thing from the past week.

"How about if I borrow your truck?"

"I'm taking it."

"I won't be ten minutes with it." Mercer cringed to think of Gradie behind the wheel just now.

Eventually, he secured Gradie's key to the aged Studebaker pickup in return for his promise to return immediately upon unloading the mantel. Together they worked the heavy mahogany piece onto the truck bed—Mercer fretting at each threatened scrape against the rusted metal.

"Care to come along to help unload?" Mercer invited. "I got a bottle at the house."

Gradie refused the bait. "I got things to do before I go. You just get back here soon as you're finished."

Grinding dry gears, Mercer edged the pickup out of the kudzu-walled yard, and clattered away into the night.

The mantel was really too heavy for the two of them to move—Mercer could handle the weight easily enough, but the bulky piece needed two people. Linda struggled gamely with her end, but the mantel scraped and scuffed as they lowered it from the truck bed and hauled it into the house. By the time they had finished, they both were sticky and exhausted from the effort.

Mercer remembered his watch. "Christ, it's 2:30. I've got to get this heap back to Gradie."

"Why don't you wait till morning? He's probably passed out cold by not."

"I promised to get right back to him."

Linda hesitated at the doorway. "Wait a second. I'm coming."

"Thought you'd had enough of Gradie's place."

"I don't like waiting here alone this late."

"Since when?" Mercer laughed, climbing into the pickup.

"I don't like the way the kudzu crawls all up the back of the house. Something might be hiding . . ."

Gradie didn't pop out of his burrow when they rattled into his yard. Linda had been right, Mercer reflected—the old man was sleeping it off. With a pang of guilt, he hoped his fifty bucks wouldn't go toward extending this binge; Gradie had really looked bad tonight. Maybe he should look in on him tomorrow afternoon, get him to eat something.

"I'll just look in to see if he's OK," Mercer told her. "If he's asleep, I'll just leave the keys beside him."

"Leave them in the ignition," Linda argued. "Let's just go."

"Won't take a minute."

Linda swung down from the cab and scrambled after him. Fitful gushes of heat lightning spilled across the crowded yard—picking out the junk-laden stacks and shelves, crouched in fantastic distortions like a Daliesque vision of Hell. The darkness in between bursts was hot and oily, heavy with moisture, and the subdued rumble of thunder seemed like gargantuan breathing.

"Be lucky to make it back before this hits," Mercer grumbled. The screen door was unlatched. Mercer pushed it open.

"Mr. Gradie?" he called softly—not wishing to wake the old man, but remembering the shotgun. "Mr. Gradie? It's Jon."

Within, the table lamps shed a dusty glow across the cluttered room. Without, the sporadic glare of heat lightning popped on and off like a defective neon sign. Mercer squinted into the pools of shadow between cabinets and shelves. Bellies of curved glass, shoulders of polished mahogany smouldered in the flickering light. From the walls, glass eyes glinted watchfully from the mounted deer's heads and stuffed birds. "Mr. Gradie?"

"Jon. Leave the keys, and let's go."

"I'd better see if he's all right."

Mercer started toward the rear of the house, then paused a moment. One of the glass-fronted cabinets stood open; it had been closed when he was here before. Its door snagged out into the cramped aisle-space; Mercer made to close it as he edged past. It was the walnut cabinet that housed Gradie's wartime memorabilia, and Mercer paused as he closed it because one exhibit was noticeably missing: that of the monkeylike skull that was whimsically labeled "Jap General's Skull."

"Mr. Gradie?"

"Phew!" Linda crinkled her nose. "He's got something scorching on the stove!"

Mercer turned into the kitchen. An overhead bulb glared down upon a squalid confusion of mismatched kitchen furnishings, stacks of chipped, unwashed dishes, empty cans and bottles, scattered remnants of desiccated meals. Mercer winced at the thought of having drunk from these same grimy glasses. The kitchen was deserted. On the stove an overheated saucepan boiled gouts of sour steam, but for the moment Mercer's attention was on the kitchen table.

A space had been cleared by pushing away the debris of dirty dishes and stale food. In that space reposed a possum-jawed monkey's skull, with the yellowed label: "Jap General's Skull."

There was a second skull beside it on the table. Except for a few clinging tatters of dried flesh and greenish fur—the other was bleached white by the sun—this skull was identical to Gradie's Japanese souvenir: a high-domed skull the size of a large, clenched fist, with a jutting, sharp-toothed muzzle. A baboon of some sort, Mercer judged, picking it up.

A neatly typed label was affixed to the occiput: "Unknown Animal Skull. Found by Fred Morny on Grand Ave. Knoxville, Tenn. 1976."

"Someone lost a pet," Mercer mused, replacing the skull and reaching for the loose paper label that lay beside the two relics.

Linda had gone to the stove to turn off its burner. "Oh, *God!*" she gagged, recoiling from the steaming saucepan.

Mercer stepped across to the stove, followed her sickened gaze. The water had boiled low in the large saucepan, scorching the repellent broth in which the skull simmered. It was a third skull, baboonlike, identical to the others.

"He's *eating* rats!" Linda retched.

"No," Mercer said dully, glancing at the freshly typed label he had scooped from the table. "He's boiling off the flesh so he can exhibit the skull." For the carefully prepared label in his hand read: "Kudzu Devil Skull. Shot by Red Gradie in Yard, Knoxville, Tenn. June 1977."

"Jon, I'm going. This man's stark crazy!"

"Just let me see if he's all right," Mercer insisted. "Or go back by yourself."

"God, no!"

"He's probably in his bedroom then. Fell asleep while he was working on this . . . this . . ." Mercer wasn't sure what to call it. The old man *had* seemed a bit unhinged these last few days.

The bedroom was in the other rear corner of the house, leading off from the small dining room in between. Leaving the glare of the kitchen light, the dining room was lost in shadow. No one had dined here in years, obviously, for the area was another of Gradie's storerooms—stacked and double-stacked with tables, chairs and bulky items of furniture. Threading his way between the half-seen obstructions, Mercer gingerly approached the bedroom door—a darker blotch against the opposite wall.

"Mr. Gradie? It's Jon Mercer."

He thought he heard a weak groan from the darkness within.

"It's Jon Mercer, Mr. Gradie." He called more loudly. "I've brought your keys back. Are you all right?"

"Jon, let's *go!*"

"Shut up, damn it! I thought I heard him try to answer."

He stepped toward the doorway. An object rolled and crumpled under his foot. It was an empty shotgun shell. There was a strange sweet-sour stench that tugged at Mercer's belly, and he thought he could make out the shape of a body sprawled half out of the bed.

"Mr. Gradie?"

This time a soughing gasp, too liquid for a snore.

Mercer groped for a wall switch, located it, snapped it back and forth. No light came on.

"Mr. Gradie?"

Again a bubbling sigh.

"Get a lamp! Quick!" he told Linda.

"Let him alone, for Christ's sake."

"Damn it, he's passed out and thrown up! He'll strangle in his own vomit if we don't help him!"

"He had a big flashlight in the kitchen!" Linda whirled to get it, anxious to get away.

Mercer cautiously made his way into the bedroom—treading with care, for broken glass crunched under his foot. The outside shades were drawn, and the room was swallowed in inky blackness, but he was certain he could pick out Gradie's comatose form lying across the bed. Then Linda was back with the flashlight.

Gradie sprawled on his back, skinny legs flung onto the floor, the rest crosswise on the unmade bed. The flashlight beam shimmered on the spreading splotches of blood that soaked the sheets and mattress. Someone had spent a lot of time with him, using a small knife—small-bladed, for if the wounds that all but flayed him had not been shallow, he could not be yet alive.

Mercer flung the flashlight beam about the bedroom. The cluttered furnishings were overturned, smashed. He recognized the charge pattern of a shotgun blast low against one wall, spattered with bits of fur and gore. The shotgun, broken open, lay on the floor; its barrel and stock were matted with bloody fur—Gradie had used it as a club when he'd had no chance to reload. The flashlight beam probed the blackness at the base of the corner wall, where the termite-riddled floorboards had been torn away. A trail of blood crawled into the darkness beneath.

Then Mercer crouched beside Gradie, shining the light into the tortured face. The eyes opened at the light—one eye was past seeing, the other stared dully. "That you, Jon?"

"It's Jon, Mr. Gradie. You take it easy—we're getting you to the hospital. Did you recognize who did this to you?"

Linda had already caught up the telephone from where it had fallen beneath an overturned nightstand. It seemed impossible that he had survived the blood loss, but Mercer had seen drunks run off after a gut-shot that would have killed a sober man from shock.

Gradie laughed horribly. "It was the little green men. Do you think I could have told anybody about the little green men?"

"Take it easy, Mr. Gradie."

"Jon! The phone's dead!"

"Busted in the fall. Help me carry him to the truck." Mercer prodded clumsily with a wad of torn sheets, trying to remember first-aid for bleeding. Pressure points? Where? The old man was cut to tatters.

"They're little green devils," Gradie raved weakly. "And they ain't no animals—they're clever as you or me. They *live* under the kudzu. That's what the Nip was trying to tell me when he sold me the skull. Hiding down there beneath the damn vines, living off the roots and whatever they can scavenge. They nurture the goddamn stuff, he said, help it spread around, care for it just like a man looks after his garden. Winter comes, they burrow down underneath the soil and hibernate."

"Shouldn't we make a litter?"

"How? Just grab his feet."

"Let me lie! Don't you see, Jon? Kudzu was brought over here from Japan, and these damn little devils came with it. I started to put it all together when Morny found the skull—started piecing together all the little hints and suspicions. They like it here, Jon—they're taking over all the waste lots, got more food out in the wild, multiplying like rats over here and nobody knows about them."

Gradie's hysterical voice was growing weaker. Mercer gave up trying to bandage the torn limbs. "Just take it easy, Mr. Gradie. We're getting you to a doctor."

"Too late for a doctor. You scared them off, but they've done for me. Just like they done for old Morny. They're smart, Jon—that's what I didn't understand in time—smart as devils. They know that I was figuring on them, started spying on me, creeping in to see what I knew—then came to shut me up. They don't want nobody to know about them, Jon! Now they'll come after . . ."

Whatever else Gradie said was swallowed in the crimson froth that bubbled from his lips. The tortured body went rigid for an instant, then Mercer cradled a dead weight in his arms. Clumsily, he felt for a pulse, realized the blood was no longer flowing in weak spurts.

"I think he's gone."

"Oh god, Jon. The police will think we did this!"

"Not if we report it first. Come on! We'll take the truck."

"And just leave him here?"

"He's dead. This is a murder. Best not to disturb things any more than we have."

"Oh, god! Jon, whoever did this may still be around."

Mercer pulled his derringer from his pocket, flicked back the safety. His chest and arms were covered with Gradie's blood, he noticed. This was not going to be pleasant when they got to the police station. Thank god the cops never patrolled this slum, or else the shotgun blasts would have brought a squad car by now.

Warily, he led the way out of the house and into the yard. Wind was whipping the leaves now, and a few spatters of rain were starting to hit the pavement. The erratic light peopled each grotesque shadow with lurking murderers, and against the rush of the wind, Mercer seemed to hear a thousand stealthy assassins.

A flash of electric blue highlighted the yard.

"Jon! Look at the truck!"

All four tires were flat. Slashed.

"Get in! We'll run on the rims!"

Another glare of heat lightning.

All about them, the kudzu erupted from a hundred hidden lairs.

Mercer fired twice.

STICKS

I

The lashed-together framework of sticks jutted from a small cairn alongside the stream. Colin Leverett studied it in perplexity—half a dozen odd lengths of branch, wired together at cross angles for no fathomable purpose. It reminded him unpleasantly of some bizarre crucifix, and he wondered what might lie beneath the cairn.

It was spring of 1942—the kind of day to make the War seem distant and unreal, although the draft notice waited on his desk. In a few days Leverett would lock his rural studio, wonder if he would see it again—be able to use its pens and brushes and carving tools when he did return. It was good-bye to the woods and streams of upstate New York, too. No fly rods, no tramps through the countryside in Hitler's Europe. No point in putting off fishing that trout stream he had driven past once, exploring back roads of the Otselic Valley.

Mann Brook—so it was marked on the old geological survey map—ran southeast of DeRuyter. The unfrequented country road crossed over a stone bridge old before the first horseless carriage, but Leverett's Ford eased across and onto the shoulder. Taking fly rod and tackle, he included a pocket flask and tied an iron skillet to his belt. He'd work his way downstream a few miles. By afternoon he'd lunch on fresh trout, maybe some fat bullfrog legs.

It was a fine clear stream, though difficult to fish, as dense bushes hung out from the bank, broken with stretches of open water hard to work without being seen. But the trout rose boldly to his fly, and Leverett was in fine spirits.

From the bridge the valley along Mann Brook began as fairly open pasture, but half a mile downstream the land had fallen into disuse and was thick with second-growth evergreens and scrub-apple trees. Another mile, and the scrub merged with dense forest, which continued unbroken. The land here, he had learned, had been taken over by the state many years back.

As Leverett followed the stream, he noted remains of an old railroad embankment. No vestige of tracks or ties—only the embankment itself, overgrown with large trees. The artist rejoiced in the beautiful dry-wall culverts spanning the stream as it wound through the valley. To his mind it seemed eerie, this forgotten railroad running straight and true through virtual wilderness.

He could imagine an old wood-burner with a conical stack, steaming along through the valley dragging two or three wooden coaches. It must be a branch of the old Oswego Midland Rail Road, he decided, abandoned rather suddenly in the 1870s. Leverett, who had a memory for detail, knew of it from a story his grand-father told of riding the line in 1871 from Otselic to DeRuyter on his honeymoon. The engine had so labored up the steep grade over Crumb Hill that he got off to walk alongside. Probably that sharp grade was the reason for the line's abandonment.

When he came across a scrap of board nailed to several sticks set into a stone wall, his darkest thought was that it might read "No Trespassing." Curiously, though the board was weathered featureless, the nails seemed quite new. Leverett scarcely gave it a thought, until a short distance beyond he came upon another such contrivance. And another.

Now he scratched at the day's stubble on his long jaw. This didn't make sense. A prank? But on whom? A child's game? No, the arrangement was far too sophisticated. As an artist, Lever-ett appreciated the craftsmanship of the work—the calculated angles and lengths, the designed intricacy of the maddeningly inexplicable devices. There was something distinctly uncomfortable about their effect.

Leverett reminded himself that he had come here to fish, and continued downstream. But as he worked around a thicket he again stopped in puzzlement.

Here was a small open space with more of the stick lattices and an arrangement of flat stones laid out on the ground. The stones—likely taken from one of the many dry-wall culverts—made a pattern maybe twenty by fifteen feet, that at first glance resembled a ground plan for a house. Intrigued, Leverett quickly saw this was not so. If the ground plan for anything, it would have to be for a small maze.

The bizarre lattice structures were all around. Sticks from trees and bits of board nailed together in fantastic array. They defied description; no two seemed alike. Some were only one or two straight sticks lashed together in parallel or at angles. Others were worked into complicated lattices of dozens of sticks and boards. One could have been a child's tree house—it was built in three planes, but was so abstract and useless that it could be nothing more than an insane conglomeration of sticks and wire. Sometimes the contrivances were stuck in a pile of stones or a wall, maybe thrust into the railroad embankment or nailed to a tree.

It should have been ridiculous. It wasn't. Instead it seemed somehow sinister—these utterly inexplicable, meticulously con-structed stick lattices spread through a wilderness where only a tree-grown embankment or a forgotten stone wall gave evidence that man had ever passed through. Leverett forgot about trout and frog legs, instead dug into his pockets for a notebook and stub of pencil. Busily he began to sketch the more intricate structures. Perhaps someone could explain them; perhaps there was some-thing to their insane complexity that warranted closer study for his own work.

Leverett was roughly two miles from the bridge when he came upon the ruins of a house. It was an unlovely Colonial farmhouse, box-shaped and gambrel-roofed, fast falling into the ground. Windows were dark and empty; the chimneys on either end looked ready to topple. Rafters showed through open spaces in the roof, and the weathered boards of the walls had in places rotted away to reveal hewn timber beams. The foundation was stone and disproportionately massive. From the size of the unmortared stone blocks, its builder had intended the foundation to stand forever.

The house was nearly swallowed up by undergrowth and rampant lilac bushes, but Leverett could distinguish what had been a lawn with imposing shade trees. Farther back were gnarled and sickly apple trees and an overgrown garden where a few lost flowers still bloomed—wan and serpentine from years in the wild. The stick lattices were everywhere—the lawn, the trees, even the house were covered with the uncanny structures. They reminded Leverett of a hundred misshapen spider webs grouped so closely together as to almost ensnare the entire house and clearing. Wondering, he sketched page on page of them as he cautiously approached the abandoned house.

He wasn't certain just what he expected to find inside. The aspect of the farmhouse was frankly menacing, standing as it did in gloomy desolation where the forest had devoured the works of man—where the only sign that man had been here in this century were these insanely wrought latticeworks of sticks and board. Some might have turned back at this point. Leverett, whose fascination for the macabre was evident in his art, instead was intrigued. He drew a rough sketch of the farmhouse and grounds, overrun with the enigmatic devices, with thickets of hedges and distorted flowers. He regretted that it might be years before he could capture the eeriness of the place on sketchboard or canvas.

The door was off its hinges, and Leverett gingerly stepped within, hoping that the flooring remained sound enough to bear his sparse frame. The afternoon sun pierced the empty windows, mottling the decaying floorboards with great blotches of light. Dust drifted in the sunlight. The house was empty—stripped of furnishings other than indistinct tangles of rubble mounded over with decay and the drifted leaves of many seasons.

Someone had been here, and recently. Someone who had literally covered the mildewed walls with diagrams of the mysterious lattice structures. The drawings were applied directly to the walls, crisscrossing the rotting wallpaper and crumbling plaster in bold black lines. Some of vertiginous complexity covered an entire wall, like a mad mural. Others were small, only a few crossed lines, and reminded Leverett of cuneiform glyphics.

His pencil hurried over the pages of his notebook. Leverett

noted with fascination that a number of the drawings were recognizable as schematics of lattices he had earlier sketched. Was this then the planning room for the madman or educated idiot who had built these structures? The gouges etched by the charcoal into the soft plaster appeared fresh—done days or months ago, perhaps.

A darkened doorway opened into the cellar. Were there drawings there as well? And what else? Leverett wondered if he should dare it. Except for streamers of light that crept through cracks in the flooring, the cellar was in darkness.

"Hello?" he called. "Anyone here?" It didn't seem silly just then. These stick lattices hardly seemed the work of a rational mind. Leverett wasn't enthusiastic about the prospect of encountering such a person in this dark cellar. It occurred to him that virtually anything might transpire here, and no one in the world of 1942 would ever know.

And that in itself was too great a fascination for one of Leverett's temperament. Carefully he started down the cellar stairs. They were stone and thus solid, but treacherous with moss and debris.

The cellar was enormous—even more so in the darkness. Leverett reached the foot of the steps, and paused for his eyes to adjust to the damp gloom. An earlier impression recurred to him. The cellar was too big for the house. Had another dwelling stood here originally—perhaps destroyed and rebuilt by one of lesser fortune? He examined the stonework. Here were great blocks of gneiss that might support a castle. On closer look they reminded him of a fortress—for the dry-wall technique was startlingly Mycenaean.

Like the house above, the cellar appeared to be empty, although without light Leverett could not be certain what the shadows hid. There seemed to be darker areas of shadow along sections of the foundation wall, suggesting openings to chambers beyond. Leverett began to feel uneasy in spite of himself.

There was something here—a large tablelike bulk in the center of the cellar. Where a few ghosts of sunlight drifted down to touch its edges, it seemed to be of stone. Cautiously he crossed the stone paving to where it loomed—waist high, maybe eight feet long, and less wide. A roughly shaped slab of gneiss, he judged, and supported by pillars of unmortared stone. In the darkness he could get only a vague conception of the object. He ran his hand along the slab. It seemed to have a groove along its edge.

His groping fingers encountered fabric, something cold and leathery and yielding. Mildewed harness, he guessed in distaste.

Something closed on his wrist, set icy nails into his flesh.

Leverett screamed and lunged away with frantic strength. He was held fast, but the object on the stone slab pulled upward.

A sickly beam of sunlight came down to touch one end of the slab. It was enough. As Leverett struggled backward and the thing that held him heaved up from the stone table, its face passed through the beam of light.

It was a lich's face—desiccated flesh tight over its skull. Filthy strands of hair were matted over its scalp; tattered lips were drawn away from broken yellowed teeth, and sunken in their sockets eyes that should be dead were bright with hideous life.

Leverett screamed again, desperate with fear. His free hand clawed the iron skillet tied to his belt. Ripping it loose, he smashed at the nightmarish face with all his strength.

For one frozen instant of horror the sunlight let him see the skillet crush through the mould-eaten forehead like an axe—cleaving the dry flesh and brittle bone. The grip on his wrist failed. The cadaverous face fell away, and the sight of its caved-in forehead and unblinking eyes from between which thick blood had begun to ooze would awaken Leverett from nightmares on countless nights.

But now Leverett tore free, and fled. And when his aching legs faltered as he plunged headlong through the scrub-growth, he was spurred to desperate energy by the memory of the footsteps that had stumbled up the cellar stairs behind him.

II

When Colin Leverett returned from the War, his friends marked him a changed man. He had aged. There were streaks of grey in his hair; his springy step had slowed. The athletic leanness of his body had withered to an unhealthy gauntness. There were indelible lines to his face, and his eyes were haunted.

More disturbing was an alteration of temperament. A mordant cynicism had eroded his earlier air of whimsical asceticism. His fascination with the macabre had assumed a darker mood, a morbid obsession that his old acquaintances found disquieting. But it had been that kind of war, especially for those who had fought through the Apennines.

Leverett might have told them otherwise, had he cared to discuss his nightmarish experience on Mann Brook. But Leverett kept his own counsel, and when he grimly recalled that creature he had struggled with in the abandoned cellar, he usually convinced himself it had only been a derelict—a crazy hermit whose appearance had been distorted by the poor light and his own imagination. Nor had his blow more than glanced off the man's forehead, he reasoned, since the other had recovered quickly enough to give chase. It was best not to dwell upon such matters, and this rational explanation helped restore sanity when he awoke from nightmares of that face.

Thus Colin Leverett returned to his studio, and once more plied his pens and brushes and carving knives. The pulp magazines, where fans had acclaimed his work before the War, welcomed him back with long lists of assignments. There were commissions from galleries and collectors, unfinished sculptures and wooden models. Leverett busied himself.

There were problems now. *Short Stories* returned a cover painting as "too grotesque." The publishers of a new anthology of horror stories sent back a pair of his interior drawings—"too gruesome, especially the rotted, bloated faces of those hanged men." A customer returned a silver figurine, complaining the martyred saint was too thoroughly martyred. Even *Weird Tales*, after heralding his return to its ghoul-haunted pages, began returning illustrations they considered "too strong, even for our readers."

Leverett tried halfheartedly to tone things down, found the results vapid and uninspired. Eventually the assignments stopped trickling in. Leverett, becoming more the recluse as years went by, dismissed the pulp days from his mind. Working quietly in his isolated studio, he found a living doing occasional commissioned pieces and gallery work, from time to time selling a painting or sculpture to the major museums. Critics had much praise for his bizarre abstract sculptures.

III

The War was twenty-five years history when Colin Leverett received a letter from a good friend of the pulp days—Prescott Brandon, now editor-publisher of Gothic House, a small press that specialized in books of the weird-fantasy genre. Despite a lapse in correspondence of many years, Brandon's letter began in his typically direct style:

The Eyrie / Salem, Mass. / Aug. 2

To the Macabre Hermit of the Midlands:

Colin, I'm putting together a deluxe three-volume collection of H. Kenneth Allard's horror stories. I well recall that Kent's stories were personal favorites of yours. How about shambling forth from retirement and illustrating these for me? Will need two-color jackets and a dozen line interiors each. Would hope that you can startle fandom with some especially ghastly drawings for these—something different from the hackneyed skulls and bats and werewolves carting off half-dressed ladies.

Interested? I'll send you the material and details, and you can have a free hand. Let us hear—Scotty

Leverett was delighted. He felt some nostalgia for the pulp days, and he had always admired Allard's genius in transforming visions of cosmic horror into convincing prose. He wrote Brandon an enthusiastic reply.

He spent hours rereading the stories for inclusion, making notes and preliminary sketches. No squeamish subeditors to offend here; Scotty meant what he said. Leverett bent to his task with maniacal relish.

Something different, Scotty had asked. A free hand. Leverett
studied his pencil sketches critically. The figures seemed headed
the right direction, but the drawings needed something more—
something that would inject the mood of sinister evil that per-
vaded Allard's work. Grinning skulls and leathery bats? Trite.
Allard demanded more.

The idea had inexorably taken hold of him. Perhaps because
Allard's tales evoked that same sense of horror, perhaps because
Allard's visions of crumbling Yankee farmhouses and their
depraved secrets so reminded him of that spring afternoon on
Mann Brook. . . .

Although he had refused to look at it since the day he had staggered in, half dead from terror and exhaustion, Leverett perfectly
recalled where he had flung his notebook. He retrieved it from
the back of a seldom-used file, thumbed through the wrinkled
pages thoughtfully. These hasty sketches reawakened the sense
of foreboding evil, the charnel horror of that day. Studying the
bizarre lattice patterns, it seemed impossible to Leverett that
others would not share the feeling of horror the stick structures
evoked in him.

He began to sketch bits of stick latticework into his pencil
roughs. The sneering faces of Allard's degenerate creatures took
on an added shadow of menace. Leverett nodded, pleased with
the effect.

IV

Some months afterward, a letter from Brandon informed
Leverett he had received the last of the Allard drawings and was
enormously pleased with the work. Brandon added a postscript:

For God's sake, Colin—What is it *with these insane sticks you've
got poking up everywhere in the illos! The damn things get really creepy
after awhile. How on earth did you get onto this?*

Leverett supposed he owed Brandon some explanation. Dutifully he wrote a lengthy letter, setting down the circumstances of

his experience on Mann Brook—omitting only the horror that had seized his wrist in the cellar. Let Brandon think him eccentric, but not a madman and murderer.

Brandon's reply was immediate:

Colin—Your account of the Mann Brook episode is fascinating—and incredible! It reads like the start of one of Allard's stories! I have taken the liberty of forwarding your letter to Alexander Stefroi in Pelham. Dr. Stefroi is an earnest scholar of this region's history—as you may already know. I'm certain your account will interest him, and he may have some light to shed on the uncanny affair.

Expect 1st volume, Voices from the Shadow, *to be ready from the binder next month. Pages looked great. Best—Scotty*

The following week brought a letter postmarked Pelham, Mass.:

A mutual friend, Prescott Brandon, forwarded your fascinating account of discovering curious sticks and stone artifacts on an abandoned farm in upstate New York. I found this most intriguing, and wonder if you can recall further details? Can you relocate the exact site after 30 years? If possible, I'd like to examine the foundations this spring, as they call to mind similar megalithic sites of this region. Several of us are interested in locating what we believe are remains of megalithic construction dating back to the Bronze Age, and to determine their possible use in rituals of black magic in Colonial days.

Present archeological evidence indicates that ca. 1700-2000 B.C. there was an influx of Bronze Age peoples into the Northeast from Europe. We know that the Bronze Age saw the rise of an extremely advanced culture, and that as seafarers they were to have no peers until the Vikings. Remains of a megalithic culture originating in the Mediterranean can be seen in the Lion Gate in Mycenae, in Stonehenge, and in dolmens, passage graves and barrow mounds throughout Europe. Moreover, this seems to have represented far more than a style of architecture peculiar to the era. Rather, it appears to have been a religious cult whose adherents worshipped a sort of earth-mother, served her with fertility rituals and sacrifices, and believed that immortality of the soul could be secured through interment in megalithic tombs.

That this culture came to America cannot be doubted from the hundreds of megalithic remnants found—and now recognized—in our region. The most important site to date is Mystery Hill in N.H., comprising a great many walls and dolmens of megalithic construction—most notably the Y Cavern barrow mound and the Sacrificial Table (see postcard). Less spectacular megalithic sites include the group of cairns and carved stones at Mineral Mt., subterranean chambers with stone passageways such as at Petersham and Shutesbury, and uncounted shaped megaliths and buried "monk's cells" throughout this region.

Of further interest, these sites seem to have retained their mystic aura for the early Colonials, and numerous megalithic sites show evidence of having been used for sinister purposes by Colonial sorcerers and alchemists. This became particularly true after the witchcraft persecutions drove many practitioners into the western wilderness—explaining why upstate New York and western Mass. have seen the emergence of so many cultist groups in later years.

Of particular interest here is Shadrach Ireland's "Brethren of the New Light," who believed that the world was soon to be destroyed by sinister "Powers from Outside" and that they, the elect, would then attain physical immortality. The elect who died beforehand were to have their bodies preserved on tables of stone until the "Old Ones" came forth to return them to life. We have definitely linked the megalithic sites at Shutesbury to later unwholesome practices of the New Light cult. They were absorbed in 1781 by Mother Ann Lee's Shakers, and Ireland's putrescent corpse was hauled from the stone table in his cellar and buried.

Thus I think it probable that your farmhouse may have figured in similar hidden practices. At Mystery Hill a farmhouse was built in 1826 that incorporated one dolmen in its foundations. The house burned down ca. 1848-55, and there were some unsavory local stories as to what took place there. My guess is that your farmhouse had been built over or incorporated a similar megalithic site—and that your "sticks" indicate some unknown cult still survived there. I can recall certain vague references to lattice devices figuring in secret ceremonies, but can pinpoint nothing definite. Possibly they represent a development of occult symbols to be used in certain conjurations, but this is just a guess. I suggest you consult Waite's Ceremonial Magic *or such to see if you can recognize similar magical symbols.*

Hope this is of some use to you. Please let me hear back.

Sincerely,
Alexander Stefroi

There was a postcard enclosed—a photograph of a four-and-a-half-ton granite slab, ringed by a deep groove with a spout, identified as the Sacrificial Table at Mystery Hill. On the back Stefroi had written:

You must have found something similar to this. They are not rare—we have one in Pelham removed from a site now beneath Quabbin Reservoir. They were used for sacrifice—animal and human—and the groove is to channel blood into a bowl, presumably.

Leverett dropped the card and shuddered. Stefroi's letter reawakened the old horror, and he wished now he had let the matter lie forgotten in his files. Of course, it couldn't be forgotten—even after thirty years.

He wrote Stefroi a careful letter, thanking him for his information and adding a few minor details to his account. This spring, he promised, wondering if he would keep the promise, he would try to relocate the farmhouse on Mann Brook.

V

Spring was late that year, and it was not until early June that Colin Leverett found time to return to Mann Brook. On the surface, very little had changed in three decades. The ancient stone bridge yet stood, nor had the country lane been paved. Leverett wondered whether anyone had driven past since his terror-sped flight.

He found the old railroad grade easily as he started downstream. Thirty years, he told himself—but the chill inside him only tightened. The going was far more difficult than before. The day was unbearably hot and humid. Wading through the rank underbrush raised clouds of black flies that savagely bit him.

Evidently the stream had seen severe flooding in past years, judging from piled logs and debris that blocked his path. Stretches were scooped out to barren rocks and gravel. Elsewhere, gigantic barriers of uprooted trees and debris looked like ancient and mouldering fortifications. As he worked his way down the valley, he realized that his search would yield nothing. So intense had been the force of the long-ago flood that even the course of the stream had changed. Many of the dry-wall culverts no longer spanned the brook, but sat lost and alone far back from its present banks. Others had been knocked flat and swept away, or were buried beneath tons of rotting logs.

At one point Leverett found remnants of an apple orchard groping through weeds and bushes. He thought the house must be close by, but here the flooding had been particularly severe, and evidently even those ponderous stone foundations had been toppled over and buried beneath debris.

Leverett finally turned back to his car. His step was lighter.

A few weeks later he received a response from Stefroi to his reported failure:

Forgive my tardy reply to your letter of 13 June. I have recently been pursuing inquiries which may, I hope, lead to discovery of a previously unreported megalithic site of major significance. Naturally I am disappointed that no traces remained of the Mann Brook site. While I tried not to get my hopes up, it did seem likely that the foundations would have survived. In searching through regional data, I note that there were particularly severe flash floods in the Otselic area in July 1942 and again in May 1946. Very probably your old farmhouse with its enigmatic devices was utterly destroyed not very long after your discovery of the site. This is weird and wild country, and doubtless there is much we shall never know.

I write this with a profound sense of personal loss over the death two nights ago of Prescott Brandon. This was a severe blow to me—as I am sure it was to you and to all who knew him. I only hope the police will catch the vicious killers who did this senseless act—evidently thieves surprised while ransacking his office. Police believe the killers were high on drugs, from the mindless brutality of their crime.

I had just received a copy of the third Allard volume, Unhallowed

Places. *A superbly designed book, and this tragedy becomes all the more insuperable with the realization that Scotty will give the world no more such treasures.*

> *In sorrow,*
> *Alexander Stefroi*

Leverett stared at the letter in shock. He had not received news of Brandon's death—had only a few days before opened a parcel from the publisher containing a first copy of *Unhallowed Places.* A line of Brandon's last letter recurred to him—a line that had seemed amusing at the time:

Your sticks have bewildered a good many fans, Colin, and I've worn out a ribbon answering inquiries. One fellow in particular—a Major George Leonard—has pressed me for details, and I'm afraid I told him too much. He has written several times for your address, but knowing how you value privacy I told him simply to permit me to forward any correspondence. He wants to see your original sketches, I gather, but these overbearing occult-types give me a pain. Frankly, I wouldn't care to meet the man myself.

VI

"Mr. Colin Leverett?"

Leverett studied the tall, lean man who stood smiling at the doorway of his studio. The sports car he had driven up in was black, and looked expensive. The same held for the turtleneck and leather slacks he wore, and the sleek briefcase he carried. The blackness made his thin face deathly pale. Leverett guessed his age to be in the late forties by the thinning of his hair. Dark glasses hid his eyes, black driving gloves his hands.

"Scotty Brandon told me where to find you," the stranger said.

"Scotty?" Leverett's voice was wary.

"Yes, we lost a mutual friend, I regret to say. I'd been talking with him just before . . . But I see by your expression Scotty never had time to write." He fumbled awkwardly. "I'm Dana Allard."

"Allard?"

His visitor seemed embarrassed. "Yes—H. Kenneth Allard was my uncle."

"I hadn't realized Allard left a family," mused Leverett, shaking the extended hand. He had never met the writer personally, but there was a strong resemblance to the few photographs he had seen. And Scotty had been paying royalty checks to an estate of some sort, he recalled.

"My father was Kent's half-brother. He later took his father's name, but there was no marriage, if you follow."

"Of course." Leverett was abashed. "Please find a place to sit down. And what brings you here?"

Dana Allard tapped his briefcase. "Something I'd been discussing with Scotty. Just recently I turned up a stack of my uncle's unpublished manuscripts." He unlatched the briefcase and handed Leverett a sheaf of yellowed paper. "Father collected Kent's personal effects from the state hospital as next-of-kin. He never thought much of my uncle, or his writing. He stuffed this away in our attic and forgot about it. Scotty was quite excited when I told him of my discovery."

Leverett was glancing through the manuscript—page on page of cramped handwriting, with revisions pieced throughout like an indecipherable puzzle. He had seen photographs of Allard manuscripts. There was no mistaking this.

Or the prose. Leverett read a few passages with rapt absorption. It was authentic—and brilliant.

"Uncle's mind seems to have taken an especially morbid turn as his illness drew on," Dana hazarded. "I admire his work very greatly, but I find these last few pieces . . . well, a bit *too* horrible. Especially his translation of his mythical *Book of Elders*."

It appealed to Leverett perfectly. He barely noticed his guest as he pored over the brittle pages. Allard was describing a megalithic structure his doomed narrator had encountered in the crypts beneath an ancient churchyard. There were references to "elder glyphics" that resembled his lattice devices.

"Look here." Dana pointed. "These incantations he records here from Alorri-Zrokros's forbidden tome. 'Yogth-Yugth-Sut-Hyrath-Yogng'—hell. I can't pronounce them. And he has pages of them."

"This is incredible!" Leverett protested. He tried to mouth the alien syllables. It could be done. He even detected a rhythm.

"Well, I'm relieved you approve. I'd feared these last few stories and fragments might prove a little much for Kent's fans."

"Then you're going to have them published?"

Dana nodded. "Scotty was going to. I just hope those thieves weren't searching for this—a collector would pay a fortune. But Scotty said he was going to keep this secret until he was ready for announcement." His thin face was sad. "So now I'm going to publish it myself—in a deluxe edition. And I want you to illustrate it."

"I'd feel honored!" vowed Leverett, unable to believe it.

"I really liked those drawings you did for the trilogy. I'd like to see more like those—as many as you feel like doing. I mean to spare no expense in publishing this. And those stick things . . ."

"Yes?"

"Scotty told me the story of those. Fascinating! And you have a whole notebook of them? May I see it?"

Leverett hurriedly dug the notebook from his file, returned to the manuscript.

Dana paged through the book in awe. "These are totally bizarre—and there are references to such things in the manuscript, to make it even more fantastic. Can you reproduce them all for the book?"

"All I can remember," Leverett assured him. "And I have a good memory. But won't that be overdoing it?"

"Not at all! They fit into the book. And they're utterly unique. No, put everything you've got into this book. I'm going to entitle it *Dwellers in the Earth,* after the longest piece. I've already arranged for its printing, so we begin as soon as you can have the art ready. And I know you'll give it your all."

VII

He was floating in space. Objects drifted past him. Stars, he first thought. The objects drifted closer.

Sticks. Stick lattices of all configurations. And then he was drift-

ing among them, and he saw they were not sticks—not of wood.
The lattice designs were of dead-pale substance, like streaks
of frozen starlight. They reminded him of glyphics of some
unearthly alphabet—complex, enigmatic symbols arranged to
spell . . . what? And there *was* an arrangement—a three-dimen-
sional pattern. A maze of utterly baffling intricacy . . .

Then somehow he was in a tunnel. A cramped, stone-lined
tunnel through which he must crawl on his belly. The dank,
moss-slimed stones pressed close about his wriggling form, evok-
ing shrill whispers of claustrophobic dread.

And after an indefinite space of crawling through this and
other stone-lined burrows, and sometimes through passages
whose angles hurt his eyes, he would creep forth into a subterranean chamber. Great slabs of granite a dozen feet across formed
the walls and ceiling of this buried chamber, and between the
slabs other burrows pierced the earth. Altar-like, a gigantic slab of
gneiss waited in the center of the chamber. A spring welled darkly
between the stone pillars that supported the table. Its outer edge
was encircled by a groove, sickeningly stained by the substance
that clotted in the stone bowl beneath its collecting spot.

Others were emerging from the darkened burrows that ringed
the chamber—slouched figures only dimly glimpsed and vaguely
human. And a figure in a tattered cloak came toward him from
the shadow—stretched out a claw-like hand to seize his wrist, and
draw him toward the sacrificial table. He followed unresistingly,
knowing that something was expected of him.

They reached the altar, and in the glow from the cuneiform
lattices chiselled into the gneiss slab he could see his guide's
face. A mouldering corpse-face, the rotted bone of its forehead
smashed inward upon the foulness that oozed forth . . .

And Leverett would awaken to the echo of his own screams . . .

He'd been working too hard, he told himself, stumbling about
in the darkness, getting dressed because he was too shaken to
return to sleep. The nightmares had been coming every night. No
wonder he was exhausted.

But in his studio his work awaited him. Almost fifty drawings
completed now, and he planned another score. No wonder the
nightmares.

It was a grueling pace, but Dana Allard was ecstatic with the work he had done. And *Dwellers in the Earth* was waiting. Despite problems with typesetting, with getting the special paper Dana wanted—the book only waited on him.

Though his bones ached with fatigue, Leverett determinedly trudged through the greying night. Certain features of the nightmare would be interesting to portray.

VIII

The last of the drawings had gone off to Dana Allard in Petersham, and Leverett, fifteen pounds lighter and gut-weary, converted part of the bonus check into a case of good whiskey. Dana had the offset presses rolling as soon as plates were shot from the drawings. Despite his precise planning, presses had broken down, one printer had quit for reasons not stated, there had been a bad accident at the new printer's—seemingly innumerable problems, and Dana had been furious at each delay. But production pushed along quickly for all that. Leverett wrote that the book was cursed, but Dana responded that a week would see it ready.

Leverett amused himself in his studio constructing stick lattices and trying to catch up on his sleep. He was expecting a copy of the book when he received a letter from Stefroi:

Have tried to reach you by phone last few days, but no answer at your house. I'm pushed for time just now, so must be brief. I have indeed uncovered an unsuspected megalithic site of enormous importance. It's located on the estate of a long-prominent Mass. family—and as I cannot receive authorization to visit it, I will not say where. Have investigated secretly (and quite illegally) for a short time one night and was nearly caught. Came across references to the place in collection of 17th-century letters and papers in a divinity school library. Writer denouncing the family as a brood of sorcerers and witches, reference to alchemical activities and other less savory rumors—and describes underground stone chambers, megalithic artifacts, etc. which are put to "foul usage and diabolic pracktise." Just got a quick glimpse, but his description was not exaggerated. And Colin—in creeping through the woods to get to the site, I came across dozens of your mysterious "sticks"! Brought a small one back and have it here to show you. Recently constructed and exactly like your drawings. With luck, I'll gain admittance and find out their significance—undoubtedly they have significance—though these cultists can be stubborn about sharing secrets. Will explain my interest is scientific, no exposure to ridicule—and see what they say. Will get a closer look one way or another. And so—I'm off!

> Sincerely,
> Alexander Stefroi

Leverett's bushy brows rose. Allard had intimated certain dark rituals in which the stick lattices figured. But Allard had written over thirty years ago, and Leverett assumed the writer had stumbled onto something similar to the Mann Brook site. Stefroi was writing about something current.

He rather hoped Stefroi would discover nothing more than an inane hoax.

The nightmares haunted him still—familiar now, for all that their scenes and phantasms were visited by him only in dream. Familiar. The terror that they evoked was undiminished.

Now he was walking through forest—a section of hills that seemed to be those close by. A huge slab of granite had been dragged aside, and a pit yawned where it had lain. He entered the pit without hesitation, and the rounded steps that led downward were known to his tread. A buried stone chamber, and, leading from it, stone-lined burrows. He knew which one to crawl into.

And again the underground room with its sacrificial altar and its dark spring beneath, and the gathering circle of poorly glimpsed figures. A knot of them clustered about the stone table, and as he stepped toward them he saw they pinioned a frantically writhing man.

It was a stoutly built man, white hair disheveled, flesh gouged and filthy. Recognition seemed to burst over the contorted features, and he wondered if he should know the man. But now the lich with the caved-in skull was whispering in his ear, and he tried not to think of the unclean things that peered from that cloven brow, and instead took the bronze knife from the skeletal hand,

and raised the knife high, and because he could not scream and awaken, did with the knife as the tattered priest had whispered . . .

And when after an interval of unholy madness, he at last did awaken, the stickiness that covered him was not cold sweat, nor was it nightmare the half-devoured heart he clutched in one fist.

IX

Leverett somehow found sanity enough to dispose of the shredded lump of flesh. He stood under the shower all morning, scrubbing his skin raw. He wished he could vomit.

There was a news item on the radio. The crushed body of noted archeologist, Dr. Alexander Stefroi, had been discovered beneath a fallen granite slab near Whately. Police speculated the gigantic slab had shifted with the scientist's excavations at its base. Identification was made through personal effects.

When his hands stopped shaking enough to drive, Leverett fled to Petersham—reaching Dana Allard's old stone house about dark. Allard was slow to answer his frantic knock.

"Why, good evening, Colin! What a coincidence your coming here just now! The books are ready. The bindery just delivered them."

Leverett brushed past him. "We've got to destroy them!" he blurted. He'd thought a lot since morning.

"Destroy them?"

"There's something none of us figured on. Those stick lattices—there's a cult, some damnable cult. The lattices have some significance in their rituals. Stefroi hinted once they might be glyphics of some sort; I don't know. But the cult is still alive. They don't want their secrets revealed. They killed Scotty ... they killed Stefroi. They're onto me—I don't know what they intend. They'll kill you to stop you from releasing this book!"

Dana's frown was worried, but Leverett knew he hadn't impressed him the right way. "Colin, this sounds insane. You really have been overextending yourself, you know. Look, I'll show you the books. They're in the cellar."

Leverett let his host lead him downstairs. The cellar was quite large, flagstoned and dry. A mountain of brown-wrapped bundles awaited them.

"Put them down here where they wouldn't knock the floor out," Dana explained. "They start going out to distributors tomorrow. Here, I'll sign your copy."

Distractedly Leverett opened a copy of *Dwellers in the Earth*. He gazed at his lovingly rendered drawings of rotted creatures and buried stone chambers and stained altars—and everywhere the enigmatic latticework structures. He shuddered.

"Here." Dana Allard handed Leverett the book he had signed. "And to answer your question, they *are* elder glyphics."

But Leverett was staring at the inscription in its unmistakable handwriting: "For Colin Leverett, Without whom this work could not have seen completion—H. Kenneth Allard."

Allard was speaking. Leverett saw places where the hastily applied flesh-toned makeup didn't quite conceal what lay beneath. "Glyphics symbolic of alien dimensions—inexplicable to the human mind, but essential fragments of an evocation so unthinkably vast that the 'pentagram' (if you will) is miles across. Once before we tried—but your iron weapon destroyed part of Althol's brain. He erred at the last instant—almost annihilating us all. Althol had been formulating the evocation since he fled the advance of iron four millennia past.

"Then you reappeared, Colin Leverett—you with your artist's knowledge and diagrams of Althol's symbols. And now a thousand new minds will read the evocation you have returned to us, unite with our minds as we stand in the Hidden Places. And the Great Old Ones will come forth from the earth, and we, the dead who have steadfastly served them, shall be masters of the living."

Leverett turned to run, but now they were creeping forth from the shadows of the cellar, as massive flagstones slid back to reveal the tunnels beyond. He began to scream as Althol came to lead him away, but he could not awaken, could only follow.

Afterword

Some readers may note certain similarities between characters and events in this story and the careers of real-life figures, well known to fans of this genre. This was unavoidable, and no disrespect is intended. For much of this story *did* happen, though I suppose you've heard that one before.

In working with Lee Brown Coye on Wellman's *Worse Things Waiting*, I finally asked him why his drawings so frequently included sticks in their design, Lee's work is well known to me, but I had noticed that the "sticks" only began to appear in his work for Ziff-Davis in the early '60s. Lee finally sent me a folder of clippings and letters, far more eerie than this story—and factual.

In 1938 Coye *did* come across a stick-ridden farmhouse in the desolate Mann Brook region. He kept this to himself until fall of 1962, when John Vetter passed the account to August Derleth and to antiquarian-archeologist Andrew E. Rothovius. Derleth intended to write Coye's adventure as a Lovecraft novelette, but never did so. Rothovius discussed the site's possible megalithic significance with Coye in a series of letters and journal articles on which I have barely touched. In June 1963 Coye returned to the Mann Brook site and found it obliterated. It is a strange region, as HPL knew.

Coye's fascinating presentation of their letters appeared in five weekly installments of his "Chips and Shavings" column in the *Mid-York Weekly* from August 22 to September 26, 1963. Rothovius, whose research into the New England megaliths has been published in many journals, wrote an excellent and disquieting summary of his research in Arkham House's *The Dark Brotherhood*. to which the reader is referred.

THE FOURTH SEAL

I

"I had a friend at St. Johns you would have liked to have met," observed Dr. Metzger. "At least the idea you've brought up reminds me of some of our old undergraduate bull sessions."

"Bull sessions?" responded Dr. Thackeray, his frosty brows wavering askance.

Geoff laughed easily. "Never underestimate the value of a liberal arts background, Dr. Thackeray. St. Johns men could find loftier subjects to drain a keg of beer over than the matter of a cheerleader's boobs—especially with cheerleaders in short supply.

"No, Kirk Walker was something of a medievalist—and certainly a romanticist. Fancied himself the last of the Renaissance men, or some such, I imagine. Anyway, he used to put away booze like a Viking raiding party, and often he'd kick around some impossibly half-assed ideas. Argue them with dignified tenacity through all our hooting—and you were never sure whether he was serious, or handing us another piece of outrageous whimsy.

"But one of the points he liked to bring up was this idea that modern science, as we call it, isn't all that modern. Maintained that substantial scientific knowledge and investigation have existed on a recondite basis since early history—and not just as hocus-pocus and charlatanry."

"As I have suggested," Dr. Thackeray nodded, drawing on his cigar and tilting his padded desk chair a fraction closer to overbalance.

"Pity Kirk isn't here to talk with a kindred soul," Geoff Metzger continued. "He used to drag out all manner of evidence to support his claim. Go on about Egyptian artifacts, Greek thinkers, Byzantine and later Roman writings, Islamic studies after the Roman Lake changed owners, Jewish cabalism, secret researches by certain monks, on through the Dark Ages and into the so-called Renaissance—even threw out bits of Chinese history. He'd go wild talking about the *quattrocento* and the *cinquecento* and dozens of Italian names no one else had heard of—then Central Europe and France and England, and people like Bacon and Paracelsus and Albertus Magnus. That was really the astonishing thing. I mean, all of us at St. Johns were supposed to be well read and well versed in the classics and those great and mouldy books, but Kirk was something else. God knows how much that guy must have read!"

"Your friend Walker sounds like a man I ought to meet," Dr. Thackeray broke in.

Metzger's face saddened. "I'm sorry to say you can't. Quite a tragic story about old Kirk. He went on to med school after St. Johns, too—some big Southern school of notable reputation. Wasn't happy there for some reason, and ran afoul of the administration. Left after a rather stormy scene. Died not long thereafter—Hodgkins, I believe. Everyone felt bad about it at the time."

"A pity."

"Yes, it was. I must say I'm surprised to find someone of your position giving credence to such similar ideas. Guess maybe we took Kirk more lightly than we might have. Still, he was always one for elaborate jokes. Strange guy." Geoff's eye fell to wandering along the impressively filled shelves which lined Dr. Thackeray's office. These walls of conglomerate knowledge—concentrated to blocky solidity, properly bound and systematically shelved—exuded the weighty atmosphere of learned dignity that one expected for the sanctum of the Chairman of the Department of Medicine.

"And why did your friend believe this unsuspected depth of scientific knowledge was kept in secret?" the older man asked carefully.

"Kirk was vague," returned Metzger, downing his acrid coffee before it got colder. A grimy residue stained the bottom of the

Styrofoam cup, and he reflected bitterly that hospital coffee deteriorated with every medical center he came to.

"He had several reasons, though. For one thing, he'd argue that our basic conception of the past comes through writings of the past, and that these writers viewed their world from their own particular set of terms. The idea of progress—in fact, the conception of *science* as we understand it—is a relatively modern development of thought. In another age this was altogether different. To the bulk of the populace, scientific knowledge would have been no more than a pointless exercise, useless to them. What would a serf care about a microscope? It wouldn't clothe and feed him. What would an intellectual care about the discovery of microorganisms? Plagues were the punishment of God or the work of Satan.

"And the language of the day was totally different; there simply were no words—nor even systems of thought—to convey scientific conceptions. Thus every man who studied the stars was an astrologer, while the thoughtful investigator of elemental or molecular structure was only another alchemist seeking to create gold. And to be sure, many of these men were only superstitious dabblers in the occult. With the ignorance or even hostility of most writers of the day, fool and genius were lumped together, and the early scientist was categorized as being in league with the devil. He was ignored and mocked at best, more often persecuted by the authorities of the land. We know of several brilliant thinkers who were condemned to the stake for their efforts—or had near misses, like Galileo.

"It is any wonder then that Walker's protoscientists kept their work secret, shared their discoveries only with a select brotherhood? At least, that was Kirk's theory."

Dr. Thackeray considered his cigar. "Interesting. And, as you say, tragic. Medicine needs men of his caliber—and men like yourself, Dr. Metzger."

Geoff smiled at the compliment. Coming from the Grand Old Man, it meant a lot. "I consider myself fortunate to be associated with the medical center here."

"Good. And I'll say that we're all delighted you decided to join us. You're a capable man, Dr. Metzger; your record is brilliant.

Those of us who have watched you feel certain you'll go far in medicine—farther, perhaps, than you might imagine."

"Thank you, sir."

"Not at all. I'm merely stating facts. I knew your father during my residency, you know, and he was a splendid physician himself. So I'm pleased that you decided to take a position here at the Center. It's good to learn the facilities are up to your expectations, and that you're getting your lab set up to suit you."

He gestured toward the sheaf of papers Geoff had carried with him. "I like the way you've drawn this together. I'd say it's dead certain the grant will go through."

"I'm counting on it, sir."

Dr. Thackeray brandished his cigar. "Oh, it will. It will. You've stated the scientific aspects of it beautifully—and now we'll handle the political end of things. Politics, as you'll learn, count for a great deal. A very great deal, Dr. Metzger."

"No doubt," laughed Geoff drily.

It had been a good move, thought Metzger, pausing to look over his new lab facilities. A damn good move. He could make his name here at the Center.

It was a heady feeling to be in charge of his own research project—a major project at the medical center of considerable renown—and still a young man by his colleagues' standards. But Geoffrey Metzger was inured to honors.

He was, after all, the Center's prize catch—hotly contested for by any number of major institutions. Head of his class at St. Johns and at Harvard Medical School, and he could have been one of the youngest men to finish, if he had not chosen the roundabout course of a liberal arts education, a few sojourns in Europe, and a combined M.D.-Ph.D. (biochemistry) program at Harvard. Afterward he had taken his pick of the most prestigious internships and residencies, finishing as chief resident in one of the nation's best hospital centers. Then a stint with the Public Health Service in the poverty belt—in effect voluntary, since his family connections were sufficient to keep him out of military service.

An uncle with a governorship, a brother doing Very Well in the vice-presidential ladder of a Very Big corporation, and a "good marriage," socially. Another brother was becoming known in legal medicine, and his father-in-law was partner in a string of ENT clinics in Detroit. Medicine had called members of his family for several generations. Geoff had himself followed his father into internal medicine. His father, very influential in the A.M.A., had been supposedly slated for its top post at the time of his death from a coronary.

A good record, as Dr. Thackeray had observed. And no reason why it should not continue to shine. Metzger's previous research work—extending back to his undergraduate days and assuming considerable stature during his residency—had led to numerous publications and no little acclaim. Clearly he was a man who was going places, and the Center was quite proud when he accepted their extremely generous offer. They had given him a free hand in a superbly equipped lab in their newest research facility, with a position as attending physician on the medical staff. And they had made it plain that this was merely a start for him, that there shortly would be important vacancies in the hierarchy of the Center. . . .

Yes, it had been a damn good move.

Geoff grimaced and crumpled his Styrofoam cup. And one of the first additions to his lab equipment was going to be a private coffee urn.

II

"Did you notice that ring Sid Lipton had on last night?" asked Gwen.

"What?" Geoff, a persistent headache reminding him of the cocktail party at Trelane's the night before, was trying to watch the morning news.

"Sid had on a sort of signet ring," Gwen persisted. "Did you notice?"

"What? No, guess I didn't."

"It was an ornate silver ring with a large black onyx, I think. Into the onyx was set a kind of silver medallion or seal. It looked like a fraternity ring or something, but I couldn't place it. I thought maybe you knew what it was."

"Haven't noticed it. Dr. Lipton's usually scrubbed for surgery whenever I see him—or always looks that way. Don't think I've ever seen him wear anything on his hands but rubber gloves."

"Want some more orange juice? Well, it was strange, because when I went to the girls' room I passed Sid and Brice Thackeray in the hall, and Brice seemed like he was upset or something because Sid had on the ring."

"Upset?"

"Well, maybe not. But they were talking over something in a not-very-casual manner, and it seemed like the ring was part of it. They stopped when I walked by and moved back in with the party. Did you see that slutty dress Tess Gilman had on?"

"Huh? No."

"I'll bet. A see-through blouse with her figure! You could see where her body stocking had padded inserts. And all you men ogling her like she was Raquel or somebody."

"Gwen, I'm trying to listen to the news."

Her face tightened. "Screw the news! You spend all day between the hospital and your damn lab, and when you do get home in time to talk, all you do is tell me about the hospital, tell me about your research. Damn it, you might at least try to pay a little attention to me over the breakfast table!"

"Sweetheart, they're talking about Senator Hollister. He had a CVA last night and died. Forgive me if I find the death of the front-running liberal candidate for the next Presidential election of somewhat greater interest than your rehash of the highlights of another boring cocktail party!"

"Well I'm sorry if you find spending an evening with your wife boring!" she returned hotly.

The news moved on to the latest catastrophe in Pakistan.

"Gwen, honey, that wasn't what I meant."

"Well, goddamn it, Geoff! You don't have to brush off everything I say. I put up with that miserable last year of Harvard, and then your internship in that filthy city—gone all the time, and home every other night just to sleep. Then that endless residency period, when everything was supposed to get better and you'd have more free time—but you didn't, because you were doing work on your own in that lab. And Jesus, that miserable stay in the heartland of coal mines and grits while you played the medical missionary! And all this was supposed to lead up to when you could be the big man in the big medical complex, and name your own hours, and pay some attention to me for a change. Remember me? I'm your wife! Would you like to stuff me away with some of those damn virus cultures you're forever playing with!"

I've heard this before, thought Geoff, knowing that he would hear it again. And she wasn't being all that unfair, he also realized. But he was running late, and this lingering hangover left him in no mood to talk things out again.

"Honey, it happens that I'm at a crucial stage right now, and I really have to keep at it," he offered by way of reconciliation. "Besides, we went to the cocktail party at Trelane's last night, didn't we? We were together then, weren't we?"

"Big deal," Gwen sniffled. "It was a lousy party. All you talked about was medicine."

Geoff sighed, and glanced at his watch. "Look, I don't want to make this sound too dramatic, but what I'm working on now could be big—I mean *big*. How big it might be I haven't even told my colleagues—I don't want to look like a fool if it doesn't work out. But, honey, I think it *is* going to work out, and if it does, I'll have made a breakthrough like no one since . . . Well, it will be a breakthrough."

"Swell! You mean you'll have discovered a whole new way to implant zits on a monkey's navel, or some other thrilling discovery that all the journals can argue about!" Gwen was not to be placated.

Giving it up, Geoff bent to kiss her. She turned her face, and he got a mouthful of brown curls. "Baby, it really could be big. If it is, well, things could get a whole lot different for us in a hurry."

"I'll take any change—the sooner the better," she murmured, raising her chin a little.

"Trust me, sweetheart. Hey look, you were fussing about your party dress last night. Why don't you go out today and pick out a new one—something nice, whatever you like. OK?"

"Mmmff," decided his wife, letting him kiss her cheek.

"What news today?"

Geoff glanced up from his stack of electron photomicrographs. "Oh, hi, Dave." And to atone for the trace of irritation in his voice, he added, "Have a cup of coffee?"

"Muchos grassy-ass," his visitor replied, turning to the large coffee urn Geoff had inveigled for his lab. He spooned in half a cupful of sugar and powdered cream substitute, and raised the steaming container immediately to his lips—one of those whose mouths seem impervious to scalding temperatures.

"Don't know why it is, but even when you brew your own, it ends up tasting rancid like all other hospital coffee," Geoff commented, half covering his pile of photographs.

"Unh," Dr. Froneberger acceded. "Know what you mean— that's why I gave up drinking it black. Rot your liver if you don't cut it with powdered goo. I think it's the water. Hospital water is shot full of chemicals, rays, gases, dead bugs. Very healthfully unhealthful.

"What you got there, Geoff?" he queried, moving over to the desk.

Reluctantly, Metzger surrendered the photomicrographs. Froneberger's own lab was at the other end of the hall, and it would be impolitic to affront his neighbor. Still, he vaguely resented the frequent contacts that their proximity afforded. Not that Dave was any more than ordinarily obnoxious, but the other's research with influenza viruses impinged closely enough on some areas of his own work to raise the touchy problem of professional jealousy.

"Unh," Froneberger expounded, tapping a hairy finger across several of the photos. "Right here, buddy. I can see it too. You got that same twisted grouping along the nuclear membrane, and on these two you can definitely see the penetration. And you can make a good argument with this one that here's the same grouping on the chromosome. Hey, this is good stuff you're getting here, Geoff buddy."

"I think I'm making some progress," offered Metzger testily, rankled at the other's appropriation of data he had spent countless hours working toward. It would never do for Froneberger to insinuate himself into this thing with matters such as they were.

"Where's it leading you, buddy? Got anything backing this besides what the editors like to brush off as 'artifacts of electron microscopy'?"

"I couldn't say," Geoff replied evasively. "I'm getting some new data off these labeled cultures that may lead somewhere."

"May, and again may not, that's the way it always is. I know the feeling, believe you me. Been a few times, buddy, when I damn near thought I . . . But, hell, maybe all the cherries will roll up for you this time, you never know. Looks impressive so far, my fran. Could be we're hearing the Nobel boys sniffing outside the door."

"I think that's your telephone."

"Shit, it is that. And my secretary's on break. Better catch it. Chow!" He lumbered off.

"Damn!" Geoff breathed, resorting his photographs with fumbling touch.

III

"Too late for you to help him, eh?"

"How's that?" Geoff looked up from his evening paper and turned toward the man who was seating himself opposite him. It was Ira Festung, who busily rearranged his cafeteria tray, smiling cheerfully as he smothered his hospital pot roast in catsup. He should have taken the paper back to the lab to finish reading, Geoff reflected. He had promised Gwen he would be home before too late, and he could lose half an hour trying to break away from the garrulous epidemiologist.

"I noticed you were reading the headlines about the Supreme Court Justice," said Dr. Festung, doing nothing to clarify his greeting.

"I was," Geoff admitted, glancing again at the lead article, which told of Justice Freeport's death from cancer that morning. "Freeport was a good man. The second justice to die in the last few months, and both of them liberals. They'll have a hard time replacing them—especially with the Administration we have right now."

Festung snorted into his ice water. "Oh, they'll probably find another couple Commies to fill their seats. Don't see how you can seriously regret Freeport and Lloyd, after the stands those leftists took on socialized medicine. Sure it sounds great to be the bleeding-heart humanitarian, but tell me how much of this fancy research you'd be doing as a salaried pill-pusher. Hell, look at the disaster in Britain! Is that the kind of medical care you want to dish out to the public?"

If this got started again, Geoff knew he could plan to spend the whole evening in the hospital cafeteria. And afterward he'd have a sore throat, and his grey-haired colleagues would shake their heads condescendingly and despair of his political judgment.

"What did you mean by what you said when you sat down?" he asked instead, hoping to steer the epidemiologist away from another great debate.

"That?" Festung wiped catsup from his full lips.

Whiskers, and he'd look like President Taft, Metzger decided.

"Well, Freeport had multiple myeloma, and from what I hear, aren't you about to come up with the long-sought breakthrough in cancer?" Festung's watery eyes were suddenly keen.

Goddamn that sonofabitch Froneberger! Geoff fought to hold a poker face. Let word go around that the Boy Wonder thought he had a cure for cancer, and he'd be a laughingstock if this research didn't pan out!

"Oh, is that the scuttlebutt these days?" He smiled carefully. "Well, I'm glad to hear somebody has even greater optimism for my project than I do. Maybe I ought to trade notes with him."

"If we didn't have rumors to play with, wouldn't this medical center be a dull place to live," Dr. Festung pronounced.

Geoff laughed dutifully, although he had his own opinion of the back-stabbing gossip that filled so many conversations here.

"Waste of time trying to cure cancer anyway," the epidemiologist continued. "Nature would only replace it with another scourge just as deadly, and then we'd have to begin all over again. Let it run its course and be done, I say."

"Well, that's your specialty," Geoff said with a thin smile, uncertain how serious his companion meant to be taken.

"Common sense," confided Festung. "Common sense and simple arithmetic—that's all there is to epidemiology. Every Age has its deadly plague, far back as you care to trace it.

"The great plagues of the ancient world—leprosy, cholera, the Black Death. They all came and went, left millions dead before they were finished, and for most of them we can't even say for certain what disease it may have been."

"Those were primitive times," Geoff shrugged. "Plagues were expected—and accepted. No medicine, and filthy living conditions. Naturally a plague would go unchecked—until it either killed all those who were susceptible, or something like the London Fire came along to cauterize the centers of contagion."

"More often the plagues simply ran their course and vanished," Dr. Festung went on in a tone of dismissal. "Let's take modern times, civilized countries, then—after your London Fire (actually it was a change of dominant species of rat) and the ebbing of the bubonic plague. Comes the Industrial Revolution to Europe, and with it strikes smallpox and then tuberculosis. A little later, and you get the picture in this country too. OK, you finally vaccinate against smallpox, but what about TB? Where did TB come from, anyway? Industrialization? No sir, because TB went on the wane at the height of industrialization. And why did it? Biggest killer of its day, and now it's a rare disease. And you know medicine had damn little to do with its disappearance. Then influenza. Killed millions, and not just because medical conditions weren't what we have now. Hell, we still can't do much about the flu. Froneberger tells me his research indicates there are two or three wholly new influenza strains 'born' (if you will) each year—that we know about. Hell, we still aren't really sure what strain was the great killer at the early part of the century. And talk about confusion, why, when you say 'flu,' you can mean anything from several bacteria to any number of viral strains and substrains."

"Well, how about polio?" challenged Metzger, digging for a cigarette. Festung hated tobacco smoke.

"Polio? Exactly. Another killer plague that appeared from nowhere. Sure, this time we came up with a vaccine. But so we know where it went—where did polio come from, though? Each generation seems to have its nemesis. When I was your age, the big killer was stomach cancer. Like bad weather, we talked a lot about stomach cancer, but nothing much was ever done, and it faded into the background just the same. Instead, we had heart disease. Now there's the number one killer for these many years—the reason for billions of government dollars doled out for research. And what have we really done about it? Dietary fads, a few ghoulish transplants, and a pile of Rube Goldberg gadgetry that can keep things pumping for a few extra years. Sum total: too close to nothing to bother caring. But that's all right too, because now heart disease is on the way out, and for now our great slayer of mankind is cancer.

"History and figures tell the story, young man. Cancer is here for the moment. And maybe all your research will do something about it, then more likely it won't. But it doesn't matter in the long run, because cancer will have its heyday and fade like its predecessors at the scythe handle, and then we'll find something new to die of. Wonder what it'll be."

"Someone else's worry, that's what it'll be. I suppose, as they say, you got to die of something." Geoff pushed his chair back from the table. "Meanwhile I'll chase after today's problems. And one of the most immediate concerns a scintillation counter run that ought to be gone through by now. See you, Ira."

"Sure. Hey, how about leaving that paper, if you're finished reading it."

Dr. Thackeray was waiting in the lab when Geoff returned. The Great Man was leaning over Metzger's desk, idly looking through several days' loose data and notes. A long white lab coat, stylishly ragged after the Center's peculiar snobbery, covered his sparse frame. A little imagination and he could make a good Hallowe'en phantom, mused Geoff, watching the blue cigar smoke swirl about his hawklike face.

Geoff stepped into his office alcove. "Keeping late hours, Dr. Thackeray?" The Chairman of Medicine has no first name within the walls of his domain.

"Good evening, Dr. Metzger," returned his superior. "No, not particularly. I wanted to see how things were going with you, and

I felt it likely you'd still be here. Your devotion to your work has caused some comment—even among our staff. Most commendable, but I hope you aren't working yourself into an early grave."

"I'll manage," Geoff promised. "I feel like I'm really getting somewhere right now though, and I hate to let up."

"Yes. I see you've made progress, Dr. Metzger." His eyes black in the sterile glare of the fluorescents, Dr. Thackeray let his gaze gesture about the crowded laboratory. "Very significant progress in the year you've been with us here at the Center."

Geoff framed his words with care. "I don't like to put myself down as saying—even off the record—just how far what I'm doing here might lead, Dr. Thackeray. You've seen what I've accomplished so far, read the preliminary reports. But in the last few months I've . . . well, made a few unexpected breakthroughs. I think I know what it will mean, but I want absolute evidence to substantiate my findings before I speculate openly with regard to what I've learned. Forgive me if this seems melodramatic, but I've no desire to be labeled a fool, nor would I care to bring derision upon the Center."

"Again commendable, Dr. Metzger. I appreciate your position, naturally. As you know, there's been some speculation among the staff relating to your most recent work—enough that some of us can understand what you're trying to lead up to."

"I'm making no preliminary claims," Geoff repeated. "Between the two of us, I feel certain of my ground. But too many overeager researchers have gone off half cocked and regretted it when their errors were immediately apparent to more careful workers."

"To be sure!" Dr. Thackeray turned his piercing eyes into Geoff's. "I truly admire your discretion. Untold damage might result from foolish disclosures at this point. I agree."

"Thank you, sir."

"Not at all." Dr. Thackeray waved his hand. His expression darkened. "It's because of the position you find yourself in right now that I've left these two papers on your desk."

Surprised, Geoff noticed for the first time the two dull black binders waiting beside a tangle of data tapes. Their vinyl covers bore no title—then, on closer glance, he was aware of a tiny silver seal embossed on either spine.

"It required considerable effort to obtain those two copies," Dr. Thackeray advised. "Needless to say, I'll expect you to examine them with care—the data is confidential, of course—and return them to me when you've finished. Reading them is explanation enough for the present, so I'll say no more for now.

"I think you'll want to discuss your thoughts on this with me. How about tomorrow morning at 8:00? I think you will have read through them to your satisfaction by then."

"Certainly," agreed Metzger in bewilderment. "If you feel this is important to my project . . ."

"It's extremely important, Dr. Metzger, I assure you. Very well, then. We'll talk this over at eight."

With a bizarre sense of foreboding, Geoff took up the first of the black folders.

IV

Dr. Thackeray's secretary was not present when Metzger entered the Department of Medicine offices the following morning—his nerves jagged after a sleepless night. Since he knew he was expected, he knocked and entered the Chairman's office. *Sanctum sanctorum,* soul of the Center, he thought with a tinge of hysteria.

"Dr. Thackeray, I've been trying to get in touch with you all night . . ." He halted, startled to find the Chairman of Surgery seated within.

"It's all right, Dr. Metzger," pronounced Dr. Thackeray. "Dr. Lipton is a party to . . . this matter we have to discuss."

Numbly Geoff dropped into the room's vacant chair. The two older men faced him with carefully composed mien—eyes alert as birds of prey.

Geoff thumped a fist against the black vinyl folders in his lap. "God, it's all here!" His eyes were feverish. "Everything I've done, all I'd hoped to establish—a number of aspects I'd never considered!"

Dr. Thackeray nodded, eyes unblinking.

"Well, Christ, where did you get this? If you knew someone

else was working in my field, why didn't you tell me earlier? Hell, this is too important for professional jealousy. I'll gladly share any of my data with these researchers. To hell with who gets official credit!"

His voice began to shake. "This research—this information! My god—it means a definite cure for almost every form of human cancer! Why, this delineates each etiological factor involved in cancer—pinpoints two definite stages where the causative agent can be destroyed, the disease process completely arrested! This research marks the triumph of medicine over leukemia, most of the systemic dysplasias—individual organ involvement will be virtually eradicated!"

"Quite true," Dr. Lipton agreed. His long surgeon's fingers toyed with the silver-and-onyx ring he wore.

"Well, no more suspense, please! Whose work is this? Where's it being done?" Geoff's excitement was undiminished by the coolness of the other two physicians.

"One paper was prepared from the work of Dr. C. Johnson Taggart," Dr. Thackeray told him.

"Taggart? No wonder it's . . . But Taggart died ten years ago—brain tumor! You mean they've taken this long to piece together his notes?"

"The other paper, as you've noticed, is considerably older. Most of it was the work of Sir David Aubrey," Dr. Thackeray concluded.

Geoff stared at them to determine whether they were playing some horribly sick joke. "Aubrey died at the turn of the century."

"True again. But he was responsible for most of the pioneer work in this field," Dr. Lipton added with a tone of reproof.

The overweighted shelves of accumulated knowledge seemed to press down on Geoff's soul. A windowless room in the center of the complex, like a chamber of the vast heart of some monstrous entity. "I don't understand," he whispered in a choked voice. "Why hasn't this information been used before now? Why were millions left to die?"

"Perhaps the world wasn't ready for a cure to cancer," Dr. Thackeray replied.

"That's . . . that's insane! I don't understand," quavered Geoff, noticing now that Dr. Thackeray wore a ring similar to Dr. Lipton's. There was a seal set into the onyx. He had seen it before. It was stamped on the spines of the black binders.

"You can understand," Dr. Thackeray was saying. "This will be strange—traumatic perhaps, at first. But think carefully. Would it be wise to circulate a total cure for cancer just now?"

"Are you serious? You can't be! The lives, the suffering . . ."

"The price of power, Dr. Metzger. The price of power—just as every empire is built upon the lives and suffering of the expendable." Dr. Lipton's voice was pitiless as the edge of his scalpels, excising without rancor the organism's defective tissue.

"Think of cancer in more rational terms," Dr. Thackeray went on. "Have you any conception of the money invested every day in cancer research, in treatment of cancer patients? It's incalculable, I assure you. Do you think the medical profession can sacrifice this wealth, this enormous power, just for a humanitarian gesture?"

"But a physician's role is to heal!" screamed Metzger, abstractly noting how thoroughly the endless shelves muffled sound.

"Of course. And he does heal," put in Dr. Lipton. "But where would a physician be if there were no sickness to be healed?"

They were mad, Geoff realized. Or he was. He had been overworking. This was a dream, a paranoid fantasy.

This knowledge made him calmer. He would follow this mad logic—at least until he could be certain with whom the insanity lay. "But some diseases are eradicated," he protested.

"When they become expendable," Dr. Thackeray told him. "Some, of course, simply die out, or fall victim to nonmedical intervention. Others we announce a cure for—makes the profession look good. The world has restored faith in medicine, praises its practitioners, and pours more money into research. The prestige a physician enjoys in the community is an essential factor to us."

Lipton's frown furrowed into his close-cropped hair where it grew low on his brow. "And sometimes we slip up, and some fool announces a major cure without our awareness. Thank God, there's less of that now with the disappearance of independent research. As it is, we've had some damn close calls—took a lot of work to discredit a few of these thoughtless meddlers."

Geoff remembered some of them. And now he knew fear. Fear greater than his dread of insanity; fear that these men were all too sane. "I suppose something can happen to some of these researchers who might cause difficulty."

"You make it sound like a line from a gangster movie, but yes," Dr. Thackeray acknowledged. "Quite a number of them die from some sudden illness, and the scientific community regrets that they left their brilliant promise unfulfilled."

"It's a way of avoiding other dilemmas as well, as I think you'll follow me," Dr. Lipton growled. "Meddlers who become aware of our existence. Fools who would destroy the medical profession with Communistic laws and regulations, endanger the social structure with ruinous legislation.

"And don't look shocked, young man. Think instead just what kind of doctor you might be right now, if some of these late and unlamented wild-eyed liberals could have done all they intended to this country and to the medical profession."

"Murder . . ." breathed Geoff weakly.

"Not actually," Dr. Thackeray broke in. "After all, as physicians we have to see human society as a living organism. The social organism is subject to disease just like any other entity. To be trite, it isn't murder to excise a cancerous growth. Regulation treatment—sometimes drastic treatment—is essential if the organism is not to perish. This is the rationale behind all forms of government; the alternative is chaos. I think you'll agree that an educated elite is best suited to direct the social destiny of us all. After all, an epithelial cell is scarcely suited to handle the functions of a nerve cell. It functions smoothly, dies when its time comes—all because the brain, of which it has no conception, directs its course. How else would you have it?"

"You can't suppress medical knowledge indefinitely," Geoff returned defiantly. "Someday someone will eradicate cancer. They were aware of its etiology as far back as Aubrey . . ."

"Certainly."

"In fact, it's amazing that Aubrey understood cancer so thoroughly—considering the relatively crude apparatus of the day."

Dr. Thackeray smiled. "Ah, but we've talked earlier about the possibility of what I believe you termed 'recondite scientific knowledge.' And besides, Aubrey had several advantages over moderns as to the matter of his starting point."

Horror was damp on Metzger's face. The air was stifling, charged with hideous revelation. "You said he was a pioneer. . . ."

"Yes," Lipton rumbled impatiently. "A pioneer in the *development* of the disease process."

"Oh my god," whispered Geoff. *"Oh my god!"*

"I know this is a great deal to comprehend," Dr. Thackeray offered sympathetically. "But use your intelligence. To have significant power, a physician must have an essential role—and what is more compelling than the power of life and death? If there were no diseases, there would be no need for physicians. Therefore at certain times throughout history it has been necessary to develop and introduce to the general population new forms of disease."

"But accidental deaths—traffic accidents . . ." Geoff countered, striving to follow his resolve to argue the situation by their own insane reasoning.

Dr. Lipton laughed shortly. "If you only knew half our efforts toward keeping cars and highways unsafe! Or the medications we release for the public to abuse. Or the chemical additives we've developed . . ."

"Who? Who are you?" His nerve was going to shatter in another instant. This dispassionate, insane . . .

"There are a number of us," Dr. Thackeray announced. "A small, highly select order of medicine's elite. An ancient order, I might point out. After all, the art of medicine is as old as human suffering, is it not?

"And of course, our order has grown in power with the passage of time. Today, our society is custodian of an astonishing body of medical and scientific knowledge; our research facilities are the best in the world. We have a certain hierarchy—democratically established, of course—to oversee our operations, direct the use of our wealth, to make those decisions vital to maintaining the order's power and security.

"And naturally you can see why we've been so interested in you, Dr. Metzger."

Under their relentless stare, Geoff struggled desperately to maintain exterior calm, while underneath his mind grappled with ideas too nightmarish for conception. "What do you want from me?" he grated, dreading the answer.

"Come now, young man," Dr. Thackeray spoke reassuringly. "This isn't a high tribunal. We wish to bestow a great honor upon you—an honor reserved for only those most worthy. We want you to join in our order."

"This is insane, of course," Geoff murmured without conviction. "You want me to become part of a society of inhuman despots? God! This is the most debased treachery to mankind that any mind could ever conceive!"

"It will take a certain period for your thinking to adjust to this new awareness," Dr. Lipton interceded with some rancor. "It might change matters if you knew your father was one of us."

"I can't believe that!" But from the dim recesses of his memory came the phantom image of a ring he once saw his father wear—a black onyx ring, set with a peculiar signet.

"True, nonetheless," Dr. Thackeray said. "I knew him well. His untimely death was a great setback to us."

"So 'untimely death' can even strike your council of petty gods!"

"There are occasional power struggles within our ..." Dr. Lipton began. He was silenced by a glare from Dr. Thackeray.

"Naturally we protect ourselves from our own, ah, methods," Dr. Thackeray proceeded. "As a member of our order, you will have access to medical techniques beyond the dream of those outside. Only rarely does something untoward occur."

"Why did you pick me?"

"That should be obvious. It was essential to stop your present line of research, certainly. But that could have been a simple matter. No, we've had our attention on you for a great while. As I say, your father was high in our order. Your family connections are invaluable. Your own contributions to medicine would have singled you out, even had your background been quite plebeian. You're a brilliant man, Dr. Metzger. It would be difficult to postulate a candidate better qualified for membership in our order."

"I suppose I'm immensely flattered."

"You should be," the surgeon growled.

"And you shall be," Dr. Thackeray assured him. "You will

naturally want a certain length of time to consider. This is quite understandably a devastating blow to your past conceptions and ideals. We are pleased to offer you time to consider, to re-evaluate your position in light of this new awareness. You're an intelligent man, Dr. Metzger. I feel certain your decision will be the rational one—once you've had time to reconsider your former prejudices and misconceptions."

"Suppose I decide to tell the world of your unspeakable conspiracy?"

"Who would ever believe you?"

"It's not that unusual for an overwrought researcher to suffer a nervous collapse," Dr. Lipton told him. "In such cases, immediate institutional treatment is available. We become very sympathetic, and work very hard to help our stricken fellow—but I'm afraid our cure ratio is somewhat grim."

Geoff remembered, and fear tightened a chill coil around his heart. "I have to think," he muttered, his thoughts searching frantically for some release to this nightmare. "God, I have to think!"

"Of course." Dr. Thackeray's smile was one of paternal sympathy. "We'll wait for your decision."

Not very many minutes after Geoff Metzger had dazedly fled Dr. Thackeray's office, a section of the book-lined wall pivoted open. The two noted physicians looked expectantly to the heavy-set man who waited within the hidden niche.

"Well, Dr. Royce?"

The eminent psychiatrist grimly studied the monitoring devices focused on the room's vacant chair.

"No," he pronounced.

v

By habit Geoff stumbled back to his lab. A wounded beast returns to his lair, he thought morbidly.

None of his lab workers had appeared. No doubt they had been instructed to take a day off. His phone worked—at least there was a dial tone. But then they couldn't disconnect every phone in the

Center. Besides, who could he tell? Gwen? She might believe him. More likely she'd call a psychiatrist at the first discreet moment. And even without believing him, her knowledge would endanger her life as well.

It was monstrous. Surrounded by a sterile labyrinth of tile and cinder block and stainless steel, shelves of gleaming lab equipment, banks of humming research apparatus—watchful in the dead white glare of the fluorescents . . . God, he'd never realized how sinister a research lab could be. Suddenly he felt like some ancient sorcerer, surrounded by the abhorrent paraphernalia of his evil delvings—a sorcerer who had suddenly succeeded with his conjurations, who now held the bleak knowledge of what demonic powers had claimed his soul.

To become a partner in this inhuman conspiracy was unthinkable. Perhaps its arrogant, ruthless rationality would appeal to certain of his colleagues. But never to him. He could never endure the knowledge of so monstrous a betrayal. He would not become a traitor to mankind.

The alternative? Death, almost certainly. Countless others had died for suspecting, for so much as entertaining ideas which might lead to exposing this secret order. *He knew.* They would show him no mercy. What chance did one man have against a hidden society that had held remorseless power for centuries?

There was a slim chance. His only chance. He might pretend to acquiesce. He could agree to join them in their dread order. Of course, they would suspect; he would be carefully watched. But in time they would accept him. For such enormous stakes he could afford to bide his time, wait patiently for years perhaps. During that period he could plan, build up unassailable evidence, learn their names—lay preparations for the day when he might expose their dark treason to the unsuspecting world. . . .

"Hey, buddy, you look gloomy. Wife troubles, I bet. They don't go for their man spending all his time with the test tubes, I should know. How about some coffee?" Dave Froneberger was grinning at him, already fiddling with the urn.

Geoff blinked at him dumbly. After the ordeal of these last few hours, Froneberger with his insinuating banalities and petty gossip seemed almost an ally. Perhaps he could be one.

"Thanks, Dave," he muttered, accepting the Styrofoam cup. He was too shaken even to feel his customary disgust with the bitter coffee. Yes, Froneberger with his prying interest in his research might be an ally. At least he could be one other party to this new cancer data. They couldn't murder and discredit the entire Center staff.

"You know, Dave," Geoff began. "I'm glad you dropped by just now. It strikes me that your own research is similar to mine in enough aspects that you might have some fresh insight into some problems I've run into. If you'd care to take time, I'd like to go over some of my notes with you, and see what you think."

"I don't think you'll have time," smiled Froneberger. He reached for Geoff's empty coffee cup, dropped it into a pocket of his lab coat.

"What do you mean?" asked Geoff thickly, coughing suddenly. There was pain deep, deep in his throat. Another racking cough filled his mouth with blood.

And he knew what Froneberger meant.

MORE SINNED AGAINST

Theirs was a story so commonplace that it balanced uneasily between the maudlin and the sordid—a cliché dipped in filth.

Her real name was Katharina Oglethorpe and she changed that to Candace Thornton when she moved to Los Angeles, but she was known as Candi Thorne in the few films she ever made— the ones that troubled to list credits. She came from some little Baptist church and textile mill town in eastern North Carolina, although later she said she came from Charlotte. She always insisted that her occasional and transient friends call her Candace, and she signed her name Candace in a large, legible hand for those occasional and compulsive autographs. She had lofty aspirations and only minimal talent. One of her former agents perhaps stated her *mot juste*: a lady with a lot of guts, but too much heart. The police records gave her name as Candy Thorneton.

There had been money once in her family, and with that the staunch pride that comes of having more money than the other thousand or so inhabitants of the town put together. Foreign textiles eventually closed the mill: unfortunate investments leeched the money. Pride of place remained.

By the time that any of her past really matters, Candace had graduated from an area church-supported junior college, where she was homecoming queen, and she'd won one or two regional beauty contests and was almost a runner-up in the Miss North Carolina pageant. Her figure was good, although more for a truck-stop waitress than suited to a model's requirements, and her acting talents were wholehearted, if marginal. Her parents believed she was safely enrolled at U.C.L.A., and they never quite forgave her when they eventually learned otherwise.

Their tuition checks kept Candace afloat as an aspiring young actress/model through a succession of broken promises, phony deals, and predatory agents. Somewhere along the way she sacrificed her cherished virginity a dozen times over, enough so that it no longer pained her, even as the next day dulled the pain of the promised break that never materialized. Her family might have taken back, if not welcomed, their prodigal daughter, had Candace not begged them for money for her first abortion. They refused, Candace got the money anyway, and her family had no more to do with her ever.

He called himself Richards Justin, and there was as much truth to that as to anything else he ever said. He met Candace when she was just on the brink of putting her life together, although he never blamed himself for her subsequent crash. He always said that he was a man who learned from the mistakes of others, and had he said "profited" instead, he might have told the truth for once.

They met because they were sleeping with the same producer, both of them assured of a part in his next film. The producer failed to honor either bargain, and he failed to honor payment for a kilo of coke, after which a South American entrepreneur emptied a Browning Hi-Power into him. Candace and Richards Justin consoled one another over lost opportunity, and afterward he moved in with her.

Candace was sharing a duplex in Venice with two cats and a few thousand roaches. It was a cottage of rotting pink stucco that resembled a gingerbread house left out in the rain. Beside it ran a refuse-choked ditch that had once been a canal. The shack two doors down had been burned out that spring in a shootout between rival gangs of bikers. The neighborhood was scheduled for gentrification, but no one had decided yet whether this should entail restoration or razing. The rent was cheaper than an apartment, and against the house grew a massive clump of jade plant that Candace liked to pause before and admire.

At this time Candace was on an upswing and reasonably confident of landing the part of a major victim in a minor stalk-and-slash film. Her face and teeth had always been good; afternoons in the sun and judicious use of rinses on her mousy hair had transformed her into a passable replica of a Malibu blonde. She had that sort of ample figure that looks better with less clothing and best with none at all, and she managed quite well in a few photo spreads in some of the raunchier skin magazines. She was not to be trusted with a speaking part, but some voice and drama coaching might have improved that difficulty in time.

Richards Justin—Rick to his friends—very studiously was a hunk, to use the expression of the moment. He stood six foot four and packed about 215 pounds of health club-nurtured muscle over wide shoulders and lean hips. His belly was quite hard and flat, his thighs strong from jogging, and an even tan set off the generous dark growth of body hair. His black hair was neatly permed, and the heavy mustache added virility to features that stopped just short of being pretty. He seemed designed for posing in tight jeans, muscular arms folded across hairy chest, and he often posed just so. He claimed to have had extensive acting experience in New York before moving to Los Angeles, but somehow his credentials were never subject to verification.

Candace was a type who took in stray animals, and she took in Richards Justin. She had survived two years on the fringes of Hollywood, and Rick was new to Los Angeles—still vulnerable in his search for the elusive Big Break. She was confident that she knew some friends who could help him get started, and she really did need a roommate to help with the rent—once he found work, of course. Rick loaded his suitcase and possessions into her aging Rabbit, with room to spare, and moved in with Candace. He insisted that he pay his share of expenses, and borrowed four hundred bucks to buy some clothes—first appearances count everything in an interview.

They were great together in bed, and Candace was in love. She recognized the sensitive, lonely soul of the artist hidden beneath his macho exterior. They were both painfully earnest about their acting careers—talking long through the nights of films and actors, great directors and theories of drama. They agreed that one must never compromise art for commercial considerations, but that sometimes it might be necessary to make small compromises in order to achieve the Big Break.

The producer of the stalk-and-slash flick decided that Candace retained too much southern accent for a major role. Having just gone through her savings, Candace spent a vigorous all-night interview with the producer and salvaged a minor role. It wasn't strictly nonspeaking, as she got to scream quite a lot while the deranged killer spiked her to a barn door with a pitchfork. It was quite effective, and a retouched still of her big scene was used for the posters of *Camp Hell!* It was the highwater mark of her career.

Rick found the Big Break even more elusive than a tough, cynical, street-wise hunk like himself had envisioned. It discouraged the artist within him, just as it embarrassed his virile nature to have to live off Candace's earnings continually. Fortunately coke helped restore his confidence, and unfortunately coke was expensive. They both agreed, however, that coke was a necessary expense, career-wise. Coke was both inspiration and encouragement; besides, an actor who didn't have a few grams to flash around was as plausible as an outlaw biker who didn't drink beer.

Candace knew how discouraging this all must be for Rick. In many ways she was so much wiser and tougher than Rick. Her concern over his difficulties distracted her from the disappointment of her own faltering career. Granted, Rick's talents were a bit raw—he was a gem in need of polishing. Courses and workshops were available, but these cost money, too. Candace worked her contacts and changed her agent. If she didn't mind doing a little T&A, her new agent felt sure he could get her a small part or two in some soft-R films. It was money.

Candace played the dumb southern blonde in *Jiggle High* and she played the dumb southern cheerleader in *Cheerleader Superbowl* and she played the dumb southern stewardess in *First Class Only* and she played the dumb southern nurse in *Sex Clinic* and she played the dumb southern hooker in *Hard Streets,* but always this was Candi Thorne who played these roles, and not Candace Thornton, and somehow this made the transition from soft-R to hard-R films a little easier to bear.

They had their first big quarrel when Candace balked over her part in *Malibu Hustlers.* She hadn't realized they were shooting it in both R- and X-rated versions. Prancing about in the buff and faking torrid love scenes was one thing, but Candace drew the line at actually screwing for the close-up cameras. Her agent swore he was through if she backed out of the contract. Rick yelled at her and slapped her around a little, then broke into tears. He hadn't meant to lose control—it was just that he was so close to getting his break, and without money all they'd worked so hard together for, all they'd hoped and prayed for . . .

Candace forgave him, and blamed herself for being thoughtless and selfish. If she could ball off camera to land a role, she could give the same performance on camera. This once.

Candace never did find out what her agent did with her check from *Malibu Hustlers,* nor did the police ever manage to find her agent. The producer was sympathetic, but not legally responsible. He did, however, hate to see a sweet kid burned like that, and he offered her a lead role in *Hot 'n' Horny.* This one would be straight X—or XXX, as they liked to call them now—but a lot of talented girls had made the big time doing their stuff for the screen, and Candi Thorne just might be the next super-X superstar. He had the right connections, and if she played it right with him . . .

It wasn't the Big Break Candace had dreamed of, but it was money. And they *did* need money. She worried that this would damage her chances for a legitimate acting career, but Rick told her to stop being a selfish prude and to think of their future together. His break was coming soon, and then they'd never have to worry again about money. Besides, audiences were already watching her perform in *Malibu Hustlers,* so what did she have left to be shy about?

The problem with coke was that Rick needed a lot of it to keep him and his macho image going. The trouble with a lot of coke was that Rick tended to get wired a little too tight, and then he needed downers to mellow out. Smack worked best, but the trouble with smack was that it was even more expensive. Still, tomorrow's male sex symbol couldn't go about dropping ludes and barbs like some junior high punker. Smack was status in this game—everybody did coke. Not to worry: Rick had been doing a little heroin ever since his New York days—no needle work, just some to toot. He could handle it.

Candace could not—either the smack or the expense. Rick was gaining a lot of influential contacts. He had to dress well, show up at the right parties. Sometimes they decided it would be better for his career if he went alone. They really needed a better place to live, now that they could afford it.

After making *Wet 'n' Willing* Candace managed to rent a small house off North Beverly Glen Boulevard—not much of an improvement over her duplex in Venice, but the address was a quantum leap in class. Her biggest regret was having to leave her cats: no pets allowed. Her producer had advanced her some money to cover immediate expenses, and she knew he'd be getting it back in pounds of flesh. There were parties for important friends, and Candace felt quite casual about performing on camera after some of the things she'd been asked to do on those nights. And that made it easier when she was asked to do them again on camera.

Candace couldn't have endured it all if it weren't for her selfless love for Rick, and for the coke and smack and pills and booze. Rick expressed concern over her increasing use of drugs, especially when they were down to their last few lines. Candace economized by shooting more—less waste and a purer high than snorting.

She was so stoned on the set for *Voodoo Vixens* that she could barely go through the motions of the minimal plot. The director complained; her producer reminded her that retakes cost money, and privately noted that her looks were distinctly taking a shop-worn plunge. When she threw up in her co-star's lap, he decided that Candi Thorne really wasn't star material.

Rick explained that he was more disappointed than angry with her over getting canned, but this was after he'd bloodied her lip. It wasn't so much that this financial setback stood to wreck his career just as the breaks were falling in place for him, as it was that her drug habit had left them owing a couple thou to the man, and how were they going to pay that?

Candace still had a few contacts to fall back on, and she was back before the cameras before the bruises had disappeared. These weren't the films that made the adult theater circuits. These were the fifteen-minute-or-so single-takes shot in motel rooms for the 8-mm. home projector/porno peepshow audiences. Her contacts were pleased to get a semi-name porno queen, however semi and however shopworn, even if the films seldom bothered to list credits or titles. It was easier to work with a pro than some drugged-out runaway or amateur hooker, who might ruin a take if the action got rough or she had a phobia about Dobermans.

It was quick work and quick bucks. But not enough bucks.

Rick was panic-stricken when two large black gentlemen stopped him outside a singles bar one night to discuss his credit and to share ideas as to the need to maintain intact kneecaps in this cruel world. They understood a young actor's difficulties in meeting financial obligations, but felt certain Rick could make a substantial payment within forty-eight hours.

Candace hit the streets. It was that, or see Rick maimed. After the casting couch and exotic partners under floodlights, somehow it seemed so commonplace doing quickies in motel rooms and car seats. She missed the cameras. It all seemed so transient without any playback.

The money was there, and Rick kept his kneecaps. Between her work on the streets and grinding out a few 8-mm. films each month, Candace could about meet expenses. The problem was that she really needed the drugs to keep her going, and the more drugs she needed meant the more work to pay for them. Candace knew her looks were slipping, and she appreciated Rick's concern for her health. But for Rick the Big Break was coming soon. She no longer minded when he had other women over while she was on the streets, or when he stayed away for a day or two without calling her. She was selling her body for his career, and she must understand that sometimes it was necessary for Rick, too, to sleep around. In the beginning, some small compromises are to be expected.

A pimp beat her up one night. He didn't like freelance chippies taking johns from his girls on his turf. He would have just scared her, had she agreed to become one of his string, but she needed all her earnings for Rick, and the truth was the pimp considered her just a bit too far gone to be worth his trouble. So he worked her over but didn't mess up her face too badly, and Candace was able to work again after only about a week.

She tried another neighborhood and got busted the second night out; paid her own bail, got busted again a week later. Rick got her out of jail—she was coming apart without the H, and he couldn't risk being implicated. He had his career to think about, and it was thoughtless of Candace to jeopardize his chances through her own sordid lifestyle.

He would have thrown her out, but Candace paid the rent. Of course, he still loved her. But she really ought to take better care of herself. She was letting herself go. Since her herpes scare they seldom made love, although Candace understood that Rick was often emotionally and physically drained after concentrating his energy on some important interview or audition.

They had lived together almost two years, and Candace was almost 25, but she looked almost 40. After a client broke her nose and a few teeth in a moment of playfulness, she lost what little remained of her actress/model good looks. They got the best cosmetic repair she could afford, but after that neither the johns nor the sleaze producers paid her much attention. When she saw herself on the screen at fifth-rate porno houses, in the glimpses between ducking below the rows of shabby seats, she no longer recognized herself.

But Rick's career was progressing all the while, and that was what made her sacrifice worthwhile. A part of Candace realized now that her dreams of Hollywood stardom had long since washed down the gutter, but at least Rick was almost on the verge of big things. He'd landed a number of modeling jobs and already had made some commercials for local TV. Some recent roles in what Rick termed "experimental theater" promised to draw the attention of talent scouts. Neither of them doubted that the Big Break was an imminent certainty. Candace kept herself going through her faith in Rick's love and her confidence that better times lay ahead. Once Rick's career took off, she'd quit the streets, get off the drugs. She'd look ten years younger if she could just rest and eat right for a few months, get a better repair on her nose. By then Rick would be in a position to help her resume her own acting career.

Candace was not too surprised when Rick came in one morning and shook her awake with the news that he'd lined up a new film for her. It was something about devil worshipers called *Satan's Sluts*—X-rated, of course, but the money would be good, and Candace hadn't appeared even in a peepshow gangbang in a couple months. The producer, Rick explained, remembered her in *Camp Hell!* and was willing to take a chance on giving her a big role.

Candace might have been more concerned about filming a scene with so small a crew and in a cellar made over into a creepy B&D dungeon, but her last films had been shot in cheap motel rooms with a home video camera. She didn't like being strapped to an inverted cross and hung before a black-draped altar, but Rick was there—snorting coke with the half-dozen members of the cast and crew.

When the first few whip lashes cut into her flesh, it took Candace's drugged consciousness several moments to be aware of the pain, and to understand the sort of film for which Rick had sold her. By the time they had heated the branding iron and brought in the black goat, Candace was giving the performance of her life.

She passed out eventually, awoke another day in their bed, vaguely surprised to be alive. It was a measure of Rick's control over Candace that they hadn't killed her. No one was going to pay much attention to anything Candace might say—a burned out porno star and drug addict with an arrest record for prostitution. Rick had toyed with selling her for a snuff film, but his contacts there preferred anonymous runaways and wetbacks, and the backers of *Satan's Sluts* had paid extra to get a name actress, however faded, to add a little class to the production—especially a star who couldn't cause problems afterward.

Rick stayed with her just long enough to feel sure she wouldn't die from her torture, and to pack as many of his possessions as he considered worth keeping. Rick had been moving up in the world on Candace's earnings—meeting the right people, making the right connections. The money from *Satan's Sluts* had paid off his debts with enough left over for a quarter-ounce of some totally awesome rock, which had so impressed his friends at a party that a rising TV director wanted Rick to move in with her while they discussed a part for him in a much talked-about new miniseries.

The pain when he left her was the worst of all. Rick had counted on this, and he left her with a gram of barely cut heroin, deciding to let nature take its course.

Candace had paid for it with her body and her soul, but at last this genuinely was the Big Break. The primetime soaper miniseries, *Destiny's Fortune*, ran for five nights and topped the ratings each night. Rick's role as the tough steelworker who romanced the mill owner's daughter in parts four and five, while not a major part, attracted considerable attention and benefited from the huge success of the series itself. Talent scouts saw a new hunk in Richards Justin, most talked-about young star from the all-time hit, *Destiny's Fortune*.

Rick's new agent knew how to hitch his Mercedes to a rising star. Richards Justin made the cover of *TV Guide* and *People*, the centerfold of *Playgirl*, and then the posters. Within a month it was evident from the response to *Destiny's Fortune* that Richards Justin was a hot property. It was only a matter of casting him for the right series. Network geniuses juggled together all the ingredients of recent hits and projected a winner for the new season—*Colt Savage, Soldier of Fortune*.

They ran the pilot as a two-hour special against a major soaper and a TV-movie about teenage prostitutes, and *Colt Savage* blew the other two networks away in that night's ratings. *Colt Savage* was The New Hit, blasting to the top of the Nielsen's on its first regular night. The show borrowed from everything that had already been proven to work—"an homage to the great adventure classics of the '30s" was how its producers liked to describe it.

Colt Savage, as portrayed by Richards Justin, was a tough, cynical, broad-shouldered American adventurer who kept busy dashing about the cities and exotic places of the 1930s—finding lost treasures, battling spies and sinister cults, rescuing plucky young ladies from all manner of dire fates. Colt Savage was the *protégé* of a brilliant scientist who wished to devote his vast fortune and secret inventions to fighting Evil. He flew an autogiro and drove a streamlined speedster—both decked out with fantastic weapons and gimmickry rather in advance of the technology of the period. He had a number of exotic assistants and, inevitably, persistent enemies—villains who somehow managed to escape the explosion of their headquarters in time to pop up again two episodes later.

Colt Savage was pure B-movie corn. In a typical episode, Colt would meet a beautiful girl who would ask him for help, then be kidnapped. Following that there would be fights, car chases, air battles, captures and escapes, derring-do in exotic locales, rescues and romance—enough to fill an hour show. The public loved it. Richards Justin was a new hero for today's audiences—the new Bogart, a John Wayne for the '80s. The network promoted *Colt Savage* with every excess at its command. The merchandising rights alone were bringing in tens of millions.

Rick dumped the director who had given him his start in *Destiny's Fortune* long before he moved into several million bucks worth of Beverly Hills real estate. The tabloids followed his numerous love affairs with compulsive and imaginative interest.

Candace blamed it all on the drugs. She couldn't bring herself to believe that Rick had never loved her, that he had simply used her until she had no more to give. Her mind refused to accept that. It was she who had let Rick down, let drugs poison his life and destroy hers. Drugs had ruined her acting career, had driven her onto the streets to pay for their habit. They could have made it, if she hadn't ruined everything for them.

So she quit, cold turkey. Broken in body and spirit, the miseries of withdrawal made little difference to her pain. She lived ten years of hell over the next few days, lying in an agonized delirium that barely distinguished consciousness from unconsciousness. Sometimes she managed to crawl to the bathroom or to the refrigerator, mostly she just curled herself into a fetal pose of pain and shivered beneath the sweaty sheets and bleeding sores. In her nightmares she drifted from lying in Rick's embrace to writhing in torture on Satan's altar, and the torment of either delirium was the same to her.

As soon as she was strong enough to face it, Candace cut the heroin Rick had left her to make five grams and sold it to one of her friends who liked to snort it and wouldn't mind the cut. It gave her enough money to cover bills until Candace was well enough to go back on the streets. She located the pimp who had once beat her up; he didn't recognize her, and when Candace asked to work for him, he laughed her out of the bar.

After that she drifted around Los Angeles for a month or two, turning tricks whenever she could. She was no longer competitive, even without the scars, but she managed to scrape by, somehow making rent for the place on North Beverly Glen. It held her memories of Rick, and if she let that go, she would have lost even that shell of their love. She even refused to throw out any of his discarded clothing and possessions; his toothbrush and an old razor still lay by the sink.

The last time the cops busted her, Candace had herpes, a penicillin-resistant clap, and no way of posting bail. Jail meant losing her house and its memories of Rick, and there would be nothing left for her after that. Rick could help her now, but she couldn't manage to reach him. An old mutual friend finally did, but when he came to visit Candace he couldn't bear to give her Rick's message, and so he paid her bail himself and told her the money came from Rick, who didn't want to risk getting his name involved.

She had to have a legitimate job. The friend had a friend who owned interest in a plastic novelties plant, and they got Candace a factory job there. By now she had very little left of herself to sell in the streets, but at least she was off the drugs. Somewhat to the surprise of all concerned, Candace settled down on the line and turned out to be a good worker. Her job paid the bills, and at night she went home and read about Richards Justin in the papers and magazines, played back video cassettes of him nights when he wasn't on live.

The cruelest thing was that Candace still nurtured the hope that she could win Rick back, once she got her own act together. Regular meals, decent hours, medication and time healed some wounds. That face that looked back at her from mirrors no longer resembled a starved plague victim. Some of the men at the plant were beginning to stare after her, and a couple of times she'd been asked to go out. She might have got over Richards Justin in time, but probably not.

The friend of a friend pulled some strings and called in some favors, and so the plant where Candace worked secured the merchandising rights to the Colt Savage, Soldier of Fortune Action Pak. This consisted of a plastic Colt Savage doll, complete with weapons and action costumes, along with models of Black Blaze, his supersonic autogiro, and Red Lightning, the supercar. The merchandising package also included dolls of his mentor and regular assistants, as well as several notable villains and their sinister weaponry. The plant geared into maximum production to handle the anticipated rush of orders for the Christmas market.

Candace found herself sitting at the assembly line, watching thousands of plastic replicas of Richards Justin roll past her.

She just had to see Rick, but the guards at the gate had instructions not to admit her. He wouldn't even talk to her over the phone or answer her letters. The way he must remember her, Candace couldn't really blame him. It would be different now.

His birthday was coming up, and she knew he would be having a party. She wrote him several times, sent messages via old contacts, begging Rick to let her come. When the printed invitation finally came, she'd already bought him a present. Candace knew that her confidence had not been a mistake, and she took a day off work to get ready for their evening together.

The party had been going strong for some time when Candace arrived, and Rick was flying high on coke and champagne. He hugged her around the shoulders but didn't kiss her, and half carried her over to where many of the guests were crowded around a projection television.

Ladies and gentlemen, here she is—our leading lady, the versatile Miss Candi Thorne.

All eyes flicked from the screen to Candace, long enough for recognition. Then the cheers and applause burst out across the room. Rick had been amusing his guests with some of her films. Just now they were watching the one with the donkey.

Candace didn't really remember how she managed to escape and find her way home.

She decided not to leave a note, and she was prying the blade out of Rick's old razor when the idea began to form. The razor was crudded with dried lather and bits of Rick's whiskers, and she wanted to get it clean before she used it on her wrists. A scene from another of her films, *Voodoo Vixens*, arose through the confusion of her thoughts. She set the razor aside carefully.

Candace made herself a cup of coffee and let the idea build in her head. She was dry-eyed now and quite calm—the hysterical energy that had driven her to suicide now directed her disordered thoughts toward another course of action.

She still had all of her mementos of Rick, and throughout the night she went over them, one by one, coolly and meticulously. She scraped all the bits of beard and skin from his razor, collected hair and dandruff from his brush and comb, pared away his toothbrush bristles for the minute residues of blood and plaque. She found a discarded handkerchief, stained from a coke-induced nosebleed, and from the mattress liner came residues of their former lovemaking. Old clothes yielded bits of hair, stains of body oils and perspiration. Candace searched the house relent-lessly, finding fragments of his nails, his hair, anything at all that retained physical residues of Rick's person.

The next day Candace called in sick. She spent the day browsing through Los Angeles' numerous occult bookshops, made a few purchases, and called up one or two of the contacts she'd made filming *Voodoo Vixens*. It all seemed straightforward enough. Even those who rationalized it all admitted that it was a matter of belief. And children have the purest belief in magic.

Candace ground up all her bits and scrapings of Richards Justin. It came to quite a pile and reminded her of a bag of Mexi-can heroin.

Candace returned to work and waited for her chance. When no one was watching, she dumped her powdered residue into the plastic muck destined to become Colt Savage dolls. Then she said a prayer of sorts.

Beneath the Christmas tree, Joshua plays with his new Colt Savage doll. *Pow!* An electron cannon knocks Colt out of the sky, crashes him to the rocks below!

Jason pits Colt Savage against his model dinosaurs. *Yahhh!* The dinosaur stomps him!

David is racing Colt Savage in his car. Red Lightning. *Ker-blam!* Colt drives off the cliff at a hundred miles an hour!

Billy is still too young to play with his Colt Savage doll, but he likes to chew on it.

Mark decides to see if Colt Savage and Black Blaze can withstand the attack of his atomic bomb firecrackers.

Jessica is mad at her brother. She sees his Colt Savage doll and stomps on it as hard as she can.

Tyrone is bawling. He pulled the arms off his Colt Savage doll, and he can't make them go back on.

Richards Justin collapsed on set, and only heavy sedation finally stilled his screams. It quickly became apparent that his seizures were permanent, and he remains under sedation in a psychiatric institution. Doctors have attributed his psychotic break to long-term drug abuse.

Nothing excites the public more than a fallen hero. *Richards Justin: The Untold Story,* by Candace Thornton, rose quickly on the best-seller charts. Reportedly she was recently paid well over a million for the film rights to her book.

.220 SWIFT

I

Within, there was musty darkness and the sweet-stale smell of damp earth.

Crouched at the opening, Dr. Morris Kenlaw poked his head into the darkness and snuffled like a hound. His spadelike hands clawed industriously, flinging clods of dirt between his bent knees. Steadying himself with one hand, he wriggled closer to the hole in the ground and craned his neck inward.

He stuck out a muddy paw. "Give me back the light, Brandon." His usually overloud voice was muffled.

Brandon handed him that big flashlight and tried to look over Kenlaw's chunky shoulder. The archeologist's blocky frame completely stoppered the opening as he hunched forward.

"Take hold of my legs!" came back his words, more muffled still.

Shrugging, Brandon knelt down and pinioned Kenlaw's stocky legs. He had made a fair sand-lot fullback not too many years past, and his bulk was sufficient to anchor the overbalanced archeologist. Thus supported, Kenlaw crawled even farther into the tunnel. From the way his back jerked, Brandon sensed he was burrowing again, although no hunks of clay bounced forth.

Brandon pushed back his lank white hair with his forearm and looked up. His eyes were hidden behind mirror sunglasses, but his pale eyebrows made quizzical lines toward Dell Warner. Dell had eased his rangy denim-clad frame onto a limestone knob. Dan made a black-furred mound at his feet, tail thumping whenever his master looked down at him. The young farmer dug a crumpled pack of cigarettes out of his shirt pocket, watching in amused interest.

"Snake going to reach out, bite his nose off," Dell ventured, proffering the cigarettes to Brandon, selecting one himself when the other man declined.

The cool mountain breeze whisked his lighter flame, whipped the high weeds that patchworked the sloping pasture. Yellow grass and weeds—cropped closely here, there a verdant blotch to mark a resorbed cow-pie. Not far above them dark pines climbed to the crest of the ridge; a good way below, the slope leveled to a neat field of growing corn. Between stretched the steep bank of wild pasture, terraced with meandering cow paths and scarred with grey juts of limestone. The early summer breeze had a cool, clean taste. It was not an afternoon to poke one's head into dank pits in the ground.

Kenlaw heaved convulsively, wriggling back out of the hole. He banged down the flashlight and swore; dirt hung on his black mustache. "Goddamn hole's nothing but a goddamn groundhog burrow!" Behind his smudged glasses his bright-black eyes were accusing.

Dell's narrow shoulders lifted beneath his blue cotton work shirt. "Groundhog may've dug it out, now—but I remember clear it was right here my daddy told me granddad filled the hole in. Losing too much stock, stepping off into there."

Kenlaw snorted and wiped his glasses with a big handker-chief. "Probably just a hole leading into a limestone cave. This area's shot through with caves. Got a smoke? Mine fell out of my pocket."

"Well, my dad said Granddad told him it was a tunnel mouth of some sort, only all caved in. Like an old mine shaft that's been abandoned years and years."

Ill-humoredly snapping up his host's cigarette, Kenlaw scowled. "The sort of story you'd tell to a kid. These hills are shot through with yarns about the mines of the ancients, too. God knows how many wild goose chases I've been after these last couple days."

Dell's eyes narrowed. "Now all I know is what I was told, and I was told this here was one of the mines of the ancients."

Puffing at his cigarette, Kenlaw wisely forbore to comment.

"Let's walk back to my cabin." Brandon suggested quickly. "Dr. Kenlaw, you'll want to wash up, and that'll give me time to set out some drinks."

"Thanks, but I can't spare the time just now," Dell grunted, sliding off the rock suddenly. The Plott hound scrambled to its feet. "Oh, and Ginger says she's hoping you'll be down for supper this evening."

"I'd like nothing better," Brandon assured him, his mind forming a pleasant image of the farmer's copper-haired sister.

"See you at supper then, Eric."

"So long, Dr. Kenlaw. Hope you find what you're after."

The archeologist muttered a good-bye as Warner and his dog loped off down the side of the pasture.

Brandon recovered his heavy Winchester Model 70 in .220 Swift. He had been looking for woodchucks when he'd come upon Dell Warner and his visitor. From a flap pocket of his denim jacket he drew a lens cover for the bulky Leupold 3x9 telescopic sight.

"Did you say whether you cared for that drink?"

Kenlaw nodded. "Jesus, that would be good. Been a long week up here, poking into every groundhog hole some hillbilly thinks is special."

"That doesn't happen to be one there," Brandon told him, hefting the rifle. "I've scouted it several times for chucks—never anything come out."

"You just missed seeing it—or else it's an old burrow," Kenlaw judged.

"It's old," Brandon agreed, "or there'd be fresh-dug earth scattered around. But there's no sign of digging, just this hole in the hillside. Looks more like it was dug out from below."

II

The cabin that Eric Brandon rented stood atop a low bluff about half a mile up a dirt road from the Warner farmhouse. Dell had made a show of putting the century-old log structure into such state of repair that he might rent it out to an occasional venturesome tourist. The foot-thick poplar logs that made its rough-hewn walls were as solid as the day some antebellum Warner had levered them into place. The grey walls showed rusty streaks where Dell had replaced the mud chinks with mortar, made from river sand hauled up from the Pigeon as it rushed past below the bluff. The massive riverrock fireplace displayed fresh mortar as well, and the roof was bright with new galvanized sheet metal. Inside was one large puncheon-floored room, with a low loft overhead making a second half-story. There were no windows, but a back door opened onto a roofed porch overlooking the river below.

Dell had brought in a power line for lighting, stove and refrigerator. There was cold water from a line to the spring on the ridge above, and an outhouse farther down the slope. The cabin was solid, comfortable—but a bit too rustic for most tourists. Occasionally someone less interested in heated pools and color television found out about the place, and the chance rent helped supplement the farm's meager income. Brandon, however, had found the cabin available each of the half-dozen times over the past couple years when he had desired its use.

While the archeologist splashed icy water into the sink at the cabin's kitchen end, Brandon removed a pair of fired cartridges from the pocket of his denim jacket. He inspected the finger-sized casings carefully for evidence of flowing, then dropped them into a box of fired brass destined for reloading.

Toweling off, Kenlaw watched him sourly. "Ever worry about ricochets, shooting around all this rock like you do?"

"No danger," Brandon returned, cracking an ice tray briskly. "Bullet's moving too fast—disintegrates on impact. One of the nice things about the .220 Swift. Rum and Coke OK?" He didn't care to lavish his special Planter's Punch on the older man.

Moving to the porch, Kenlaw took a big mouthful from the tall glass and dropped onto a ladderback chair. The Jamaican rum seemed to agree with him; his scowl eased into a contemplative frown.

"Guess I was a little short with Warner," he volunteered.

When Brandon did not contradict him, he went on. "Frustrating business, though, this trying to sort the thread of truth out of a snarl of superstition and hearsay. But I guess I'm not telling you anything new."

The woven white-oak splits of the chair bottom creaked as Kenlaw shifted his ponderous bulk. The Pigeon River, no more than a creek this far upstream, purled a cool, soothing rush below. Downstream the Canton papermills would transform its icy freshness into black and foaming poison.

Brandon considered his guest. The archeologist had a sleek roundness to his frame that reminded Brandon of young Charles Laughton in *Island of Lost Souls*. There was muscle beneath the pudginess, judging by the energy with which he moved. His black hair was unnaturally sleek, like a cheap toupee, and his bristly mustache looked glued on. His face was round and inno-cent; his eyes, behind round glasses, round and wet. Without the glasses, Brandon thought they seemed tight and shrewd; perhaps this was a squint.

Dr. Morris Kenlaw had announced himself the day before with a peremptory rap at Brandon's cabin door. He had started at Brandon's voice behind him—the other man had been watching from the ridge above as Kenlaw's dusty Plymouth drove up. His round eyes had grown rounder at the thick-barrelled rifle in Bran-don's hands.

Dr. Kenlaw, it seemed, was head of the Department of Anthro-pology at some Southern college, and perhaps Brandon was familiar with his work. No? Well, they had told him in Waynes-ville that the young man staying at the Warner's cabin was study-ing folklore and Indian legends and such things. It seemed Mr. Brandon might have had cause to read this or that article by Dr. Kenlaw. . . . No? Well, he'd have to send him a few reprints, then, that might be of interest.

The archeologist had appropriated Brandon's favorite seat and drunk a pint of his rum before he finally asked about the lost mines of the ancients. And Brandon, who had been given little chance before to interrupt his visitor's rambling discourse, abruptly found the other's flat stare fixed attentively on him.

Brandon dutifully named names, suggested suggestions; Kenlaw scribbled notes eagerly. Mission accomplished, the archeologist pumped his hand and hustled off like a hound on a scent. Brandon had not expected to see the man again. But Dell Warner's name was among those in Kenlaw's notes, and today Brandon had run into them—Kenlaw, having introduced himself as a friend of Brandon, had persuaded Dell to show him his family's version of the lost mines. And that trail, it would seem, had grown cold again.

The chunky reddish-grey squirrel—they called them boomers—that had been scrabbling through the pine needle sod below them, suddenly streaked for the bushy shelter of a Virginia pine. Paying no attention, Dan romped around the corner of the cabin and bounded onto the porch. Brandon scratched the Plott hound's black head and listened. After a moment he could hear the whine and rattle as a pickup lurched up the dirt road.

"That'll be Dell," he told Kenlaw. "Dan knew he was headed here and took the short-cut up the side of the ridge. Dog's one of the smartest I've seen."

Kenlaw considered the panting black hound. "He's a bear hound, isn't he?"

"A damn good one," Brandon asserted.

"A bear killed young Warner's father, if I heard right," Kenlaw suggested. "Up near where we were just now. How dangerous are the bears they have up here?"

"A black bear doesn't seem like much compared to a grizzly," Brandon said, "but they're quite capable of tearing a man apart—as several of these stupid tourists find out every summer. Generally they won't cause trouble, although now and then you get a mean one. Trouble is, the bears over in the Smokies have no fear of man, and the park rangers tend to capture the known troublemakers and release them in the more remote sections of the mountains. So every now and then one of these renegades wanders out of the park. Unafraid of man and unaccustomed to foraging in the wild, they can turn into really nasty stock killers. Probably what killed Bard Warner that night. He'd been losing stock and had the bad sense to wait out with a bottle and his old 8-mm Mannlicher. Bolt on the Mannlicher is too damn slow for close work. From what I was told, Bard's first shot didn't do it, and he never got off his second. Found what was left pulled under a rock ledge the next morning."

Dell's long legs stuck out from the battered door of his old Chevy pickup. He emerged from the cab balancing several huge tomatoes in his hands; a rolled newspaper was poked under one arm.

"These'll need to go into the refrigerator, Eric," he advised. "They're dead ripe. Get away, Dan!" The Plott hound was leaping about his legs.

Brandon thanked him and opened the refrigerator. Finger-combing his wind-blown sandy hair, Dell accepted his offer of a rum and Coke. "Brought you the Asheville paper," he indicated. "And you got a letter."

"Probably my advisor wondering what progress I've made on my dissertation," Brandon guessed, setting the letter with no return address carefully aside. He glanced over the newspaper while his friend uncapped an RC and mixed his own drink. Inflation, Africa, the Near East, a new scandal in Washington, and, in New York, a wave of gang-land slayings following the sniping death of some syndicate kingpin. In this century-old cabin in the ancient hills, all this seemed distant and unreal.

"Supper'll be a little late," Dell was saying. "Faye and Ginger took off to Waynesville to get their hair done." He added: "We'd like to have you stay for supper too, Dr. Kenlaw."

The redhead's temper had cooled so that he remembered mountain etiquette. Since Kenlaw was still here, he was Brandon's guest, and a supper invitation to Brandon must include Brandon's company as well—or else Brandon would be in an awkward position. Had Kenlaw already left, there would have been no obligation. Brandon sensed that Dell had waited to see if the archeologist would leave, before finally driving up.

"Thanks, I'd be glad to," Kenlaw responded, showing some manners himself. Either he felt sheepish over his brusque behavior earlier, or else he realized he'd better use some tact if he wanted any further help in his research here.

Brandon refilled his and Kenlaw's glasses before returning to the porch. Dell was standing uncertainly, talking with the archeologist, so Brandon urged him to take the other porch chair. Taking hold with one hand of the yard-wide section of white-oak log that served as a low table, he slid it over the rough planks to a corner post and sat down. He sipped the drink he had been carrying in his free hand, and leaned back. It was cool and shady on the porch, enough so that he would have removed his mirror sunglasses had he been alone. Brandon, a true albino, was self-conscious about his pink eyes.

As it was, Kenlaw was all but gawking at his host. The section of log that Brandon had negligently slewed across the uneven boards probably weighed a couple hundred pounds. Dell, who had seen the albino free his pickup from a ditch by the straight-forward expedient of lifting the mired rear wheel, appeared not to notice.

"I was asking Dr. Kenlaw what it was he was looking for in these mines," Dell said.

"If mines they are," Brandon pointed out.

"Oh, they're mines, sure enough," the archeologist asserted. "You should be convinced of that, Brandon." He waved a big hand for emphasis. Red clay made crescents beneath untrimmed nails.

"Who were the 'ancients' who dug them?" Dell asked. "Were they the same Indians who put up all those mounds you see around here and Tennessee?"

"No, the mound builders were a lot earlier," Kenlaw explained. "The mines of the ancients were dug by Spaniards—or more exactly, by the Indian slaves of the conquistadors. We know that de Soto came through here in 1540 looking for gold. The Chero-kees had got word of what kind of thieves the Spaniards were, though, and while they showed the strangers polite hospitality, they took pains not to let them know they had anything worth stealing. De Soto put them down as not worth fooling with, and moved on. But before that he sank a few mine shafts to see what these hills were made of."

"Did he find anything?" Dell wanted to know.

"Not around here. Farther south along these mountains a little ways, though, he did find some gold. In northern Georgia you can find vestiges of their mining shafts and camps. Don't know how much they found there, but there's evidence the Spaniards were still working that area as late as 1690."

"Must not have found much gold, or else word would have spread. You can't keep gold a secret."

"Hard to say. They must have found something to keep coming back over a century and a half. There was a lot of gold coming out of the New World, and not much of it ever reached Spain in the hands of those who discovered it. Plenty of reason to keep the discovery secret. And, of course, later on this area produced more gold than any place in the country before the Western gold rush. But all those veins gave out long before the Civil War."

"So you think the Spaniards were the ones that dug the mines of the ancients," Dell said.

"No doubt about it," stated Kenlaw, bobbing his head fiercely.

"Maybe that's been settled for northern Georgia," Brandon interceded, "although I'd had the impression this was only con-jecture. But so far as I know, no one's ever proved the conquista-dors mined this far north. For that matter, I don't believe anyone's ever made a serious study of the lost mines of the ancients in the North Carolina and Tennessee hills."

"Exactly why I'm here," Kenlaw told him impatiently. "I'm hoping to prove the tie-in for my book on the mines of the ancients. Only, so far I've yet to find proof of their existence in this area."

"Well, you may be looking for a tie-in that doesn't exist," Brandon returned. "I've studied this some, and my feeling is that the mines go back far beyond the days of the conquistadors. The Cherokees have legends that indicate the mines of the ancients were here already when the Cherokees migrated down from the north in the thirteenth century."

"This is the first I've heard about it then," Kenlaw scoffed. "Who do you figure drove these mines into the hills, if it wasn't the conquistadors? Don't tell me the Indians did it. I hardly think they would have been that interested in gold."

"Didn't say it was the Indians," Brandon argued.

"Who was it then?"

"The Indians weren't the first people here. When the Chero-kees migrated into the Tellico region not far from here, they encountered a race of white giants—fought them and drove the survivors off, so their legends say."

"You going to claim the Vikings were here?" Kenlaw snorted.

"The Vikings, the Welsh, the Phoenicians, the Jews—there's

good evidence that on several occasions men from the Old World reached North America long before Columbus set out. Doubtless there were any number of pre-Columbian contacts of which we have no record, only legends."

"If you'll forgive me, I'll stick to facts that are on record."

"Then what about the Melungeons over in Tennessee? They're not Indians, though they were here before the first pioneers, and even today anthropologists aren't certain of their ancestry."

Brandon pressed on. "There are small pockets of people all across the country—not just in these mountains—whose ethnic origins defy pinning down. And there are legends of others—the Shonokins, for example...."

"Now you're dealing with pure myth!" Kenlaw shut him off. "That's the difference between us, Brandon. I'm interested in collecting historical fact, and you're a student of myths and legends. Science and superstition shouldn't be confused."

"Sometimes the borderline is indistinct," Brandon countered.

"My job is to make it less so."

"But you'll have to concede there's often a factual basis for legend," Brandon argued doggedly. "And the Cherokees have a number of legends about the caves in these mountains, and about the creatures who live within. They tell about giant serpents, like the Uktena and the Uksuhi, that lair inside caves and haunt lonely ridges and streams, or the intelligent panthers that have townhouses in secret caves. Then there's the Nunnehi, an immortal race of invisible spirits that live beneath the mounds and take shape to fight the enemies of the Cherokee—these were supposedly seen as late as the Civil War. Or better still, there's the legend of the Yunwi Tsunsdi, the Little People who live deep inside the mountains."

"I'm still looking for that 'factual basis,'" Kenlaw said with sarcasm.

"Sometimes it's there to find. Ever read John Ashton's *Curious Creatures in Zoology*? In his chapter on pygmies he quotes from three sources that describe the discovery of entire burying grounds of diminutive stone sarcophagi containing human skeletons under two feet in length—adult skeletons, by their teeth. Several such burial grounds—ranging upwards to an acre and a half—were found in White County, Tennessee, in 1828, as well as an ancient town site near one of the burials. General Milroy found similar graves in Smith County, Tennessee, in 1866, after a small creek had washed through the site and exposed them. Also, Weller in his *Romance of Natural History* makes reference to other such discoveries in Kentucky as well as Tennessee. Presumably a race of pygmies may have lived in this region before the Cherokees, who remember them only in legend as the Yunwi Tsunsdi. Odd, isn't it, that there are so many Indian legends of a pygmy race?"

"Spare me from Victorian amateur archeology!" Kenlaw dismissed him impatiently. "What possible bearing have these half-baked superstitions on the mines of the ancients? I'm talking about archeological realities, like the pits in Mitchell County, like the Sink Hole mine near Bakersville. That's a pit forty feet wide and forty feet deep, where the stone shows marks of metal tools and where stone tools were actually uncovered. General Thomas Clingman studied it right after the Civil War, and he counted three hundred rings on the trees he found growing on the mine workings. That clearly puts the mines back into the days of the conquistadors. There's record of one Tristan de Luna, who was searching for gold and silver south of there in 1560; the Sink Hole mine contained mica, and quite possibly he was responsible for digging it and the other mines of that area."

"I've read about the Sink Hole mine in Creecy's *Grandfather's Tales*," Brandon told him. "And as I recall the early investigators there were puzzled by the series of passageways that connected the Sink Hole with other nearby pits—passageways that were only fourteen inches wide."

The archeologist sputtered in his drink. "Well, Jesus Christ, man!" he exploded after a moment. "That doesn't have anything to do with Indian legends! Don't you know anything about mining? They would have driven those connecting tunnels to try to cut across any veins of gold that might have lain between the pits."

Brandon spread his big hands about fourteen inches apart. He said: "Whoever dug the passageways would have had to have been rather small."

III

Afternoon shadows were long when Dell drove the other two men down to the house in his pickup. The farmhouse was a two-story board structure with stone foundation, quite old, but in neat repair. Its wide planks showed the up-and-down saw marks that indicated its construction predated the more modern circular sawmill blade. The front was partially faced with dark mountain stone, and the foundation wall extended to make a flagstone veranda, shaded and garlanded by bright-petaled clematis.

Another truck was parked beside Kenlaw's Plymouth—a battered green 1947 Ford pickup that Brandon recognized as belonging to Dell's father-in-law, Olin Reynolds. Its owner greeted them from the porch as they walked up. He was a thin, faded man whose bony frame was almost lost in old-fashioned overalls. His face was deeply lined, his hair almost as white as Brandon's. Once he had made the best moonshine whiskey in the region, but his last stay in Atlanta had broken him. Now he lived alone on his old homestead bordering the Pisgah National Forest. He often turned up about dinner time, as did Brandon.

"Hello, Eric," Olin called in his reedy voice. "You been over to get that 'chuck that's been after my little girl's cabbages yet?"

"Hi, Olin," Brandon grinned. "Shot him yesterday morning from over across by that big white pine on the ridge."

"That's near a quarter-mile," the old man figured.

Brandon didn't say anything because Ginger Warner just then stepped out onto the porch. Dell's younger sister was recently back from finishing her junior year at Western Carolina in nearby Cullowhee. She was tall and willowy, green-eyed and quick to smile. Her copper hair was cut in a boyish shag instead of the unlovely bouffant most country women still clung to. Right now she had smudges of flour on her freckled face.

"Hi, Eric," she grinned, brushing her hands on her jeans. "Supper'll be along soon as the biscuits go in. You sure been keeping to yourself lately."

"Putting together some of my notes for the thesis," he apologized, thinking he'd eaten dinner here just three nights ago.

"Liar. You've been out running ridges with Dan."

"That's relaxation after working late at night."

Ginger gave him a skeptical look and returned to her biscuits.

With a ponderous grunt, Dr. Kenlaw sank onto one of the wide-armed porch rockers. He swung his feet up onto the rail and gazed thoughtfully out across the valley. Mist was obscuring the hills beyond, now, and the fields and pasture closer at hand filled with hazy shadow. Hidden by trees, the Pigeon River rushed its winding course midway through the small valley. Kenlaw did not seem at ease with what he saw. He glowered truculently at the potted flowers that lined the porch.

"What the hell!" Kenlaw suddenly lurched from his rocker. The other three men broke off their conversation and stared. Balancing on the rail, the archeologist yanked down a hanging planter and dumped its contents into the yard.

"Where the hell did this come from!" he demanded, examining the rusted metal dish that an instant before had supported a trailing begonia.

Dell Warner bit off an angry retort.

"For god's sake, Kenlaw!" Brandon broke the stunned reaction.

"Yeah, for god's sake!" Kenlaw was too excited to be nonplussed. "This is a Spanish morion! What's it doing hanging here full of petunias?"

Ginger stepped onto the porch to announce dinner. Her freckled face showed dismay. "What on earth . . . ?"

Kenlaw was abashed. "Sorry. I forgot myself when I saw this. Please excuse me—I'll replace your plant if it's ruined. But, where did you get this?"

"That old bowl? It's lain around the barn for years. I punched holes along the rim, and it made a great planter for my begonia." She glanced over the rail and groaned.

"It's a morion—a conquistador's helmet!" Kenlaw blurted in disbelief. Painstakingly he studied the high-crested bowl of rusted iron with its flared edges that peaked at either end. "And genuine too—or I'm no judge. Show me where this came from originally, and I'll buy you a pickup full of begonias."

Ginger wrinkled her forehead. "I really don't know where it

came from—I didn't even know it was anything. What's a Spanish helmet doing stuck back with all Dad's junk in our barn? There's an old iron pot with a hole busted in it where I found this. Want to look at it and tell me if it's Montezuma's bullet-proof bathtub?"

Kenlaw snorted. "Here, Brandon. You look at this and tell me I'm crazy."

The albino examined the helmet. It was badly pitted, but solid. It could not have lain outside, or it would have rusted entirely away centuries ago. "It's a morion, of course," he agreed. "Whether it dates to conquistador days or not, I'm not the one to tell. But it does seem equally unlikely that a careful reproduction would be lying around your barn."

"Hell, I know where that come from," Olin cut in, craning his long neck to see. "I was with your-all's daddy time he found it."

Kenlaw stared at the old mountain man, his eyes intent behind thick glasses. "For god's sake—where?"

Olin worked his pointed chin in a thoughtful circle, eyeing Dell questioningly. The younger man shrugged.

"Place up on Old Field Mountain," Olin told him, "near Tanasee Bald in what's now Pisgah National Forest. There's a sort of cave there, and I guess it won't do no harm now telling you a couple of old boys named Brennan used to make a little blockade from a still they'd built back inside. Me and Bard used to stop up there times and maybe carry wood and just set around. Well, one time Bard goes back inside a ways, and we worried some because he'd had a little—and after a while he comes back carrying that thing there and calling it an Indian pot 'cause he found it with a lot of bones way back in there. He liked to keep arrowheads and axe-heads and such-like when he found them, and so he carried that there back and put it with some other stuff, and I guess it's all just laid there and been scattered around the barn since."

"You can find the place still?" Kenlaw pounced. "Can you take me there tomorrow? Who else knows about this?"

"Why, don't guess there's nobody knows. The Brennans is all out of these parts now and gone—never did amount to much. Hardin Brennan got hisself shot one night arguing with a customer, and they said his brother Earl busted his head in a rock fall back there in the cave. Earl's wife had left him, and there was just his boy Buck and a daughter Laurie. She was half-wild and not right in the head; young as she was, she had a baby boy they said must've been by her own kin, on account everybody else was half afraid of her. They all went up north somewheres—I heard to live with their mother. There's other Brennans still around that might be distant kin, but far as I know nobody's gone around that cave on Old Field Mountain since Buck and his sister left here better than twenty years back."

Kenlaw swore in excitement. "Nobody knows about it, then? Fantastic! What time tomorrow do you want to go? Better make it early. Seven?"

"Say about six instead," Olin suggested. "You'll need the whole day. How about coming up to the cabin—if that's all right with you, Eric? Shouldn't go back in there by yourself, and Lord knows my old bones are too brittle for scrambling around such places."

"Sure. I'll go along," Brandon agreed. "Sounds interesting."

"No need to," Kenlaw told him. "I've done my share of spelunking."

"Then you know it's dangerous to go in alone. Besides, I'm intrigued by all this."

"You all coming in to eat?" Faye Warner pushed open the screen. "Ginger, I thought you'd gone to call them. Everything's ready."

IV

There was chicken and ham, cornbread and gravy, tomatoes and branch lettuce, bowls of field peas, snap beans, corn and other garden vegetables. Kenlaw's scowl subsided as he loaded his plate a second time. Shortly after dinner the archeologist excused himself. "Been a long day, and we'll be up early enough tomorrow."

Olin drove away not long after, and when Dell went off to see to some chores, Brandon had the porch to himself. He was half-asleep when Ginger came out to join him.

"Did I startle you?" she apologized, sliding onto the porch swing beside him. "You're jumpy as a cat. Is that what living in the city does to your nerves?"

"Keeps you alert, I guess," Brandon said sheepishly.

Coppery hair tickled his shoulder. "Then you ought to get out of New York after you finish your project or whatever it is. Sounds like you must spend most of your time travelling around from one place to another as it is."

"That's known as field research."

"Ha! Dell says you don't do anything but laze around the cabin, or go out hunting. No wonder you still don't have your doctorate. Must be nice to get a government grant to run around the country studying folklore."

"Well, part of the time I'm organizing my notes, and part of the time I'm relaxing from the tension of writing."

"I can see how lugging that cannon of a rifle around would be exercise. Why don't you use that little air pistol instead?"

"What air pistol?"

"You know. You use it sometimes, because once I saw you shoot a crow with it that was making a fuss in the apple tree in front of the cabin. I saw you point it, and there wasn't a sound except the crow gave a squawk, and then feathers everywhere. My cousin has an air pistol too, so I knew what happened."

"Little spy." His arm squeezed her shoulder with mock roughness.

"Wasn't spying," Ginger protested, digging her chin into his shoulder. "I was walking up to help Dell chop tobacco."

When Brandon remained silent, she spoke to break the rhythmic rasp of the porch swing. "What do you think of Dr. Kenlaw?"

"A bit too pig-headed and pushy. They raise them that way up north."

"That's one, coming from a New Yorker! Or are you from New York originally? You have less accent than Dr. Kenlaw."

"Hard to say. I grew up in a foster home; I've lived a lot of places since."

"Well, folks around here like you well enough. They don't much like Dr. Kenlaw."

"I expect he's too aggressive. Some of these obsessive researchers are like that."

Ginger lined her freckles in a frown. "You're a researcher. Is Dr. Kenlaw?"

Brandon went tense beneath her cheek. "What do you mean?"

"I mean, have you ever heard of him? If you're both studying the same subjects pretty much . . . ?"

"I don't know his work, if that's what you mean." Brandon's muscles remained steel-tight. "But then, he knows his subject well enough. Why?"

"He seems to be more interested in gold than in archeology," Ginger told him. "At least, that's the way his questions strike most folks he talks to."

Brandon laughed and seemed to relax again. "Well, there's more acclaim in discovering a tomb filled with gold relics than in uncovering a burial of rotted bones and broken pot shards, regardless of the relative value to archeological knowledge. That's why King Tutankhamen's tomb made headlines, while the discovery of a primitive man's jawbone gets squeezed in with the used car ads."

"There was a curse on King Tut's tomb," Ginger reminded him dourly.

"Even better, if you're fighting for a grant."

"Grants!" Ginger sniffed. "Do you really mean to get that degree, or do you just plan to make a career of living off grants?"

"There's worse ways to make a living," Brandon assured her.

"Somehow I can't see you tied down to some university job. That's what you'll do when you get your doctorate, isn't it? Teach?"

"There's a lot of Ph.D.'s out there looking for jobs once the grants dry up." Brandon shrugged. "If there's an opening some-where, I suppose so."

"There might be an opening at Western Carolina," Ginger hinted.

"There might."

"And why not?" You like it down here—or else you wouldn't keep coming back. And people like you. You seem to fit right in—not like most of these loud New York types."

"It does feel like coming home again when I get back here," Brandon acknowledged. "Guess I've never stayed in one place long enough to call it home. Would you like for me to set up shop in Cullowhee?"

"I just might."

Brandon decided she had waited long enough for her kiss, and did something about it. Shadows crept together to form misty darkness, and the cool mountain breeze carried the breath of entwined clematis and freshly turned earth. The creak of the porch swing measured time like an arthritic grandfather's clock, softened by the rustle of the river. A few cows still lowed, and somewhere a chuck-will's-widow called to its mate. The quiet was dense enough so that they could hear Dan gnawing a bone in the yard below.

Ginger finally straightened, stretched cozily from her cramped position. "Mmm," she purred; then: "Lord, what is that dog chewing on so! We didn't have more than a plate of scraps for him after dinner."

"Maybe Dan caught himself a rabbit. He's always hunting."

"Oh! Go see! He killed a mother rabbit last week, and I know her babies all starved."

"Dan probably saw that they didn't." Brandon rose to go look. "What you got there, boy?"

Ginger saw him stiffen abruptly. "Oh, no! Not another mamma bunny!"

She darted past Brandon's arm before he could stop her.

Dan thumped his tail foolishly and returned her stare. Between his paws was a child's arm.

v

Olin Reynolds shifted his chaw reflectively. "I don't wonder Ginger came to carry on such a fit," he allowed. "What did you figure it was?"

"Certainly not a child's arm," Brandon said. "Soon as you got it into good light you could see it was nothing human. It had to have been some type of monkey, and the resemblance gave me a cold chill at first glance, too. Pink skin with just a frost of dirty white fur, and just like a little kid's arm except it was all muscle and sinew instead of baby fat. And it was a sure enough hand, not a paw, though the fingers were too long and sinewy for any child's hand, and the nails were coarse and pointed like an animal's claws."

"Wonder where old Dan come to catch him a monkey," Olin put in.

"Somebody's pet. Tourists, maybe—they carry everything they own in those damn campers. Thing got away; or more likely, died and they buried it, and Dan sniffed it out and dug it up. He'd been digging, from the look of him."

"What did you finally do with it?"

"Dell weighted it down in an old gunny sack and threw it into a deep hole in the river there. Didn't want Dan dragging it back again to give the ladies another bad start."

"Just as well," Olin judged. "It might have had somebody come looking for to see what come of it. I suspect that'll be Dr. Kenlaw coming up the hill now."

Kenlaw's Plymouth struggled into view through the pines. Brandon glanced at his watch, noted it was past seven. He stretched himself out of Olin's ladderback chair and descended the porch steps to greet the archeologist.

"Had a devil of a time finding the turn-off," Kenlaw complained, squeezing out from behind the wheel. "Everything set?"

"Throw your stuff in my pickup, and we'll get going," Olin told him. "Where we're headed, ain't no kind of road any car can follow up."

"Will that old bucket make it up a hill?" Kenlaw laughed, opening his trunk to take out a coil of rope and two powerful flashlights.

"This here old Ford's got a Marmon-Herrington all-wheel-drive conversion," Olin said coldly. "She can ride up the side of a bluff and pull out a cedar stump while your feet are hanging straight out the back window of the cab."

Kenlaw laughed easily, shoving spare batteries and a geologist's pick into the ample pockets of the old paratrooper's jacket he wore. Brandon helped him stow his gear into the back of the truck, then climbed into the cab beside Reynolds.

It was a tight squeeze in the cab after Dr. Kenlaw clambered in, and once they reached the blacktop road the whine of the gears and fan made conversation like shouting above a gale. Olin drove along in moody silence, answering Kenlaw's occasional questions in few words. After a while they left the paved roads, and then it was a long kidney-bruising ride as the dual-sprung truck attacked rutted mountain paths that bored ever upward through the shouldering pines. Kenlaw cursed and braced himself with both arms. Brandon caught a grin in Olin's faded eyes.

The road they followed led on past a tumbledown frame house, lost within a yard that had gone over to first-growth pine and scrub. A few gnarled apple trees made a last stand, and farther beneath the encroaching forest, Brandon saw the hulking walls of a log barn—trees spearing upward past where the roof had once spread. He shivered. The desolation of the place seemed to stir buried memories.

Beyond the abandoned farmhouse the road deteriorated into little more than a cow path. It had never been more than a timber road, scraped out when the lumber barons dragged down the primeval forest from the heights half a century or more ago. Farm vehicles had kept it open once, and now an occasional hunter's truck broke down the young trees that would otherwise have choked it.

Olin's pickup strained resolutely upward, until at length they shuddered into an overgrown clearing. Reynolds cut the engine. "Watch for snakes," he warned, stepping down.

The clearing was littered beneath witch's broom and scrub with a scatter of rusted metal and indistinct trash. A framework of rotted lumber and a corroded padlock faced against the hillside. Several of the planks had fallen inward upon the blackness within.

Olin Reynolds nodded. "That's the place. Reckon the Brennans boarded it over before they moved on to keep stock from falling in. Opening used to just lie hidden beneath the brush."

Dr. Kenlaw prodded the eroded timbers. The padlock hasp hung from rusted nails over the space where the board had rotted away. At a bolder shove, the entire framework tore loose and tumbled inward.

Sunlight spilled in past the dust. The opening was squeezed between ledges of rock above and below, wide enough for a man to stoop and drop through. Beyond was a level floor, littered now with the debris of boards.

"Goes back like that a ways, then it narrows down to just a crack," Olin told them.

Kenlaw grunted in a self-satisfied tone and headed back for the pickup to get his equipment.

"Coming with us?" Brandon asked.

Olin shook his head firmly. "I'll just wait here. These old bones are too eat up with arthuritis to go a-crawling through that snaky hole."

"Wait with him. Eric, if you like," Kenlaw suggested. "I probably won't be long about this. No point you getting yourself all dirty messing around on what's likely to be just another wild goose chase."

"I don't mind," Brandon countered. "If that morion came out of this cave, I'm curious to see what else lies hidden back there."

"Odds are, one of those Brennans found it someplace else and just chucked it back in there. Looks like this place has been used as a dump."

Kenlaw cautiously shined his light across the rubble beneath the ledge. Satisfied that no snakes were evident, the archeologist gingerly squeezed his corpulent bulk past the opening and lowered himself to the floor of the cavern. Brandon dropped nimbly beside him.

Stale gloom filled a good-sized antechamber. Daylight trickled in from the opening, and a patch of blackness at the far end marked where the cavern narrowed and plunged deeper into the side of the mountain. Brandon took off his mirror sunglasses and glanced about the chamber—the albino's eyes were suited to the dank gloom.

The wreckage of what had once been a moonshine still cluttered the interior of the cavern. Copper coil and boiler had long ago been carried off, as had anything else of any value. Broken barrels, rotted mounds of sacks, jumbles of firewood, misshapen sculptures of galvanized metal. Broken bits of Mason jars and crockery shards crunched underfoot; dead ashes made a sodden raisin pudding. Kenlaw flung his light overhead and disclosed only sooty rock and somnolent bats.

"A goddamn dump," he muttered petulantly. "Maybe something farther back in."

The archeologist swung his light toward the rear of the chamber. A passage led farther into the mountain. Loose stones and more piled debris half blocked the opening. Pushing his way past this barricade, Kenlaw entered the narrow tunnel.

The passage was cramped. They ducked their heads, twisted about to avoid contact with the dank rock. Kenlaw carefully examined the walls of the cavern as they shuffled on. To Brandon's eye, there was nothing to indicate that man's tools had shaped the shaft. Alter a time, the sunlight from behind them disappeared, leaving them with their flashlights to guide them. The air grew stale with a sourness of animal decay, and as the passage seemed to lead downward, Brandon wondered whether they might risk entering a layer of noxious gases.

"Hold on here!" Kenlaw warned, stopping abruptly.

Darkness met their probing flashlight beams several yards ahead of their feet, as the floor of the passage disappeared. Kenlaw wiped his pudgy face and caught his breath, as they shined their lights down into the sudden pit that confronted them.

"Must be thirty-forty feet to the bottom," Kenlaw estimated. "Cavern's big enough for a high school gym. The ledge we're standing on creeps on down that fault line toward the bottom. We can make it if you'll just watch your step."

"Is the air OK?" Brandon wondered.

"Smells fresh enough to me," Kenlaw said. He dug a crumpled cigarette pack from his pocket, applied his lighter. The flame fanned outward along the direction they had come. Kenlaw dropped the burning wad of paper over the edge. It fell softly through the blackness, showering sparks as it hit the floor.

"Still burning," the archeologist observed. "I'm going on down."

"Nice if that was natural gas down there," Brandon muttered.

"This isn't a coal mine. Just another natural cavern, for my money."

Clinging to the side of the rock for support, they cautiously felt their way down the steep incline. Although an agile climber could negotiate the descent without ropes, the footing was treacherous, and a missed step could easily mean a headlong plunge into the darkness.

They were halfway down when Kenlaw paused to examine the rock wall. Switching hands with his flashlight, he drew his geologist's pick and tapped against the stone.

"Find something?" Brandon turned his light onto the object of the archeologist's scrutiny, saw a band of lighter stone running along the ledge.

"Just a sample of stratum," Kenlaw explained, hastily breaking free a specimen and shoving it into one of his voluminous pockets. "I'll have to examine it back at my lab—study it for evidence of tool marks and so on."

The floor of the pit appeared little different from the chamber through which they had entered the cavern, save that it lacked the accumulated litter of human usage. The air was cool and fresh enough to breathe, although each lungful carried the presence of a sunless place deep beneath the mountains.

"Wonder when the last time was anyone came down here?" Brandon said, casting his light along the uneven floor. The bottom was strewn with broken rock and detritus, with a spongy paste of bat guano and dust. Footprints would be hard to trace after any length of time.

"Hard to say," Kenlaw answered, scooping up a handful of gravel and examining it under his light. "Sometimes the Confederates worked back into places like this after saltpetre. Maybe Bard Warner came down here, but I'm betting that morion was just something some dumb hillbilly found someplace else and got tossed onto the dump."

"Are these bones human?" Brandon asked.

Kenlaw stuffed the gravel into a jacket pocket and scrambled over to where Brandon crouched. There was a fall of broken rock against the wall of the pit opposite their point of descent. Interspersed with the chunks of stone were fragments of mouldering bone. The archeologist dug out a section of rib. It snapped easily in his hand, showing whiteness as it crumbled.

"Dead a long time," Kenlaw muttered, pulling more of the rocks aside. "Maybe Indian."

"Then it's a human skeleton?"

"Stone burial cairn, at a guess. But it's been dug up and the bones scattered about. These long bones are all smashed apart."

"Maybe he was killed in a rock slide."

Kenlaw shook his head. "Look how this femur is split apart. I'd say more likely something broke open the bones to eat the marrow."

"An animal?"

"What else would it have been?"

Kenlaw suddenly bent forward, clawed at the detritus. His thick fingers locked onto what looked to be the edge of a flat rock. Grunting, he hauled back and wrenched forth a battered sheet of rusted iron.

"Part of a breastplate! Damned if this isn't the original skeleton in armor! Give me a hand with the rest of these rocks."

Together they dragged away the cairn of rubble—Kenlaw puffing energetically as he flung aside the stones and fragments of bone. Brandon, caught up in the excitement of discovery himself, reflected with a twinge that this was hardly a careful piece of excavation. Nonetheless, Kenlaw's anxious scrabbling continued until they had cleared a patch of bare rock.

The archeologist squatted on a stone and lit a cigarette. "Doesn't tell me much," he complained. "Just broken bones and chunks of rust. Why was he here? Were there others with him? Who were they? What were they seeking here?"

"Isn't it enough that you've found the burial of a conquistador?"

"Can't prove that until I've run some tests," Kenlaw grumbled. "Could have been a Colonial—breastplates were still in use in European armies until this century. Or an Indian buried with some tribal heirlooms."

"There's another passage back of here," Brandon called out.

He had been shining his light along the fall of rock, searching for further relics from the cairn. Behind where they had cleared away some of the loose rocks, a passageway pierced the wall of the pit. Brandon rolled aside more of the stone, and the mouth of the passage took shape behind the crest of the rock pile.

Kenlaw knelt and peered within. "Not much more than a crawl space," he announced, "but it runs straight on for maybe twenty or thirty feet, then appears to open onto another chamber."

Brandon played his flashlight around the sides of the pit, then back to where they stood. "I don't think this is just a rock slide.

I think someone piled all these rocks here to wall up the tunnel mouth."

"If they didn't want it found, then they must have found something worth hiding," the archeologist concluded. "I'll take a look. You wait here in case I get stuck."

Brandon started to point out that his was the slimmer frame, but already Kenlaw had plunged headfirst into the tunnel—his thick buttocks blocking Brandon's view as he squeezed his way through. Brandon thought of a fat old badger ducking down a burrow. He kept his light on the shaft. Wheezing and scuffling, the other man managed to force his bulk through the passage. He paused at the far end and called back something, but his words were too muffled for Brandon to catch.

A moment later Kenlaw's legs disappeared from view, and then his flushed face bobbed into Brandon's light. "I'm in another chamber about like the one you're standing in," he called back. "I'll take a look around."

Brandon sat down to wait impatiently. He glanced at his watch. To his surprise, they had been in the cavern some hours. The beam of his flashlight was yellowing; Brandon cut the switch to save the batteries, although he carried spares in his pockets. The blackness was as total as the inside of a grave, except for an occasional wan flash as Kenlaw shined his light past the tunnel mouth from the pit beyond. Brandon held his hand before his face, noted that he could dimly make out its outline. The albino had always known he could see better in the dark than others could, and it had seemed a sort of recompense for the fact that bright light tormented his pink eyes. He had read that hemeralopia did not necessarily coincide with increased night vision, and his use of infrared rifle scopes had caused him to wonder whether his eyes might not be unusually receptive to light from the infrared end of the spectrum.

Kenlaw seemed to be taking his time. At first Brandon had heard the sharp tapping of his geologist's pick from time to time. Now there was only silence. Brandon flipped his light back on, consulted his watch. It had been half an hour.

"Dr. Kenlaw?" he called. He thrust his shoulders into the passage and called again, louder. There came no reply.

Less anxious than impatient, Brandon crawled into the tunnel and began to wriggle forward, pushing his light ahead of him. Brandon was stocky, and it was a tight enough squeeze. The crawl space couldn't be much more than two feet square at its widest point. Brandon reflected that it was fortunate that he was not one of those bothered by claustrophobia.

Halfway through the tunnel, Brandon suddenly halted to study its walls. No natural passage; those were tool marks upon the stone—not even Kenlaw could doubt now. The regularity of the passage had already made Brandon suspicious. Cramped as it was, it reminded him of a mine shaft, and he thought again about the mention in Creecy's *Grandfather's Tales* of the interconnecting tunnels found at the Sink Hole pits.

The tunnel opened onto another chamber much like the one he had just quitted. It was a short drop to the floor, and Brandon lowered himself headfirst from the shaft. There was no sign of Kenlaw's light. He stood for a moment uneasily, swinging his flash about the cavern. Perhaps the archeologist had fallen into a hidden pit, smashed his light.

"Dr. Kenlaw?" Brandon called again. Only echoes answered.

No. There was another sound. Carried through the rock in the subterranean stillness. A sharp tapping. Kenlaw's geologist's pick.

Brandon killed his flash. A moment passed while his eyes adjusted to the blackness, then he discerned a faint haze of light visible only because of the total darkness. Switching his own light back on, Brandon directed it toward the glimmer. It came from the mouth of yet another passageway cut against the wall opposite.

He swung his light about the pit. Knowing what to look for now, Brandon thought he could see other such passages, piercing the rock face at all levels. It came to him that they began to run a real risk of losing their way if they were able to progress much farther within these caverns. Best to get Kenlaw and keep together after this, he decided.

The new shaft was a close copy of the previous one—albeit somewhat more cramped. Brandon scraped skin against its confines as he crawled toward the sound of Kenlaw's pick.

The archeologist was so engrossed in what he was doing that he hadn't noticed Brandon's presence, until the other wriggled out onto the floor of the pit and hailed him. Spotlighted by Brandon's flash, Kenlaw glowered truculently. The rock face where he was hammering threw back a crystalline reflection.

"I was worried something had happened," Brandon said, approaching.

"Sorry. I called to you that I was going on, but you must not have heard." Kenlaw swept up handfuls of rock samples and stuffed them into the already bulging pockets of his paratrooper's jacket. "We'd best be getting back before we get lost. Reynolds will be wondering about us."

"What *is* this place? Don't tell me all of this is due to natural formation!" Brandon swept his light around. More diminutive tunnels pierced the sides of this pit also. He considered the broken rock that littered the floor.

"This *is* a mine of some sort, isn't it. Congratulations, Dr. Kenlaw—you really *have* found one of the lost mines of the ancients! Christ, you'll need a team of spelunkers to explore these pits if they keep going on deeper into the mountain!"

Kenlaw laughed gruffly. "Lost mines to the romantic imagination, I suppose—but not to the trained mind. This is a common enough formation—underground streams have forced their way through faults in the rock, hollowed out big chambers wherever they've encountered softer stone. Come on, we've wasted enough time on this one."

"Soft rock?" Brandon pushed past him. "Hell, this is quartz!"

He stared at the quartz dike where Kenlaw had been working. Under the flashlight beam, golden highlights shimmered from the chipped matrix.

"Oh my god." Brandon managed to whisper.

These were good words for a final prayer, although Kenlaw probably had no such consideration in mind. The rush of motion from the darkness triggered some instinctive reflex. Brandon started to whirl about, and the pick of the geologist's hammer only tore a furrow across his scalp instead of plunging into his skull.

The glancing blow was enough. Brandon went down as if

pole-axed. Crouching over him, Kenlaw raised the hammer for the *coup de grâce.*

When Brandon made no move, the murderous light in the other man's eyes subsided to cunning. Brandon was still breathing, although bare bone gleamed beneath the blood-matted hair. Kenlaw balanced the geologist's pick pensively.

"Got to make this look like an accident," he muttered. "Can't risk an investigation. Tell them you took a bad fall. Damn you, Brandon! You would have to butt in the one time I finally found what I was after! This goddamn mountain is made out of gold, and that's going to be my secret until I can lock up the mining rights."

He hefted a rock—improvising quickly, for all that his attack had been born of the moment. "Just as well the pick only grazed you. Going to have to look like you busted your head on the rocks. Can't have it happen in here, though—this has to be kept hidden. Out there on the ledge where we first climbed down— that's where you fell. I'll block the tunnel entrance back up again. All they'll know is that we found some old bones in a cave, and you fell to your death climbing back up."

He raised the rock over Brandon's head, then threw it aside. "Hell, you may never wake up from that one there. Got to make this look natural as possible. If they don't suspect now, they might later on. Push you off the top of the ledge headfirst, and it'll just be a natural accident."

Working quickly, Kenlaw tied a length of rope to Brandon's ankles. The man was breathing hoarsely, his pulse erratic. He had a concussion, maybe worse. Kenlaw debated again whether to kill him now, but considered it unlikely that he would regain consciousness before they reached the ledge. An astute coroner might know the difference between injuries suffered through a fatal fall and trauma inflicted upon a lifeless body—they always did on television.

Brandon was heavy, but Kenlaw was no weakling for all his fat. Taking hold of the rope, he dragged the unconscious body across the cavern floor—any minor scrapes would be attributed to the fall. At the mouth of the tunnel he paused to pay out his coil of rope. Once on the other side, he could haul in Brandon's limp form like a fish on a line. It would only take minutes to finish the job.

The tunnel seemed far more cramped as he wriggled into it. The miners must have had small frames, but then people were smaller four centuries ago. Moreover, the Spaniards, who almost certainly would have used slave labor to drive these shafts, weren't men to let their slaves grow fat.

It *was* tighter, Kenlaw realized with growing alarm. For a moment he attempted to pass it off to claustrophobia, but as he reached a narrower section of the tunnel, the crushing pressure on his stout sides could not be denied. Panic whispered through his brain, and then suddenly he understood. He had crammed his baggy jacket pockets with rock samples and chunks of ore from the quartz dike; he was a good twenty pounds heavier and inches bulkier now than when he had crawled through before.

He could back out, but to do so would lose time. Brandon might revive; Reynolds might come looking for them. Gritting his teeth against the pressure on his ribs, Kenlaw pushed his light on ahead and forced his body onward. This was the tightest point, and beyond that the way would be easier. He sucked in his breath and writhed forward another foot or more. His sides ached, but he managed yet another foot with all his strength.

No farther. He was stuck.

His chest aching, Kenlaw found scant breath to curse. No need to panic. Just back out and take off the jacket, push it in ahead of him and try again. He struggled to work his corpulent body backward from the tunnel. The loose folds of his paratrooper's jacket rolled up as he wriggled backward, bunching against the bulging pockets. Jammed even tighter against his flesh and against the rock walls, the laden coat bunched up into a wedge. Kenlaw pushed harder, setting his teeth against the pain, as rock samples gouged into his body.

He couldn't move an inch farther. Backward or forward.

He was stuck midway in the tunnel.

Still Kenlaw fought down his panic. It was going to cost him some bruises and some torn skin, no doubt, but he'd work his way free in good time. He must above all else remain calm, be patient. A fraction of an inch forward, a fraction of an inch backward. He would take his time, work his way loose bit by bit, tear free of the jacket or smooth out its bunched-up folds. At worst, Reynolds would find him, bring help. Brandon might be dead by then, or have no memory of the blow that felled him; he could claim he was only trying to drag his injured companion to safety.

Kenlaw noticed that the light from his flashlight was growing dim. He had meant to replace the batteries earlier; now the spares were part of the impedimenta that pinioned him here. No matter; he didn't need light for this—only to be *lighter*. Kenlaw laughed shakily at his own joke, then the chuckle died.

The flashlight was fast dwindling, but its yellowing beam was enough to pick out the pink reflections of the many pairs of eyes that watched him from the mouth of the tunnel—barely glimpsed shapes that grew bolder as the light they feared grew dim.

And then Kenlaw panicked.

VI

The throbbing ache in his skull was so intense that it was some time before Brandon became aware that he was conscious. By gradual increments, as one awakens from a deep dream, he came to realize that something was wrong, that there was a reason for the pain and clouded state of awareness. An elusive memory whispered of a treacherous attack, a blow from behind. . . .

Brandon groaned as he forced himself to sit up, goaded to action as memory returned. His legs refused to function, and after a moment of confusion, he realized that his ankles were tied together. He almost passed out again from the effort to lean forward and fumble with the knots, and more time dragged past as he clumsily worked to free his ankles.

His brain refused to function clearly. He knew that it was dark, that he could see only dimly, but he could not think where his flashlight might be, nor marvel that his albino eyes had so accommodated to give him preternatural vision in a lightless cavern. Remembering Kenlaw's attack, he began to wonder where the other man had gone; only disjointedly did he understand the reasons behind the archeologist's actions and the probable consequences of his own plight.

The knots at last came loose. Brandon dully considered the rope—his thoughts groping with the fact that someone had tied it to his ankles. Tied him to what? Brandon pulled on the rope, drew coils of slack through the darkness, until there was tension from the other end. He tugged again. The rope was affixed to something beyond. With great effort, Brandon made it to his feet, staggered forward to lean against the rock face beneath which he had lain. The rope was tied to the wall. No, it entered the wall, into the tunnel. It was affixed to something within the narrow passage.

Brandon knelt forward and followed the rope into the crawl space. Dimly he remembered that this was the shaft by which he had entered—or so he hoped. He had hardly crawled forward for more than a body-length, when his fingers clawed against boots. Brandon groped and encountered damp cloth and motionless legs—the rope pressing on beneath their weight.

"Kenlaw?" he called out in a voice he scarcely recognized. He shook the man's feet, but no response came. Bracing himself against the narrow passage, Brandon grasped the other man's ankles and hauled back. For a moment there was resistance, then the slack body slid backward under his tugging. Backing out of the tunnel, Brandon dragged the archeologist's motionless form behind him. The task was an easy one for him, despite that the pain in his skull left Brandon nauseated and weak.

Emerging from the shaft, he rested until the giddiness subsided. Kenlaw lay where he had released him, still not moving. Brandon could only see the man as a dim outline, but vague as that impression was, something seemed wrong about the silhouette. Brandon bent forward, ran his hands over the archeologist's face, groping for a pulse.

His fingers encountered warm wetness across patches of slick hardness and sticky softness, before skidding into empty eye sockets. Most of the flesh of Kenlaw's face and upper body had been stripped from the bone.

Brandon slumped against the wall of the cavern, trying to comprehend. His brain struggled drunkenly to think, but the agony of his skull kept making his thoughts tumble apart again just as understanding seemed to be there. Kenlaw was dead. He, Brandon, was in a bad way. This much he could hold in his mind, and with that, the recognition that he had to get out of this place.

That meant crawling back through the narrow shaft where Kenlaw had met his death. Brandon's mind was too dazed to feel the full weight of horror. Once again he crawled into the tunnel and inched his way through the cramped darkness. The rock was damp, and now he knew with what wetness, but he forced himself to wriggle across it.

His hands encountered Kenlaw's flashlight. He snapped its switch without effect, then remembered the fresh batteries in his pockets. Crawling from the tunnel and onto the floor of the chamber beyond, he fumbled to open the flashlight, stuff in new batteries. He thumbed the switch, again without result. His fingers groped across the lens, gashed against broken glass. The bulb was smashed, the metal dented; tufts of hair and dried gore caked the battered end. Kenlaw had found service from the flashlight as a club, and it was good for little else now. Brandon threw it away from him with a curse.

The effort had taxed his strength, and Brandon passed from consciousness to unconsciousness and again to consciousness without really being aware of it. When he found himself capable of thought once again, he had to remember all over again how he had come to this state. He wondered how much time had passed, touched his watch, and found that the glare from the digital reading hurt his eyes.

Setting his teeth against the throbbing that jarred his skull, Brandon made it to his feet again, clutching at the wall of the pit for support. Olin, assuming he was getting anxious by now, might not find the passage that led from the first pit. To get help, Brandon would have to cross this cavern, crawl through the shaft back into the first pit, perhaps climb up along the ledge and into the passageway that led to the outer cavern. In his condition it wouldn't have been easy even if he had a light.

Brandon searched his pockets with no real hope. A non-smoker, he rarely carried matches, nor did he now. His eyes seemed to have accommodated as fully to the absence of light as their abnormal sensitivity would permit. It was sufficient to discern the shape of objects close at hand as shadowy forms distinct from the engulfing darkness—little enough, but preferable to total blindness. Brandon stood with his back to the shaft through which he had just crawled. The other tunnel had seemed to be approximately opposite, and if he walked in a straight line he ought to strike the rock face close enough to grope for the opening.

With cautious steps, Brandon began to cross the cavern. The floor was uneven, and loose stones were impossible for him to see. He tried to remember if his previous crossing had revealed any pitfalls within this chamber. A fall and a broken leg would leave him helpless here, and slowly through his confused brain was creeping the shrill warning that Kenlaw's death could hardly have been from natural causes. A bear? There were persistent rumors of mountain lions being sighted in these hills. Bobcats, which were not uncommon, could be dangerous under these circumstances. Brandon concentrated on walking in a straight line, much like a drunk trying to walk a highway line for a cop, and found that the effort demanded his entire attention.

The wall opposite loomed before him—Brandon was aware of its darker shape an instant before he blundered into it. He rested against its cool solidity for a moment, his knees rubbery, head swimming after the exertion. When he felt stronger once again, he began to inch his way along the rock face, fumbling for an opening in the wall of the pit.

There—a patch of darkness less intense opened out of the stone. He dared not even consider the possibility that this might not be the shaft that was hidden behind the cairn. Brandon fought back unconsciousness as it surged over him once more, forced his muscles to respond. Once through this passage, Olin would be able to find him. He stopped to crawl into the tunnel, and the rock was coated with a musty stickiness.

Brandon wriggled forward across the moist stone. The sensation was already too familiar, when his out-thrust fingers clawed against a man's boot. Kenlaw's boot. Kenlaw's body. In the shaft ahead of him.

Brandon was too stunned to feel terror. His tortured mind

struggled to comprehend. Kenlaw's body lay in the farther chamber, beyond the other passage by which he had returned. And Brandon knew a dead man when he came upon one. Had he circled the cavern, gone back the way he had come? Or was he delirious, his injured brain tormented by a recurring nightmare?

He clutched the lifeless feet and started to haul them back, as he had done before, or thought he had done. The boots were abruptly dragged out of his grasp.

Brandon slumped forward on his face, pressing against the stone to hold back the waves of vertigo and growing fear. Kenlaw's body disappeared into the blackness of the tunnel. How serious was his head injury? Had he imagined that Kenlaw was dead? Or was it Kenlaw ahead of him now in this narrow passage?

Brandon smothered a cackling laugh. It must not be Kenlaw. Kenlaw was dead, after all. It was Olin Reynolds, or someone else, come to search for him.

"Here I am!" Brandon managed to shout. "In here!"

His lips tasted of blood, and Brandon remembered the wetness he had pressed his face against a moment gone. It was too late to call back his outcry.

New movement scurried in the tunnel, from either end. Then his night vision became no blessing, for enough consciousness remained for Brandon to know that the faces that peered at him from the shaft ahead were not human faces.

VII

Olin Reynolds was a patient man. Age and Atlanta had taught him that. When the sun was high, he opened a tin of Vienna sausages and a pack of Lance crackers, munched them slowly, then washed them down with a few swallows from a Mason jar of blockade. Sleepy after his lunch, he stretched out on the seat and dozed.

When he awoke, the sun was low, and his joints complained as he slid from the cab and stretched. Brandon and Kenlaw should have returned by now, he realized with growing unease. Being a patient man, he sat on the running board of his truck, smoked two cigarettes and had another pull from the jar of whiskey. By then dusk was closing, and Reynolds decided it was time for him to do something.

There was a flashlight in the truck. Its batteries were none too fresh, but Reynolds dug it out and tramped toward the mouth of the cave. Stooping low, he called out several times, and, when there came no answer to his hail, he cautiously let himself down into the cavern.

The flashlight beam was weak, but enough to see that there was nothing here but the wreckage of the moonshine still that had been a going concern when he last set foot within the cavern. Reynolds didn't care to search farther with his uncertain light, but the chance that the others might have met with some accident and be unable to get back was too great for him to ignore. Still calling out their names, he nervously picked his way along the passage that led from the rear of the antechamber.

His batteries held out long enough for Reynolds to spot the sudden drop-off before he blundered across the edge and into space. Standing as close to the brink as he dared, Reynolds pointed his flashlight downward into the pit. The yellow beam was sufficient to pick out a broken heap of a man on the rocks below the ledge. Reynolds had seen death often enough before, and he didn't expect an answer when he called out into the darkness of the pit.

As quickly as his failing light permitted, Reynolds retraced his steps out into the starry darkness of the clearing. Breathing a prayer that one of the men might have survived the fall, he sent his truck careening down the mountain road in search of help.

Remote as the area was, it was well into the night before rescue workers in four-wheel-drive vehicles were able to converge upon the clearing before the cavern. Men with lights and emergency equipment hurried into the cave and climbed down into the pit beyond. There they found the broken body of Dr. Morris Kenlaw—strangely mutilated, as if set upon by rats after he fell to his death. They loaded his body onto a stretcher, and continued to search for his companion.

Eric Brandon they never found.

They searched the cavern and the passageway and the pit from corner to crevice. They found the wreckage of an old still and, within the pit, Kenlaw's body—and that was all. Later, when there were more lights, someone thought he saw evidence that a rock fall against the far wall of the pit might be a recent one; but after they had turned through this for a while, it was obvious that only bare rock lay underneath.

By morning, news of the mystery had spread. One man dead, one man vanished. Local reporters visited the scene, took photographs, interviewed people. Curiosity seekers joined the search. The day wore on, and still no sign of Brandon. By now the State Bureau of Investigation had sent men into the area in addition to the local sheriff's deputies—not that foul play was suspected so much, but a man had been killed and his companion had disappeared. And since it was evident that Brandon was not to be found inside the cavern, the mystery centered upon his disappearance—and why.

There were many conjectures. The men had been attacked by a bear, Brandon's body carried off. Brandon had been injured, had crawled out for help after Olin Reynolds had driven off; had subsequently collapsed, or become lost in the forest, or was out of his mind from a head injury. Some few suggested that Kenlaw's death had not been accidental, although no motive was put forward, and that Brandon had fled in panic while Reynolds was asleep. The mountainside was searched, and searched more thoroughly the next day. Dogs were brought in, but by now too many people had trampled over the site.

No trace of the missing man was discovered.

It became necessary that Brandon's family and associates be notified, and here the mystery continued. Brandon seemed to have no next-of-kin, but then, he had said once that he was an orphan. At his apartment in New York, he was almost unknown; the landlord could only note that he paid his rent promptly—and often by mail, since he evidently travelled a great deal. The university at which he had mentioned he was working on his doctorate (when asked once) had no student on record named Eric Brandon, and no one could remember if he had ever told them the name of the grant that was supporting his folklore research.

In their need to know *something* definite about the vanished man, investigators looked through the few possessions and personal effects in his cabin. They found no names or addresses with which Brandon might be connected—nothing beyond numerous reference works and copious notes that showed he had indeed been a serious student of regional folklore. There was his rifle, and a handgun—a Walther PPK in .380 ACP—still nothing to excite comment (the Walther was of pre-War manufacture, its serial number without American listing), until someone forced the lock on his *attaché* case and discovered the Colt Woodsman. The fact that this .22-calibre pistol incorporated a silencer interested the FBI, and, after fingerprints had been sent through channels, was of even greater interest to the FBI.

"They were manufactured for the OSS," the agent explained, indicating the Colt semi-automatic with its bulky silencer. "A few of them are still in use, although the Hi-Standard HD is more common now. There's no way of knowing how this one ended up in Brandon's possession—it's illegal for a private citizen to own a silencer of any sort, of course. In the hands of a good marksman, it's a perfect assassination gun—about all the sound it makes is that of the action functioning, and a clip of .22 hollow points placed right will finish about any job."

"Eric wouldn't have killed anyone!" Ginger Warner protested angrily. The FBI agent reminded her of a too-scrubbed Bible salesman. She resented the high-handed way he and the others had appropriated Brandon's belongings.

"That's the thing about these sociopathic types: they seem perfectly normal human beings, but it's only a mask." He went on: "We'll run ballistics on this and see if it matches with anything on file. Probably not. This guy was good. Real good. What we have on him now is purely circumstantial, and if we turn him up, I'm not sure we can nail him on anything more serious than firearms violations. But putting together all the things we know and that won't stand up in court, your tenant is one of the top hit men in the business."

"Brandon—a hit man!" scoffed Dell Warner.

"Brandon's not his real name," the agent went on, ticking off his information. "He's set up other identities too, probably. We ran his prints: took some looking, but we finally identified him. His name was Ricky Brennan when he was turned over to a New York state foster home as a small child. Father unknown; mother one Laurie Brennan, deceased. Records say his mother was from around here originally, by the way—maybe that's why he came back. Got into a bit of trouble in his early teens; had a fight with some other boys in the home. One died from a broken neck as a result, but since the others had jumped Brennan, no charges were placed. But out of that, we did get his prints on record—thanks to an institutional blunder when they neglected to expunge his juvenile record. They moved him to another facility, where they could handle his type; shortly after that, Brennan ran away, and there the official record ends."

"Then how can you say that Eric is a hired killer!" Ginger demanded. "You haven't any proof! You've said so yourself."

"No proof that'll stand up in court, I said," the agent admitted. "But we've known for some time of a high-priced hit man who likes to use a high-powered rifle. One like this."

He hefted Brandon's rifle. "This is a Winchester Model 70, chambered for the .220 Swift. That's the fastest commercially loaded cartridge ever made. Factory load will move a 48-grain bullet out at a velocity of over 4100 feet per second on a trajectory flat as a stretched string. Our man has killed with head shots from distances that must have been near three hundred yards, in reconstructing some of his hits. The bullet virtually explodes on impact, so there's nothing left for ballistics to work on.

"But it's a rare gun for a hit man to use, and that's where Brandon begins to figure. It demands a top marksman, as well as a shooter who can handle this much gun. You see, the .220 Swift has just too much power. It burned out the old nickel steel barrels when the cartridge was first introduced, and it's said that the bullet itself will disintegrate if it hits a patch of turbulent air. The .220 Swift may have fantastic velocity, but it also has a tendency to self-destruct."

"Eric used that as a varmint rifle," Dell argued. "It's a popular cartridge for varmint shooters, along with a lot of other small-calibre high-velocity cartridges. And as for that silenced Colt, Eric isn't the first person I've heard of who owned a gun that's considered illegal."

"As I said, we don't have a case—yet. Just pieces of a puzzle, but more pieces start to fall into place once you make a start. There's more than just what I've told you, you can be sure. And we'll find out a lot more once we find Brandon. At a guess, he killed Kenlaw—who may have found out something about him—then panicked and fled."

"Sounds pretty clumsy for a professional killer," Dell commented.

The agent frowned, then was all official politeness once more. These hillbillies were never known for their cooperation with Federal agents. "We'll find out what happened when we find Brandon."

"If you find him."

VIII

Brandon seemed to be swirling through pain-fogged delirium—an endless vertigo in which he clutched at fragments of dream as a man caught in a maelstrom is flung against flotsam of his broken ship. In rare moments his consciousness surfaced enough for him to wonder whether portions of the dreams might be reality.

Most often, Brandon dreamed of limitless caverns beneath the mountains, caverns through which he was borne along by partially glimpsed dwarfish figures. Sometimes Kenlaw was with him in this maze of tunnels—crawling after him, his face a flayed mask of horror, a bloody geologist's pick brandished in one fleshless fist.

At other times Brandon sensed his dreams were visions of the past, visions that could only be born of his obsessive study of the folklore of this region. He looked upon the mountains of a primeval age, when the boundless forest was untouched by the iron bite and poisoned breath of white civilization. Copper-hued savages hunted game along these ridges, to come upon a race of diminutive white-skinned folk who withdrew shyly into the shelter of hidden caverns. The Indians were in awe of these little people, whose origins were beyond the mysteries of their oldest legends, and so they created new legends to explain them.

With the successive migrations of Indians through these mountains, the little people remained in general at peace, for they were wise in certain arts beyond the comprehension of the red man—who deemed them spirit-folk—and their ways were those of secrecy and stealth.

Then came a new race of men: white skins made bronze by the sun, their faces bearded, their flesh encased in burnished steel. The conquistadors enslaved the little folk of the hills as they had enslaved the races of the south, tortured them to learn the secrets of their caves beneath the mountains, forced them to mine the gold from pits driven deep into the earth. Then followed a dream of mad carnage, when the little people arose from their tunnels in unexpected force, to entrap their masters within the pits, and to drive those who escaped howling in fear from that which they had called forth from beneath the mountains.

Then came the white settlers in a wave that never receded, driving before them the red man, and finally the game. Remembering the conquistadors, the little people retreated farther into their hidden caverns, hating the white man with his guns and his settlements. Seldom now did they venture into the world above, and then only by night. Deep within the mountains, they found sustenance from the subterranean rivers and the beds of fungoid growths they nourished, feeding as well upon other cave creatures and such prey as they might seek above on starless nights. With each generation, the race slipped farther back into primordial savagery, forgetting the ancient knowledge that had once been theirs. Their stature became dwarfish and apelike, their faces brutish as the devolution of their souls; their flesh and hair assumed the dead pallor of creatures that live in eternal darkness, even as their vision and hearing adapted to their subterranean existence.

They remembered their hatred of the new race of men. Again and again Brandon's dreams were red with visions of stealthy ambush and lurid slaughter of those who trespassed upon their hidden domain, of those who walked mountain trails upon nights when the stars were swallowed in cloud. He saw children snatched from their blankets, women set upon in lonely places. For the most part, these were nightmares from previous centuries, although there was a recurrent dream in which a vapid-faced girl gave herself over willingly to their obscene lusts, until the coming of men with flashlights and shotguns drove them from her cackling embrace.

These were dreams that Brandon through his comatose delirium could grasp and understand. There were far more visions that defied his comprehension.

Fantastic cities reeled and shattered as the earth tore itself apart, thrusting new mountains toward the blazing heavens, opening vast chasms that swallowed rivers and spat them forth as shrieking steam. Oceans of flame melted continents into leaden seas, wherein charred fragments of a world spun frenziedly upon chaotic tides and whirlpools, riven by enormous bolts of raw energy that coursed like fiery cobwebs from the cyclopean orb that filled the sky.

Deep within the earth, fortress cities were shaken and smashed by the Hell that reigned miles above. From out of the ruins, survivors crept to attempt to salvage some of the wonders of the age that had died and left them exiles in a strange world. Darkness and savagery stole from them their ideals, even as monstrous dwellers from even greater depths of the earth drove them from their buried cities and upward through caverns that opened onto an alien surface. In the silent halls of vanished greatness, nightmarish shapes crawled like maggots, while the knowledge of that godlike age was a fading memory to the degenerate descendants of those who had fled.

How long the dreams endured, Brandon could not know. It was the easing of the pain in his skull that eventually convinced Brandon that he had passed from dream into reality, although it was into a reality no less strange than that of delirium.

They made a circle about where he lay—so many of them that Brandon could not guess their number. Their bodies were stunted, but lacking the disproportion of torso to limbs of human dwarfs. The thin white fur upon their naked pink flesh combined to give them something of the appearance of lemurs. Brandon thought of elves and of feral children, but their faces were those of demons. Broad nostrils and outthrust, tusked jaws stopped just short of being muzzles, and within overlarge red-pupiled eyes glinted the malign intelligence of a fallen angel.

They seemed in awe of him.

Brandon slowly raised himself on one arm, giddy from the effort. He saw that he lay upon a pallet of dried moss and crudely cured furs, that his naked body seemed thin from long fever. He touched the wound on his scalp and encountered old scab and new scar. Beside him, water and what might be broth or emollients filled bowls which might have been formed by human hands, and perhaps not.

Brandon stared back at the vast circle of eyes. It occurred to him to wonder that he could see them; his first thought was that there must be a source of dim light from somewhere. It then came to him to wonder that these creatures had spared him; his first thought was that as an albino they had mistakenly accepted him as one of their race. In the latter, he was closer to the truth than with the former.

Then slowly, as his awakening consciousness assimilated all that he now knew, Brandon understood the truth. And, in understanding at last, Brandon knew who he was, and why he was.

IX

There was only a sickle of moon that night, but Ginger Warner, feeling restless, threw on a wrap and slipped out of the house.

On some nights sleep just would not come, although such nights came farther apart now. Walking seemed to help, although she had forgone these nocturnal strolls for a time, after once when she realized someone was following her. As it turned out, her unwelcome escort was a Federal agent—they thought she would lead them to where her lover was hiding—and Ginger's subsequent anger was worse than her momentary fear. But in time even the FBI decided that the trail was a cold one, and the investigation into the disappearance of a suspected hired killer was pushed into the background.

It was turning autumn, and the thin breeze made her shiver beneath her dark wrap. Ginger wished for the company of Dan, but her brother had taken the Plott hound off on a weekend bear hunt. The wind made a lonely sound as it moved through the trees, chattering the dead leaves so that even the company of her own footsteps was denied her.

Only the familiarity of the tone let her stifle a scream, when someone called her name from the darkness ahead.

Ginger squinted into the darkness, wishing now she'd brought a light. She whispered uncertainly: "Eric?"

And then he stepped out from the shadow of the rock out-cropping that overhung the path along the ridge, and Ginger was in his arms.

She spared only a moment for a kiss, before warning him in one breathless outburst: "Eric, you've got to be careful! The police—the FBI—they've been looking for you all summer! They think you're some sort of criminal!"

In her next breath, she found time to look at him more closely. "Eric, where have you been? What's happened to you?"

Only the warm pressure of his arms proved to her that Brandon was not a phantom of dream. The wind whipped through his long white hair and beard, and there was just enough moonlight for her to make out the streak of scar that creased his scalp. He was shirtless: his only attire a ragged pair of denim jeans and battered boots. Beneath his bare skin, muscles bunched in tight masses that were devoid of fleshy padding. About his neck he wore a peculiar amulet of gold, and upon his belt hung a conquis-tador's sword.

"I've been walking up and down in the earth," he said. "Is summer over, then? It hadn't seemed so long. I wonder if time moves at a different pace down there."

Both his words and his tone made her stare at him anew. "Eric! God, Eric! What's happened to you?"

"I've found my own kind," Brandon told her, with a laugh that gave her a chill. "But I was lonely among them as well, and so I came back. I knew there must be an open passageway some-where on your land here, and it didn't take me long to find it."

"You've been hiding out in some caves?" Ginger wondered.

"Not hiding out. They recognized me for who I am, don't you understand? They've forgotten so much over the ages, but not all of the old wisdom has left them. They're not quite beasts yet!"

Ginger considered the scar on his head, and remembered that

he must have been wandering in some undiscovered system of caverns for many weeks, alone in the darkness.

"Eric," she said gently, "I know you've been hurt, that you've been alone for a long time. Now I want you to come back with me to the house. You need to have a doctor look at your head where you hurt it."

"It's certain to sound strange to you, I realize," Brandon smiled. "I still sometimes wonder if it isn't all part of my dreams. There's gold down there—more gold than the conquistadors ever dreamed—and hoards of every precious stone these mountains hold. But there's far greater treasure than any of this. There's a lost civilization buried down below, its ruins guarded by entities that transcend any apocalyptic vision of Hell's demons. It's been ages since any of my people have dared to enter the hidden strongholds—but I've dared to enter there, and I've returned."

Ginger compressed her lips and tried to remember all she'd learned in her psychology course last year.

"Eric, you don't have to be worried about what I said about the police. They know you weren't to blame for Dr. Kenlaw's death, and they admitted to us that they didn't have any sort of evidence against you on all that other nonsense."

She hoped that was all still true. Far better to have Eric turn himself in and let a good lawyer take charge, than to allow him to wander off again in this condition. They had good doctors at the center in Morganton who could help him recover.

"Come back?" Brandon's face seemed suddenly satanic. "You'd have me come back to the world of men and be put in a cell? I think instead I'll rule in Hell!"

Ginger did not share in his laughter at his allusion. There were soft rustlings among the leaves alongside the trail, and the wind was silent.

She cried out when she saw their faces, and instinctively pressed against Brandon for protection.

"Don't be afraid," he soothed, gripping her tightly. "These are my people. They've fallen far, but I can lead them back along the road to their ancient greatness.

"Our people," Brandon corrected himself, "Persephone."

THE RIVER OF NIGHT'S DREAMING

Everywhere: greyness and rain.

The activities bus with its uniformed occupants. The wet pavement that crawled along the crest of the high bluff. The storm-fretted waters of the bay far below. The night itself, gauzy with grey mist and traceries of rain, feebly probed by the wan headlights of the bus.

Greyness and rain merged in a slither of skidding rubber and a protesting bawl of brakes and tearing metal.

For an instant the activities bus paused upon the broken guard-rail, hung half-swallowed by the greyness and rain upon the edge of the precipice. Then, with thirty voices swelling a chorus to the screams of rubber and steel, the bus plunged over the edge.

Halfway down it struck glancingly against the limestone face, shearing off wheels amidst a shower of glass and bits of metal, its plunge unchecked. Another carom, and the bus began to break apart, tearing open before its final impact onto the wave-frothed jumble of boulders far below. Water and sound surged upward into the night, as metal crumpled and split open, scattering bits of humanity like seeds flung from a bursting melon.

Briefly those trapped within the submerging bus made despairing noises—in the night they were no more than the cries of kittens, tied in a sack and thrown into the river. Then the waters closed over the tangle of wreckage, and greyness and rain silenced the torrent of sound.

She struggled to the surface and dragged air into her lungs in a shuddering spasm. Treading water, she stared about her—her actions still automatic, for the crushing impact into the dark waters had all but knocked her unconscious. Perhaps for a moment she *had* lost consciousness; she was too dazed to remember anything very clearly. Anything.

Fragments of memory returned. The rain and the night, the activities bus carrying them back to their prison. Then the plunge into darkness, the terror of her companions, metal bursting apart. Alone in another instant, flung helplessly into the night, and the stunning embrace of the waves.

Her thoughts were clearing now. She worked her feet out of her tennis shoes and tugged damp hair away from her face, trying to see where she was. The body of the bus had torn open, she vaguely realized, and she had been thrown out of the wreckage and into the bay. She could see the darker bulk of the cliff looming out of the greyness not far from her, and dimly came the moans and cries of other survivors. She could not see them, but she could imagine their presence, huddled upon the rocks between the water and the vertical bluff.

Soon the failure of the activities bus to return would cause alarm. The gap in the guard rail would be noticed. Rescuers would come, with lights and ropes and stretchers, to pluck them off the rocks and hurry them away in ambulances to the prison's medical ward.

She stopped herself. Without thought, she had begun to swim toward the other survivors. But why? She took stock of her situation. As well as she could judge, she had escaped injury. She could easily join the others where they clung to the rocks, await rescue—and once the doctors were satisfied she was whole and hearty, she would be back on her locked ward again. A prisoner, perhaps until the end of her days.

Far across the bay, she could barely make out the phantom glimmering of the lights of the city. The distance was great—in miles, two? three? more?—for the prison was a long drive beyond the outskirts of the city and around the sparsely settled shore of the bay. But she was athletically trim and a strong swimmer—she exercised regularly to help pass the long days. How many days, she could not remember. She only knew she would not let them take her back to that place.

The rescue workers would soon be here. Once they'd taken care of those who clung to the shoreline, they'd send divers to raise the bus—and when they didn't find her body among those in the wreckage, they'd assume she was drowned, her body washed away. There would surely be others who were missing, others whose bodies even now drifted beneath the bay. Divers and boatmen with drag hooks would search for them. Some they might never find.

Her they would never find.

She turned her back to the cliff and began to swim out into the bay. Slow, patient strokes—she must conserve her strength. This was a dangerous act, she knew, but then they would be all the slower to suspect when they discovered she was missing. The rashness of her decision only meant that the chances of escape were all the better. Certainly, they would search along the shoreline close by the wreck—perhaps use dogs to hunt down any who might have tried to escape along the desolate stretch of high cliffs. But they would not believe that one of their prisoners would attempt to swim across to the distant city—and once she reached the city, no bloodhounds could seek her out there.

The black rise of rock vanished into the grey rain behind her, and with it dwindled the sobbing wails of her fellow prisoners. No longer her fellows. She had turned her back on that existence. Beyond, where lights smeared the distant greyness, she would find a new existence for herself.

For a while she swam a breast stroke, switching to a back stroke whenever she began to tire. The rain fell heavily onto her upturned face; choppy waves spilled into her mouth, forcing her to abandon the back stroke each time before she was fully rested. Just take it slow, take your time, she told herself. Only the distant lights gave any direction to the greyness now. If she tried to turn back, she might swim aimlessly through the darkness, until . . .

Her dress, a drab prison smock, was weighting her down. She hesitated a moment—she would need clothing when she reached the shore, but so encumbered she would never reach the city. She could not waste strength in agonizing over her dilemma. There was no choice. She tugged at the buttons. A quick struggle, and she was able to wrench the wet dress over her head and pull it free. She flung the shapeless garment away from her, and it sank into the night. Another struggle, and her socks followed.

She struck out again for the faraway lights. Her bra and panties were no more drag than a swimsuit, and she moved through the water cleanly—berating herself for not having done this earlier. In the rain and the darkness it was impossible to judge how far she had swum. At least halfway, she fervently hoped. The adrenalin that had coursed through her earlier with its glib assurances of strength was beginning to fade, and she became increasingly aware of bruises and wrenched muscles suffered in the wreck.

The lights never appeared to come any closer, and by now she had lost track of time, as well. She wondered whether the flow of the current might not be carrying her away from her destination whenever she rested, and that fear sent new power into her strokes. The brassiere straps chafed her shoulders, but this irritation was scarcely noticed against the gnawing ache of fatigue. She fought down her growing panic, concentrating her entire being upon the phantom lights in the distance.

The lights seemed no closer than the stars might have been— only the stars were already lost in the greyness and rain. At times the city lights vanished as well, blotted out as she labored through a swell. She was cut off from everything in those moments, cut off from space and from time and from reality. There was only the greyness and the rain, pressing her deeper against the dark water. Memories of her past faded—she had always heard that a drowning victim's life flashes before her, but she could scarcely remember any fragment of her life before they had shut her away. Perhaps that memory would return when at last her straining muscles failed, and the water closed over her face in an unrelinquished kiss.

But then the lights *were* closer—she was certain of it this time. True, the lights were fewer than she had remembered, but she knew it must be far into the night after her seemingly endless swim. Hope sped renewed energy into limbs that had moved like a mechanical toy, slowly winding down. There was a current here, she sensed, seeking to drive her away from the lights and back into the limitless expanse she had struggled to escape.

As she fought against the current, she found she could at last make out the shoreline before her. Now she felt a new rush of fear. Sheer walls of stone awaited her. The city had been built along a bluff. She might reach the shore, but she could never climb its rock face.

She had fought too hard to surrender to despair now. Grimly she attacked the current, working her way along the shoreline. It was all but impossible to see anything—only the looming wall of blackness that cruelly barred her from the city invisible upon its heights. Then, beyond her in the night, the blackness seemed to recede somewhat. Scarcely daring to hope, she swam toward this break in the wall. The current steadily increased. Her muscles stabbed with fatigue, but now she had to swim all the harder to keep from being swept away.

The bluff was indeed lower here, but as a defense against the floods, they had built a wall where the natural barrier fell away. She clutched at the mossy stones in desperation—her clawing fingers finding no purchase. The current dragged her back, denying her a moment's respite.

She sobbed a curse. The heavy rains had driven the water to highest levels, leaving no rim of shoreline beneath cliff or dike. But since there was no escape for her along the direction she had come, she forced her aching limbs to fight on against the current. The line of the dike seemed to be curving inward, and she thought surely she could see a break in the barrier of blackness not far ahead.

She made painful progress against the increasing current, and at length was able to understand where she was. The seawall rose above a river that flowed through the city and into the bay. The city's storm sewers swelling its stream, the river rushed in full flood against the man-made bulwark. Its force was almost more than she could swim against now. Again and again she clutched at the slippery face of the wall, striving to gain a hold. Each time the current dragged her back again.

Storm sewers, some of them submerged now, poured into the river from the wall—their cross currents creating whirling eddies that shielded her one moment, tore at her the next, but allowed her to make desperate headway against the river itself. Bits of debris, caught up by the flood, struck at her invisibly. Rats, swimming frenziedly from the flooded sewers, struggled past her, sought to crawl onto her shoulders and face. She hit out at them, heedless of their bites, too intent on fighting the current herself to feel new horror.

A sudden eddy spun her against a recess in the sea wall, and in the next instant her legs bruised against a submerged ledge. She half swam, half crawled forward, her fingers clawing slime-carpeted steps. Her breath sobbing in relief, she dragged herself out of the water and onto a flight of stone steps set out from the face of the wall.

For a long while she was content to press herself against the wet stone, her aching limbs no longer straining to keep her afloat, her chest hammering in exhaustion. The flood washed against her feet, its level still rising, and a sodden rat clawed onto her leg—finding refuge as she had done. She crawled higher onto the steps, becoming aware of her surroundings once more.

So. She had made it. She smiled shakily and looked back toward the direction she had come. Rain and darkness and distance made an impenetrable barrier, but she imagined the rescue workers must be checking off the names of those they had found. There would be no checkmark beside her name.

She hugged her bare ribs. The night was chill, and she had no protection from the rain. She remembered now that she was almost naked. What would anyone think who saw her like this? Perhaps in the darkness her panties and bra would pass for a bikini—but what would a bather be doing out at this hour and in this place? She might explain that she had been sunbathing, had fallen asleep, taken refuge from the storm, and had then been forced to flee from the rising waters. But when news of the bus wreck spread, anyone who saw her would remember.

She must find shelter and clothing—somewhere. Her chance to escape had been born of the moment; she had not had time yet to think matters through. She only knew she could not let them recapture her now. Whatever the odds against her, she would face them.

She stood up, leaning against the face of the wall until she felt her legs would hold her upright. The flight of steps ran diagonally down from the top of the seawall. There was no railing on the outward face, and the stone was treacherous with slime and streaming water. Painfully, she edged her way upward, trying not to think about the rushing waters below her. If she slipped, there was no way she could check her fall; she would tumble down into the black torrent, and this time there would be no escape.

The climb seemed as difficult as had her long swim, and her aching muscles seemed to rebel against the task of bearing her up the slippery steps, but at length she gained the upper landing and stumbled onto the storm-washed pavement atop the sea wall. She blinked her eyes uncertainly, drawing a long breath. The rain pressed her black hair to her neck and shoulders, sluiced away the muck and filth from her skin.

There were no lights to be seen along here. A balustrade guarded the edge of the seawall, with a gap to give access to the stairs. A street, barren of any traffic at this hour, ran along the top of the wall, and, across the empty street, rows of brick buildings made a second barrier. Evidently she had come upon a district of warehouses and such—and, from all appearances, this section was considerably run-down. There were no streetlights here, but even in the darkness she could sense the disused aspect of the row of buildings with their boarded-over windows and filthy fronts, the brick street with its humped and broken paving.

She shivered. It was doubly fortunate that none were here to mark her sudden appearance. In a section like this, and dressed as she was, it was unlikely that anyone she might encounter would be of Good Samaritan inclinations.

Clothing. She had to find clothing. Any sort of clothing. She darted across the uneven paving and into the deeper shadow of the building fronts. Her best bet would be to find a shop: perhaps some sordid second-hand place such as this street might well harbor, a place without elaborate burglar alarms, if possible. She could break in, or at worst find a window display and try her luck at smash and grab. Just a simple raincoat would make her far less vulnerable. Eventually she would need money, shelter and food, until she could leave the city for someplace faraway.

As she crept along the deserted street, she found herself wondering whether she could find anything at all here. Doorways were padlocked and boarded over; behind rusted gratings, windows showed rotting planks and dirty shards of glass. The waterfront street seemed to be completely abandoned—a deserted row of ancient buildings enclosing forgotten wares, cheaper to let rot than to haul away, even as it was cheaper to let these brick hulks stand than to pull them down. Even the expected winos and derelicts seemed to have deserted this section of the city. She began to wish she might encounter at least a passing car.

The street had not been deserted by the rats. Probably they had been driven into the night by the rising waters. Once she began to notice them, she realized there were more and more of them—creeping boldly along the street. Huge, knowing brutes; some of them large as cats. They didn't seem afraid of her, and at times she thought they might be gathering in a pack to follow her. She had heard of rats attacking children and invalids, but surely . . . She wished she were out of this district.

The street plunged on atop the riverside, and still there were no lights or signs of human activity. The rain continued to pour down from the drowned night skies. She began to think about crawling into one of the dark warehouses to wait for morning, then thought of being alone in a dark, abandoned building with a closing pack of rats. She walked faster.

Some of the empty buildings showed signs of former grandeur, and she hoped she was coming toward a better section of the river-front. Elaborate entranceways of fluted columns and marble steps gave onto the street. Grotesque Victorian facades and misshapen statuary presented imposing fronts to buildings filled with the same musty decay as the brick warehouses. She must be reaching the old merchants' district of the city, although these structures as well appeared long abandoned, waiting only for the wrecking ball of urban renewal. She wished she could escape this street, for there seemed to be more rats in the darkness behind her than she could safely ignore.

Perhaps she might find an alleyway between buildings that would let her flee this waterfront section and enter some inhabited neighborhood—for it became increasingly evident that this street had long been derelict. She peered closely at each building, but never could she find a gap between them. Without a light, she dared not enter blindly and try to find her way through some ramshackle building.

She paused for a moment and listened. For some while she

had heard a scramble of wet claws and fretful squealings from the darkness behind her. Now she heard only the rain. Were the rats silently closing about her?

She stood before a columned portico—a bank or church?—and gazed into the darker shadow, wondering whether she might seek shelter. A statue—she supposed it was of an angel or some symbolic figure—stood before one of the marble columns. She could discern little of its features, only that it must have been malformed—presumably by vandalism—for it was hunched over and appeared to be supported against the column by thick cables or ropes. She could not see its face.

Not liking the silence, she hurried on again. Once past the portico, she turned quickly and looked back—to see if the rats were creeping after her. She saw no rats. She could see the row of columns. The misshapen figure was no longer there.

She began to run then. Blindly, not thinking where her panic drove her.

To her right, there was only the balustrade, marking the edge of the wall, and the rushing waters below. To her left, the unbroken row of derelict buildings. Behind her, the night and the rain, and something whose presence had driven away the pursuing rats. And ahead of her—she was close enough to see it now—the street made a dead end against a rock wall.

Stumbling toward it, for she dared not turn back the way she had run, she saw that the wall was not unbroken—that a stairway climbed steeply to a terrace up above. Here the bluff rose high against the river once again, so that the seawall ended against the rising stone. There were buildings crowded against the height, fronted upon the terrace a level above. In one of the windows, a light shone through the rain.

Her breath shook in ragged gasps and her legs were rubbery, but she forced herself to half run, half clamber up the rain-slick steps to the terrace above. Here, again a level of brick paving and a balustrade to guard the edge. Boarded windows and desolate facades greeted her from a row of decrepit houses, shouldered together on the rise. The light had been to her right, out above the river.

She could see it clearly now. It beckoned from the last house on the terrace—a looming Victorian pile built over the bluff. A casement window, level with the far end of the terrace, opened out onto a neglected garden. She climbed over the low wall that separated the house from the terrace, and crouched outside the curtained window.

Inside, a comfortable-looking sitting room with old-fashioned appointments. An older woman was crocheting, while in a chair beside her a young woman, dressed in a maid's costume, was reading aloud from a book. Across the corner room, another casement window looked out over the black water far below.

Had her fear and exhaustion been less consuming, she might have taken a less reckless course, might have paused to consider what effect her appearance would make. But she remembered a certain shuffling sound she had heard as she scrambled up onto the terrace, and the way the darkness had seemed to gather upon the top of the stairway when she glanced back a moment gone. With no thought but to escape the night, she tapped her knuckles sharply against the casement window.

At the tapping at the window, the older woman looked up from her work, the maid let the yellow-bound volume drop onto her white apron. They stared at the casement, not so much frightened as if uncertain of what they had heard. The curtain inside veiled her presence from them.

Please! she prayed, without voice to cry out. She tapped more insistently, pressing herself against the glass. They would see that she was only a girl, see her distress.

They were standing now, the older woman speaking too quickly for her to catch the words. The maid darted to the window, fumbled with its latch. Another second, and the casement swung open, and she tumbled into the room.

She knelt in a huddle on the floor, too exhausted to move any farther. Her body shook and water dripped from her bare flesh. She felt like some half-drowned kitten, plucked from the storm to shelter. Vaguely, she could hear their startled queries, the protective clash as the casement latch closed out the rain and the curtain swept across the night.

The maid had brought a coverlet and was furiously toweling her dry. Her attentions reminded her that she must offer some sort of account of herself—before her benefactors summoned the police, whose investigation would put a quick end to her freedom.

"I'm all right now," she told them shakily. "Just let me get my breath back, get warm."

"What's your name, child?" the older woman inquired solicitously. "Camilla, bring some hot tea."

She groped for a name to tell them. "Cassilda." The maid's name had put this in mind, and it was suited to her surroundings. "Cassilda Archer." Dr. Archer would indeed be interested in *that* appropriation.

"You poor child! How did you come here? Were you ... attacked?"

Her thoughts worked quickly. Satisfy their curiosity, but don't make them suspicious. Justify your predicament, but don't alarm them.

"I was hitchhiking." She spoke in uncertain bursts. "A man picked me up. He took me to a deserted section near the river. He made me take off my clothes. He was going to ..." She didn't need to feign her shudder.

"Here's the tea, Mrs. Castaigne. I've added a touch of brandy."

"Thank you, Camilla. Drink some of this, dear."

She used the interruption to collect her thoughts. The two women were alone here, or else any others would have been summoned.

"When he started to pull down his trousers ... I hurt him. Then I jumped out and ran as hard as I could. I don't think he came after me, but then I was wandering, lost in the rain. I couldn't find anyone to help me. I didn't have anything with me except my underwear. I think a tramp was following me. Then I saw your light and ran toward it.

"Please, don't call the police!" She forestalled their obvious next move. "I'm not hurt. I know I couldn't face the shame of a rape investigation. Besides, they'd never be able to catch that man by now."

"But surely you must want me to contact someone for you."

"There's no one who would care. I'm on my own. That man has my pack and the few bucks in my handbag. If you could please let me stay here for the rest of the night, lend me some clothes just for tomorrow, and in the morning I'll phone a friend who can wire me some money."

Mrs. Castaigne hugged her protectively. "You poor child! What you've been through! Of course you'll stay with us for the night—and don't fret about having to relive your terrible ordeal for a lot of leering policemen! Tomorrow there'll be plenty of time for you to decide what you'd like to do.

"Camilla, draw a nice hot bath for Cassilda. She's to sleep in Constance's room, so see that there's a warm comforter, and lay out a gown for her. And you, Cassilda, must drink another cup of this tea. As badly chilled as you are, child, you'll be fortunate indeed to escape your death of pneumonia!"

Over the rim of her cup, the girl examined the room and its occupants more closely. The sitting room was distinctly old-fashioned—furnished like a parlor in an old photograph, or like a set from some movie that was supposed to be taking place at the turn of the century. Even the lights were either gas or kerosene. Probably this house hadn't changed much since years ago, before the neighborhood had begun to decay. Anyone would have to be a little eccentric to keep staying on here, although probably this place was all Mrs. Castaigne had, and Mr. Castaigne wasn't in evidence. The house and property couldn't be worth much in this neighborhood, although the furnishings might fetch a little money as antiques—she was no judge of that, but everything looked to be carefully preserved.

Mrs. Castaigne seemed well fitted to this room and its furnishings. Hers was a face that might belong to a woman of forty or of sixty—well featured, but too stern for a younger woman, yet without the lines and age marks of an elderly lady. Her figure was still very good, and she wore a tight-waisted, ankle-length dress that seemed to belong to the period of the house. The hands that stroked her bare shoulders were strong and white and unblemished, and the hair she wore piled atop her head was as black as the girl's own.

It occurred to her that Mrs. Castaigne must surely be too young for this house. Probably she was a daughter, or, more likely, a granddaughter of its original owners—a widow who lived alone with her young maid. And who might Constance be, whose room she was to sleep in?

"Your bath is ready now, Miss Archer." Camilla reappeared. Wrapped in the coverlet, the girl followed her. Mrs. Castaigne helped support her, for her legs had barely strength to stand, and she felt ready to pass out from fatigue.

The bathroom was spacious—steamy from the vast, claw-footed tub, and smelling of bath salts. Its plumbing and fixtures were no more modern than the rest of the house. Camilla entered with her, and, to her surprise, helped her remove her scant clothing and assisted her into the tub. She was too tired to feel ill at ease at this unaccustomed show of attention, and when the maid began to rub her back with scented soap, she sighed at the luxury.

"Who else lives here?" she asked casually.

"Only Mrs. Castaigne and myself, Miss Archer."

"Mrs. Castaigne mentioned someone—Constance?—whose room I am to have."

"Miss Castaigne is no longer with us, Miss Archer."

"Please call me Cassilda. I don't like to be so formal."

"If that's what you wish to be called, of course . . . Cassilda." Camilla couldn't be very far from her own age, she guessed. Despite the old-fashioned maid's outfit—black dress and stockings with frilled white apron and cap—the other girl was probably no more than in her early twenties. The maid wore her long blonde hair in an upswept topknot like her mistress, and she supposed she only followed Mrs. Castaigne's preferences. Camilla's figure was full—much more buxom than her own boyish slenderness—and her cinch-waisted costume accented this. Her eyes were a bright blue, shining above a straight nose and wide-mouthed face.

"You've hurt yourself." Camilla ran her fingers tenderly along the bruises that marred her ribs and legs.

"There was a struggle. And I fell in the darkness—I don't know how many times."

"And you've cut yourself." Camilla lifted the other girl's black hair away from her neck. "Here on your shoulders and throat. But I don't believe it's anything to worry about." Her fingers carefully touched the livid scrapes. "Are you certain there isn't someone whom we should let know of your safe whereabouts?"

"There is no one who would care. I am alone."

"Poor Cassilda."

"All I want is to sleep," she murmured. The warm bath was easing the ache from her flesh, leaving her deliciously sleepy.

Camilla left her, to return with large towels. The maid helped her from the tub, wrapping her in one towel as she dried her with another. She felt faint with drowsiness, allowed herself to relax against the blonde girl. Camilla was very strong, supporting her easily as she towelled her small breasts. Camilla's fingers found the parting of her thighs, lingered, then returned again in a less than casual touch.

Her dark eyes were wide as she stared into Camilla's luminous blue gaze, but she felt too pleasurably relaxed to object when the maid's touch became more intimate. Her breath caught, and held.

"You're very warm, Cassilda."

"Hurry, Camilla." Mrs. Castaigne spoke from the doorway. "The poor child is about to drop. Help her into her nightdress."

Past wondering, she lifted her arms to let Camilla drape the beribboned lawn nightdress over her head and to her ankles. In another moment she was being ushered into a bedroom, furnished in the fashion of the rest of the house, and to an ornate brass bed whose mattress swallowed her up like a wave of foam. She felt the quilts drawn over her, sensed their presence hovering over her, and then she slipped into a deep sleep of utter exhaustion.

"Is there no one?"

"Nothing at all."

"Of course. How else could she be here? She is ours."

Her dreams were troubled by formless fears—deeply disturbing as experienced, yet their substance was already forgotten when she awoke at length on the echo of her outcry. She stared about her anxiously, uncertain where she was. Her disorientation was the same as when she awakened after receiving shock, only this place wasn't a ward, and the woman who entered the room wasn't one of her wardens.

"Good morning, Cassilda." The maid drew back the curtains to let long shadows streak across the room. "I should say, good evening, as it's almost that time. You've slept throughout the day, poor dear."

Cassilda? Yes, that was she. Memory came tumbling back in a confused jumble. She raised herself from her pillows and looked about the bedchamber she had been too tired to examine before. It was distinctly a woman's room—a young woman's—and she remembered that it had been Mrs. Castaigne's daughter's room. It scarcely seemed to have been unused for very long: the brass bed was brightly polished, the walnut of the wardrobe, the chests of drawers and the dressing table made a rich glow, and the gay pastels of the curtains and wallpaper offset the gravity of the high, tinned ceiling and parquetry floor. Small oriental rugs and pillows upon the chairs and chaise longue made bright points of color. Again she thought of a movie set, for the room was altogether lacking in anything modern. She knew very little about antiques, but she guessed that the style of furnishings must go back before the First World War.

Camilla was arranging a single red rose in a crystal bud vase upon the dressing table. She caught her gaze in the mirror. "Did you sleep well, Cassilda? I thought I heard you cry out, just as I knocked."

"A bad dream, I suppose. But I slept well. I don't, usually." They had made her take pills to sleep.

"Are you awake, Cassilda? I thought I heard your voices." Mrs. Castaigne smiled from the doorway and crossed to her bed. She was dressed much the same as the night before.

"I didn't mean to sleep so long," she apologized.

"Poor child! I shouldn't wonder that you slept so, after your dreadful ordeal. Do you feel strong enough to take a little soup?"

"I really must be going. I can't impose any further."

"I won't hear any more of that, my dear. Of course you'll stay with us until you're feeling stronger." Mrs. Castaigne sat beside her on the bed, placed a cold hand against her brow. "Why, Cassilda, your face is simply aglow. I do hope you haven't taken a fever. Look, your hands are positively trembling!"

"I feel all right." In fact, she did not. She did feel as if she were running a fever, and her muscles were so sore that she wasn't sure she could walk. The trembling didn't concern her: the injections they gave her every two weeks made her shake, so they gave her little pills to stop the shaking. Now she didn't have those pills, but since it was time again for another shot, the injection and its side effects would soon wear off.

"I'm going to bring you some tonic, dear. And Camilla will bring you some good nourishing soup, which you must try to take. Poor Cassilda, if we don't nurse you carefully, I'm afraid you may fall dangerously ill."

"But I can't be such a nuisance to you," she protested, as a matter of form. "I really must be going."

"Where to, dear child?" Mrs. Castaigne held her hands gravely. "Have you someplace else to go? Is there someone you wish us to inform of your safety?"

"No," she admitted, trying to make everything sound right. "I've no place to go; there's no one who matters. I was on my way down the coast, hoping to find a job during the resort season. I know one or two old girlfriends who could put me up until I get settled."

"See there. Then there's no earthly reason why you can't just stay here until you're feeling strong again. Why, perhaps I might find a position for you myself. But we shall discuss these things later, when you're feeling well. For the moment, just settle back on your pillow and let us help you get well."

Mrs. Castaigne bent over her, kissed her on the forehead. Her lips were cool. "How lovely you are, Cassilda," she smiled, patting her hand.

She smiled back, and returned the other woman's firm grip. She'd seen no sign of a television or radio here, and an old eccentric like Mrs. Castaigne probably didn't even read the newspapers. Even if Mrs. Castaigne had heard about the bus wreck, she plainly was too overjoyed at having a visitor to break her lonely routine to concern herself with a possible escapee—assuming they hadn't just listed her as drowned. She couldn't have hoped for a better place to hide out until things cooled off.

The tonic had a bitter licorice taste and made her drowsy, so that she fell asleep not long after Camilla carried away her tray. Despite her long sleep throughout that day, fever and exhaustion drew her back down again—although her previous sleep robbed this one of restful oblivion. Again came troubled dreams, this time cutting more harshly into her consciousness.

She dreamed of Dr. Archer—her stern face and mannish shoulders craning over her bed. Her wrists and ankles were fixed to each corner of the bed by padded leather cuffs. Dr. Archer was speaking to her in a scolding tone, while her wardens were pulling up her skirt, dragging down her panties. A syringe gleamed in Dr. Archer's hand, and there was a sharp stinging in her buttock.

She was struggling again, but to no avail. Dr. Archer was shouting at her, and a stout nurse was tightening the last few buckles of the straitjacket that bound her arms to her chest in a loveless hug. The straps were so tight she could hardly draw breath, and while she could not understand what Dr. Archer was saying, she recognized the spurting needle that Dr. Archer thrust into her.

She was strapped tightly to the narrow bed, her eyes staring at the grey ceiling as they wheeled her through the corridors to Dr. Archer's special room. Then they stopped; they were there, and Dr. Archer was bending over her again. Then came the sting in her arm as they penetrated her veins, the helpless headlong rush of the drug—*and Dr. Archer smiles and turns to her machine, and the current blasts into her tightly strapped skull and her body arches and strains against the restraints and her scream strangles against the rubber gag clenched in her teeth.*

But the face that looks into hers now is not Dr. Archer's, and the hands that shake her are not cruel.

"Cassilda! Cassilda! Wake up! It's only a nightmare!"

Camilla's blonde-and-blue face finally focused into her awakening vision.

"Only a nightmare," Camilla reassured her. "Poor darling." The hands that held her shoulders lifted to smooth her black hair from her eyes, to cup her face. Camilla bent over her, kissed her gently on her dry lips.

"What is it?" Mrs. Castaigne, wearing her nightdress and carrying a candle, came anxiously into the room.

"Poor Cassilda has had bad dreams." Camilla told her. "And her face feels ever so warm."

"Dear child!" Mrs. Castaigne set down her candlestick. "She must take some more tonic at once. Perhaps you should sit with her, Camilla, to see that her sleep is untroubled."

"Certainly, madame. I'll just fetch the tonic."

"Please, don't bother . . ." But the room became a vertiginous blur as she tried to sit up. She slumped back and closed her eyes tightly for a moment. Her body *did* feel feverish, her mouth dry, and the trembling when she moved her hand to take the medicine glass was so obvious that Camilla shook her head and held the glass to her lips herself. She swallowed dutifully, wondering how much of this was a reaction to the Prolixin still in her flesh. The injection would soon be wearing off, she knew, for when she smiled back at her nurses, the sharp edges of color were beginning to show once again through the haze the medication drew over her perception.

"I'll be all right soon," she promised them.

"Then do try to sleep, darling." Mrs. Castaigne patted her arm. "You must regain your strength. Camilla will be here to watch over you.

"Be certain that the curtains are drawn against any night vapors," she directed her maid. "Call me, if necessary."

"Of course, madame. I'll not leave her side."

She was dreaming again—or dreaming still.

Darkness surrounded her like a black leather mask, and her body shook with uncontrollable spasms. Her naked flesh was slick with chill sweat, although her mouth was burning dry. She moaned and tossed—striving to awaken order from out of the damp blackness, but the blackness only embraced her with smothering tenacity.

Cold lips were crushing her own, thrusting a cold tongue into her feverish mouth, bruising the skin of her throat. Fingers, slender and strong, caressed her breasts, held her nipples to hungry lips. Her hands thrashed about, touched smooth flesh. It came to her that her eyes were indeed wide open, that the darkness was so profound she could no more than sense the presence of other shapes close beside her.

Her own movements were languid, dreamlike. Through the spasms that racked her flesh, she became aware of a perverse thrill of ecstasy. Her fingers brushed somnolently against the cool flesh that crouched over her, with no more purpose or strength than the drifting limbs of a drowning victim.

A compelling lassitude bound her, even as the blackness blinded her. She seemed to be drifting away, apart from her body, apart from her dream, into deeper, even deeper darkness. The sensual arousal that lashed her lost reality against the lethargy and fever that held her physically, and rising out of the eroticism of her delirium shrilled whispers of underlying revulsion and terror.

One pair of lips imprisoned her mouth and throat now, sucking at her breath, while other lips crept down across her breasts, hovered upon her navel, then pounced upon the opening of her thighs. Her breath caught in a shudder, was sucked away by the lips that held her mouth, as the coldness began to creep into her burning flesh.

She felt herself smothering, unable to draw breath, so that her body arched in panic, her limbs thrashed aimlessly. Her efforts to break away were as ineffectual as was her struggle to awaken. The lips that stole her breath released her, but only for a moment. In the darkness she felt other flesh pinion her tossing body, move against her with cool strength. Chill fire tormented her loins, and as she opened her mouth to cry out, or to sigh, smooth thighs pressed down onto her cheeks, and coldness gripped her breath. Mutely, she obeyed the needs that commanded her, that overwhelmed her, and through the darkness blindly flowed her silent scream of ecstasy and of horror.

Cassilda awoke.

Sunlight spiked into her room—the colored panes creating a false prism effect. Camilla, who had been adjusting the curtains, turned and smiled at the sound of her movement.

"Good morning, Cassilda. Are you feeling better this morning?"

"A great deal better." Cassilda returned her smile. "I feel as if I'd slept for days." She frowned slightly, suddenly uncertain.

Camilla touched her forehead. "Your fever has left you; Mrs.

Castaigne will be delighted to learn that. You've slept away most of yesterday and all through last night. Shall I bring your break-fast tray now?"

"Please—I'm famished. But I really think I should be getting up."

"After breakfast, if you wish. And now I'll inform madame that you're feeling much better."

Mrs. Castaigne appeared as the maid was clearing away the breakfast things. "How very much better you look today, Cas-silda. Camilla tells me you feel well enough to sit up."

"I really can't play the invalid and continue to impose upon your hospitality any longer. Would it be possible that you might lend me some clothing? My own garments . . ." Cassilda frowned, trying to remember why she had burst in on her benefactress virtually naked.

"Certainly, my dear." Mrs. Castaigne squeezed her shoulder. "You must see if some of my daughter's garments won't fit you. You cannot be very different in size from Constance, I'm certain. Camilla will assist you."

She was lightheaded when first she tried to stand, but Cassilda clung to the brass bedposts until her legs felt strong enough to hold her. The maid was busying herself at the chest of drawers, removing items of clothing from beneath neat coverings of tissue paper. A faint odor of dried rose petals drifted from a sachet beneath the folded garments.

"I do hope you'll overlook it if these are not of the latest mode," Mrs. Castaigne was saying. "It has been some time since Constance was with us here."

"Your daughter is . . . ?"

"Away."

Cassilda declined to intrude further. There was a dressing screen behind which she retired, while Mrs. Castaigne waited upon the chaise longue. Trailing a scent of dried roses from the garments she carried, Camilla joined her behind the screen and helped her out of her nightdress.

There were undergarments of fine silk, airy lace and gauzy pastels. Cassilda found herself puzzled, both from their un-familiarity and at the same time their familiarity, and while her thoughts struggled with the mystery, her hands seemed to dress her body with practiced movements. First the chemise, knee length and trimmed with light lace and ribbons. Seated upon a chair, she drew on pale stockings of patterned silk, held at mid-thigh by beribboned garters. Then silk knickers, open front and back and tied at the waist, trimmed with lace and ruching where they flared below her stocking tops. A frilled petticoat fell almost to her ankles.

"I won't need that," Cassilda protested. Camilla had presented her with a boned corset of white-and-sky *broche.*

"Nonsense, my dear," Mrs. Castaigne directed, coming around the dressing screen to oversee. "You may think of me as old fashioned, but I insist that you not ruin your figure."

Cassilda submitted, suddenly wondering why she had thought anything out of the ordinary about it. She hooked the straight busk together in front, while Camilla gathered the laces at the back. The maid tugged sharply at the laces, squeezing out her breath. Cassilda bent forward and steadied herself against the back of the chair, as Camilla braced a knee against the small of her back, pulling the laces as tight as possible before tying them. Once her corset was secured, she drew over it a camisole of white cotton lace trimmed with ribbon, matching her petticoat. Somewhat dizzy, Cassilda sat stiffly before the dressing table, while the maid brushed out her long, black hair and gathered it in a loose knot atop her head, pinning it in place with tortoise-shell combs. Opening the wardrobe, Camilla found her a pair of shoes with high heels that mushroomed outward at the bottom, which fit her easily.

"How lovely, Cassilda!" Mrs. Castaigne approved. "One would scarcely recognize you as the poor drowned thing that came out of the night!"

Cassilda stood up and examined herself in the full-length dressing mirror. It was as if she looked upon a stranger, and yet she knew she looked upon herself. The corset constricted her waist and forced her slight figure into an "S" curve—hips back, bust forward—imparting an unexpected opulence, further enhanced by the gauzy profusion of lace and silk. Her face, dark-eyed and finely boned, returned her gaze watchfully from beneath a lustrous pile of black hair. She touched herself, almost in wonder, almost believing that the reflection in the mirror was a photograph of someone else.

Camilla selected for her a long-sleeved linen shirtwaist, buttoned at the cuffs and all the way to her throat, then helped her into a skirt of some darker material that fell away from her cinched waist to her ankles. Cassilda studied herself in the mirror, while the maid fussed about her.

I look like someone in an old illustration—a Gibson girl, she thought, then puzzled at her thought.

Through the open window she could hear the vague noises of the city, and for the first time she realized that intermingled with these familiar sounds was the clatter of horses' hooves upon the brick pavement.

"You simply must not say anything more about leaving us, Cassilda," Mrs. Castaigne insisted, laying a hand upon the girl's knee as she leaned toward her confidentially.

Beside her on the settee, Cassilda felt the pressure of her touch through the rustling layers of petticoat. It haunted her, this flowing whisper of sound that came with her every movement, for it seemed at once strange and again familiar—a shivery sigh of silk against silk, like the whisk of dry snow sliding across stone. She smiled, holding her teacup with automatic poise, and wondered that such little, commonplace sensations should seem at all out of the ordinary to her. Even the rigid embrace of her corset seemed quite familiar to her now, so that she sat gracefully at ease, listening to her benefactress, while a part of her thoughts stirred in uneasy wonder.

"You have said yourself that you have no immediate prospects," Mrs. Castaigne continued. "I shouldn't have to remind you of the dangers the city holds for unattached young women. You were extremely fortunate in your escape from those white slavers who had abducted you. Without family or friends to question your disappearance—well, I shan't suggest what horrible fate awaited you."

Cassilda shivered at the memory of her escape—a memory as formless and uncertain, beyond her *need* to escape, as that of her life prior to her abduction. She had made only vague replies to Mrs. Castaigne's gentle questioning, nor was she at all certain which fragments of her story were half-truths, or lies.

Of one thing she was certain beyond all doubt: the danger from which she had fled awaited her beyond the shelter of this house.

"It has been so lonely here since Constance went away," Mrs. Castaigne was saying. "Camilla is a great comfort to me, but nonetheless she has her household duties to occupy her, and I have often considered engaging a companion. I should be only too happy if you would consent to remain with us in this posi-tion—at least for the present time."

"You're much too kind! Of course I'll stay."

"I promise you that your duties shall be no more onerous than to provide amusements for a rather old-fashioned lady of retiring disposition. I hope it won't prove too dull for you, my dear."

"It suits my own temperament perfectly," Cassilda assured her. "I am thoroughly content to follow quiet pursuits within doors."

"Wonderful!" Mrs. Castaigne took her hands. "Then it's set-tled. I know Camilla will be delighted to have another young spirit about the place. And you may relieve her of some of her tasks."

"What shall I do?" Cassilda begged her, overjoyed at her good fortune.

"Would you read to me, please, my dear? I find it so relaxing to the body and so stimulating to the mind. I've taken up far too much of Camilla's time from her chores, having her read to me for hours on end."

"Of course." Cassilda returned Camilla's smile as she entered the sitting room to collect the tea things. From her delight, it was evident that the maid had been listening from the hallway. "What would you like for me to read to you?"

"That book over there beneath the lamp." Mrs. Castaigne indi-cated a volume bound in yellow cloth. "It is a recent drama—and a most curious work, as you shall quickly see. Camilla was read-ing it to me on the night you came to us."

Taking up the book, Cassilda again experienced a strange sense of unaccountable *déjà vu*, and she wondered where she might previously have read *The King in Yellow*, if indeed she ever had.

"I believe we are ready to begin the second act," Mrs. Castaigne told her.

Cassilda was reading in bed when Camilla knocked tentatively at her door. She set aside her book with an almost furtive movement. *"Entrez vous."*

"I was afraid you might already be asleep," the maid explained, "but then I saw light beneath your door. I'd forgotten to bring you your tonic before retiring."

Camilla, *en déshabille*, carried in the medicine glass on a silver tray. Her fluttering lace and pastels seemed a pretty contrast to the black maid's uniform she ordinarily wore.

"I wasn't able to go to sleep just yet," Cassilda confessed, sitting up in bed. "I was reading."

Camilla handed her the tonic. "Let me see. Ah, yes. What a thoroughly wicked book to be reading in bed!"

"Have you read *The King in Yellow*?"

"I have read it through aloud to madame, and more than once. It is a favorite of hers."

"It is sinful and more than sinful to imbue such decadence with so compelling a fascination. I cannot imagine that anyone could have allowed it to be published. The author must have been mad to pen such thoughts."

"And yet, you read it."

Cassilda made a place for her on the edge of the bed. "Its fascination is too great a temptation to resist. I wanted to read further after Mrs. Castaigne bade me good night."

"It was Constance's book." Camilla huddled close beside her against the pillows. "Perhaps that is why madame cherishes it so."

Cassilda opened the yellow-bound volume to the page she had been reading. Camilla craned her blonde head over her shoulder to read with her. She had removed her corset, and her ample figure swelled against her beribboned chemise. Cassilda in her nightdress felt almost scrawny as she compared her own small bosom to the other girl's.

"Is it not strange?" she remarked. "Here in this decadent drama we read of Cassilda and Camilla."

"I wonder if we two are very much like them," Camilla laughed.

"They are such very dear friends."

"And so are we, are we not?"

"I do so want us to be."

"But you haven't read beyond the second act, dear Cassilda. How can you know what may their fate be?"

"Oh, Camilla!" Cassilda leaned her face back against Camilla's perfumed breasts. "Don't tease me so!"

The blonde girl hugged her fiercely, stroking her back. "Poor, lost Cassilda."

Cassilda nestled against her, listening to the heartbeat beneath her cheek. She was feeling warm and sleepy, for all that the book had disturbed her. The tonic always carried her to dreamy oblivion, and it was pleasant to drift to sleep in Camilla's soft embrace.

"Were you and Constance friends?" she wondered.

"We were the very dearest of friends."

"You must miss her very much."

"No longer."

Cassilda sat at the escritoire in her room, writing in the journal she had found there. Her petticoats crowded against the legs of the writing table as she leaned forward to reach the inkwell. From time to time she paused to stare pensively past the open curtains of her window, upon the deepening blue of the evening sky as it met the angled rooftops of the buildings along the waterfront below.

"I think I should feel content here," she wrote. "Mrs. Castaigne is strict in her demands, but I am certain she takes a sincere interest in my own well-being, and that she has only the kindliest regard for me. My duties during the day are of the lightest nature and consist primarily of reading to Mrs. Castaigne or of singing at the piano while she occupies herself with her needlework, and in all other ways making myself companionable to her in our simple amusements.

"I have offered to assist Camilla at her chores, but Mrs.

Castaigne will not have it that I perform other than the lightest household tasks. Camilla is a very dear friend to me, and her sweet attentions easily distract me from what might otherwise become a tedium of sitting about the house day to day. Nonetheless, I have no desire to leave my situation here, nor to adventure into the streets outside the house. We are not in an especially attractive section of the city here, being at some remove from the shops and in a district given over to waterfront warehouses and commercial establishments. We receive no visitors, other than the tradesmen who supply our needs, nor is Mrs. Castaigne of a disposition to wish to seek out the society of others.

"Withal, my instincts suggest that Mrs. Castaigne has sought the existence of a recluse out of some very great emotional distress which has robbed life of its interests for her. It is evident from the attention and instruction she has bestowed upon me that she sees in me a reflection of her daughter, and I am convinced that it is in the loss of Constance where lies the dark secret of her self-imposed withdrawal from the world. I am sensible of the pain Mrs. Castaigne harbors within her breast, for the subject of her daughter's absence is never brought into our conversations, and for this reason I have felt loath to question her, although I am certain that this is the key to the mystery that holds us in this house."

Cassilda concluded her entry with the date: June 7th, 189—

She frowned in an instant's consternation. What *was* the date? How silly. She referred to a previous day's entry, then completed the date. For a moment she turned idly back through her journal, smiling faintly at the many pages of entries that filled the diary, each progressively dated, each penned in the same neat hand as the entry she had just completed.

Cassilda sat at her dressing table in her room. It was night, and she had removed her outer clothing preparatory to retiring. She gazed at her reflection—the gauzy paleness of her chemise, stockings and knickers was framed against Camilla's black maid's uniform as the blonde girl stood behind her, brushing out her dark hair.

Upon the dressing table she had spread out the contents of a tin box she had found in one of the drawers, and she and Camilla had been looking over them as she prepared for bed. There were paper dolls, valentines and greeting cards, illustrations clipped from magazines, a lovely cutout of a swan. She also found a crystal ball that rested upon an ebony cradle. Within the crystal sphere was a tiny house, covered with snow, with trees and a frozen lake and a young girl playing. When Cassilda picked it up, the snow stirred faintly in the transparent fluid that filled the globe. She turned the crystal sphere upside down for a moment, then quickly righted it, and a snowstorm drifted down about the tiny house.

"How wonderful it would be to dwell forever in a crystal fairyland just like the people in this little house," Cassilda remarked, peering into the crystal ball.

Something else seemed to stir within the swirling snowflakes, she thought, but when the snow had settled once more, the tableau was unchanged. No: there was a small mound, there beside the child at play, that she was certain she had not seen before. Cassilda overturned the crystal globe once again, and peered more closely. There it was. Another tiny figure spinning amidst the snowflakes. A second girl. She must have broken loose from the tableau. The tiny figure drifted to rest upon the frozen lake, and the snowflakes once more covered her from view.

"Where is Constance Castaigne?" Cassilda asked.

"Constance ... became quite ill," Camilla told her carefully. "She was always subject to nervous attacks. One night she suffered one of her fits, and she ..."

"Camilla!" Mrs. Castaigne's voice from the doorway was stern. "You know how I despise gossip—especially idle gossip concerning another's misfortunes."

The maid's face was downcast. "I'm very sorry, madame. I meant no mischief."

The older woman scowled as she crossed the room. Cassilda wondered if she meant to strike the maid. "Being sorry does not pardon the offense of a wagging tongue. Perhaps a lesson in behavior will improve your manners in the future. Go at once to your room."

"Please, madame ..."

"Your insolence begins to annoy me, Camilla."

"Please, don't be harsh with her!" Cassilda begged, as the maid hurried from the room. "She was only answering my question." Standing behind the seated girl, Mrs. Castaigne placed her hands upon her shoulders and smiled down at her. "An innocent question, my dear. However, the subject is extremely painful to me, and Camilla well knows the distress it causes me to hear it brought up. I shall tell you this now, and that shall end the matter. My daughter suffered a severe attack of brain fever. She is confined in a mental sanatorium."

Cassilda crossed her arms over her breasts to place her hands upon the older woman's wrists. "I'm terribly sorry."

"I'm certain you can appreciate how sorely this subject distresses me." Mrs. Castaigne smiled, meeting her eyes in the mirror.

"I shan't mention it again."

"Of course not. And now, my dear, you must hurry and make yourself ready for bed. Too much exertion so soon after your illness will certainly bring about a relapse. Hurry along now, while I fetch your tonic."

"I'm sure I don't need any more medicine. Sometimes I think it must bring on evil dreams."

"Now don't argue, Cassilda dear." The fingers on her shoulders tightened their grip. "You must do as you're told. You can't very well perform your duties as companion if you lie about ill all day, now can you? And you *do* want to stay."

"Certainly!" Cassilda thought this last had not been voiced as a question. "I want to do whatever you ask."

"I know you do, Cassilda. And I only want to make you into a perfect young lady. Now let me help you into your night things."

Cassilda opened her eyes into complete darkness that swirled about her in an invisible current. She sat upright in her bed, fighting back the vertigo that she had decided must come from the tonic they gave her nightly. Something had wakened her. Another bad dream? She knew she often suffered them, even though the next morning she was unable to recall them. Was she about to be sick? She was certain that the tonic made her feel drugged.

Her wide eyes stared sleeplessly at the darkness. She knew

sleep would not return easily, for she feared to lapse again into the wicked dreams that disturbed her rest and left her lethargic throughout the next day. She could not even be certain that this, now, might not be another of those dreams.

In the absolute silence of the house, she could hear her heart pulse, her breath stir anxiously.

There was another sound, more distant, and of almost the same monotonous regularity. She thought she heard a woman's muffled sobbing.

Mrs. Castaigne, she thought. The talk of her daughter had upset her terribly. Underscoring the sobbing came a sharp, rhythmic crack, as if a rocker sounded against a loose board.

Cassilda felt upon the nightstand beside her bed. Her fingers found matches. Striking one, she lit the candle that was there— her actions entirely automatic. Stepping down out of her bed, she caught up the candlestick and moved cautiously out of her room.

In the hallway, she listened for the direction of the sound. Her candle forced a small nimbus of light against the enveloping darkness of the old house. Cassilda shivered and drew her nightdress closer about her throat; its gauzy lace and ribbons were no barrier to the cold darkness that swirled about her island of candlelight.

The sobbing seemed no louder as she crept down the hallway toward Mrs. Castaigne's bedroom. There, the bedroom door was open, and within was only silent darkness.

"Mrs. Castaigne?" Cassilda called softly, without answer.

The sound of muffled sobbing continued, and now seemed to come from overhead. Cassilda followed its sound to the end of the hallway, where a flight of stairs led to the maid's quarters in the attic. Cassilda paused fearfully at the foot of the stairway, thrusting her candle without effect against the darkness above. She could still hear the sobbing, but the other sharp sound had ceased. Her head seemed to float in the darkness as she listened, but, despite her dreamlike lethargy, she knew her thoughts raced too wildly now for sleep. Catching up the hem of her nightdress, Cassilda cautiously ascended the stairs.

Once she gained the landing above, she could see the blade of yellow light that shone beneath the door to Camilla's room, and from within came the sounds that had summoned her. Quickly

Cassilda crossed to the maid's room and knocked softly upon the door.

"Camilla? It's Cassilda. Are you all right?"

Again no answer, although she sensed movement within. The muffled sobs continued.

Cassilda tried the doorknob, found it was not locked. She pushed the door open and stepped inside, dazzled a moment by the bright glare of the oil lamp.

Camilla, dressed only in her corset and undergarments, stood bent over the foot of her bed. Her ankles were lashed to the base of either post, her wrists tied together and stretched forward by a rope fixed to the headboard. Exposed by the open-style knickers, her buttocks were crisscrossed with red welts. She turned her head to look at Cassilda, and the other girl saw that Camilla's cries were gagged by a complicated leather bridle strapped about her head.

"Come in, Cassilda, since you wish to join us," said Mrs. Castaigne from behind her. Cassilda heard her close the door and lock it, before the girl had courage enough to turn around. Mrs. Castaigne wore no more clothing than did Camilla, and she switched her riding crop anticipatorily. Looking from mistress to maid, Cassilda saw that both pairs of eyes glowed alike with the lusts of unholy pleasure.

For a long interval Cassilda resisted awakening, hovering in a languor of unformed dreaming despite the rising awareness that she still slept. When she opened her eyes at last, she stared at the candlestick on her nightstand, observing without comprehension that the candle had burned down to a misshapen nub of cold wax. Confused memories came to her, slipping away again as her mind sought to grasp them. She had dreamed . . .

Her mouth seemed bruised and sour with a chemical taste that was not the usual anisette aftertaste of the tonic, and her limbs ached as if sore from too strenuous exercise the day before. Cassilda hoped she was not going to have a relapse of the fever that had stricken her after she had fled the convent that stormy night so many weeks ago.

She struggled for a moment with that memory. The sisters in

black robes and white aprons had intended to wall her up alive in her cell because she had yielded to the temptation of certain unspeakable desires ... The memory clouded and eluded her, like a fragment of some incompletely remembered book.

There were too many elusive memories, memories that died unheard ... Had she not read that? *The King in Yellow* lay open upon her nightstand. Had she been reading, then fallen asleep to such dreams of depravity? But dreams, like memories, faded miragelike whenever she touched them, leaving only tempting images to beguile her.

Forcing her cramped muscles to obey her, Cassilda climbed from her bed. Camilla was late with her tray this morning, and she might as well get dressed to make herself forget the dreams. As she slipped out of her nightdress, she looked at her reflection in the full length dressing mirror.

The marks were beginning to fade now, but the still painful welts made red streaks across the white flesh of her shoulders, back and thighs. Fragments of repressed nightmare returned as she stared in growing fear. She reached out her hands, touching the reflection in wonder. There were bruises on her wrists, and unbidden came a memory of her weight straining against the cords that bound her wrists to a hook from an attic rafter.

Behind her, in the mirror, Mrs. Castaigne ran the tip of her tongue along her smiling lips.

"Up and about already, Cassilda? I hope you've made up your mind to be a better young lady today. You were most unruly last night."

Her brain reeling under the onrush of memories, Cassilda stared mutely. Camilla, obsequious in her maid's costume, her smile a cynical sneer, entered carrying a complex leather harness of many straps and buckles.

"I think we must do something more to improve your posture, Cassilda," Mrs. Castaigne purred. "You may think me a bit old-fashioned, but I insist that a young lady's figure must be properly trained if she is to look her best."

"What are you doing to me?" Cassilda wondered, feeling panic.

"Only giving you the instruction a young lady must have if

she is to serve as my companion. And you *do* want to be a proper young lady, don't you, Cassilda?"

"I'm leaving this house. Right now."

"We both know why you can't. Besides, you don't really want to go. You quite enjoy our cozy little *menage à trois.*"

"You're deranged."

"And you're one to talk, dear Cassilda." Mrs. Castaigne's smile was far more menacing than any threatened blow. "I think, Camilla, the scold's bridle will teach this silly girl to mind that wicked tongue."

A crash of thunder broke her out of her stupor. Out of reflex, she tried to dislodge the hard rubber ball that filled her mouth, choked on saliva when she failed. Half strangled by the gag strapped over her face, she strained in panic to sit up. Her wrists and ankles were held fast, and, as her eyes dilated in unreasoning fear, a flash of lightning beyond the window rippled down upon her spread-eagled body, held to the brass bedposts by padded leather cuffs.

Images, too chaotic and incomprehensive to form coherent memory, exploded in bright shards from her shattered mind.

She was being forced into a straitjacket, flung into a padded cell, and they were bricking up the door . . . no, it was some bizarre corset device, forcing her neck back, crushing her abdomen, arms laced painfully into a single glove at her back . . . Camilla was helping her into a gown of satin and velvet and lace, and then into a hood of padded leather that they buckled over her head as they led her to the gallows . . . and the nurses held her down while Dr. Archer penetrated her with a grotesque syringe of vile poison, and Mrs. Castaigne forced the yellow tonic down her throat as she pinned her face between her thighs . . . and Camilla's lips dripped blood as she rose from her kiss, and her fangs were hypodermic needles, injecting poison, sucking life . . . they were wheeling her into the torture chamber, where Dr. Archer awaited her ("It's only a frontal lobotomy, just to relieve the pressure on these two diseased lobes.") and plunges the bloody scalpel deep between her thighs . . . and they were strapping her into the metal chair in the death cell, shoving the rubber gag between her teeth and blinding her with the leather hood, and Dr. Archer grasps the thick black handle of the switch and pulls it down and sends the current ripping through her nerves . . . she stands naked in shackles before the black-masked judges, and Dr. Archer gloatingly exposes the giant needle ("Just an injection of my elixir, and she's quite safe for two more weeks.") . . . and the nurses in rubber aprons hold her writhing upon the altar, while Dr. Archer adjusts the hangman's mask and thrusts the electrodes into her breast . . . ("Just a shot of my prolixir, and she's quite sane for two more weeks.") . . . then the judge in wig and mask and black robe smacks down the braided whip and screams "She must be locked away forever!" . . . she tears away the mask and Mrs. Castaigne screams "She must be locked in here forever!" . . . she tears away the mask and her own face screams "She must be locked in you forever!" . . . then Camilla and Mrs. Castaigne lead her back into her cell, and they strap her to her bed and force the rubber gag between her teeth, and Mrs. Castaigne adjusts her surgeon's mask while Camilla clamps the electrodes to her nipples, and the current rips into her and her brain screams and screams unheard . . . "I think she no longer needs to be drugged." Mrs. Castaigne smiled, and her lips are bright with blood. "She's one of us now. She always has been one with us" . . . and they leave her alone in darkness on the promise "We'll begin again tomorrow" and the echo, "She'll be good for two more weeks."

She moaned and writhed upon the soiled sheets, struggling to escape the images that spurted like foetid purulence from her tortured brain. With the next explosive burst of lightning, her naked body lifted in a convulsive arc from the mattress, and her scream against the gag was like the first agonized outcry of the newborn.

The spasm passed. She dropped back limply onto the sodden mattress. Slippery with sweat and blood, her relaxed hand slid the rest of the way out of the padded cuff. Quietly, in the darkness, she considered her free hand—suddenly calm, for she knew she had slipped wrist restraints any number of times before this.

Beneath the press of the storm, the huge house lay in darkness and silence. With her free hand she unbuckled the other wrist cuff, then the straps that held the gag in place, and the restraints that pinned her ankles. Her tread no louder than a phantom's, she glided from bed and crossed the room. A flicker of lightning revealed shabby furnishings and a disordered array of fetishist garments and paraphernalia, but she threw open the window and looked down upon the black waters of the lake and saw the cloud waves breaking upon the base of the cliff, and when she turned away from that vision her eyes knew what they beheld and her smile was that of a lamia.

Wraithlike she drifted through the dark house, passing along the silent rooms and hallways and stairs, and when she reached the kitchen she found what she knew was the key to unlock the dark mystery that bound her here. She closed her hand upon it, and her fingers remembered its feel.

Camilla's face was tight with sudden fear as she awakened at the clasp of fingers closed upon her lips, but she made no struggle as she stared at the carving knife that almost touched her eyes.

"What happened to Constance?" The fingers relaxed to let her whisper, but the knife did not waver.

"She had a secret lover. One night she crept through the sitting room window and ran away with him. Mrs. Castaigne showed her no mercy."

"Sleep now," she told Camilla, and kissed her tenderly as she freed her with a swift motion that her hand remembered.

In the darkness of Mrs. Castaigne's room she paused beside the motionless figure on the bed.

"Mother?"

"Yes, Constance?"

"I've come home."

"You're dead."

"I remembered the way back."

And she showed her the key and opened the way

It only remained for her to go. She could no longer find shelter in this house. She must leave as she had entered.

She left the knife. That key had served its purpose. Through the hallways she returned, in the darkness her bare feet sometimes treading upon rich carpets, sometimes dust and fallen plaster. Her naked flesh tingled with the blood that had freed her soul.

She reached the sitting room and looked upon the storm that lashed the night beyond. For one gleam of lightning the room seemed festooned with torn wallpaper; empty wine bottles littered the floor and dingy furnishings. The flickering mirage passed, and she saw that the room was exactly as she remembered. She must leave by the window.

There was a tapping at the window.

She started, then recoiled in horror as another repressed memory escaped into consciousness.

The figure that had pursued her through the darkness on that night she had sought refuge here. It waited for her now at the window. Half-glimpsed before, she saw it now fully revealed in the glare of the lightning.

Moisture glistened darkly upon its rippling and exaggerated musculature. Its uncouth head and shoulders hunched forward bullishly; its face was distorted with insensate lust and drooling madness. A grotesque phallus swung between its misshapen legs—serpentine, possessed of its own life and volition. Like an obscene worm, it stretched blindly toward her, blood oozing from its toothless maw.

She raised her hands to ward it off, and the monstrosity pawed at the window, mocking her every terrified movement as it waited there on the other side of the rain-slick glass.

The horror was beyond enduring. There was another casement window to the corner sitting room, the one that overlooked the waters of the river. She spun about and lunged toward it—noticing from the corner of her eye that the creature outside also whirled about, sensing her intent, flung itself toward the far window to forestall her.

The glass of the casement shattered, even as its blubbery hands stretched out toward her. There was no pain in that release, only a dreamlike vertigo as she plunged into the greyness and the rain. Then the water and the darkness received her falling body, and she set out again into the night, letting the current carry her, she knew not where.

*

"A few personal effects remain to be officially disposed of, Dr. Archer—since there's no one to claim them. It's been long enough now since the bus accident, and we'd like to be able to close the files on this catastrophe."

"Let's have a look." The psychiatrist opened the box of personal belongings. There wasn't much; there never was in such cases, and had there been anything worth stealing, it was already unofficially disposed of.

"They still haven't found a body," the ward superintendent wondered. "Do you suppose . . . ?"

"Callous as it sounds, I rather hope not," Dr. Archer confided. "This patient was a paranoid schizophrenic—and dangerous."

"Seemed quiet enough on the ward."

"Thanks to a lot of ECT—and to depot phenothiazines. Without regular therapy, the delusional system would quickly regain control, and the patient would become frankly murderous."

There were a few toiletry items and some articles of clothing, a brassiere and pantyhose. "I guess send this over to Social Services. These shouldn't be allowed on a locked ward—" the psychiatrist pointed to the nylons "—nor these smut magazines."

"They always find some way to smuggle the stuff in," the ward superintendent sighed, "and I've been working here at Coastal State since back before the War. What about these other books?"

Dr. Archer considered the stack of dog-eared gothic romance novels. "Just return these to the Patients' Library. What's this one?"

Beneath the paperbacks lay a small hardcover volume, bound in yellow cloth, somewhat soiled from age.

"Out of the Patients' Library too, I suppose. People have donated all sorts of books over the years, and if the patients don't tear them up, they just stay on the shelves forever."

"*The King in Yellow,*" Dr. Archer read from the spine, opening the book. On the flyleaf a name was penned in a graceful script: *Constance Castaigne.*

"Perhaps the name of a patient who left it here," the superintendent suggested. "Around the turn of the century this was a private sanitarium. Somehow, though, the name seems to ring a distant bell."

"Let's just be sure this isn't vintage porno."

"I can't be sure—maybe something the old-timers talked about when I first started here. I seem to remember there was some famous scandal involving one of the wealthy families in the city. A murderess, was it? And something about a suicide, or was it an escape? I can't recall . . ."

"Harmless nineteenth-century romantic nonsense," Dr. Archer concluded. "Send it on back to the library."

The psychiatrist glanced at a last few lines before closing the book:

Cassilda: I tell you, I am lost! Utterly lost!

Camilla (terrified herself): You have seen the King . . . ?

Cassilda: And he has taken from me the power to direct or to escape my dreams.

BEYOND ANY MEASURE

I

"In the dream I find myself alone in a room. I hear musical chimes—a sort of music-box tune—and I look around to see where the sound is coming from.

"I'm in a bedroom. Heavy curtains close off the windows, and it's quite dark, but I can sense that the furnishings are entirely antique—late Victorian, I think. There's a large four-poster bed, with its curtains drawn. Beside the bed is a small night table upon which a candle is burning. It is from here that the music seems to be coming.

"I walk across the room toward the bed, and as I stand beside it I see a gold watch resting on the night table next to the candle-stick. The music-box tune is coming from the watch, I realize. It's one of those old pocket-watch affairs with a case that opens. The case is open now, and I see that the watch's hands are almost at midnight. I sense that on the inside of the watch case there will be a picture, and I pick up the watch to see whose picture it is.

"The picture is obscured with a red smear. It's fresh blood.

"I look up in sudden fear. From the bed, a hand is pulling aside the curtain.

"That's when I wake up."

"Bravo!" applauded someone.

Lisette frowned momentarily, then realized that the comment was directed toward another of the chattering groups crowded into the gallery. She sipped her champagne; she must be a bit tight, or she'd never have started talking about the dreams.

"What do you think. Dr. Magnus?"

It was the gala reopening of Covent Garden. The venerable fruit, flower and vegetable market, preserved from the dem-olition crew, had been renovated into an airy mall of expensive shops and galleries: "London's new shopping experience." Lisette thought it an unhappy hybrid of born-again Victorian exhibition hall and trendy "shoppes." Let the dead past bury its dead. She wondered what they might make of the old Billingsgate fish market, should SAVE win its fight to preserve that landmark, as now seemed unlikely.

"Is this dream, then, a recurrent one, Miss Seyrig?"

She tried to read interest or skepticism in Dr. Magnus' pale blue eyes. They told her nothing.

"Recurrent enough."

To make me mention it to Danielle, she finished in her thoughts. Danielle Borland shared a flat—she'd stopped terming it an apartment even in her mind—with her in a row of terrace houses in Bloomsbury, within an easy walk of London University. The gallery was Maitland Reddin's project: Danielle was another. Whether Maitland really thought to make a business of it, or only intended to showcase his many friends' not always evident talents was not open to discussion. His gallery in Knightsbridge was cer-tainly successful, if that meant anything.

"How often is that?" Dr. Magnus touched his glass to his blonde-bearded lips. He was drinking only Perrier water, and, at that, was using his glass for little more than to gesture.

"I don't know. Maybe half a dozen times since I can remember. And then, that many again since I came to London."

"You're a student at London University, I believe Danielle said?"

"That's right. In art. I'm over here on fellowship."

Danielle had modelled for an occasional session—Lisette now was certain it was solely from a desire to display her body rather than due to any financial need—and when a muttered profanity at a dropped brush disclosed a common American heritage, the two *émigrés* had rallied at a pub afterward to exchange news and views. Lisette's bed-sit near the Museum was impossible, and Danielle's roommate had just skipped to the Continent with two months' owing. By closing time it was settled.

"How's your glass?"

Danielle, finding them in the crowd, shook her head in mock dismay and refilled Lisette's glass before she could cover it with her hand.

"And you, Dr. Magnus?"

"Quite well, thank you."

"Danielle, let me give you a hand?" Maitland had charmed the two of them into acting as hostesses for his opening.

"Nonsense, darling. When you see me starting to pant with the heat, then call up the reserves. Until then, do keep Dr. Magnus from straying away to the other parties."

Danielle swirled off with her champagne bottle and her smile. The gallery, christened "Such Things May Be" after Richard Burton (*not* Liz Taylor's ex, Danielle kept explaining, and got laughs each time), was ajostle with friends and well-wishers as were most of the shops tonight: private parties with evening dress and champagne, only a scattering of displaced tourists, gaping and photographing. She and Danielle were both wearing slit-to-thigh crepe de Chine evening gowns and could have passed for sisters: Lisette blonde, green-eyed, with a dust of freckles: Danielle light brunette, hazel-eyed, acclimated to the extensive facial makeup London women favored: both tall without seeming coltish, and close enough of a size to wear each other's clothes.

"It must be distressing to have the same nightmare over and again," Dr. Magnus prompted her.

"There have been others as well. Some recurrent, some not. Similar in that I wake up feeling like I've been through the sets of some old Hammer film."

"I gather you were not actually troubled with such nightmares until recently?"

"Not really. Being in London seems to have triggered them. I suppose it's repressed anxieties over being in a strange city." It was bad enough that she'd been taking some of Danielle's pills in order to seek dreamless sleep.

"Is this, then, your first time in London, Miss Seyrig?"

"It is." She added, to seem less the typical American student: "Although my family was English."

"Your parents?"

"My mother's parents were both from London. They emigrated to the States just after World War I."

"Then this must have been rather a bit like coming home for you."

"Not really. I'm the first of our family to go overseas. And I have no memory of Mother's parents. Grandmother Keswicke died the morning I was born." Something Mother never was able to work through emotionally, Lisette added to herself.

"And have you consulted a physician concerning these nightmares?"

"I'm afraid your National Health Service is a bit more than I can cope with." Lisette grimaced at the memory of the night she had tried to explain to a Pakistani intern why she wanted sleeping medications.

She suddenly hoped her words hadn't offended Dr. Magnus, but then, he scarcely looked the type who would approve of socialized medicine. Urbane, perfectly at ease in formal evening attire, he reminded her somewhat of a blonde-bearded Peter Cushing. Enter Christopher Lee, in black cape, she mused, glancing toward the door. For that matter, she wasn't at all certain just what sort of doctor Dr. Magnus might be. Danielle had insisted she talk with him, very likely had insisted that Maitland invite him to the private opening: "The man has such *insight*! And he's written a number of books on dreams and the subconscious—and not just rehashes of Freudian silliness!"

"Are you going to be staying in London for some time, Miss Seyrig?"

"At least until the end of the year."

"Too long a time to wait to see whether these bad dreams will go away once you're back home in San Francisco, don't you agree? It can't be very pleasant for you, and you really should look after yourself."

Lisette made no answer. *She* hadn't told Dr. Magnus she was from San Francisco. So then, Danielle had already talked to him about her.

Dr. Magnus smoothly produced his card, discreetly offered it to her. "I should be most happy to explore this further with you on a professional level, should you so wish."

"I don't really think it's worth . . ."

"Of course it is, my dear. Why otherwise would we be talking? Perhaps next Tuesday afternoon? Is there a convenient time?"

Lisette slipped his card into her handbag. If nothing else, perhaps he could supply her with some barbs or something. "Three?"

"Three it is, then."

II

The passageway was poorly lighted, and Lisette felt a vague sense of dread as she hurried along it, holding the hem of her nightgown away from the gritty filth beneath her bare feet. Peeling scabs of wallpaper blotched the leprous plaster, and, when she held the candle close, the gouges and scratches that patterned the walls with insane graffiti seemed disquietingly non-random. Against the mottled plaster, her figure threw a double shadow: distorted, one crouching forward, the other following.

A full-length mirror panelled one segment of the passageway, and Lisette paused to study her reflection. Her face appeared frightened, her blonde hair in disorder. She wondered at her nightgown—pale, silken, billowing, of an antique mode—not remembering how she came to be wearing it. Nor could she think how it was that she had come to this place.

Her reflection puzzled her. Her hair seemed longer than it should be, trailing down across her breasts. Her finely chiselled features, prominent jawline, straight nose—her face, except the expression, was not hers: lips fuller, more sensual, redder than her lip-gloss, glinted; teeth fine and white. Her green eyes, intense beneath level brows, cat-cruel, yearning.

Lisette released the hem of her gown, raised her fingers to her reflection in wonder. Her fingers passed through the glass, touched the face beyond.

Not a mirror. A doorway. Of a crypt.

The mirror-image fingers that rose to her face twisted in her hair, pulled her face forward. Glass-cold lips bruised her own. The dank breath of the tomb flowed into her mouth.

Dragging herself from the embrace, Lisette felt a scream rip from her throat . . .

. . . And Danielle was shaking her awake.

III

The business card read *Dr. Ingmar Magnus,* followed simply by *Consultations* and a Kensington address. Not Harley Street, at any rate. Lisette considered it for the hundredth time, watching for street names on the corners of buildings as she walked down Kensington Church Street from the Notting Hill Gate station. No clue as to what type of doctor, nor what sort of consultations; wonderfully vague, and just the thing to circumvent licensing laws, no doubt.

Danielle had lent her one of his books to read; *The Self Reborn,* put out by one of those minuscule scholarly publishers clustered about the British Museum. Lisette found it a bewildering *mélange* of occult philosophy and lunatic-fringe theory—all evidently having something to do with reincarnation—and gave it up after the first chapter. She had decided not to keep the appointment, until her nightmare Sunday night had given force to Danielle's insistence.

Lisette wore a loose silk blouse above French designer jeans and ankle-strap sandal-toe high heels. The early summer heat wave now threatened rain, and she would have to run for it if the grey skies made good. She turned into Holland Street, passed the recently closed Equinox bookshop, where Danielle had purchased various works by Aleister Crowley. A series of back streets—she consulted her map of Central London—brought her to a modestly respectable row of nineteenth-century brick houses, now done over into offices and flats. She checked the number on the brass plaque with her card, sucked in her breath and entered.

Lisette hadn't known what to expect. She wouldn't have been surprised, knowing some of Danielle's friends, to have been greeted with clouds of incense, Eastern music, robed initiates. Instead she found a disappointingly mundane waiting room, rather small but expensively furnished, where a pretty Eurasian receptionist took her name and spoke into an intercom. Lisette noted that there was no one else—patients? clients?—in the waiting room. She glanced at her watch and noticed she was several minutes late.

"Please do come in, Miss Seyrig." Dr. Magnus stepped out of his office and ushered her inside. Lisette had seen a psychiatrist briefly a few years before, at her parents' demand, and Dr. Magnus's office suggested the same—from the tasteful, relaxed decor, the shelves of scholarly books, down to the traditional psychoanalyst's couch. She took a chair beside the modern, rather carefully arranged desk, and Dr. Magnus seated himself comfortably in the leather swivel chair behind it.

"I almost didn't come," Lisette began, somewhat aggressively.

"I'm very pleased that you did decide to come." Dr. Magnus smiled reassuringly. "It doesn't require a trained eye to see that something is troubling you. When the unconscious tries to speak to us, it is foolhardy to attempt to ignore its message."

"Meaning that I may be cracking up?"

"I'm sure that must concern you, my dear. However, very often dreams such as yours are evidence of the emergence of a new level of self-awareness—sort of growing pains of the psyche, if you will—and not to be considered a negative experience by any means. They distress you only because you do not understand them—even as a child kept in ignorance through sexual repression is frightened by the changes of puberty. With your cooperation, I hope to help you come to understand the changes of your growing self-awareness, for it is only through a complete realization of one's self that one can achieve personal fulfillment and thereby true inner peace."

"I'm afraid I can't afford to undergo analysis just now."

"Let me begin by emphasizing to you that I am not suggesting psychoanalysis; I do not in the least consider you to be neurotic, Miss Seyrig. What I strongly urge is an *exploration* of your unconsciousness—a discovery of your whole self. My task is only to guide you along the course of your self-discovery, and for this privilege I charge no fee."

"I hadn't realized the National Health Service was this inclusive."

Dr. Magnus laughed easily. "It isn't, of course. My work is supported by a private foundation. There are many others who wish to learn certain truths of our existence, to seek answers where mundane science has not yet so much as realized there are questions. In that regard I am simply another paid researcher, and the results of my investigations are made available to those who share with us this yearning to see beyond the stultifying boundaries of modern science."

He indicated the book-lined wall behind his desk. Much of one shelf appeared to contain books with his own name prominent upon their spines.

"Do you intend to write a book about me?" Lisette meant to put more of a note of protest in her voice.

"It is possible that I may wish to record some of what we discover together, my dear. But only with scrupulous discretion, and, needless to say, only with your complete permission."

"My dreams." Lisette remembered the book of his that she had tried to read. "Do you consider them to be evidence of some previous incarnation?"

"Perhaps. We can't be certain until we explore them further. Does the idea of reincarnation smack too much of the occult for your liking, Miss Seyrig? Perhaps we should speak in more fashionable terms of Jungian archetypes, genetic memory or mental telepathy. The fact that the phenomenon has so many designations is ample proof that dreams of a previous existence are a very real part of the unconscious mind. It is undeniable that many people have experienced, in dreams or under hypnosis, memories that cannot possibly arise from their personal experience. Whether you believe that the immortal soul leaves the physical body at death to be reborn in the living embryo, or prefer to attribute it to inherited memories engraved upon DNA, or whatever explanation—this is a very real phenomenon and has been observed throughout history.

"As a rule, these memories of past existence are entirely buried within the unconscious. Almost everyone has experienced *déjà vu*. Subjects under hypnosis have spoken in languages and archaic dialects of which their conscious mind has no knowledge, have recounted in detail memories of previous lives. In some cases these submerged memories burst forth as dreams; in these instances, the memory is usually one of some emotionally laden experience, something too potent to remain buried. I believe that this is the case with your nightmares—the fact that they are recurrent being evidence of some profound significance in the events they recall."

Lisette wished for a cigarette; she'd all but stopped buying cigarettes with British prices, and from the absence of ashtrays here, Dr. Magnus was a nonsmoker.

"But why have these nightmares only lately become a problem?"

"I think I can explain that easily enough. Your forebears were from London. The dreams became a problem after you arrived in London. While it is usually difficult to define any relationship between the subject and the remembered existence, the timing and the force of your dream regressions would seem to indicate that you may be the reincarnation of someone—an ancestress, perhaps—who lived here in London during this past century."

"In that case, the nightmares should go away when I return to the States."

"Not necessarily. Once a doorway to the unconscious is opened, it is not so easily closed again. Moreover, you say that you had experienced these dreams on rare occasions prior to your coming here. I would suggest that what you are experiencing ts a natural process—a submerged part of your self is seeking expression, and it would be unwise to deny this shadow stranger within you. I might further argue that your presence here in London is hardly coincidence—that your decision to study here was determined by that part of you who emerges in these dreams."

Lisette decided she wasn't ready to accept such implications just now. "What do you propose?"

Dr. Magnus folded his hands as neatly as a bishop at prayer. "Have you ever undergone hypnosis?"

"No." She wished she hadn't made that sound like two syllables.

"It has proved to be extraordinarily efficacious in a great number of cases such as your own, my dear. Please do try to put from your mind the ridiculous trappings and absurd mumbo-jumbo with which the popular imagination connotes hypnotism. Hypnosis is no more than a technique through which we may release the entirety of the unconscious mind to free expression, unrestricted by the countless artificial barriers that make us strangers to ourselves."

"You want to hypnotize me?" The British inflection came to her, turning her statement into both question and protest.

"With your fullest cooperation, of course. I think it best. Through regressive hypnosis we can explore the significance of these dreams that trouble you, discover the shadow stranger within your self. Remember—this is a part of *you* that cries out for conscious expression. It is only through the full realization of one's identity, of one's total self, that true inner tranquillity may be achieved. Know thyself, and you will find peace."

"Know myself?"

"Precisely. You must put aside this false sense of guilt, Miss Seyrig. You are not possessed by some alien and hostile force. These dreams, these memories of another existence—this is you."

IV

"Some bloody weirdo made a pass at me this afternoon," Lisette confided.

"On the tube, was it?" Danielle stood on her toes, groping along the top of their bookshelf. Freshly showered, she was wearing only a lace-trimmed teddy—cami-knickers, they called them in the shops here—and her straining thigh muscles shaped her buttocks nicely.

"In Kensington, actually. After I had left Dr. Magnus's office." Lisette was lounging in an old satin slip she'd found at a stall in Church Street. They were drinking Bristol Cream out of brandy snifters. It was an intimate sort of evening they loved to share together, when not in the company of Danielle's various friends.

"I was walking down Holland Street, and there was this seedy-looking creep all dressed out in punk regalia, pressing his face against the door where that Equinox bookshop used to be. I made the mistake of glancing at him as I passed, and he must have seen my reflection in the glass, because he spun right around, looked straight at me, and said: 'Darling! What a lovely surprise to see you!' "

Lisette sipped her sherry. "Well, I gave him my hardest stare, and would you believe the creep just stood there smiling like he knew me, and so I yelled, 'Piss off!' in my loudest American accent, and he just froze there with his mouth hanging open."

"Here it is," Danielle announced. "I'd shelved it beside Roland Franklyn's *We Pass from View*—that's another you ought to read. I must remember someday to return it to that cute Liverpool writer who lent it to me."

She settled cozily beside Lisette on the couch, handed her a somewhat smudged paperback, and resumed her glass of sherry. The book was entitled *More Stately Mansions: Evidences of the Infinite* by Dr. Ingmar Magnus, and bore an affectionate inscription from the author to Danielle. "This is the first. The later printings had two of his studies deleted; I can't imagine why. But these are the sort of sessions he was describing to you."

"He wants to put *me* in one of his books," Lisette told her with an extravagant leer. "Can a woman trust a man who writes such ardent inscriptions to place her under hypnosis?"

"Dr. Magnus is a perfect gentleman," Danielle assured her, somewhat huffily. "He's a distinguished scholar and is thoroughly dedicated to his research. And besides, I've let him hypnotize me on a few occasions."

"I didn't know that. Whatever for?"

"Dr. Magnus is always seeking suitable subjects. I was fascinated by his work, and when I met him at a party I offered to undergo hypnosis."

"What happened?"

Danielle seemed envious. "Nothing worth writing about, I'm afraid. He said I was either too thoroughly integrated, or that my previous lives were too deeply buried. That's often the case, he says, which is why absolute proof of reincarnation is so difficult to demonstrate. After a few sessions I decided I couldn't spare the time to try further."

"But what was it like?"

"As adventurous as taking a nap. No caped Svengali staring

into my eyes. No lambent girasol ring. No swirling lights. Quite dull, actually. Dr. Magnus simply lulls you to sleep."

"Sounds safe enough. So long as I don't get molested walking back from his office."

Playfully, Danielle stroked her hair. "You hardly look the punk rock type. You haven't chopped off your hair with garden shears and dyed the stubble green. And not a single safety pin through your cheek."

"Actually I suppose he may not have been a punk rocker. Seemed a bit too old, and he wasn't garish enough. It's just that he was wearing a lot of black leather, and he had gold earrings and some sort of medallion."

"In front of the Equinox, did you say? How curious."

"Well, I think I gave him a good start. I glanced in a window to see whether he was trying to follow me, but he was just standing there looking stunned."

"*Might* have been an honest mistake. Remember the old fellow at Midge and Fiona's party who kept insisting he knew you?"

"And who was pissed out of his skull. Otherwise he might have been able to come up with a more original line."

Lisette paged through *More Stately Mansions* while Danielle selected a Tangerine Dream album from the stack and placed it on her stereo at low volume. The music seemed in keeping with the grey drizzle of the night outside and the coziness within their sitting room. Seeing she was busy reading, Danielle poured sherry for them both and stood studying the bookshelves—a hodgepodge of occult and metaphysical topics stuffed together with art books and recent paperbacks in no particular order. Wedged between Aleister Crowley's *Magick in Theory and Practice* and *How I Discovered My Infinite Self* by "An Initiate," was Dr. Magnus's most recent book, *The Shadow Stranger*. She pulled it down, and Dr. Magnus stared thoughtfully from the back of the dust jacket.

"Do you believe in reincarnation?" Lisette asked her.

"I do. Or rather, I do some of the time." Danielle stood behind the couch and bent over Lisette's shoulder to see where she was reading. "Midge Vaughn assures me that in a previous incarnation I was hanged for witchcraft."

"Midge should be grateful she's living in the twentieth century."

"Oh, Midge says we were sisters in the same coven and were hanged together; that's the reason for our close affinity."

"I'll bet Midge says that to all the girls."

"Oh, I like Midge." Danielle sipped her sherry and considered the rows of spines. "Did you say that man was wearing a medallion? Was it a swastika or that sort of thing?"

"No. It was something like a star in a circle. And he wore rings on every finger."

"Wait! Kind of greasy black hair slicked back from a widow's peak to straight over his collar in back? Eyebrows curled up into points like they've been waxed?"

"That's it."

"Ah, Mephisto!"

"Do you know him, then?"

"Not really. I've just seen him a time or two at the Equinox and a few other places. He reminds me of some ham actor playing Mephistopheles. Midge spoke to him once when we were by there, but I gather he's not part of her particular coven. Probably hadn't heard that the Equinox had closed. Never impressed me as a masher; very likely he actually did mistake you for someone."

"Well, they do say that everyone has a double. I wonder if mine is walking somewhere about London, being mistaken for me?"

"And no doubt giving some unsuspecting classmate of yours a resounding slap on the face."

"What if I met her suddenly?"

"Met your double—your *Doppelgänger*? Remember William Wilson? Disaster, darling—*disaster*!"

V

There really wasn't much to it; no production at all. Lisette felt nervous, a bit silly and perhaps a touch cheated.

"I want you to relax," Dr. Magnus told her. "All you have to do is just relax."

That's what her gynecologist always said, too, Lisette thought with a sudden tenseness. She lay on her back on Dr. Magnus's analyst's couch: her head on a comfortable cushion, legs stretched primly out on the leather upholstery (she'd deliberately worn jeans again), fingers clenched damply over her tummy. A white gown instead of jeans, and I'll be ready for my coffin, she mused uncomfortably.

"Fine. That's it. You're doing fine, Lisette. Very fine. Just relax. Yes, just relax, just like that. Fine, that's it. Relax."

Dr. Magnus's voice was a quiet monotone, monotonously repeating soothing encouragements. He spoke to her tirelessly, patiently, slowly dissolving her anxiety.

"You feel sleepy, Lisette. Relaxed and sleepy. Your breathing is slow and relaxed, slow and relaxed. Think about your breathing now, Lisette. Think how slow and sleepy and deep each breath comes. You're breathing deeper, and you're feeling sleepier. Relax and sleep, Lisette, breathe and sleep. Breathe and sleep . . ."

She *was* thinking about her breathing. She counted the breaths; the slow monotonous syllables of Dr. Magnus's voice seemed to blend into her breathing like a quiet, tuneless lullaby. She *was* sleepy, for that matter, and it was very pleasant to relax here, listening to that dim, droning murmur while he talked on and on. How much longer until the end of the lecture . . .

"You are asleep now, Lisette. You are asleep, yet you can still hear my voice. Now you are falling deeper, deeper, deeper into a pleasant, relaxed sleep, Lisette. Deeper and deeper asleep. Can you still hear my voice?"

"Yes."

"You are asleep, Lisette. In a deep, deep sleep. You will remain in this deep sleep until I shall count to three. As I count to three, you will slowly arise from your sleep until you are fully awake once again. Do you understand?"

"Yes."

"But when you hear me say the word *amber*, you will again fall into a deep, deep sleep, Lisette, just as you are asleep now. Do you understand?"

"Yes."

"Listen to me as I count, Lisette. One. Two. Three."

Lisette opened her eyes. For a moment her expression was blank, then a sudden confusion. She looked at Dr. Magnus seated beside her, then smiled ruefully. "I was asleep, I'm afraid. Or was I . . . ?"

"You did splendidly, Miss Seyrig." Dr. Magnus beamed reassurance. "You passed into a simple hypnotic state, and as you can see now, there was no more cause for concern than in catching an afternoon nap."

"But I'm sure I just dropped off." Lisette glanced at her watch. Her appointment had been for three, and it was now almost four o'clock.

"Why not just settle back and rest some more, Miss Seyrig. That's it, relax again. All you need is to rest a bit, just a pleasant rest."

Her wrist fell back onto the cushions, as her eyes fell shut.

"Amber."

Dr. Magnus studied her calm features for a moment. "You are asleep now, Lisette. Can you hear me?"

"Yes."

"I want you to relax, Lisette. I want you to fall deeper, deeper, deeper into sleep. Deep, deep sleep. Far, far, far into sleep."

He listened to her breathing, then suggested: "You are thinking of your childhood now, Lisette. You are a little girl, not even in school yet. Something is making you very happy. You remember how happy you are. Why are you so happy?"

Lisette made a childish giggle. "It's my birthday party, and Ollie the Clown came to play with us."

"And how old are you today?"

"I'm five." Her right hand twitched, extended fingers and thumb.

"Go deeper now, Lisette. I want you to reach farther back. Far, far back into your memories. Go back to a time before you were a child in San Francisco. Far, farther back, Lisette. I want you to go back to the time of your dreams."

He studied her face. She remained in a deep hypnotic trance, but her expression registered sudden anxiousness. It was as if she lay in normal sleep—reacting to some intense nightmare. She moaned.

"Deeper, Lisette. Don't be afraid to remember. Let your mind flow back to another time."

Her features still showed distress, but she seemed less agitated as his voice urged her deeper.

"Where are you?"

"I'm . . . I'm not certain." Her voice came in a well-bred English accent. "It's quite dark. Only a few candles are burning. I'm frightened."

"Go back to a happy moment," Dr. Magnus urged her, as her tone grew sharp with fear. "You are happy now. Something very pleasant and wonderful is happening to you."

Anxiety drained from her features. Her cheeks flushed: she smiled pleasurably.

"Where are you now?"

"I'm dancing. It's a grand ball to celebrate Her Majesty's Diamond Jubilee, and I've never seen such a throng. I'm certain Charles means to propose to me tonight, but he's ever so shy, and now he's simply fuming that Captain Stapledon has the next two dances. He's so dashing in his uniform. Everyone is watching us together."

"What is your name?"

"Elisabeth Beresford."

"Where do you live, Miss Beresford?"

"We have a house in Chelsea . . ."

Her expression abruptly changed. "It's dark again. I'm all alone. I can't see myself, although surely the candles shed sufficient light. There's something there in the candlelight. I'm moving closer."

"One."

"It's an open coffin." Fear edged her voice.

"Two."

"God in Heaven!"

"Three."

VI

"We," Danielle announced grandly, "are invited to a party."

She produced an engraved card from her bag, presented it to Lisette, then went to hang up her damp raincoat.

"Bloody English summer weather!" Lisette heard her from the kitchen. "Is there any more coffee made? Oh, fantastic!"

She reappeared with a cup of coffee and an opened box of cookies—Lisette couldn't get used to calling them biscuits. "Want some?"

"No, thanks. Bad for my figure."

"And coffee on an empty tummy is bad for the nerves," Danielle said pointedly.

"*Who* is Beth Garrington?" Lisette studied the invitation.

"Um." Danielle tried to wash down a mouthful of crumbs with too-hot coffee. "Some friend of Midge's. Midge dropped by the gallery this afternoon and gave me the invitation. A costume revel. Rock stars to royalty among the guests. Midge promises that it will be super fun; said the last party Beth threw was unbridled debauchery—there was cocaine being passed around in an antique snuff box for the guests. Can you imagine that much coke!"

"And how did Midge manage the invitation?"

"I gather the discerning Ms. Carrington had admired several of my drawings that Maitland has on display—yea, even unto so far as to purchase one. Midge told her that she knew me and that we two were ornaments for any debauchery."

"The invitation is in both our names."

"Midge *likes* you."

"Midge despises me. She's jealous as a cat."

"Then she must have told our depraved hostess what a lovely couple we make. Besides, Midge is jealous of everyone—even dear Maitland, whose interest in me very obviously is not of the flesh. But don't fret about Midge—English women are naturally bitchy toward 'foreign' women. They're oh-so proper and fashionable, but they never shave their legs. That's why I love mah fellow Americans."

Danielle kissed her chastely on top of her head, powdering Lisette's hair with biscuit crumbs. "And I'm cold and wet and dying for a shower. How about you?"

"A masquerade?" Lisette wondered. "What sort of costume? Not something that we'll have to trot off to one of those rental places for, surely?"

"From what Midge suggests, anything goes so long as it's wild. Just create something divinely decadent, and we're sure to knock them dead." Danielle had seen *Cabaret* half a dozen times. "It's to be in some back alley stately old home in Maida Vale, so there's no danger that the tenants downstairs will call the cops."

When Lisette remained silent, Danielle gave her a playful nudge. "Darling, it's a party we're invited to, not a funeral. What is it—didn't your session with Dr. Magnus go well?"

"I suppose it did." Lisette smiled without conviction. "I really can't say; all I did was doze off. Dr. Magnus seemed quite excited about it, though. I found it all . . . well, just a little bit scary."

"I thought you said you just dropped off. *What* was scary?"

"It's hard to put into words. It's like when you're starting to have a bad trip on acid: there's nothing wrong that you can explain, but somehow your mind is telling you to be afraid."

Danielle sat down beside her and squeezed her arm about her shoulders. "That sounds to me like Dr. Magnus is getting somewhere. I felt just the same sort of free anxiety the first time I underwent analysis. It's a good sign, darling. It means you're beginning to understand all those troubled secrets the ego keeps locked away."

"Perhaps the ego keeps them locked away for some perfectly good reason."

"Meaning hidden sexual conflicts, I suppose." Danielle's fingers gently massaged Lisette's shoulders and neck. "Oh, Lisette. You mustn't be shy about getting to know yourself. *I* think it's exciting."

Lisette curled up against her, resting her cheek against Danielle's breast while the other girl's fingers soothed the tension from her muscles. She supposed she was overreacting. After all, the nightmares were what distressed her so: Dr. Magnus seemed completely confident that he could free her from them.

"Which of your drawings did our prospective hostess buy?" Lisette asked, changing the subject.

"Oh, didn't I tell you?" Danielle lifted up her chin. "It was that charcoal study I did of you."

Lisette closed the shower curtains as she stepped into the tub.

It was one of those long, narrow, deep tubs beloved of English bathrooms that always made her think of a coffin for two. A Rube Goldberg plumbing arrangement connected the hot and cold faucets, and from the common spout was affixed a rubber hose with a shower head which one might either hang from a hook on the wall or hold in hand. Danielle had replaced the ordinary shower head with a shower massage when she moved in, but she left the previous tenant's shaving mirror—a bevelled glass oval in a heavily enameled antique frame—hanging on the wall above the hook.

Lisette glanced at her face in the steamed-over mirror. "I shouldn't have let you display that at the gallery."

"But why not?" Danielle was shampooing, and lather blinded her as she turned about. "Maitland thinks it's one of my best."

Lisette reached around her for the shower attachment. "It seems a bit personal somehow. All those people looking at me. It's an invasion of privacy."

"But it's thoroughly modest, darling. Not like some topless billboard in Soho."

The drawing was a charcoal and pencil study of Lisette, done in what Danielle described as her David Hamilton phase. In sitting for it, Lisette had piled her hair in a high chignon and dressed in an antique cotton camisole and drawers with lace insertions that she'd found at a shop in Westbourne Grove. Danielle called it *Dark Rose*. Lisette had thought it made her look fat.

Danielle grasped blindly for the shower massage, and Lisette placed it in her hand. "It just seems a bit too personal to have some total stranger owning my picture." Shampoo coursed like sea foam over Danielle's breasts. Lisette kissed the foam.

"Ah, but soon she won't be a total stranger," Danielle reminded her, her voice muffled by the pulsing shower spray.

Lisette felt Danielle's nipples harden beneath her lips. The brunette still pressed her eyes tightly shut against the force of the shower, but the other hand cupped Lisette's head encouragingly. Lisette gently moved her kisses downward along the other girl's slippery belly, kneeling as she did so. Danielle murmured, and when Lisette's tongue probed her drenched curls, she shifted her legs to let her knees rest beneath the blonde girl's shoulders. The shower massage dropped from her fingers.

Lisette made love to her with a passion that surprised her—spontaneous, suddenly fierce, unlike their usual tenderness together. Her lips and tongue pressed into Danielle almost ravenously, her own ecstasy even more intense than that which she was drawing from Danielle. Danielle gasped and clung to the shower rail with one hand, her other fist clenched upon the curtain, sobbing as a long orgasm shuddered through her.

"Please, darling!" Danielle finally managed to beg. "My legs are too wobbly to hold me up any longer!"

She drew away. Lisette raised her face.

"Oh!"

Lisette rose to her feet with drugged movements. Her wide eyes at last registered Danielle's startled expression. She touched her lips and turned to look in the bathroom mirror.

"I'm sorry," Danielle put her arm about her shoulder. "I must have started my period. I didn't realize . . ."

Lisette stared at the blood-smeared face in the fogged shaving mirror.

Danielle caught her as she started to slump.

VII

She was conscious of the cold rain that pelted her face, washing from her nostrils the too-sweet smell of decaying flowers. Slowly she opened her eyes onto darkness and mist. Rain fell steadily, spiritlessly, gluing her white gown to her drenched flesh. She had been walking in her sleep again.

Wakefulness seemed forever in coming to her, so that only by slow degrees did she become aware of herself, of her surroundings. For a moment she felt as if she were a chess-piece arrayed upon a board in a darkened room. All about her, stone monuments crowded together, their weathered surfaces streaming with moisture. She felt neither fear nor surprise that she stood in a cemetery.

She pressed her bare arms together across her breasts. Water ran over her pale skin as smoothly as upon the marble tombstones, and though her flesh felt as cold as the drenched marble, she did not feel chilled. She stood barefoot, her hair clinging to her shoulders above the low-necked cotton gown that was all she wore.

Automatically, her steps carried her through the darkness, as if following a familiar path through the maze of glistening stone. She knew where she was: this was Highgate Cemetery. She could not recall how she knew that, since she had no memory of ever having been to this place before. No more could she think how she knew her steps were taking her deeper into the cemetery instead of toward the gate.

A splash of color trickled onto her breast, staining its paleness as the rain dissolved it into a red rose above her heart.

She opened her mouth to scream, and a great bubble of unswallowed blood spewed from her lips.

"Elisabeth! Elisabeth!"

"Lisette! Lisette!"

Whose voice called her?

"Lisette! You can wake up now, Lisette."

Dr. Magnus's face peered into her own. Was there sudden concern behind that urbane mask?

"You're awake now, Miss Seyrig. Everything is all right."

Lisette stared back at him for a moment, uncertain of her reality, as if suddenly awakened from some profound nightmare.

"I . . . I thought I was dead." Her eyes still held her fear.

Dr. Magnus smiled to reassure her. "Somnambulism, my dear. You remembered an episode of sleepwalking from a former life. Tell me, have you yourself ever walked in your sleep?"

Lisette pressed her hands to her face, abruptly examined her fingers. "I don't know. I mean, I don't think so."

She sat up, searched in her bag for her compact. She paused for a moment before opening the mirror.

"Dr. Magnus, I don't think I care to continue these sessions." She stared at her reflection in fascination, not touching her makeup, and when she snapped the case shut, the frightened strain began to relax from her face. She wished she had a cigarette.

Dr. Magnus sighed and pressed his fingertips together, leaning back in his chair; watched her fidget with her clothing as she sat nervously on the edge of the couch.

"Do you really wish to terminate our exploration? We have, after all, made excellent progress during these last few sessions."

"Have we?"

"We have, indeed. You have consistently remembered incidents from the life of one Elisabeth Beresford, a young English lady living in London at the close of the last century. To the best of your knowledge of your family history, she is not an ancestress."

Dr. Magnus leaned forward, seeking to impart his enthusiasm. "Don't you see how important this is? If Elisabeth Beresford was not your ancestress, then there can be no question of genetic memory being involved. The only explanation must therefore be reincarnation—proof of the immortality of the soul. To establish this I must first confirm the existence of Elisabeth Beresford, and from that demonstrate that no familial bond exists between the two of you. We simply must explore this further."

"Must we? I meant, what progress have we made toward helping me, Dr. Magnus? It's all very good for you to be able to confirm your theories of reincarnation, but that doesn't do anything for me. If anything, the nightmares have grown more disturbing since we began these sessions."

"Then perhaps we dare not stop."

"What do you mean?" Lisette wondered what he might do if she suddenly bolted from the room.

"I mean that the nightmares will grow worse regardless of whether you decide to terminate our sessions. Your unconscious self is struggling to tell you some significant message from a previous existence. It will continue to do so no matter how stubbornly you will yourself not to listen. My task is to help you listen to this voice, to understand the message it must impart to you—and with this understanding and self-awareness, you will experience inner peace. Without my help . . . Well, to be perfectly frank, Miss Seyrig, you are in some danger of a complete emotional breakdown."

Lisette slumped back against the couch. She felt on the edge of panic and wished Danielle were here to support her.

"Why are my memories always nightmares?" Her voice shook, and she spoke slowly to control it.

"But they aren't always frightening memories, my dear. It's

just that the memory of some extremely traumatic experience often seeks to come to the fore. You would expect some tremendously emotional laden memory to be a potent one."

"Is Elisabeth Beresford . . . dead?"

"Assuming she was approximately twenty years of age at the time of Queen Victoria's Diamond Jubilee, she would have been past one hundred today. Besides, Miss Seyrig, her soul has been born again as your own. It must therefore follow . . ."

"Dr. Magnus. I don't *want* to know how Elisabeth Beresford died."

"Of course," Dr. Magnus told her gently. "Isn't that quite obvious?"

VIII

"For a wonder, it's forgot to rain tonight."

"Thank god for small favors," Lisette commented, thinking July in London had far more to do with monsoons than the romantic city of fogs celebrated in song. "All we need is to get these rained on."

She and Danielle bounced about on the back seat of the black Austin taxi, as their driver democratically seemed as willing to challenge lorries as pedestrians for right-of-way on the Edgeware Road. Feeling a bit self-conscious, Lisette tugged at the hem of her patent leather trench coat. They had decided to wear brightly embroidered Chinese silk lounging pyjamas that they'd found at one of the vintage clothing shops off the Portobello Road—gauzy enough for stares, but only a demure trouser-leg showing beneath their coats. "We're going to a masquerade party," Lisette had felt obliged to explain to the driver. Her concern was needless, as he hadn't given them a second glance. Either he was used to the current Chinese look in fashion, or else a few seasons of picking up couples at discos and punk rock clubs had inured him to any sort of costume.

The taxi turned into a series of side streets off Maida Vale and eventually made a neat U-turn that seemed almost an automotive pirouette. The frenetic beat of a new wave rock group clattered past the gate of an enclosed courtyard: something Mews—the iron plaque on the brick wall was too rusted to decipher in the dark—but from the lights and noise it must be the right address. A number of expensive-looking cars—Lisette recognized a Rolls or two and at least one Ferrari—were among those crowded against the curb. They squeezed their way past them and made for the source of the revelry, a brick-fronted town-house of three or more storeys set at the back of the courtyard.

The door was opened by a girl in an abbreviated maid's costume. She checked their invitation while a similarly clad girl took their coats, and a third invited them to select from an assortment of masks and indicated where they might change. Lisette and Danielle chose sequined domino masks that matched the dangling scarves they wore tied low across their brows.

Danielle withdrew an ebony cigarette holder from her bag and considered their reflections with approval. "Divinely decadent," she drawled, gesturing with her black-lacquered nails. "All that time for my eyes, and just to cover them with a mask. Perhaps later—when it's cock's-crow and all unmask . . . Forward, darling."

Lisette kept at her side, feeling a bit lost and out of place. When they passed before a light, it was evident that they wore nothing beneath the silk pyjamas, and Lisette was grateful for the strategic brocade. As they came upon others of the newly arriving guests, she decided there was no danger of outraging anyone's modesty here. As Midge had promised, anything goes so long as it's wild, and while their costumes might pass for street wear, many of the guests needed to avail themselves of the changing rooms upstairs.

A muscular young man clad only in a leather loincloth and a sword belt with broadsword descended the stairs leading a buxom girl by a chain affixed to her wrists; aside from her manacles, she wore a few scraps of leather. A couple in punk rock gear spat at them in passing; the girl was wearing a set of panties with dangling razor blades for tassels and a pair of black latex tights that might have been spray paint. Two girls in vintage Christian Dior New Look evening gowns ogled the seminude swordsman from the landing above; Lisette noted their pronounced shoulders and

Adam's apples and felt a twinge of jealousy that hormones and surgery could let them show a better cleavage than she could.

A new wave group called the Needle was performing in a large first-floor room—Lisette supposed it was an actual ballroom, although the house's original tenants would have considered tonight's ball a *danse macabre*. Despite the fact that the decibel level was well past the threshold of pain, most of the guests were congregated here, with smaller, quieter parties gravitating into other rooms. Here, about half were dancing, the rest standing about trying to talk. Marijuana smoke was barely discernible within the harsh haze of British cigarettes.

"There's Midge and Fiona," Danielle shouted in Lisette's ear. She waved energetically and steered a course through the dancers.

Midge was wearing an elaborate medieval gown—a heavily brocaded affair that ran from the floor to midway across her nipples. Her blonde hair was piled high in some sort of conical headpiece, complete with flowing scarf. Fiona waited upon her in a page boy's costume.

"Are you just getting here?" Midge asked, running a deprecative glance down Lisette's costume. "There's champagne over on the sideboard. Wait, I'll summon one of the cute little French maids."

Lisette caught two glasses from a passing tray and presented one to Danielle. It was impossible to converse, but then she hadn't anything to talk about with Midge, and Fiona was no more than a shadow.

"Where's our hostess?" Danielle asked.

"Not down yet," Midge managed to shout. "Beth always waits to make a grand entrance at her little do's. You won't miss her."

"Speaking of entrances ..." Lisette commented, nodding toward the couple who were just coming onto the dance floor. The woman wore a Nazi SS officer's hat, jackboots, black trousers and braces across her bare chest. She was astride the back of her male companion, who wore a saddle and bridle in addition to a few other bits of leather harness.

"I can't decide whether that's kinky or just tacky," Lisette said.

"Not like your little sorority teas back home, is it?" Midge smiled.

"Is there any coke about?" Danielle interposed quickly.

"There was a short while ago. Try the library—that's the room just down from where everyone's changing."

Lisette downed her champagne and grabbed a refill before following Danielle upstairs. A man in fish-net tights, motorcycle boots and a vest comprised mostly of chain and bits of Nazi medals caught at her arm and seemed to want to dance. Instead of a mask, he wore about a pound of eye shadow and black lipstick. She shouted an inaudible excuse, held a finger to her nostril and sniffed, and darted after Danielle.

"That was Eddie Teeth, lead singer for the Trepans, whom you just cut," Danielle told her. "Why didn't he grab *me!*"

"You'll get your chance," Lisette told her. "I think he's following us."

Danielle dragged her to a halt halfway up the stairs.

"Got toot right here, loves." Eddie Teeth flipped the silver spoon and phial that dangled amidst the chains on his vest.

"Couldn't take the noise in there any longer," Lisette explained.

"Needle's shit." Eddie Teeth wrapped an arm about either waist and propelled them up the stairs. "You gashes sisters? I can dig incest."

The library was pleasantly crowded—Lisette decided she didn't want to be cornered with Eddie Teeth. A dozen or more guests stood about, sniffing and conversing energetically. Seated at a table, two of the ubiquitous maids busily cut lines onto mirrors and set them out for the guests, whose number remained more or less constant as people wandered in and left. A cigarette box offered tightly rolled joints.

"That's Thai." Eddie Teeth groped for a handful of the joints, stuck one in each girl's mouth, the rest inside his vest. Danielle giggled and fitted hers to her cigarette holder. Unfastening a silver tube from his vest, he snorted two thick lines from one of the mirrors. "Toot your eyeballs out, loves," he invited them.

One of the maids collected the mirror when they had finished and replaced it with another—a dozen lines of cocaine neatly arranged across its surface. Industriously she began to work a chunk of rock through a sifter to replenish the empty mirror. Lisette watched in fascination. This finally brought home to her the wealth this party represented: all the rest simply seemed to her like something out of a movie, but dealing out coke to more than a hundred guests was an extravagance she could relate to.

"Danielle Borland, isn't it?"

A man dressed as Mephistopheles bowed before them. "Adrian Tregannet. We've met at one of Midge Vaughn's parties, you may recall."

Danielle stared at the face below the domino mask. "Oh, yes. Lisette, it's Mephisto himself."

"Then this is Miss Seyrig, the subject of your charcoal drawing that Beth so admires." Mephisto caught Lisette's hand and bent his lips to it. "Beth is so much looking forward to meeting you both."

Lisette retrieved her hand. "Aren't you the . . ."

"The rude fellow who accosted you in Kensington some days ago," Tregannet finished apologetically. "Yes, I'm afraid so. But you really must forgive me for my forwardness. I actually did mistake you for a very dear friend of mine, you see. Won't you let me make amends over a glass of champagne?"

"Certainly." Lisette decided that she had had quite enough of Eddie Teeth, and Danielle was quite capable of fending for herself if she grew tired of having her breasts squeezed by a famous pop star.

Tregannet quickly returned with two glasses of champagne. Lisette finished another two lines and smiled appreciatively as she accepted a glass. Danielle was trying to shotgun Eddie Teeth through her cigarette holder, and Lisette thought it a good chance to slip away.

"Your roommate is tremendously talented," Tregannet suggested. "Of course, she chose so charming a subject for her drawing."

Slick as snake oil, Lisette thought, letting him take her arm. "How very nice of you to say so. However, I really feel a bit embarrassed to think that some stranger owns a portrait of me in my underwear."

"Utterly chaste, my dear—as chaste as the *Dark Rose* of its title. Beth chose to hang it in her boudoir, so I hardly think it is on public display. I suspect from your garments in the drawing that you must share Beth's appreciation for the dress and manners of this past century."

Which is something I'd never suspect of our hostess, judging from this party, Lisette considered. "I'm quite looking forward to meeting her. I assume then that Ms. is a bit too modern for one of such quiet tastes. Is it Miss or Mrs. Garrington?"

"Ah, I hadn't meant to suggest an impression of a genteel dowager. Beth is entirely of your generation—a few years older than yourself, perhaps. Although I find Ms. too suggestive of American slang, I'm sure Beth would not object. However, there's no occasion for such formality here."

"You seem to know her well, Mr. Tregannet."

"It is an old family. I know her aunt, Julia Weatherford, quite well through our mutual interest in the occult. Perhaps you, too . . . ?"

"Not really; Danielle is the one you should chat with about that. My field is art. I'm over here on fellowship at London University." She watched Danielle and Eddie Teeth toddle off for the ballroom and jealously decided that Danielle's taste in her acquaintances left much to be desired. "Could I have some more champagne?"

"To be sure. I won't be a moment."

Lisette snorted a few more lines while she waited. A young man dressed as an Edwardian dandy offered her his snuff box and gravely demonstrated its use. Lisette was struggling with a sneezing fit when Tregannet returned.

"You needn't have gone to all the bother," she told him. "These little French maids are dashing about with trays of champagne."

"But those glasses have lost the proper chill," Tregannet explained. "To your very good health."

"Cheers." Lisette felt lightheaded, and promised herself to go easy for a while. "Does Beth live here with her aunt, then?"

"Her aunt lives on the Continent; I don't believe she's visited London for several years. Beth moved in about ten years ago. Theirs is not a large family, but they are not without wealth, as you can observe. They travel a great deal as well, and it's fortunate that Beth happened to be in London during your stay here. Incidentally, just how long will you be staying in London?"

"About a year is all." Lisette finished her champagne. "Then it's back to my dear, dull family in San Francisco."

"Then there's no one here in London . . . ?"

"Decidedly not, Mr. Tregannet. And now if you'll excuse me, I think I'll find the ladies'."

Cocaine might well be the champagne of drugs, but cocaine and champagne didn't seem to mix well, Lisette mused, turning the bathroom over to the next frantic guest. Her head felt really buzzy, and she thought she might do better if she found a bedroom somewhere and lay down for a moment. But then she'd most likely wake up and find some man on top of her, judging from this lot. She decided she'd lay off the champagne and have just a line or two to shake off the feeling of having been sandbagged.

The crowd in the study had changed during her absence. Just now it was dominated by a group of guests dressed in costumes from *The Rocky Horror Show,* now closing out its long run at the Comedy Theatre in Piccadilly. Lisette had grown bored with the fad the film version had generated in the States, and pushed her way past the group as they vigorously danced the Time Warp and bellowed out songs from the show.

" 'Give yourself over to absolute pleasure,' " someone sang in her ear as she industriously snorted a line from the mirror. " 'Erotic nightmares beyond any measure,' " the song continued.

Lisette finished a second line, and decided she had had enough. She straightened from the table and broke for the doorway. The tall transvestite dressed as Frankie barred her way with a dramatic gesture, singing ardently: " 'Don't dream it—be it!' "

Lisette blew him a kiss and ducked around him. She wished she could find a quiet place to collect her thoughts. Maybe she should find Danielle first—if she could handle the ballroom that long.

The dance floor was far more crowded than when they'd come in. At least all these jostling bodies seemed to absorb some of the decibels from the blaring banks of amplifiers and speakers. Lisette looked in vain for Danielle amidst the dancers, succeeding only in getting champagne sloshed on her back. She caught sight of Midge, recognizable above the mob by her conical medieval headdress, and pushed her way toward her.

Midge was being fed caviar on bits of toast by Fiona while she talked with an older woman who looked like the pictures Lisette had seen of Marlene Dietrich dressed in men's formal evening wear.

"Have you seen Danielle?" Lisette asked her.

"Why, not recently, darling," Midge smiled, licking caviar from her lips with the tip of her tongue. "I believe she and that rock singer were headed upstairs for a bit more privacy. I'm sure she'll come collect you once they're finished."

"Midge, you're a cunt," Lisette told her through her sweetest smile. She turned away and made for the doorway, trying not to ruin her exit by staggering. Screw Danielle—she needed to have some fresh air.

A crowd had gathered at the foot of the stairway, and she had to push through the doorway to escape the ballroom. Behind her, the Needle mercifully took a break. "She's coming down!" Lisette heard someone whisper breathlessly. The inchoate babel of the party fell to a sudden lull that made Lisette shiver.

At the top of the stairway stood a tall woman, enveloped in a black velvet cloak from her throat to her ankles. Her blonde hair was piled high in a complex variation of the once-fashionable French twist. Strings of garnets entwined in her hair and edged the close-fitting black mask that covered the upper half of her face. For a hushed interval she stood there, gazing imperiously down upon her guests.

Adrian Tregannet leapt to the foot of the stairway. He signed to a pair of maids, who stepped forward to either side of their mistress.

"Milords and miladies!" he announced with a sweeping bow. "Let us pay honor to our bewitching mistress whose feast we celebrate tonight! I give you the lamia who haunted Adam's dreams—Lilith!"

The maids smoothly swept the cloak from their mistress' shoulders. From the multitude at her feet came an audible intake of breath. Beth Garrington was attired in a strapless corselette of gleaming black leather, laced tightly about her waist. The rest of her costume consisted only of knee-length, stiletto-heeled tight boots, above-the-elbow gloves, and a spiked collar around her throat—all of black leather that contrasted starkly against her white skin and blonde hair. At first Lisette thought she wore a bull-whip coiled about her body as well, but then the coils moved, and she realized that it was an enormous black snake.

"Lilith!" came the shout, chanted in a tone of awe. "Lilith!"

Acknowledging their worship with a sinuous gesture, Beth Garrington descended the staircase. The serpent coiled from gloved arm to gloved arm, entwining her cinched waist; its eyes considered the revellers imperturbably. Champagne glasses lifted in a toast to Lilith, and the chattering voice of the party once more began to fill the house.

Tregannet touched Beth's elbow as she greeted her guests at the foot of the stairway. He whispered into her ear, and she smiled graciously and moved away with him.

Lisette clung to the staircase newel, watching them approach. Her head was spinning, and she desperately needed to lie down in some fresh air, but she couldn't trust her legs to carry her outside. She stared into the eyes of the serpent, hypnotized by its flickering tongue.

The room seemed to surge in and out of focus. The masks of the guests seemed to leer and gloat with the awareness of some secret jest; the dancers in their fantastic costumes became a grotesque horde of satyrs and wanton demons, writhing about the ballroom in some witches' sabbat of obscene mass copulation. As in a nightmare, Lisette willed her legs to turn and run, realized that her body was no longer obedient to her will.

"Beth, here's someone you've been dying to meet," Lisette heard Tregannet say. "Beth Garrington, allow me to present Lisette Seyrig."

The lips beneath the black mask curved in a pleasurable smile. Lisette gazed into the eyes behind the mask, and discovered that she could no longer feel her body. She thought she heard Danielle cry out her name.

The eyes remained in her vision long after she slid down the newel and collapsed upon the floor.

IX

The Catherine Wheel was a pub on Kensington Church Street. They served good pub lunches there, and Lisette liked to stop in before walking down Holland Street for her sessions with Dr. Magnus. Since today was her final such session, it seemed appropriate that they should end the evening here.

"While I dislike repeating myself," Dr. Magnus spoke earnestly, "I really do think we should continue."

Lisette drew on a cigarette and shook her head decisively. "No way, Dr. Magnus. My nerves are shot to hell. I mean, look—when I freak out at a costume party and have to be carted home to bed by my roommate! It was like when I was a kid and got hold of some bad acid: the whole world was some bizarre and sinister freak show for weeks. Once I got my head back on, I said: No more acid."

"That was rather a notorious circle you were travelling in. Further, you were, if I understand you correctly, overindulging a bit that evening."

"A few glasses of champagne and a little toot never did anything before but make me a bit giggly and talkative." Lisette sipped her half of lager; she'd never developed a taste for English bitter, and at least the lager was chilled. They sat across from each other at a table the size of a hubcap: she in the corner of a padded bench against the wall, he at a chair set out into the room, pressed in by a wall of standing bodies. A foot away from her on the padded bench, three young men huddled about a similar table, talking animatedly. For all that, she and Dr. Magnus might have been all alone in the room. Lisette wondered if the psychologist who had coined the faddish concept of "space" had been inspired in a crowded English pub.

"It isn't just that I fainted at the party. It isn't just the nightmares." She paused to find words. "It's just that everything somehow seems to be drifting out of focus, out of control. It's . . . well, it's frightening."

"Precisely why we must continue."

"Precisely why we must not." Lisette sighed. They'd covered this ground already. It had been a moment of weakness when she agreed to allow Dr. Magnus to buy her a drink afterward instead of heading back to the flat. Still, he had been so distressed when she told him she was terminating their sessions.

"I've tried to cooperate with you as best I could, and I'm certain you are entirely sincere in your desire to help me." Well, she wasn't all *that* certain, but no point in going into that. "However, the fact remains that since we began these sessions, my nerves have gone to hell. You say they'd be worse without the sessions, I say the sessions have made them worse, and maybe there's no connection at all—it's just that my nerves have gotten worse, so now I'm going to trust my intuition and try life without these sessions. Fair enough?"

Dr. Magnus gazed uncomfortably at his barely tasted glass of sherry. "While I fully understand your rationale, I must in all conscience beg you to reconsider, Lisette. You are running risks that . . ."

"Look. If the nightmares go away, then terrific. If they don't, I can always pack up and head back to San Francisco. That way I'll be clear of whatever it is about London that disagrees with me, and if not, I'll see my psychiatrist back home."

"Very well, then." Dr. Magnus squeezed her hand. "However, please bear in mind that I remain eager to continue our sessions at any time, should you change your mind."

"That's fair enough, too. And very kind of you."

Dr. Magnus lifted his glass of sherry to the light. Pensively, he remarked: "Amber."

X

"Lisette?"

Danielle locked the front door behind her and hung up her inadequate umbrella in the hallway. She considered her face in the mirror and grimaced at the mess of her hair. "Lisette? Are you here?"

No answer, and her rain things were not in the hallway. Either she was having a late session with Dr. Magnus, or else she'd wisely decided to duck under cover until this bloody rain let up. After she'd had to carry Lisette home in a taxi when she passed out at the party, Danielle was starting to feel real concern over her state of health.

Danielle kicked off her damp shoes as she entered the living room. The curtains were drawn against the greyness outside, and she switched on a lamp to brighten the flat a bit. Her dress clung to her like a clammy fish-skin; she shivered, and thought about a cup of coffee. If Lisette hadn't returned yet, there wouldn't be any brewed. She'd have a warm shower instead, and after that she'd see to the coffee—if Lisette hadn't returned to set a pot going in the meantime.

"Lisette?" Their bedroom was empty. Danielle turned on the overhead light. Christ, it was gloomy! So much for long English summer evenings—with all the rain, she couldn't remember when she'd last seen the sun. She struggled out of her damp dress, spread it flat across her bed with the vague hope that it might not wrinkle too badly, then tossed her bra and tights onto a chair.

Slipping into her bathrobe, Danielle padded back into the living room. Still no sign of Lisette, and it was past nine. Perhaps she'd stopped off at a pub. Crossing to the stereo, Danielle placed the new Blondie album on the turntable and turned up the volume. Let the neighbors complain—at least this would help dispel the evening's gloom.

She cursed the delay needed to adjust the shower temperature to satisfaction, then climbed into the tub. The hot spray felt good, and she stood under it contentedly for several minutes—initially revitalized, then lulled into a delicious sense of relaxation. Through the rush of the spray, she could hear the muffled beat of the stereo. As she reached for the shampoo, she began to move her body with the rhythm.

The shower curtain billowed as the bathroom door opened. Danielle risked a soapy squint around the curtain—she knew the flat was securely locked, but after seeing *Psycho* . . . It was only Lisette, already undressed, her long blonde hair falling over her breasts.

"Didn't hear you come in with the stereo going," Danielle greeted her. "Come on in before you catch cold."

Danielle resumed lathering her hair as the shower curtain

parted and the other girl stepped into the tub behind her. Her eyes squeezed shut against the soap, she felt Lisette's breasts thrust against her back, her flat belly press against her buttocks. Lisette's hands came around her to cup her breasts gently.

At least Lisette had gotten over her silly tiff about Eddie Teeth. She'd explained to Lisette that she'd ditched that greasy slob when he'd tried to dry hump her on the dance floor, but how do you reason with a silly thing who faints at the sight of a snake?

"Jesus, you're chilled to the bone!" Danielle complained with a shiver. "Better stand under the shower and get warm. Did you get caught in the rain?"

The other girl's fingers continued to caress her breasts, and instead of answering, her lips teased the nape of Danielle's neck. Danielle made a delighted sound deep in her throat, letting the spray rinse the lather from her hair and over their embraced bodies. Languidly she turned about to face her lover, closing her arms about Lisette's shoulders for support.

Lisette's kisses held each taut nipple for a moment, teasing them almost painfully. Danielle pressed the other girl's face to her breasts, sighed as her kisses nibbled upward to her throat. She felt weak with arousal, and only Lisette's strength held her upright in the tub. Her lover's lips upon her throat tormented her beyond enduring; Danielle gasped and lifted Lisette's face to meet her own.

Her mouth was open to receive Lisette's red-lipped kiss, and it opened wider as Danielle stared into the eyes of her lover. Her first emotion was one of wonder.

"You're not Lisette!"

It was nearly midnight when Lisette unlocked the door to their flat and quietly let herself in. Only a few lights were on, and there was no sign of Danielle—either she had gone out, or, more likely, had gone to bed.

Lisette hung up her raincoat and wearily pulled off her shoes. She'd barely caught the last train. She must have been crazy to let Dr. Magnus talk her into returning to his office for another session that late, but then he was quite right: as serious as her problems were, she really did need all the help he could give her.

She felt a warm sense of gratitude to Dr. Magnus for being there when she so needed his help.

The turntable had stopped, but a light on the amplifier indicated that the power was still on. Lisette cut it off and closed the lid over the turntable. She felt too tired to listen to an album just now.

She became aware that the shower was running. In that case, Danielle hadn't gone to bed. She supposed she really ought to apologize to her for letting Midge's bitchy lies get under her skin. After all, she had ruined the party for Danielle; poor Danielle had had to get her to bed and had left the party without ever getting to meet Beth Garrington, and she was the one Beth had invited in the first place.

"Danielle? I'm back." Lisette called through the bathroom door. "Do you want anything?"

No answer. Lisette looked into their bedroom, just in case Danielle had invited a friend over. No, the beds were still made up; Danielle's clothes were spread out by themselves.

"Danielle?" Lisette raised her voice. Perhaps she couldn't hear over the noise of the shower. "Danielle?" Surely she was all right.

Lisette's feet felt damp. She looked down. A puddle of water was seeping beneath the door. Danielle must not have the shower curtains closed properly.

"Danielle! You're flooding us!"

Lisette opened the door and peered cautiously within. The curtain was closed, right enough. A thin spray still reached through a gap, and the shower had been running long enough for the puddle to spread. It occurred to Lisette that she should see Danielle's silhouette against the translucent shower curtain.

"Danielle!" She began to grow alarmed. "Danielle! Are you all right?"

She pattered across the wet tiles and drew aside the curtain. Danielle lay in the bottom of the tub, the spray falling on her upturned smile, her flesh paler than the porcelain of the tub.

XI

It was early afternoon when they finally allowed her to return to the flat. Had she been able to think of another place to go, she probably would have gone there. Instead, Lisette wearily slumped onto the couch, too spent to pour herself the drink she desperately wanted.

Somehow she had managed to phone the police through her hysteria and make them understand where she was. Once the squad car arrived, she had no further need to act out of her own initiative; she simply was carried along in the rush of police investigation. It wasn't until they were questioning her at New Scotland Yard that she realized she herself was not entirely free from suspicion.

The victim had bled to death, the medical examiner ruled, her blood washed down the tub drain. A safety razor used for shaving legs had been opened, its blade removed. There were razor incisions along both wrists, directed lengthwise, into the radial artery, as opposed to the shallow, crosswise cuts utilized by suicides unfamiliar with human anatomy. There was, in addition, an incision in the left side of the throat. It was either a very determined suicide, or a skillfully concealed murder. In view of the absence of any signs of forced entry or of a struggle, more likely the former. The victim's roommate did admit to a recent quarrel. Laboratory tests would indicate whether the victim might have been drugged or rendered unconscious through a blow. After that, the inquest would decide.

Lisette had explained that she had spent the evening with Dr. Magnus. The fact that she was receiving emotional therapy, as they interpreted it, caused several mental notes to be made. Efforts to reach Dr. Magnus by telephone proved unsuccessful, but his secretary did confirm that Miss Seyrig had shown up for her appointment the previous afternoon. Dr. Magnus would get in touch with them as soon as he returned to his office. No, she did not know why he had cancelled today's appointments, but it was not unusual for Dr. Magnus to dash off suddenly when essential research demanded immediate attention.

After a while they let Lisette make phone calls. She phoned her parents, then wished she hadn't. It was still the night before in California, and it was like turning back the hands of time to no avail. They urged her to take the next flight home, but of course it wasn't all that simple, and it just wasn't feasible for either of them to fly over on a second's notice, since after all there really was nothing they could do. She phoned Maitland Reddin, who was stunned at the news and offered to help in any way he could, but Lisette couldn't think of any way. She phoned Midge Vaughn, who hung up on her. She phoned Dr. Magnus, who still couldn't be reached. Mercifully, the police took care of phoning Danielle's next of kin.

A physician at New Scotland Yard had spoken with her briefly and had given her some pills—a sedative to ease her into sleep after her ordeal. They had driven her back to the flat after impressing upon her the need to be present at the inquest. She must not be concerned should any hypothetical assailant yet be lurking about, inasmuch as the flat would be under surveillance.

Lisette stared dully about the flat, still unable to comprehend what had happened. The police had been thorough—measuring, dusting for fingerprints, leaving things in a mess. Bleakly, Lisette tried to convince herself that this was only another nightmare, that in a moment Danielle would pop in and find her asleep on the couch. Christ, what was she going to do with all of Danielle's things? Danielle's mother was remarried and living in Colorado; her father was an executive in a New York investment corporation. Evidently he had made arrangements to have the body shipped back to the States.

"Oh, Danielle." Lisette was too stunned for tears. Perhaps she should check into a hotel for now. No, she couldn't bear being all alone with her thoughts in a strange place. How strange to realize now that she really had no close friends in London other than Danielle—and what friends she did have were mostly people she'd met through Danielle.

She'd left word with Dr. Magnus's secretary for him to call her once he came in. Perhaps she should call there once again, just in case Dr. Magnus had missed her message. Lisette couldn't think what good Dr. Magnus could do, but he was such an understanding person, and she felt much better whenever she spoke with him.

She considered the bottle of pills in her bag. Perhaps it would be best to take a couple of them and sleep around the clock. She felt too drained just now to have energy enough to think.

The phone began to ring. Lisette stared at it for a moment without comprehension, then lunged up from the couch to answer it. "Is this Lisette Seyrig?"

It was a woman's voice—one Lisette didn't recognize. "Yes. Who's calling, please?"

"This is Beth Garrington, Lisette. I hope I'm not disturbing you."

"That's quite all right."

"You poor dear! Maitland Redding phoned to tell me of the tragedy. I can't tell you how shocked I am. Danielle seemed such a dear from our brief contact, and she had such a great talent."

"Thank you. I'm sorry you weren't able to know her better." Lisette sensed guilt and embarrassment at the memory of that brief contact.

"Darling, you can't be thinking about staying in that flat alone. Is there someone there with you?"

"No, there isn't. That's all right. I'll be fine."

"Don't be silly. Listen, I have enough empty bedrooms in this old barn to open a hotel. Why don't you just pack a few things and come straight over?"

"That's very kind of you, but I really couldn't."

"Nonsense! It's no good for you to be there all by yourself. Strange as this may sound, but when I'm not throwing one of these invitational riots, this is a quiet little backwater and things are dull as church. I'd love the company, and it will do you a world of good to get away."

"You're really very kind to invite me, but I . . ."

"Please, Lisette—be reasonable. I have guest rooms here already made up, and I'll send the car around to pick you up. All you need do is say yes and toss a few things into your bag. After a good night's sleep, you'll feel much more like coping with things tomorrow."

When Lisette didn't immediately reply, Beth added carefully: "Besides, Lisette. I understand the police haven't ruled out the possibility of murder. In that event, unless poor Danielle simply forgot to lock up, there is a chance that whoever did this has a key to your flat."

"The police said they'd watch the house."

"He might also be someone you both know and trust, someone Danielle invited in."

Lisette stared wildly at the sinister shadows that lengthened about the flat. Her refuge had been violated. Even familiar objects seemed tainted and alien. She fought back tears. "I don't know what to think." She realized she'd been clutching the receiver for a long, silent interval.

"Poor dear! There's nothing you need think about! Now listen. I'm at my solicitor's tidying up some property matters for Aunt Julia. I'll phone right now to have my car sent around for you. It'll be there by the time you pack your toothbrush and pyjamas, and whisk you straight off to bucolic Maida Vale. The maids will plump up your pillows for you, and you can have a nice nap before I get home for dinner. Poor darling, I'll bet you haven't eaten a thing. Now, say you'll come."

"Thank you. It's awfully good of you. Of course I will."

"Then it's done. Don't worry about a thing, Lisette. I'll see you this evening."

XII

Dr. Magnus hunched forward on the narrow seat of the taxi, wearily massaging his forehead and temples. It might not help his mental fatigue, but maybe the reduced muscle tension would ease his headache. He glanced at his watch. Getting on past ten. He'd had no sleep last night, and it didn't look as if he'd be getting much tonight. If only those girls would answer their phone!

It didn't help matters that his conscience plagued him. He had broken a sacred trust. He should never have made use of post-hypnotic suggestion last night to persuade Lisette to return for a further session. It went against all principles, but there had been no other course: the girl was adamant, and he had to know—he was so close to establishing final proof. If only for one final session of regressive hypnosis . . .

Afterward he had spent a sleepless night, too excited for rest, at work in his study trying to reconcile the conflicting elements of Lisette's released memories with the historical data his research had so far compiled. By morning he had been able to pull together just enough facts to deepen the mystery. He had phoned his secretary at home to cancel all his appointments, and had spent the day at the tedious labor of delving through dusty municipal records and newspaper files, working feverishly as the past reluctantly yielded one bewildering clue after another.

By now Dr. Magnus was exhausted, hungry and none too clean, but he had managed to establish proof of his theories. He was not elated. In doing so he had uncovered another secret, something undreamt of in his philosophies. He began to hope that his life work was in error.

"Here's the address, sir."

"Thank you, driver." Dr. Magnus awoke from his grim reverie and saw that he had reached his destination. Quickly, he paid the driver and hurried up the walk to Lisette's flat. Only a few lights were on, and he rang the bell urgently—a helpless sense of foreboding making his movements clumsy.

"Just one moment, sir!"

Dr. Magnus jerked about at the voice. Two men in plain clothes approached him briskly from the pavement.

"Stand easy! We're police."

"Is something the matter, officers?" Obviously, something was.

"Might we ask what your business here is, sir?"

"Certainly. I'm a friend of Miss Borland and Miss Seyrig. I haven't been able to reach them by phone, and as I have some rather urgent matters to discuss with Miss Seyrig, I thought perhaps I might try reaching her here at her flat." He realized he was far too nervous.

"Might we see some identification, sir?"

"Is there anything wrong, officers?" Magnus repeated, producing his wallet.

"Dr. Ingmar Magnus." The taller of the pair regarded him quizzically. "I take it you don't keep up with the news, Dr. Magnus."

"Just what is this about!"

"I'm Inspector Bradley, Dr. Magnus, and this is Detective Sergeant Wharton. CID. We've been wanting to ask you a few questions, sir, if you'll just come with us."

★

It was totally dark when Lisette awoke from troubled sleep. She stared wide-eyed into the darkness for a moment, wondering where she was. Slowly memory supplanted the vague images of her dream. Switching on a lamp beside her bed, Lisette frowned at her watch. It was close to midnight. She had overslept.

Beth's Rolls had come for her almost before she had had time hastily to pack her overnight bag. Once at the house in Maida Vale, a maid—wearing a more conventional uniform than those at her last visit—had shown her to a spacious guest room on the top floor. Lisette had taken a sedative pill and gratefully collapsed onto the bed. She'd planned to catch a short nap, then meet her hostess for dinner. Instead she had slept for almost ten solid hours. Beth must be convinced she was a hopeless twit after this.

As so often happens after an overextended nap, Lisette now felt restless. She wished she'd thought to bring a book. The house was completely silent. Surely it was too late to ring for a maid. No doubt Beth had meant to let her sleep through until morning, and by now would have retired herself. Perhaps she should take another pill and go back to sleep herself.

On the other hand, Beth Garrington hardly seemed the type to make it an early night. She might well still be awake, perhaps watching television where the noise wouldn't disturb her guest. In any event, Lisette didn't want to go back to sleep just yet.

She climbed out of bed, realizing that she'd only half undressed before falling asleep. Pulling off bra and panties, Lisette slipped into the antique nightdress of ribbons and lace she'd brought along. She hadn't thought to pack slippers or a robe, but it was a warm night, and the white cotton gown was modest enough for a peek into the hall.

There was a ribbon of light edging the door of the room at the far end of the hall. The rest of the hallway lay in darkness. Lisette stepped quietly from her room. Since Beth hadn't mentioned other guests, and the servants' quarters were elsewhere, presumably the light was coming from her hostess's bedroom and indicated she might still be awake. Lisette decided she really should make the effort to meet her hostess while in a conscious state.

She heard a faint sound of music as she tiptoed down the hallway. The door to the room was ajar, and the music came from within. She was in luck; Beth must still be up. At the doorway she knocked softly.

"Beth? Are you awake? It's Lisette."

There was no answer, but the door swung open at her touch.

Lisette started to call out again, but her voice froze in her throat. She recognized the tune she heard, and she knew this room. When she entered the bedroom, she could no more alter her actions than she could control the course of her dreams.

It was a large bedroom, entirely furnished in the mode of the late Victorian period. The windows were curtained, and the room's only light came from a candle upon a night table beside the huge four-poster bed. An antique gold pocket watch lay upon the night table also, and the watch was chiming an old music-box tune.

Lisette crossed the room, praying that this was no more than another vivid recurrence of her nightmare. She reached the night table and saw that the watch's hands pointed toward midnight. The chimes stopped. She picked up the watch and examined the picture that she knew would be inside the watch case.

The picture was a photograph of herself.

Lisette let the watch clatter onto the table, stared in terror at the four-poster bed.

From within, a hand drew back the bed curtains.

Lisette wished she could scream, could awaken.

Sweeping aside the curtains, the occupant of the bed sat up and gazed at her.

And Lisette stared back at herself.

"Can't you drive a bit faster than this?"

Inspector Bradley resisted the urge to wink at Detective Sergeant Wharton. "Sit back, Dr. Magnus. We'll be there in good time. I trust you'll have rehearsed some apologies for when we disrupt a peaceful household in the middle of the night."

"I only pray such apologies will be necessary," Dr. Magnus said, continuing to sit forward as if that would inspire the driver to go faster.

It hadn't been easy, Dr. Magnus reflected. He dare not tell them the truth. He suspected that Bradley had agreed to making a late night call on Beth Garrington more to check out his alibi than from any credence he gave to Magnus's improvised tale.

Buried all day in frenzied research, Dr. Magnus hadn't listened to the news, had ignored the tawdry London tabloids with their lurid headlines: "Naked Beauty Slashed in Tub" "Nude Model Slain in Bath" "Party Girl Suicide or Ripper's Victim?" The shock of learning of Danielle's death was seconded by the shock of discovering that he was one of the "important leads" police were following.

It had taken all his powers of persuasion to convince them to release him—or, at least, to accompany him to the house in Maida Vale. Ironically, he and Lisette were the only ones who could account for each other's presence elsewhere at the time of Danielle's death. While the CID might have been sceptical as to the nature of their late night session at Dr. Magnus's office, there were a few corroborating details. A barman at the Catherine Wheel had remembered the distinguished gent with the beard leaving after his lady friend had dropped off of a sudden. The cleaning lady had heard voices and left his office undisturbed. This much they'd already checked, in verifying Lisette's where-abouts that night. Half a dozen harassed records clerks could testify as to Dr. Magnus's presence for today.

Dr. Magnus grimly reviewed the results of his research. There was an Elisabeth Beresford, born in London in 1879, of a well-to-do family who lived in Cheyne Row on the Chelsea Embank-ment. Elisabeth Beresford married a Captain Donald Stapledon in 1899 and moved to India with her husband. She returned to London, evidently suffering from consumption contracted while abroad, and died in 1900. She was buried in Highgate Cemetery. That much Dr. Magnus had initially learned with some difficulty. From that basis he had pressed on for additional corroborating details, both from Lisette's released memories and from research into records of the period.

It had been particularly difficult to trace the subsequent branches of the family—something he must do in order to establish that Elis-abeth Beresford could not have been an ancestress of Lisette Seyrig. And it disturbed him that he had been unable to locate Elisabeth Stapledon née Beresford's tomb in Highgate Cemetery.

Last night he had pushed Lisette as relentlessly as he dared. Out of her resurfacing visions of horror he finally found a clue. These were not images from nightmare, not symbolic representations of buried fears. They were literal memories.

Because of the sensation involved and the considerable station of the families concerned, public records had discreetly avoided reference to the tragedy, as had the better newspapers. The yellow journals were less reticent, and here Dr. Magnus began to know fear.

Elisabeth Stapledon had been buried alive.

At her final wishes, the body had not been embalmed. The papers suggested that this was a clear premonition of her fate, and quoted passages from Edgar Allan Poe. Captain Stapledon paid an evening visit to his wife's tomb and discovered her wandering in a dazed condition about the graves. This was more than a month after her entombment.

The newspapers were full of pseudo-scientific theories, spiritualist explanations and long accounts of Indian mystics who had remained in a state of suspended animation for weeks on end. No one seems to have explained exactly how Elisabeth Stapledon escaped from both coffin and crypt, but it was supposed that desperate strength had wrenched loose the screws, while providentially the crypt had not been properly locked after a previous visit.

Husband and wife understandably went abroad immediately afterward, in order to escape publicity and for Elisabeth Stapledon to recover from her ordeal. This she very quickly did, but evidently the shock was more than Captain Stapledon could endure. He died in 1902, and his wife returned to London soon after, inheriting his extensive fortune and properties, including their house in Maida Vale. When she later inherited her own family's estate—her sole brother fell in the Boer War—she was a lady of great wealth.

Elisabeth Stapledon became one of the most notorious hostesses of the Edwardian era and on until the close of the First World War. Her beauty was considered remarkable, and men marvelled while her rivals bemoaned that she scarcely seemed to age with the passing years. After the War she left London to travel about the exotic East. In 1924 news came of her death in India.

Her estate passed to her daughter, Jane Stapledon, born abroad
in 1901. While Elisabeth Stapledon made occasional references to
her daughter, Jane was raised and educated in Europe and never
seemed to have come to London until her arrival in 1925. Some
had suggested that the mother had wished to keep her daughter
pure from her own Bohemian life style, but when Jane Stapledon
appeared, it seemed more likely that her mother's motives for
her seclusion had been born of jealousy. Jane Stapledon had all
her mother's beauty—indeed, her older admirers vowed she was
the very image of Elisabeth in her youth. She also had inherited
her mother's taste for wild living; with a new circle of friends
from her own age group, she took up where her mother had left
off. The newspapers were particularly scandalized by her association with Aleister Crowley and others of his circle. Although
her dissipations bridged the years of Flaming Youth to the Lost
Generation, even her enemies had to admit she carried her years
extremely well. In 1943 Jane Stapledon was missing and presumed
dead after an air raid levelled and burned a section of London
where she had gone to dine with friends.

Papers in the hands of her solicitor left her estate to a daughter living in America, Julia Weatherford, born in Miami in 1934.
Evidently her mother had enjoyed a typical whirlwind resort
romance with an American millionaire while wintering in Flor-
ida. Their marriage was a secret one, annulled following Julia's
birth, and her daughter had been left with her former husband.
Julia Weatherford arrived from the States early in 1946. Any
doubts as to the authenticity of her claim were instantly ban-
ished, for she was the very picture of her mother in her younger
days. Julia again seemed to have the family's wild streak, and she
carried on the tradition of wild parties and bizarre acquaintances through the Beat Generation to the Flower Children. Her
older friends thought it amazing that Julia in a minidress might
easily be mistaken as being of the same age group as her young,
pot-smoking, hippie friends. But it may have been that at last her
youth began to fade, because since 1967 Julia Weatherford had
been living more or less in seclusion in Europe, occasionally visited by her niece.

Her niece, Beth Garrington, born in 1950, was the orphaned

daughter of Julia's American half-sister and a wealthy young Englishman from Julia's collection. After her parents' death in a plane crash in 1970, Beth had become her aunt's *protegée,* and carried on the mad life in London. It was apparent that Beth Garrington would inherit her aunt's property as well. It was also apparent that she was the spitting image of her Aunt Julia when the latter was her age. It would be most interesting to see the two of them together. And that, of course, no one had ever done.

At first Dr. Magnus had been unwilling to accept the truth of the dread secret he had uncovered. And yet, with the knowledge of Lisette's released memories, he knew there could be no other conclusion.

It was astonishing how thoroughly a woman who thrived on notoriety could avoid having her photographs published. After all, changing fashions and new hair styles, careful adjustments with cosmetics, could only do so much, and while the mind's eye had an inaccurate memory, a camera lens did not. Dr. Magnus did succeed in finding a few photographs through persistent research. Given a good theatrical costume and makeup crew, they all might have been taken of the same woman on the same day.

They might also all have been taken of Lisette Seyrig.

However, Dr. Magnus knew that it *would* be possible to see Beth Garrington and Lisette Seyrig together.

And he prayed he would be in time to prevent this.

With this knowledge tormenting his thoughts, it was a miracle that Dr. Magnus had held onto sanity well enough to persuade New Scotland Yard to make this late night drive to Maida Vale—desperate, in view of what he knew to be true. He had suffered a shock as severe as any that night when they told him at last where Lisette had gone.

"She's quite all right. She's staying with a friend."

"Might I ask where?"

"A chauffeured Rolls picked her up. We checked registration, and it belongs to a Miss Elisabeth Garrington in Maida Vale."

Dr. Magnus had been frantic then, had demanded that they take him there instantly. A telephone call informed them that Miss Seyrig was sleeping under sedation and could not be disturbed; she would return his call in the morning.

Controlling his panic, Dr. Magnus had managed to contrive a disjointed tangle of half-truths and plausible lies—anything to convince them to get over to the Garrington house as quickly as possible. They already knew he was one of those occult kooks. Very well, he assured them that Beth Garrington was involved in a secret society of drug fiends and satanists (all true enough), that Danielle and Lisette had been lured to their most recent orgy for unspeakable purposes. Lisette had been secretly drugged, but Danielle had escaped to carry her roommate home before they could be used for whatever depraved rites awaited them—perhaps ritual sacrifice. Danielle had been murdered—either to shut her up or as part of the ritual—and now they had Lisette in their clutches as well.

All very melodramatic, but enough of it was true. Inspector Bradley knew of the sex and drugs orgies that took place there, but there was firm pressure from higher up to look the other way. Further, he knew enough about some of the more bizarre cult groups in London to consider that ritual murder was quite feasible, given the proper combination of sick minds and illegal drugs. And while it hadn't been made public, the medical examiner was of the opinion that the slashes to the Borland girl's throat and wrists had been an attempt to disguise the fact that she had already bled to death from two deep punctures through the jugular vein.

A demented killer, obviously. A ritual murder? You couldn't discount it just yet. Inspector Bradley had ordered a car.

"Who are you, Lisette Seyrig, that you wear my face?"

Beth Garrington rose sinuously from her bed. She was dressed in an off-the-shoulder nightgown of antique lace, much the same as that which Lisette wore. Her green eyes—the eyes behind the mask that had so shaken Lisette when last they'd met—held her in their spell.

"When first faithful Adrian swore he'd seen my double, I thought his brain had begun to reel with final madness. But after he followed you to your little gallery and brought me there to see your portrait, I knew I had encountered something beyond even my experience."

Lisette stood frozen with dread fascination as her nightmare came to life. Her twin paced about her, appraising her coolly as a serpent considers its hypnotized victim.

"Who are you, Lisette Seyrig, that yours is the face I have seen in my dreams, the face that haunted my nightmares as I lay dying, the face that I thought was my own?"

Lisette forced her lips to speak. "*Who* are you?"

"My name? I change that whenever it becomes prudent for me to do so. Tonight I am Beth Garrington. Long ago I was Elisabeth Beresford."

"How can this be possible?" Lisette hoped she was dealing with a madwoman, but knew her hope was false.

"A spirit came to me in my dreams and slowly stole away my mortal life, in return giving me eternal life. You understand what I say, even though your reason insists that such things cannot be."

She unfastened Lisette's gown and let it fall to the floor, then did the same with her own. Standing face to face, their nude bodies seemed one a reflection of the other.

Elisabeth took Lisette's face in her hands and kissed her full on the lips. The kiss was a long one; her breath was cold in Lisette's mouth. When Elisabeth released her lips and gazed longingly into her eyes, Lisette saw the pointed fangs that now curved downward from her upper jaw.

"Will you cry out, I wonder? If so, let it be in ecstasy and not in fear. I shan't drain you and discard you as I did your silly friend. No, Lisette, my new-found sister. I shall take your life in tiny kisses from night to night—kisses that you will long for with your entire being. And in the end you shall pass over to serve me as my willing chattel—as have the few others I have chosen over the years."

Lisette trembled beneath her touch, powerless to break away. From the buried depths of her unconscious mind, understanding slowly emerged. She did not resist when Elisabeth led her to the bed and lay down beside her on the silken sheets. Lisette was past knowing fear.

Elisabeth stretched her naked body upon Lisette's warmer flesh, lying between her thighs as would a lover. Her cool fingers caressed Lisette; her kisses teased a path from her belly across her breasts and to the hollow of her throat.

Elisabeth paused and gazed into Lisette's eyes. Her fangs gleamed with a reflection of the inhuman lust in her expression.

"And now I give you a kiss sweeter than any passion your mortal brain dare imagine, Lisette Seyrig—even as once I first received such a kiss from a dream-spirit whose eyes stared into mine from my own face. Why have you haunted my dreams, Lisette Seyrig?"

Lisette returned her gaze silently, without emotion. Nor did she flinch when Elisabeth's lips closed tightly against her throat, and the only sound was a barely perceptible tearing, like the bursting of a maidenhead, and the soft movement of suctioning lips.

Elisabeth suddenly broke away with an inarticulate cry of pain. Her lips smeared with scarlet, she stared down at Lisette in bewildered fear. Lisette, blood streaming from the wound on her throat, stared back at her with a smile of unholy hatred.

"*What* are you, Lisette Seyrig?"

"I am Elisabeth Beresford." Lisette's tone was implacable. "In another lifetime you drove my soul from my body and stole my flesh for your own. Now I have come back to reclaim that which once was mine."

Elisabeth sought to leap away, but Lisette's arms embraced her with sudden, terrible strength—pulling their naked bodies together in a horrid imitation of two lovers at the moment of ecstasy.

The scream that echoed into the night was not one of ecstasy.

At the sound of the scream—afterward they never agreed whether it was two voices together or only one—Inspector Bradley ceased listening to the maid's outraged protests and burst past her into the house.

"Upstairs! On the double!" he ordered needlessly. Already Dr. Magnus had lunged past him and was sprinting up the stairway.

"I think it came from the next floor up! Check inside all the rooms!" Later he cursed himself for not posting a man at the door, for by the time he was again able to think rationally, there was no trace of the servants.

In the master bedroom at the end of the third-floor hallway, they found two bodies behind the curtains of the big four-poster bed. One had only just been murdered; her nude body was drenched in the blood from her torn throat—seemingly far too much blood for one body. The other body was a desiccated corpse, obviously dead for a great many years. The dead girl's limbs obscenely embraced the mouldering cadaver that lay atop her, and her teeth, in final spasm, were locked in the lich's throat. As they gaped in horror, clumps of hair and bits of dried skin could be seen to drop away.

Detective Sergeant Wharton looked away and vomited on the floor.

"I owe you a sincere apology, Dr. Magnus." Inspector Bradley's face was grim. "You were right. Ritual murder by a gang of sick degenerates. Detective Sergeant! Leave off that, and put out an all-points bulletin for Beth Garrington. And round up anyone else you find here! Move, man!"

"If only I'd understood in time," Dr. Magnus muttered. He was obviously to the point of collapse.

"No, *I* should have listened to you sooner," Bradley growled. "We might have been in time to prevent this. The devils must have fled down some servants' stairway when they heard us burst in. I confess I've bungled this badly."

"She was a vampire, you see," Dr. Magnus told him dully, groping to explain. "A vampire loses its soul when it becomes one of the undead. But the soul is deathless; it lives on even when its previous incarnation has become a soulless demon. Elisabeth Beresford's soul lived on, until Elisabeth Beresford found reincarnation in Lisette Seyrig. Don't you see? Elisabeth Beresford met her own reincarnation, and that meant destruction for them both."

Inspector Bradley had been only half listening. "Dr. Magnus, you've done all you can. I think you should go down to the car with Detective Sergeant Wharton now and rest until the ambulance arrives."

"But you must see that I was right!" Dr. Magnus pleaded. Madness danced in his eyes. "If the soul is immortal and infinite, then time has no meaning for the soul. Elisabeth Beresford was haunting herself."

AFTERWORD

To Be Read, If Ever, After Reading *In A Lonely Place*

This *Afterword* was written for the special Scream/Press edition of *In A Lonely Place* at the suggestion of editor/publisher Jeff Conner, who thought that some readers might be interested in the story behind the story of the eight contemporary horror tales collected here. Without delving into profundities, this is basically an anecdotal attempt to answer a few of those old favorite questions: How do you write? Where do you get your ideas? What were you on when you wrote that, and what were you on about?

The unglamorous truth is that there are no secrets: whatever works for the writer works for that writer. I write using a pencil and lined notebook paper, laboriously typing the final draft with one finger on my trusty Royal manual portable. Some writers insist on writing every day, others write when the mood is upon them. I'm one of the latter school, feeling that if the mood isn't right for me, it won't be for the reader either. Ideas are where you find them. Making them work is the business of a writer. Words are a medium of communication, and a writer should be able to recreate his vision within the imagination of the reader. All that is required of the writer is to have that vision within his own imagination and to master the techniques of communicating this to the reader. None of this is very practical advice. All I can really tell you is how these eight stories came into being.

"In the Pines" was written over a period of months in 1968. The setting is based upon a vacation cabin once owned by my uncle in Sunshine, Tennessee. Description of the decaying resort area, the cabin and its furnishings is factual. It's been twenty years since my uncle owned the place, and I imagine the tottery old cabin has tumbled down the side of the mountain by now. Uncle

Bill still insists I owe him a cut of the royalties. Inspiration to use this setting for a story came from the song, "In the Pines," which we had on an old Tennessee Ernie Ford album. It is an eerie song, especially when heard in the right setting. I later discovered that my friend, Manly Wade Wellman, had also been inspired by this song to write one of his John the Balladeer stories, "Shiver in the Pines"—although Wellman knew the song from its folk roots.

The original version of "In the Pines" ran to about 16,500 words. I tried it on the few fantasy markets that existed in the late 1960s, but without success. The manuscript went back into my files. I had avoided sending it to *Fantasy & Science Fiction* because I didn't think they'd go for a haunted house story. After *F&SF* continued to bounce every story I sent them that I thought was right for them, I finally decided to try them with this story that I didn't think was right. Ed Ferman returned the manuscript, suggesting I abridge it. This I did in 1972, cutting out a long stream-of-consciousness flashback and much of the purple prose, ending up with a much tighter story at 12,000 words. Ferman bought it. His advice was sound, and the version here is as it appeared in *F&SF*, with the addition of the short prologue which was omitted from the *F&SF* publication.

"The Fourth Seal" was written in October, 1971—during the period after which I had dropped out of medical school and out of a Ph.D. program in neurobiology. The story pretty well reflects my bitterness toward the medical profession, and the briefly mentioned character, Kirk Walker, is a thin disguise of the author's persona. The story was inspired by a series of lectures in epidemiology concerning the cyclical nature of deadly diseases. This much of "The Fourth Seal" is factual, as are many of the conversations and political sentiments expressed by the characters. This latter exemplified the repressive attitudes in medical education during the late 1960s from which I had turned in disgust with the goal of making a career in writing.

"The Fourth Seal" did not sell to the fantasy markets of the day, which was one of the many failures that forced me to return to medicine after a couple years and complete work on my M.D. One editor wrote back that the premise was too fantastic, while another suggested that I had never sat and listened to real fanatics.

I returned the story to the files, and it might have remained there had not Dr. Stuart David Schiff started the fantasy magazine, *Whispers*. The first two years of dental school are very much the same as the first two years of medical school. Schiff recognized the medical basis and the characters thus portrayed; he snapped up "The Fourth Seal" for *Whispers* and later reprinted it in his hardcover anthology, *Mad Scientists*. Currently I am at work on expanding "The Fourth Seal" into novel length.

Stuart David Schiff was directly responsible for "Sticks," which I wrote especially for *Whispers* in January, 1974. The story is really Lee Brown Coye's and is about Lee Brown Coye, as the *Afterword* to "Sticks" (contained within *In A Lonely Place*) explains. I had met Coye through his work for Carcosa, and he was a good friend to those of us concerned with Carcosa and to Stuart. Coye had described the events upon which "Sticks" is based to me, and when Schiff decided to bring out a special Lee Brown Coye issue of *Whispers,* I stole time from my final few months of medical school to write a story inspired by Coye's experiences. "Sticks" is shot through with in-jokes and references which the serious fantasy/horror fan will recognize. I wrote the story as a favor and tribute to Lee, and I never expected it to be read by anyone beyond the thousand or so fans who read *Whispers.* To my surprise, "Sticks" became one of my best known and best liked stories. It won the British Fantasy Award and was a runner-up in the World Fantasy Award for best short fiction. The story has been anthologized numerous times and translated into several languages. It was broadcast on National Public Radio on Halloween, 1982 and was to have been produced for the short-lived television series, *The Darkroom*. Not bad for an in-joke.

There are only two things to add to the story's published *Afterword*. The January, 1978 issue of *Smithsonian* includes an article on Michael Singer, an artist who creates vast stick lattices in natural settings, many of them in New York and New England. In June of 1974 David Drake and I visited Coye and returned with him to the Mann Brook site. The road was a new one, but Lee found the old overgrown orchard, now far more overgrown, and we started to make our way through the thick underbrush that had swallowed the old railroad bed. Before long we encountered a sign that warned: No Trespassing For Any Purposes. After finding the third of these curiously worded postings, we turned back.

"Where The Summer Ends" is one of a number of stories that I worked on by fits and starts over a period of years. According to my notes, I began writing the story in September, 1974—just before beginning my psychiatric residency—and eventually completed it between March and July of 1977. I forget which anthology it was intended for—by this time I only wrote short fiction after some editor had requested a story from me, not that that editor always accepted it—but as usual I was way past deadline, and my agent, Kirby McCauley, simply held the story for his own anthology, *Dark Forces*.

The setting for "Where the Summer Ends" is again factual as described. During the 1960s and 1970s I had a number of close friends who were living in the student area around the University of Tennessee in downtown Knoxville. Some of these friends were the basis of the characters in "Where the Summer Ends," and I've since talked with a number of readers from the Knoxville student quarter who were able to pinpoint the houses and settings described in the story. The old junkyard did exist, although last reports I heard from friends who lived nearby said that the old dealer had abandoned his yard and that the kudzu had covered everything. At the time I wrote the story I had forgotten that northern readers were not familiar with kudzu—a vine that will grow a foot a day during the summer and simply overwhelm anything in its path. Old joke: How do you plant kudzu? Throw the seeds over your shoulder, and run like hell. Much of the decaying urban neighborhood of "Where the Summer Ends" was razed for the Knoxville World's Fair in 1982 and blacktopped over for parking space. These lots stand empty now, and the kudzu is swiftly reclaiming its lost ground.

".220 Swift" is another story that remained on the back burner for a long time: I began writing it in May, 1973 and eventually finished it in June, 1979. At one point during all this I had intended it for one or another of Ramsey Campbell's anthologies—probably missing deadlines on both *Superhorrors* and *New Tales of the Cthulhu Mythos*. I just did manage to get it to Campbell in time for his *New Terrors* anthology, the first of the two volumes (abridged to one volume in the American edition). The story was held up in the mail due to the British postal strike, and Ramsey very nearly missed getting it in time. His editors at Pan Books were somewhat staggered at receiving an 18,000-word last-minute addition, and they wanted to abridge the novella through such means as cutting out the passage in which Brandon lifts the heavy table across his porch—an indication that he is not quite human. Campbell, who has the same opinion of editorial meddling as I do, insisted that the story be published as written.

In the summer of 1969 I lived in a cabin in Haywood County, North Carolina while working in a medical clinic there. The cabin and mountain settings are those in which I was living during this time. The legends of the Lost Mines of the Ancients, as described in ".220 Swift," are not pseudohistory as one critic suggested, but are historical fact—or mystery. Manly Wade Wellman, a noted writer and scholar of southern history and folklore, kindly gave me the use of his own research material regarding this archeological mystery, and over the years I was able to include some research of my own. The books and sources referred to in this regard are all actual materials, as are the legends and Indian myths. As Wellman has for many years demonstrated in his own writing, history and folklore often propose mysteries far greater than any writer's imagination can provide.

Quite often dreams—or nightmares, depending on taste—will provide inspiration for a story. Such was the case with "The River of Night's Dreaming." The story is based upon a dream I had during the early morning hours of June 30, 1979. As do many writers, I keep a commonplace book of notes, ideas, etc. for possible use in my work—and, when I manage to struggle out of bed to do so, I make notes on particularly vivid dreams. The story is very close to my dream, in which I was an observer of the events—the only difference being that my dream protagonist was escaping from a prison camp—until the protagonist began to have fears concerning the house of apparent refuge. At that point I woke up. I worked on the story for about a year, finally completing it rather past deadline for one of Charles L. Grant's *Shadows* anthologies. Grant had been asking me for a story and this time was actually holding the anthology for me. To his dismay, "The River of Night's Dreaming" was not only late but so long that he would have had to cut a story or two already slated for the book in order to make room. Further, the rather explicit sexual content of the story was not for the young readers/library audience that Doubleday had in mind for *Shadows*. Fortunately, Stuart David Schiff had already violated Doubleday's taboos with his *Whispers* anthology series, and the story found a place there. Schiff was vindicated when "The River of Night's Dreaming" was a runner-up for the World Fantasy Award.

The title, of course, is taken from Richard O'Brien's song in *The Rocky Horror Picture Show:* "The darkness must flow down the river of night's dreaming . . ." Fantasy fans will no doubt recognize the thread of references to Robert W. Chambers' *The King in Yellow*. Rock music fans may recognize certain parallels to Jim Morrison's song, "The End." Only a few readers seem to have realized that the protagonist of "The River of Night's Dreaming" is actually male, but perceiving himself as female in his psychotic state—and the reality of the story is from his/her point of view. The story is deliberately set upon two levels, supernatural and psychotic, and the levels merge and interchange.

"Beyond Any Measure," written between July, 1980 and July, 1981, again explores the relationships of eroticism and horror—and again the title is from Richard O'Brien's *The Rocky Horror Picture Show:* "Erotic nightmares beyond any measure and sensual daydreams to treasure forever." The settings are contemporary London streets and shops, and I'm indebted to author/editor Michael Parry for the tour of Covent Garden on the night of its reopening as a trendy shopping mall. "Beyond Any Measure" was written as an intended screenplay, and the story contains cinematic references and homages beyond counting. Fans of *The Avengers* television series will be quick to recognize the play on the infamous "A Touch of Brimstone" episode, shown only in later reruns on American TV.

"Beyond Any Measure" was written specifically for Stuart David Schiff's magazine, *Whispers*. Stuart was used to late manuscripts from me, and after "The River of Night's Dreaming" he was ready to expect anything. When "Beyond Any Measure" won the World Fantasy Award, Stuart must have felt his audacity in publishing the story had been worth it all.

Well, Stuart David Schiff knew what to expect from me, as have most of the editors who have requested stories from me. This is not to boast; I do not have a backlog of unpublished material. I am a very slow writer, and short fiction represents a very small proportion of my work. I cannot waste time and energy in writing a story on spec (as I was doing a decade ago), and I have to decline most requests for short fiction simply because I cannot find time to write the stuff. In view of this, probably the worst mistake possible for an editor is to ask me for a story and to give me *carte blanche* to write contemporary horror as I personally interpret the genre—without ever having read enough of my work to know what I might produce.

Such was the case with "More Sinned Against," published in the Scream/Press edition of *In A Lonely Place* for the first time. The story was written during the spring of 1984 for an anthology of original horror stories whose editor claimed to have read *In A Lonely Place* and who asked me for a story—no guidelines, just my interpretation of contemporary horror. And so I wrote "More Sinned Against"—somewhat experimental in its hardboiled journalistic technique, but basically a horror story about people using people. As usual, I was late and the story was longer than anticipated, but the editor returned "More Sinned Against" with sincere regrets on the fundamental grounds that the heroine had been able to profit from her ordeal with drugs, and that this might tempt some young reader to experiment with drugs.

Personally I thought I was putting an exact opposite message across in the story, but no matter. And was it voodoo or was it drugs? A writer shouldn't have to tell a reader anything. Or an editor.

Perhaps a final word on this collection as a whole. *In A Lonely Place* was a very important book for me. Any writer of short stories faces the frustration of knowing that his work will most likely languish and perish in the magazines or anthologies that publish it. The only real hope is to publish a collection of stories, giving such scattered short fiction the sanctuary of A Book. Unfortunately, book publishers want novels, not collections of stories. *In*

A Lonely Place was made possible thanks to the dogged efforts of Kirby McCauley and the generous help of Peter Straub.

The title, *In A Lonely Place,* is a tip of the hat to the Dorothy B. Hughes mystery novel of that title, and to the Nicholas Ray film based on her novel, starring Humphrey Bogart and Gloria Grahame—concerning a writer who is a little too close to the edge. But more than this, some readers will have recognized its source from Walter de la Mare's poem, "I Met At Eve"—

> *I met at eve the Prince of Sleep,*
> *His was a still and lovely face.*
> *He wandered through a valley steep.*
> *Lovely in a lonely place.*

—Karl Edward Wagner, July 1984

Made in the USA
Monee, IL
28 October 2024

68852632R00156